RED FEVER

Dr. Joan M Savage

ISBN: 979-8-9889548-9-7

RED FEVER

Dr. Joan M Savage

Contents

PROLOGUE   9

CHAPTER 1:   REMEMBERED PIECES – WRITING WRONGS   11

CHAPTER 2:   COPS AND ROBBERS   24

CHAPTER 3:   RISING PHOENIX   29

CHAPTER 4:   A MILLION DESIGNS FOR REVENGE   35

CHAPTER 5:   IN THE MIX   47

CHAPTER 6:   SHEDDING SKIN   53

CHAPTER 7:   BEAUTY AND ASHES   60

CHAPTER 8:   STORM CHASER   68

CHAPTER 9:   A MATTER OF LIFE AND DEBT   77

CHAPTER 10: IT SMELLS LIKE BLOOD   88

CHAPTER 11: TIES THAT BOND   101

CHAPTER 12: DIVERSION TO DIVERGENCE   112

CHAPTER 13: TWO SHADES OF BLUE   124

CHAPTER 14: TRUTHFUL LIES   139

CHAPTER 15: BLACK KING. WHITE KNIGHT.   148

CHAPTER 16: DIRTY LIES AND FILTHY TIES   160

CHAPTER 17: THE DEVIL YOU KNOW   169

CHAPTER 18: "RED ROVER, RED ROVER..."   176

CHAPTER 19: REMNANTS   192

CHAPTER 20: NOT ANOTHER ONE   201

CHAPTER 21: PUSSY POLITICS   210

CHAPTER 22: FIGMENTS   216

CHAPTER 23: THE DARK THINGS   225

CHAPTER 24: THE GIRL WHO NEVER EXISTED   232

CHAPTER 25: DON'T BITE THE HAND THAT FEELS YOU 242

CHAPTER 26: WHAT YOU DON'T KNOW   255

CHAPTER 27: ALL THE KING'S HORSES AND ALL THE KING'S
MEN   262

CHAPTER 28: BLOODY TRAILS AND TALES   272

CHAPTER 29: QUID PRO QUO   277

CHAPTER 30: HAVEN AND HELL   292

CHAPTER 31: STAB AND TWIST   303

CHAPTER 32: UNTURNED STONES   310

CHAPTER 33: INNOCENCE AND GUILT   319

CHAPTER 34: PAGE FORTY SIX   331

CHAPTER 35: FANTASIES AND NIGHTMARES   339

CHAPTER 36: EPOCH OF BELIEF. BACK TO THE BEGINNING 346

Dr. Joan M Savage

Prologue

Do you think it's a sin if I don't want to live anymore? June wondered endlessly.

It was the road less traveled in reality, but mentally, she ran grooves into the ground. Should she dump all her self stock while she still could? Sell the money pit that was her life? Cut the dead weight? If anyone knew who June Shimmers really was it would be Charles Dickens, had she been alive in his lifetime.

"It was the best of times, it was the worst of times, it was the age of wisdom, it was the age of foolishness, it was the epoch of belief, it was the epoch of incredulity, it was the season of Light, it was the season of Darkness..."

June was in her season of Darkness.

Hell, she was born into it. Uniquely created for it and forged by the Darkness itself for such a time as this.

When should she cut her losses and run?

Dr. Joan M Savage

Chapter 1

Remembered Pieces – Writing Wrongs

June Shimmers sat straight up in bed gasping for breath.

It's just a dream.

Her mind locked down on trying to control her breathing. Exactly the way she was taught from a stupid mindless mindfulness video she picked out on YouTube. It wasn't until both feet hit the cold dry floor that she finally convinced herself.

"It's just a dream…" she whispered to the dark. The dark answering with the sound of an occasional car driving by.

A warm wet trickle slid down the middle of her back, sending goosebumps everywhere. As if one cue, another trickle made its way down her cheek.

It's just sweat.

Breathing deeply in and out as the bloody bodies from her nightmare began slowly fading away.

The TV from her neighbor's apartment was blaring loudly through the paper-thin walls. One of the news stations was sending out more fear, horror, gore, murder, and gang related monstrosities. It was nothing new, except…

June's ears perked up as the anchorwoman spoke of the tenth anniversary for the victims of *Red Fever* and the death of LA's most beloved Criddendane family.

Sitting on the edge of her bed, she laid her head in her hands. Sweat dripping off them and landing in a tiny pool at her feet. Her eyes peeked from behind her fingers, instantly focusing on the glistening puddle forming beneath her.

She couldn't shake it, the dreams were fucking relentless in their assault tonight. Just when she thought she pushed the darkness back into hiding, image after image forced its way back, bringing thoughts of death, bloody floors, and burning bodies. June cupped her hands over her ears, a childhood habit intended to quiet the lingering sounds of screaming zombies and rapid gunfire…

Stop. Please stop.

She begged, pleading to a nameless god. She compelled herself fully awake, ending the tug-of-war for her mind. The dreams visited whenever stress levels were high, and here it was again like a technicolor movie. She couldn't pretend anymore that her stress wasn't off the charts. Her dad, in his usual brisk and setaceous manner, decided they were moving again. This time across the world to Los Angeles. Typical Ben gave his typical twenty-four hour notice to gather her shit and somehow stuff her entire life into an allotted three medium-sized boxes.

She learned long ago to just do it. No more temper tantrums, no more running away, and no more threats. Gone were all her hateful words because nothing stopped it and nothing changed it. Any time wasted arguing was time wasted for packing and to "close down any friendships" as Ben liked to tell her. As if saying goodbye was as easy as closing a good book after reading its final chapter – sad it's over and thankful for closure.

You should be used to it by now, she chided herself. Shit, she should've expected the dreams days ago after first arriving to this new city. She knew they would come – like clockwork they always come following a move.

Tonight they were unrelenting, making up for lost time.

June pinched the soft sensitive skin under her arm, the pain grounding her. It was her saving grace when the dreams felt too lifelike. The pain gave her some weird sickening pleasurable release and a moment's peace. It had a way of freeing her from all the anxiety and fear tormenting her. It's why she chose to study martial arts – Taekwondo, Kenpo, Krav Maga…

She couldn't fight the nightmares but she learned to fight everything else. And physical pain became almost…

…euphoric.

##

It was her third night in this new apartment and Ben disappeared again. Maybe it was only a few hours... maybe a few days. Time blended into one giant depressing moment, so June made a fast and quick decision, no more depression and no more whining about this bullshit move.

She decided to make the best of it, whatever *it* was... starting with Googling the nearest home improvement store. With a wild hair up her ass, June painted her bedroom floor bright yellow hoping on nights like this, the sweat she left behind would be as bright as the floor. A yellow floor was her only link back to reality these days because it was impossible to mistake a yellow floor for a bloody floor.

Except tonight.

For some reason, under the pale moonlight and the luminous streetlamps shining through her window, the shadows on her bright yellow floor looked like puddles of blood. And yesterday's scattered clothes and books... like charred dead bodies.

She couldn't shake it, afraid to go back to sleep but unable to stay awake. June lowered herself back into bed, closing her eyes just for a second.

##

The nightmare poured over her in giant billowing clouds of black smoke, filling her nostrils with burnt hair and flesh. She was suffocating. Wherever her eyes landed, bodies were burning and people were screaming. The piles of bodies and puddles of blood lit up with flames as high as the walls around her. The fire was creeping across the floor like little snakes attacking everything in its wake.

It was nothing short of a zombie apocalypse, and she was trapped right in the middle of it.

Looking down at her pretty white shoes, they were slowly soaking up the blood from the pool she was standing in. Her feet were like two tiny sailboats in a giant crimson sea.

All around her blood was oozing from the bodies into new puddles. It was sickening. It was terrifying.

Out of the darkness, a woman dragged herself through the blood and over the stacks of bodies as if her legs were broken. She was pulling herself toward June. The wheezing sounds she made with each breath grew louder and louder, drowning out the screams and gunfire.

She was trying to say something to June, but every time she opened her mouth, a gurgling sound erupted followed by a thick flow of blood that ran down her chin. Her mouth and teeth were stained bright red like the cherry Popsicles June loved to eat in the summer.

With one final grunt, the woman pulled herself into the same bloody puddle as June. Looking up with her bulging red eyes, the woman grabbed her ankle, leaving a bloody handprint on her beautiful white shoes and frilly socks.

June wanted nothing more than to escape the monster and her bloody hand. She tried screaming but the thick black smoke was gagging her until only spit and vomit were coming out of her mouth and nose. The flames surrounding them were moving quickly and viciously like demons on a mission, grabbing body after body, alive and on the hunt. They came for the woman next…igniting everything they touched as if the blood itself was a type of flammable liquid. And like a hungry beast, it devoured the woman in one gulp.

June pulled and pulled to escape… fighting helplessly to get away from the horror she was witnessing on the woman's face – mouth open, silently screaming, eyes rolled into the back of her head as the blazing beast ravaged her. June didn't have the strength to get away. She was locked in the blood like it was quicksand, and the black burnt hand was cement.

The blaze quickly consumed the woman, her body jerking violently. And in one final attempt to scream, she coughed an explosion of the bright red Popsicle splattering June's face and arms and her pretty white dress. The living flame followed the blood, jumping from the woman to the frills on June's dress, dancing around her and ruthlessly attacking.

It took seconds before the flames began eating her alive too…

She screamed.

##

Jumping awake, June swatted at the non-existent fire burning through her pajamas, and violently kicked at the wet sheets that twisted around her trapped legs.

"Dad!?" she cried out in the dark. Shaking, gagging, coughing.

Licking her lips, she could almost taste the nightmare's dawdling odor of burnt hair and flesh in her mouth. It lingered the way campfire smoke clings to your clothes and hides in your nose.

Jesus, were dreams supposed to be so vivid? Feel so… real?

Battling sleepiness was preferable to battling flames. June got up and moved swiftly into the kitchen, slamming on the kitchen light. Out of habit, she checked her arms and feet to see if they were covered in blood and soot and burn marks. There was nothing. Only the dewy glisten of her sweaty skin.

Maybe I'm losing my mind?

She heard one of her teachers explain that mental illness can start showing itself around age fourteen. And June was fifteen, a few months shy of her sixteenth birthday. What a fucking way to spend her sweet sixteen. Mentally unstable and in a strange new city.

And alone again.

Focused breathing helped the memory to fade quicker and deep concentration on the neighbor's TV. The anchorwoman had switched topics, discussing the weather. And June was glad for the gore respite. Especially because her father wasn't home yet to help her through it.

"Loser." She threw out a verbal dagger as she glared at his open bedroom door. If he was home, the door would be closed. The mother fucker ditched her yet again. Since arriving in LA, he was not around often enough to scare off her demons and clean up the nightmares.

As far back as she could remember, it was a nightly ritual of swapping sweaty jammies and wet sheets while her dad reassured her it was only a dream.

A dream mixed in with some bad memories of all the haunted houses he used to take her to.

She wanted to be pissed at his absence of late but deep down knew it was her fault he was staying out so much. It wasn't intentional, she started asking too many questions… *again.* But June couldn't help it, the older she got, the more curiosity became her master. They grew hand in hand, and lately there were just too many unanswered questions rolling around in her brain.

Why America? And why LA?

Why only 24 hours to pack and leave? Why the rush?

And the ultimate question that seemed to drive the stake home every time.

Where's my mother?

June was happy in Asia. The United States felt foreign to her, and knowing all this Ben still chose to stay out late every night.

Where the hell is he?

Why hadn't he touched base with her yet? June checked her phone, it was 3:16am. She glanced at his bedroom when something caught her eye, something that wasn't there when she went to bed last night. A messy stack of paperwork and newspapers lay sprawled out over the kitchen counter. Clearly he came home sometime after midnight. A feeling of relief washing over her, yet, still angry that he didn't wake her or text her. Maybe he left a note?

Searching through the stack, June curiously grabbed one of the newspapers. It was a dated *L.A. Times* newspaper, roughly ten years old. She glanced up at the crooked puppy dog calendar barely hanging by a thumbtack. Yep, the newspaper was from ten years ago this week. She remembered exactly where they were living ten years ago, Beijing, China. A radical new culture and thrust in the middle of trying to learn a new language, she was utterly miserable. They were strangers in a strange place. Then again, they were *always* strangers in a strange place, what the fuck did it matter which country?

The front page was patched with articles about different local LA murders, turf wars, drug busts, gang fights, and dirty politicians. Absolutely nothing new according to the news blaring through the walls. She scanned the article titles.

Dead Body Found in Apartment Baffles Police

Dirty Pictures are the Downfall of Congressman

Chief of Police Found Dead in Warehouse Fire

Bodies Found Believed to be Gang Related

New Evidence on Warehouse Massacre

She shivered. No wonder she had nightmares about massacres and zombies. Who wouldn't after reading this shit? June folded the paper and laid it where she found it, noticing a brown buried file. She read the hand-written white label on its edge. It was her dad's handwriting.

Red Fever [5L]

Red Fever? She smiled, it sounded like a porno... or a biological weapon.

The edge of a picture was sticking out from between the folds. Out of habit, June looked around the room in case her father suddenly showed up. Ben was private to the point of obsession. In fact, as much as they moved and as secretive as he kept himself, she was utterly convinced her father was working for the CIA.

She just wanted to take a quick peek. What could it hurt?

One.

Small.

Peek.

She opened the file.

Sitting at the top was a newspaper clipping and a picture. The article's title was something about the porno, *Red Fever,* but it was the picture that caught her eye. Two men were standing side by side, smiling, arm over arm. It was an old picture, slightly faded. She recognized one of the men as her father, but it was the other... the *boy* that held her attention. He looked like a K-pop artist – fucking stunning with a unique mixed heritage, like maybe Chinese and American? Or Korean and Spanish? Whatever he was, he was seriously hot, and he couldn't be much older than June was now.

Except...

She flipped the picture, it was dated over thirteen years ago. June was just a toddler. Written on the back were their names.

Ben Shimmers and Yang Choo.

She stared at the beautiful boy for a long time, memorizing his features like he was famous. Her mind hanging onto his name, pushing all traces of the nightmare away in favor of something beautiful.

Yang Choo…

She had never seen anyone as handsome as him. Not even in a magazine. It was a quick and easy decision to steal the picture and hide it smack in the middle of her old red leather journal that she kept hidden under her pillow.

There were many pictures in that file, she reasoned, and surely her dad wouldn't miss just one? Not this one. Feeling like a little thief, she pushed the other pictures back into the file fold and tucked it back under the stack of papers.

It was nearing 4am when June crawled back into bed, everything was deathly quiet including the noises from the neighbors. The silence felt deafening now.

Pulling her legs to her chest, she held them while slowly rocking herself into peace. Her pajamas and sheets were still soaking wet, making the room feel colder than it was. Sunrise was still too far off, and the night provided very little comforting light. Just the quarter moon reflecting off her yellow floorboards.

The nightmares visited whenever she was worried, and something about this new place worried her. Or maybe it was her dad's behavior that worried her. Ben was staying out later and later, forgetting to text or not caring despite their unbreakable agreement. Their unofficial agreement stated they had to check-in with each other before midnight – no matter what. A call, a text, even a hand-scribbled note. Something.

Her favorite text from him was, '*Staying at the office late*' code for '*I got lucky, don't wait up.*' They had this arrangement for as long as she could remember…especially because he knew she had nightmares when he didn't show. She checked her phone in case she missed the ding.

Nothing.

Something felt a little off tonight. They had a fucking deal. '*No matter what,*' he'd say, '*we connect before midnight.*'

Asshole.

Standing up, June walked to her window and stood in the scarce moonlight staring out into the street. The city was usually dead by 3am after all the bars locked down. Nothing moved outside except a cat or two. She stayed standing and staring out the window like a guard at her post and as solid as a soldier at watch.

When 6am rolled around, June was cold and aching with her teeth chattering, stomach growling, and bladder screaming. She slammed her curtains closed at the first glimmer of sunrise – slamming them so hard they ripped, pulling the hinge right off the wall. Releasing a frustrated sigh, she decided to just go about her normal school day and make him pay tonight. Revenge would be swift and sweet.

Tonight we're renting my favorite movie and ordering my favorite takeout… she smiled to herself as she plotted her vengeance down to the exact extra order of fortune cookies. Obsessively, she checked her phone again.

Still nothing. Mentally adding another order of shrimp fried rice to the *IOU* list building in her head.

##

It was time for school.

High school was worse than *Lord of the Flies* and June planned on staying lord. It was purely instinctual. Survival of the fittest.

Getting dressed, color coordinating, wearing makeup…in times like these, June missed the idea of having a mother. On the rare occasion, she let her mind wander and closing her eyes, she concentrated on any memory that might provoke one of her mother. Nothing. No memories and zero information. There was absolutely nothing in any corner of her mind. It was a blank space. An empty void and one that her dad never filled. The topic was completely off limits. Taboo. No subtext. No innuendos. Ben would get tight lipped and his eyes would drift off and June immediately knew that he left the conversation despite his body being present.

One time – and only once – he told her to look in the mirror when she wanted to see her mother. And that was that and just like that the conversation was over. She didn't bother asking him anymore.

Until they arrived in LA.

June's mind was momentarily cluttered with semi-happy moments with her dad as she made herself presentable for school. That's what her dad would say, *be presentable*. And she would answer, *be available*. And they had their own special weird communication process. A threat but not really a threat. A warning but not really a warning. A demand but not really demanding. They spoke in subtext. And she loved the decoding process. It gave her brain something to do instead of worry.

Except for today.

June returned to obsessing and checking her phone like she was an addict counting the seconds until her next fix.

Where the fuck is that asshole?

She was mentally cussing at him over and over hoping somehow he would feel all the sharp mental daggers her brain was throwing at him.

It was time to leave for school! Quickly grabbing the stolen picture from her journal, she flicked at Ben's head with her finger before shoving everything into her backpack and heading out the front door. She paused for a moment as a brilliant revenge plot presented itself, and with a small glint of requite flashing across her eyes, June aggressively slid her hand over the kitchen counter scattering all the newspapers, the clippings, and files...

He'll get that message.

It gave her no relief to sabotage his stash... and somewhere in the pit of her stomach, the tiny alarm switched from bad to worse.

June flew down the apartment steps, skipping four at a time, and jumping and running full speed down all seven stories. At the bottom step, she paused momentarily realizing this was the first time leaving home without making contact with her dad. It frightened, angered, excited, and tormented her all at once.

When her feet hit the cement at ground level, the bad feeling twisted and grew twice its size forcing her to a sliding halt just outside their building. She couldn't take it anymore, deciding to reach out one more time before school.

Fuck him. I'll find another way to make him pay.

Unlocking her phone, she scrolled past the dozen or so violent and threatening messages she left him until she found the last message he sent her. It was a stupid pointless text and laced with subtext for her to decipher.

Today is National Chocolate Day and National Red Wine Day. So why not grab some chocolates and red wine for a good time.

Time stamp was around 8:24pm. The subtext? He got laid using some good old-fashioned wooing. Her response was immediate, blunt and sweet.

What goes n da lips comes out on da hips and I'm underage. Nuff said. Mic drop.

Ben had been out of contact for almost 12 hours now. Standing outside in the early morning sun made it difficult to see her on-screen keyboard, so she moved to the edge of the building for some shade, sending three letters and a question mark.

WTF?

A familiar ding from somewhere close penetrated her thoughts. Her eyes shifted past her phone to search for the receiver. But there wasn't anyone close enough. Curious, she quickly retyped it.

WTF? Send.

Ding. It sounded like it was coming from the side of her building, very near to where she was standing.

No way…

She quickly typed the three letters a third time following the ding. Excitement taking over the ball of anxiety in her gut.

He lost his phone!

She couldn't help the giggle resonating in her chest, she planned to *never* let him live this down. A small wicked grin spreading across her face.

This time she dialed, waiting, instantly hearing '*Everything is Awesome*' from the Lego movie. It was the ringtone she assigned herself on his phone, annoying as hell and super funny. She giggled louder, quickening her pace toward the music.

She followed it about six feet into the alley, searching on the ground, moving aside papers, wrappers, and broken pieces of boxes. It went to voicemail.

"Where's your stupid phone? Oh looky here… you dropped it! So… okay… you have somewhat of an excuse as to why you didn't check in, but you still owe me! And why didn't you wake me when you *dropped by*? I know you came home. You owe me big time! And I'm collecting! Don't bother coming home tonight unless you have an extra order of shrimp fried rice and an extra bag of fortune cookies!"

End. Satisfied with her threat, she dialed again, the happy ringtone leading her further into the alley. June was staring at the ground as she searched around the dumpster, kicking away debris, her foot suddenly hit a pair of perfectly polished black shoes. Startled, she almost fell backwards, quickly looking up to see her father standing in front of her.

His eyes were wide, blank. He was hanging onto the corner edge of the dumpster, and pushing off it, he started stumbling toward her like he had been drinking.

"Dad? What're you doing!? You scared me!"

Ben only stared at her in response, his eyes softening...

That's when she saw the blood on his hand. At first it was barely noticeable but the longer she looked at it, the more the blood seemed to grow... spreading rapidly over his long white sleeve dress shirt.

RED FEVER

Chapter 2

Cops and Robbers

"Shit! Did you cut yourself?" June reached out grabbing his hand to take a closer look. Her mind couldn't comprehend what she was seeing. It couldn't. The blood was spreading too quickly, saturating the entire front of him, spilling down his pants, onto his shoes, and pooling on the cement.

Everything around her was slowing down until all the trains in her brain came to a screeching halt, no… they fucking crashed. She snapped her phone shut as her father took two more steps to reach her, collapsing to his knees, and falling over onto his back. The blood continuing to pool around her feet like a giant oil spill. It was her fucking nightmare all over again.

One minute her dad was walking toward her and then he wasn't. One minute he was standing – then he was face up on the ground, all in the time it took her to blink. The tall proud world traveler reduced to a pound of flesh laying in spit and bubblegum. Disturbing as it was, it was June's response that would later come to haunt her.

She just stared. Observing the scene like a spectator. Watching. Witnessing the end of a life. Paralyzed with fear, frozen in a swirl of time and blood. As he collapsed, his eyes found and locked onto hers, red, bloodshot, bulging. They were speaking to her – saying something. Warning? Apologizing? Blaming? Forgiving? She'll never know…

Just like the woman in her nightmare.

Ben was laying in a pool of his own blood, staring at nothing. The memory of the hollow thud from his skull hitting the pavement burned permanently into her brain. Freeing herself from the trap of her own nightmare, June skidded to her knees to reach him.

##

His facial expression never changed. His eyes never blinked. They just kept staring at nothing. Nothing. June laid her hand on his chest. And for just a moment, she thought her father was looking right at her, seeing her and realizing he wasn't alone.

She touched his cheek with her finger to see if he would blink, move, flinch, do something, do anything. But there was nothing left of him.

Ben Shimmers was gone, leaving June alone... again.

"Daddy?" she whispered softly in shock and horror. She had never seen a dead body before.

Maybe in her dreams.

June jerked him tightly against her, his body offering no more resistance, his eyes permanently fixed on nothing.

"Dad?" she tried again. A rush of emotion spilling over into hysterical pleas.

"Daddy!? NO! Please no! No... no... no! Somebody help me! Dad! Daddy!" she cried out to an empty street.

"Don't leave me... please please daddy... don't! Don't leave me. Don't leave me alone. Please! Somebody help me! Help!" June begged him to get up. She pounded on his chest, shaking his body and calling to him as if she somehow had the power to wake the dead.

"Please! No! No! No, daddy, don't leave me! SOMEBODY HELP HIM!" In a last-ditch effort, she put her hand over the hole in his heart to stop the blood from gushing... or push it back in. Her hand felt nothing. No beat. No life.

She was too late.

And for one brief moment, she was that little girl in the haunted house she dreamed of most nights. She collapsed onto his chest, hugging what was left of him.

"Daddy don't leave me alone," she whispered in his ear, begging him to stay and weeping uncontrollably. Promising to be a good girl. Promising anything he wanted if he stayed with her for a little while longer. And part of her was dying right alongside him. The blood that pooled around her knees felt like it was coming from her own wounds. She rocked back and forth holding him as close as her little arms would let her, weeping, begging, pleading for his life.

##

It may have been days… maybe hours… or maybe a few seconds when she first heard the click of a camera, followed by several more clicks. Looking up, she was surrounded by nosy neighbors taking pictures and capturing the worst moment of her life. Capturing the utter loneliness, despair, helplessness, and failure of a family. Like the rich and famous with their paparazzi stalkers. She wanted to be angry and scream at them but her mind wouldn't engage in any emotion except profound grief.

June held him tightly, hiding him from the onlookers, weeping bitterly… and the people around her were murmuring like background noise in a coffee shop, like bees buzzing around a hive. Their faces a blur while they clicked their cameras with oohs and ahhs like it was all just a goddamn peep show or entertainment from street performers. And then she could hear someone screaming loudly – screaming bloody murder…

The loud screaming was coming from her own mouth. Her weeping had turned to murderous wailing. Wailing that was soon covered up by the sounds of sirens.

##

In the blink of an eye her life came to a crashing end. Why didn't it happen like the movies? Why wasn't she given time to remember every detail? Every feeling? The memory that remained most true was the blood on her hands as the EMTs pulled his body away from her. Cops. Firemen. EMTs.

Thieves.

All of them were fucking thieves.

Taking what didn't belong to them. Taking his body away and pushing her off him like she was some kind of nothing, like they were removing a blood-sucking leech. If she could just hold on to him, somehow that would be enough to stop time, stop everything from happening so fast. Maybe she could be enough to keep him alive? The blood on her hands and knees told a different story.

As they carried him away, the only thing running through June's head was the lyrics of one of her dad's stupid songs. A song he would sing to her whenever she cut herself or got hurt in one of her martial arts tournaments:

blood on the saddle

blood on the ground

great big puddles of blood all around

pity that cowboy, bloody and red

dumb old pony done stomped on his head.

The men in uniform carted his body into their truck, taking him, taking everything, taking every single part of life as she knew it.

It was like he never even existed.

Dr. Joan M Savage

Chapter 3

Rising Phoenix

Frumpled across her desk in a pile of messy red curly hair, June was laying with her arms spread straight out as if she were crucifying herself.

She was doing it again.

Three and a half years later and she still couldn't forgive herself. Popping up in frustration, she cupped her hands over her ears like she did when she was a small child. As if it would somehow silence the thoughts and the onslaught of memories. She wasn't even sixteen years old when her father was murdered. She played that party scene over and over in her head trying to remember the faces around her – the smells – everything. Anything. But the only real memory remaining was the blood. It permanently etched itself into her brain almost as if she was still there, trapped in that moment. It was fresh and warm and smelled like a bag full of copper pennies.

The cops were robbers that day, peeling her off him and tossing her aside. Nobody checked on her. Nobody asked her if she was okay. Nobody even asked who she was. So when they pushed her away, she simply stepped back as one of the crowd… watching them steal her dad. She blended in with the onlookers and spectators, acting nosy and curious, hiding her tear-smeared cheeks under her hoodie, her bloody knees with her long blue socks, and her bloody hands in her pockets. She just disappeared into the wayside.

There was no other way, she reasoned as she thought about the choices she made to get where she was. When Ben died, chronologically she was still too young to be alone in the world. She feared if anyone found her, they would put her in a home, in the system, or worse. The irony being she did exactly what her father taught her to do since before she could remember – run and disappear.

June blinked back the tears, quickly looking around the room hoping nobody noticed the childish behavior of cupping her hands over her ears. For a minute she forgot where she was, and worse, she momentarily forgot *who* she was... as far as the world was concerned June Shimmers never existed.

She became someone else. How ironic that she became the very thing she hated the most.

Standing up, June stretched all five feet six inches of her body toward the blueish-gray ceiling of the Indianapolis Police Station, rolling her neck around and around as it clicked and popped. June adjusted her uniform and straightened both her badge and its accompanying name tag. The name on the tag read *JoJo Sparks*.

Forgetting her identity now could literally land her in jail. Sighing deeply, she ran her hand over her head, only to make a face as she felt the mess of red curls that had escaped their prison bun. It was still early enough that she could probably nap at her desk at least another 30 minutes before the day shift started. Fuck the bun, she'll fix it later. A nap was preferable.

But rest was the furthest thing from her thoughts. When her ass hit the chair, her mind wandered right back to where it left off. Right when the men in uniform pried her off Ben's body and pushed her away. Without her father, there was nobody in the world around to miss her or even remember who she was...

She stared at the computer screen with a deep growing sense of despair filling her heart.

Sleep wasn't happening and for some reason memories were mercilessly bombarding her today. She typed her dad's name into the IPD case file search bar while the little cursor blinked at her. Just blinking and blinking. Waiting for her to add something else. Waiting for more information. Waiting for answers. Like the cursor on her heart, blinking, blinking, waiting, waiting. Waiting for her to rearrange the evidence – see it differently – change perspectives. To mix and match names and dates and other places. Something different. Something new. Something broken. Something blue. Any-fucking-thing. Why couldn't she remember anything? She slammed her hand down on the keyboard.

"Fuck."

It had been over three fucking years and she still had nothing to add. Nothing. Like their entire life together meant nothing. No matter what she typed into the goddamn computer, nothing came back, solidifying the possibility that Ben Shimmers was indeed in the CIA. She was one hundred percent certain of it.

Well… either the CIA or the mafia. It was a fifty-fifty guess at this point.

Massaging her temples, random memories pelted her faster than she could handle it. What triggered them? Nothing unusual happened today.

Except… night shift brought in an eight year old boy for stealing baby food.

What a fucked up world when we arrest a kid for stealing food… and for a baby.

It had to be for a baby. Any normal kid would steal candy or real food.

June knew too well, she stole her share of survival food when Ben performed his disappearing acts. She thought back to the first time she lifted some food from a local convenience store. At the ripe old age of eight years old, when hunger was at its worst, June easily stole a can of mini hotdogs… and some candy. But Jesus Christ never any baby food.

Who the hell steals baby food?

She worried her lip wondering if a small infant somewhere was going to starve tonight, once again remembering her own nights of starvation and survival. By the ripe old age of ten, she could easily pilfer a meal, and take a grown man to the ground when she got caught. At eleven years old, she knew thirty ways to kill a man, pick his pockets, and steal his car. Why could she remember all that in explicit detail, and for the life of her she couldn't remember a single face in the crowd that watched her father die in her arms? Blank. They were all blank to her. She was blank.

Suddenly feeling sorry for herself, June missed the tangible investigation board she put together with strings and drop pins that pieced together her dad's life – places, projects, people he might have known, pictures she remembered laying around. The board was plain and simple – no expectations. No demands.

Unlike the fucking blinking cursor.

It felt like it was screaming at her. Gnawing at her. Demanding more from her with little promise of return. She slammed the keyboard with her hand again. Every time she reexamined the past, an old familiar anger would grip her throat like two hands trying to choke her to death. Fuck anger – it was downright rage.

Time to shut it down… just for now.

Taking a deep breath, she ran her fingers through her hair suddenly remembering the tangled disaster on her head. She stood up arching her back like a cat, yawning indolently.

Her Indianapolis police uniform fit her perfectly – a little too perfectly – highlighting every curve and attractive feature of her athletic body. The resulting ensemble made her look like a very expensive call girl – to which the guys she worked with never let her forget.

She blossomed into a "goddamn beauty" as her Indy Captain liked to say, and something she truly resented him for. Fighting was her thing, not flirting.

F-I-G-H-T-I-N-G.

And the obsessive pursuit of her dad's murderer.

These were the reasons for her existence. The reason she became a police officer – the people she hated most for taking her dad away. And seeking revenge motivated her to get up in the morning and keep breathing. It was the *only* reason she dared to put on this uniform. Everything else was shit.

She headed to the restroom. It was time for her shift to start and her hair looked like it barely survived a hurricane.

The only thing left tying her to the past was her own fading memory.

And one other.

She found herself smiling and quickly catching herself, she glanced around to see if anyone noticed.

Thinking of the *one other* was… insidious. And the day she met him was both heaven and hell.

RED FEVER

Chapter 4

A Million Designs for Revenge

They were burying her dad.

It was completely by accident that she discovered there was a funeral for him. After waiting a few days, she was satisfied the cops didn't know about their apartment, so she crawled into her window and packed up whatever shit could fit into one of her smaller suitcases. Ben had a stash of cash taped to the bottom of his dresser.

"Emergencies only," he warned her.

I think your death counts as an emergency. She reasoned with him silently.

And sitting there on top of the stack of mail in their mail slot was an invitation to Ben's funeral.

Who the fuck even knew we lived here?

It was a formal invitation, something you would see for an expensive wedding – glorious and shiny. She couldn't possibly imagine who in the world would pay for a real funeral... they didn't know anybody. At least, *she* didn't know anybody. Would anyone come to see him?

June went to the cemetery by bus, and much to her distress, people came. Surely they were there for someone else? A simultaneous funeral of another *someone*, a famous someone, an important someone. And what a fucking shock to discover they were there to see her *someone*. People in black cars and SUVs, limousines, police cruisers, and a chain of fancy vehicles like her dad was true royalty.

And they kept coming even though it was raining.

June decided to hide until she had some privacy. She needed to be a ghost lest someone ask the wrong question or discover she was Ben's kid and toss her in a home. She was in the process of disappearing, but for the invitation to the funeral... she wanted to say goodbye. June found an oversized gravestone and carefully hid behind it. It was all she could do not to weep bitterly while waiting for her chance to say her peace.

She peeked around the stone.

Jesus, there were so many goddamn fucking people...

And they just kept coming. Coming and coming all day long. Coming and coming even after his funeral hours officially ended. Her curiosity concerning the identity of so many people nearly killed her, but fear of discovery was stronger, and the grief deeper. Twice she almost talked herself into asking one of them who they were... and twice she started panicking.

No, I'll wait.

The longer it rained, the colder it became, and the deeper her despair. And all she wanted was to say goodbye. Hours passed as she waited for some privacy. The only warmth came from her boney arms wrapping tightly around her bare knees. Her blue lips matching her school uniform with its short skirt, and suit jacket, neither of which provided any warmth. She didn't care though, maybe it was the hypothermia setting in, or maybe because the longer she thought about life alone on the run without her father, the more pointless life seemed. In fact, as far as she could see with the wisdom of her fifteen-year-old eyes, there was no life without him.

And right there she decided as soon as the place emptied, she would lay down on his grave, and wait for death. It was a good plan. She was already halfway frozen anyway.

June huddled against her knees still waiting for the last stupid person with their stupid big red umbrella to finally drive away. The dark of night poured into the sky as the sun said its goodbyes to the day making June even colder until she couldn't feel her fingers or toes, and ice cold were her cheeks and nose. Peeking around the gravestone again, she watched the final visitor drive completely out of view. Satisfied she was safely alone, she made her move to finally be with her daddy. It was all she could do to get her body moving. It was so cold, so fucking cold.

The last two hours had numbed her heart, quieting her tears. But the moment she reached his newly dug mud pile, she collapsed into it, wondering if he was feeling lonely six feet under. Or if he was cold and if he knew she was with him.

The love in her heart became unbearable, freeing a fresh new wave of tears and melting the cold that was numbing her.

June laid deep in the mud, letting it soak her up like quicksand and letting it pull her closer to him. Releasing all emotional inhibitions, she wept bitterly. Not just for his death but for the years of his constant absence only to lose him without any answers, and without any peace between them. The feeling of total aloneness and hopelessness washing over her in large billowy waves of grief.

She was grateful that her wailing was covered up by the heavy downpour. Feeling broken and fucking lost, June didn't notice that someone had walked up behind her. One minute the rain was pelting her back and neck, and the next not a drop was touching her. She looked up, blinking back the tears and the rain – staring into the face of an angel.

Or the devil.

He was standing behind her, holding his umbrella over her. And to this day, she has never seen anyone more handsome. She recognized him from the old photo she stole.

Yang Choo.

He was by far the most beautiful man she ever laid eyes on, and for a second, June really believed she was looking at an angel. She had to keep blinking back the tears and the rain to see if it was real.

Her heart quickened, while her stomach filled with butterflies. And despite being soaking wet, her mouth went dry.

The boy from the photo – the man – was carefully studying her every reaction. Even in the downpour and in the midst of the freshly dug dirt, she caught a whiff of his musky scent and delightful cologne. He was the only brightness in that dreary awful cold day, and by far even more stunning than the photo. His black handmade Italian double-breasted suit gave him the appearance of a gentleman. His emerald eyes shone brightly with noesis – a destructive, restless, piercing, chaotic force. The authority and power radiating from him suddenly warmed June from the tip of her toes to the top of her head like she was standing too close to a blazing inferno.

For one brief moment, in what felt like an eternity, June actually forgot about the pain her father caused.

Maybe it was the feeling of power and strength emanating from him. And it was strength that June coveted the most. In fact, she never wanted anything more than to have it, and would do anything for it. If for nothing else than to stop the pain she was in. Yang Choo had the power to stop pain. Maybe he was an angel after all.

##

When she could finally peel her eyes away from him, it suddenly occurred to her that he was surrounded by about 30 men – all in black suits with their black umbrellas and black sunglasses. He was like the president or some important foreign dignitary. She scanned over the little crowd of guards in black, wondering how in the hell so many people could walk right up to her without her knowing, hearing, or sensing them. She was ever so careful to wait until every last person had left the cemetery before coming out of hiding. Where did they all come from?

Each man was positioned carefully around her, standing in the cold rain like it was nothing, like they didn't even notice. Or maybe they were positioned carefully around the man in front of her – Yang Choo, leader of the LA Triads. Could this really be him? She wiped her eyes again to make sure they weren't deceiving her, leaving behind two long mud smears.

Yang smiled a cold lifeless smile, and continued studying her, almost as if he was waiting for something. He was dazzling and something warned her that despite his appearance, he was far more dangerous than dazzling.

Just about the time she was finding some courage to say something, he snatched it away when he slowly squatted down next to her, carefully laying his hand on her shoulder. Everything about him seemed restrained and guarded. She knew in theory who he was from her dad's pictures. Everyone who dabbled in any kind of illegal activity knew about the Organizations that thrived underground. Shit, anyone who listened to the news knew of the chaos happening downtown with the LA Triads sitting right in the middle of it. And right there on her dead father's mud pile, with the leader of the LA Triads squatting next to her, June Shimmers suddenly second guessed her assumption about Ben's occupation. Maybe he wasn't in the CIA after all. Maybe it was something far more sinister.

As she pondered things both past and present, the warm hand on her shoulder sent a shiver throughout her entire body, waking her from the cold friendless nightmare she was living. Somewhere in the growing up process, she forgot the value of human touch. And when he spoke, his voice was deep and rich and so goddamn reassuring that it shook her to the core and took everything she had not to fall into his arms and weep uncontrollably. Or maybe it took nothing at all because she had nothing left.

"Your... father was... a friend... a very good friend," he said, struggling with his words. "He... he'll be missed." Clearing his throat, Yang waited, studying her expression again. She could only stare up at him, blinking, mesmerized by him.

Even squatting, he towered over her, and she trembled from both the fear and the pleasure she found just from looking at him. The cold had long since disappeared from her body almost as if the hand on her shoulder was willing it away. He was fucking intoxicating and her sudden intense feelings for him were the only thing greater than the grief and despair. On any other day, in any other situation, she knew she lacked the courage to speak to someone like him. But this wasn't any other day, and this wasn't just any situation, and suddenly June had all the courage she needed. The courage to speak to him, to look at him, to indulge in his physical appearance, to be present with him. And intoxicating or not, she suddenly had the courage of a fucking dragon.

"How do you know... who... why... is this funeral... did you pay... do you know..." She had so many questions they came out in a garbled mess. She stopped and asked the one real question that mattered most, the one haunting her.

"Do you know who... who killed my father?"

The cold sweeping back in like an opened floodgate. Her teeth chattering behind blue lips, her voice was not nearly as courageous as her thoughts. From the moment she first noticed him, the only real expression to cross his face was a hint of surprise that she actually spoke to him, and for whatever reason, he answered her.

"Do you really want to know?" His voice was soothing and so soft and velvety in the rain. Standing back up, he kept them both covered with his large umbrella. The intensity of his closeness and the depth from his piercing eyes reminded her of a lion. Fierce and dangerous. She stared blankly at him, nodding, struggling to find her voice again. He sensed her hesitation, misunderstanding the pause.

"If you do, you'll never be the same. How about you let it go and live a normal life now? Hmmm? Can you do that?"

Feeling him withdraw, she managed to jump up quickly even though her joints were locked up and frozen. Dirt and mud ran down her bare legs. She shook her head, her curls forcing water to spray onto his fancy suit. He didn't seem to notice or care.

"Please! Do you know who killed him? Please tell me. I'll do whatever. I don't care. Just tell me… please."

This time she didn't have the courage to look at him, though she was standing right in front of him. In her heart, she knew she'd die for the truth. He stayed silent until she forced her eyes to slowly drift back up. Her heart beating so loudly she was sure he could hear it or at the very least see the pulse in the stupid vein on her neck.

His eyes were a cozy shade of green with few specks of yellow – a unique color for Chinese. Despite their soulfulness, they remained guarded. Yang Choo was definitely of mixed heritage, and June couldn't stop herself from studying every inch of him. In theory, she knew he was much older than the picture she memorized, yet surprisingly, he looked younger than expected. And equally handsome - maybe more so with the edge of wisdom etched into his fine features like golden streaks in granite. She guessed he was in his early thirties, and as far as she could tell, stood well over six feet. A rosy flush filled her cheeks when she realized he was studying her as intensely as she was studying him, and while they sized each other up, words simply were not enough. Her beating heart made it impossible to do or say anything else. It tied up her tongue and forced her to hold her breath. So she stood there being held hostage by her own body as everything he was – power, strength, beauty, danger, and hope – slammed into her all at once.

She tried to break the spell in a last ditch effort by stepping toward him, except the mud held her foot like a giant suction cup and she fell forward, grabbing his cashmere jacket with her muddy hands.

"Please tell me! I want the truth." It wasn't meant to be an aggressive move, but she was already mid-sentence when she fell forward. One of the men standing closest to them, yanked her off him, slamming his fist into her gut. The force knocked her back and pushed out all the air she was holding. Oddly, the pain from the punch felt better and more real to her than the weird breathlessness Yang Choo was causing. She fell back into the mud landing with a splash.

With his free hand, Yang casually waved his man away, neither punishing nor praising him, and June was certain he looked bored by the entire interaction. She could see him scanning the cemetery like he was searching for something, or maybe he was giving her time to find her footing. Refusing to help, waiting and watching while she gagged, coughed, and slipped around the mud. She never stopped fighting to stand back up, unwilling to back down. When a string of cuss words left her mouth and she forced herself to stand and face him, his eyebrow popped up seemingly impressed by her. Once she found her footing, he spoke again.

"The truth will hurt worse." His voice was laced with warning, his eyes shifting to cold and dark again. And just like that he was walking away. Still struggling to catch her breath, she willed herself to follow him.

"Please," she demanded unconvincingly, coughing and nursing her gut.

"Tell me! PLEASE!"

He spun around so abruptly, she instinctively cowered back, hands raised in self-defense.

"Goddamn right to fear me." The beautiful emerald eyes turning yet a darker shade of green.

"I don't," she didn't mean to pop off, surprising even herself. She knew better though, so she stared at her feet, glancing up only briefly to steal a peek at the Triad leader. Yang was smiling slightly, clearly amused or maybe still impressed by her, and she found her courage again when she caught the expression. She stood her ground now, waiting for him to answer.

"His killer… is a LEO."

"What?" Shaking her head, confused. She didn't understand.

"I don't… what? His name is Leo? First name? Please, I don't understand," she whispered fearfully but not backing down.

"LEO, Law Enforcement Officer." He leaned in closer and

instinctively she stepped back, lowering her gaze.

"A fucking dirty cop. Do you understand now?"

After a long silence, she did understand. He was right, it hurt worse than a hit to the gut. Holding his eyes, she searched them for the truth.

"Why? Who? Who was it? Why? Why my dad?"

Yang shook his head. "I... have very little information. And if I pursue the matter, I could lose my... *source* in the department." He was studying her face. Amusement still clinging to the edge of his eyes and the corners of his mouth. Was he taking pleasure in her confusion and pain? She couldn't stop her own features from contorting with too much emotion – none of which was amusing.

"Your source? A cop *works*... for *you?* But..." Her face slowly turned red. Should she know this? Was he going to kill her? Isn't that what villains do? They tell you all their secrets and then kill you? The brave dragon flew away and suddenly she felt truly terrified and very much alone.

The irony was that ten minutes ago she didn't care what happened to her but now something new was birthing – *desire*. A desire to fight for it. How precious and how odd is the value of a sixty second conversation. June Shimmers wanted to live, if for no other reason than to find out who killed her dad. She silently vowed to do whatever it took to find him.

Or her. Or them...

The dragon was slowly slithering back, filling up every single empty space while her mind was filling with a million designs for revenge.

"Whoever it was knew our schedules, there's another player. A dirty cop was working against your father."

"I... I don't understand... if... if you have cops working for you then... then why not ask them!? Use them? You said he was your friend." She could hear the desperation in her voice, her mind going a hundred miles an hour. What could she possibly do? Shit, she wasn't even old enough to get a goddamn job.

June had disappeared again into her own thinking. She was covered in mud, and her thoughts were now dragging her through it, reminding her of everything she didn't have and what she couldn't do. And the cold from the rain, the pain from the punch, and the grief from the day started returning blow by painful blow. She was frozen and lost again. Wrapping her arms around herself for warmth, she was so full of hopelessness and despair that she momentarily forgot she was in the presence of a mafia boss.

Yang produced a large white envelope from inside his jacket, smacking it against her arms, breaking the despairing spell.

"Everything you need."

She mechanically took the envelope. It had money in it. She could definitely feel a stack of money in it.

"I don't want your money! I want to know who killed my father," she demanded daringly, and reading the amusement in his eyes again, this pissed her off even more. The guard who punched her stepped forward drawing his fist back. Only this time, Yang stopped him with a slight tilt of his chin. The entire situation was truly impressive – a nod, a wave and these men did his bidding. Was she impressed or disgusted?

Jealous. A small voice admitted.

"Everything you need is in that envelope," he repeated. "Follow it precisely. And when I see you again, we'll take care of his murderer."

"Why not now? Why wait!? I'll do anything. Anything! Please. Why wait?"

Yang looked her up and down, pity briefly flashing in his face. She was wet, cold, and covered in mud and if she even looked half as bad as she felt, it was truly pathetic.

"Because you're not ready. And I don't do favors for free. If I pursue this matter, I'll be exposing my source. I'm not prepared to lose any *advantage* until I have a replacement, understand? Follow the instructions."

It began to dawn on her what he was asking her to do.

"What? I'm… I can't. I'm not old enough! I'm too young," she whined, arms wrapping around the envelope and her body, suddenly feeling small, childish, and afraid. He interrupted her protests.

"Not anymore." He was leaving again.

"Wait! Please… just wait… I… why me?" She half opened the envelope to take a quick peek, trying to protect the contents from the rain. She could see money, papers, and a passport. June's nose was buried deep in the package so she didn't notice when Yang turned around and stopped directly in front of her. It wasn't until she looked up to see why the rain stopped pelting her neck that she nearly bumped her forehead into his chest. Springing away to avoid him, she slipped, almost falling on her ass.

This time Yang grabbed her arm, holding her suspended between standing upwards and falling backwards.

"Because you asked," he said. They locked eyes and once again it was like looking at the face of a dangerous lion. She couldn't move, held captive by his gaze, his hand holding her suspended in place. As he spoke, he slowly pulled her upright.

"I have a few questions of my own. Like who is moving on *my* territory? Who has that kind of power? And how did they manage to stay hidden from me? You're in a perfect position to help me find my blind spots. No record. No history. No background. Nothing. June Shimmers never existed." He leaned in even closer now, pointing his finger in her face.

"You belong to me now, understand? Don't fuck it up. It's the price we pay for revenge. Never forget that."

She watched as his emerald eyes searched hers, waiting for something. *Waiting? For what?* A response? She slipped into a terrified poker face. His closeness triggering a temporary short-circuit in her brain, robbing her of any meaningful reaction, but leaving a small fire burning behind her very blue eyes, the promise of a coming storm. Taking her silence as acceptance, he released her and started walking away again.

June woke from her stupor, shaking off his effect. She deeply breathed in the earthy smells of the graveyard to erase the intoxication caused by his cologne. There was a question lingering in her soul.

"We?" She tried to sound brave. Without looking back, Yang paused a beat, his only acknowledgment of her question. She tried one more time.

"You said my father was your friend!"

He never turned back around, and she could barely hear his answer in the downpour.

"That's the only reason you're still alive. Follow the instructions precisely."

And she did.

Like the mist born of rain, Yang and his men simply disappeared into the fog, the muddy white envelope was the only proof she didn't dream up the whole thing.

June fulfilled what she set out to do that day — say goodbye and die.

She kissed her daddy's gravestone and said goodbye, letting go of everything that once was.

June Shimmers died that day and JoJo Sparks was born.

RED FEVER

Chapter 5

In The Mix

She shivered, remembering that terrible wonderful awful day and instinctively hugging her body as if she were that lost 15 year old kid again. It's been well over three years and the memory of that cold day still managed to freeze her skin. But the thought of Yang Choo warmed it right back up like drinking hot apple cider on a windy winter's day. Sweet and sour and absolutely delicious as it burned its way through you. The pain was worth the pleasure.

Shaking her head, she tried pushing away all the memories bombarding her.

She was JoJo Sparks now.

And June never existed. Yang's velvety voice reminding her.

She dug around her purse, pulling out an old battered picture from the secret hole she made especially for it – a hole impossible to find unless you knew exactly where to look. A neat little trick Ben taught her. It was the photo she stole the day he died. Yang and her dad looked so *happy.* She gripped the shirt over her heart trying to quiet the emotions suddenly rolling around. This fucking reminiscing was going to get her into a shitload of trouble if she accidentally slipped up. It was time to stop remembering. At least for now.

The workday was about to start, and her hair still had some serious management issues.

##

The halls were empty. The bathroom was empty. Her heart felt empty. JoJo stared at herself in the mirror.

"Yang Choo..." His name rolled right off her tongue, quieting the emptiness. She hadn't talked to him since the graveyard. Oh she *read* about him, saw his *handiwork* on the news and police reports. The velvety voice meant to threaten her became her reassurance.

Don't fuck it up.

She was early to arrive and last to leave, for 11 months now she held an impeccable record as a police officer. She kept her nose clean and spent her off hours continuing to study Chinese and Italian – the two languages that would assure her a position within the LAPD. When she wasn't studying, she was practicing self-defense and martial arts. Every waking hour was spent preparing... and preparing. She would find the goddamn mother fucker who killed her father... perhaps it was more than one? She'll burn the whole fucking force down to find out who.

And why. Why my dad?

She followed every explicit instruction Mr. Choo left her – starting with signing up for University the first chance she got. And two years later, walked out with a degree in criminal justice minoring in foreign languages. A week after graduation, she got an offer to join the Indianapolis Police Department.

It was a bitter taste when she put on the uniform. It went against all her principles, and it was the only time she ever actually felt dirty since teaming up with a mob boss. But it wasn't until JoJo raised her right hand and swore to protect and to serve that she truly felt disgusted with herself.

Good cops, bad cops, they were all filthy murdering pigs to her... and now she was one of them.

Don't fuck it up.

Just like that goddamn blinking cursor on her computer, she was waiting... and waiting. Waiting for her chance. Waiting for new information. She would be ready for LA when LA came calling. She would be ready for Yang Choo.

The bathroom door suddenly opened, startling JoJo and waking her from overwhelming feelings of nostalgia. It was Lena – a rookie cop.

"You're here early," she commented.

JoJo was finishing forcing her curls back into submission, and without missing a beat she spun around and slammed her shoulder into Lena as she exited the bathroom.

"So are you."

"Wait! I think the Captain wants to see you."

JoJo studied her, searching for any deceit.

"Why?"

She shrugged, "Last night I overheard him say he was looking for you. I… I just thought you should know. He isn't here yet, if you wanted to… uhm… get your shit together." She locked her eyebrows high in the air. JoJo snorted loudly.

"My shit's always together."

As JoJo returned to her desk, she wondered how much more she could possibly *get her shit together*. She performed perfectly. And did everything right. Everything.

Well…

Everything except the underground fighting… and there may or may not have been some illegal betting. It didn't matter though, she ended all of it the day she was accepted into the academy.

When Mr. Choo handed her that white muddy envelope, he was handing her a real life. An identity. A reason. A purpose. She was no longer bound by any age restrictions. And like a moth to a flame, her pleasure became underground fighting as she began reinventing herself as JoJo Sparks.

She smiled wryly.

The illegal betting was a necessary evil for her buy-in.

Sighing deeply, she suddenly missed the sound of the crowd chanting as she kicked the shit out of some poor bastard. How could she not miss it? It was the one thing she was really good at. Fighting was her saving grace from thoughts of revenge because those thoughts too quickly and too easily mutated into rage. And rage gave her fucking superpowers in the arena.

Did the Captain find out about her past? Why would he want to see her?

Maybe it's the transfer I've been asking for?

For a moment, she found herself hoping, only to watch her thoughts go straight to hell.

What if they can link me to Mr. Choo? She shook her head and laid her face in her hands.

No. No, I was impeccable with secrecy. Painstakingly accurate covering my tracks. Perfect...just like him.

Yang Choo.

The packet Mr. Choo gave her was impressive. She couldn't imagine there being any fault with her ID, not with so much at stake. Anyway, if the ID lacked authenticity in any way, it would've failed the background check at the start of her employment. She looked over her cubicle wall at the Captain's office, worrying her lip. His office light was on.

As if sensing her eyes on him, the Captain yelled her name.

"Sparks! My office. Now!" JoJo jumped straight up like a soldier coming to attention, accidentally knocking her chair backward. Nervously, she headed for his office, failing to look as nonchalant as possible by overcompensating. He was yelling at her through the open door.

"Pack your shit! Your transfer request was approved. Another fucking cop killing!? Are you sure about this? LA sounds like a shithole mess if you ask me... I guess they need your linguistic skills. I haven't processed your outgoing paperwork *yet*. You can still change your mind."

He came out of his office holding an envelope in front of him like a carrot on a stick. Like Yang Choo did when she was fifteen, offering her a life, offering her a choice. She reached for it only to have him pull it back.

"Did you hear what I said? You can still change your mind." And the world slowed down, the way it does when she's about to pass out or do something really stupid... or really brave. Even though the world slowed, her thoughts sped up, zooming by too quickly like bullet trains coming in and out of focus.

Would I ever change my mind? Was that even possible now?

As if some unseen force answered her, an absolute *NO* reverberated through her filling every part of her empty soul, ending any internal debates.

She never really had a choice, her rage would never allow it. It felt like fate.

Or destiny.

Sighing loudly, she reached for the envelope dangling in front of her. The fire in her bones demanded justice and every single day that she didn't do something about it, a little piece of her died. It was burning her alive from the inside out. Just like the nightmares.

In the furthest recesses of her mind, an ancient proverb floated through her crazy thoughts,

What have you done? Listen! Your brother's blood cries out to me from the ground.

Her father's blood was crying out to her from the streets of LA, demanding justice. No, she never really had a choice if she wanted any kind of peace. It was too late, she gave up too much, and too much had changed. Like a snake that shed its skin or a molten caterpillar leaving its chrysalis, it was impossible to go back and fit into who and what she once was. She needed the truth, and made a promise to do anything for it.

Anything.

She snatched the envelope from the Captain's hand while the world caught back up to speed. Three years was a long time to wait... and she couldn't control the smile that slowly spread across her face, nor the sudden jump start to her heart. She was fucking in the mix!

JoJo Sparks was going to LA.

RED FEVER

Chapter 6

Shedding Skin

JoJo walked through the valley of the shadow of death.

At least that's what it felt like after walking two and half hours in six layers of baggy clothes. Even in the middle of the night, LA was hotter than Hades. Yet JoJo was determined to find Mr. Choo and let him know of her arrival and her new set of orders.

It was happening.

Their plan finally forming into something real, taking shape, growing roots. It was all she could do to contain her excitement. Excitement so pure it brought her to the bliss point – light-headed, intoxicated, and feeling higher than a kite. Fuck the heat.

She was high from thoughts of finally destroying the person who killed her father, high on the fact that LA's most notorious gangster was helping her, and high on the image of seeing those two perfectly brilliant emerald eyes again.

What could go wrong?

She hadn't spoken to Yang Choo since the funeral. All this time she waited in silence without a word from him.

She smiled to herself. Although she never *spoke* to him, she did *see* Mr. Choo... once. It was during one of her Saturday night fights, and there he was, so formidable, precarious, shrewd... and absolutely fucking gorgeous, strutting in like he owned the goddamn place. JoJo could only assume that he was doing business with the owner of the Indianapolis games. Of course no one knew it was her in the fights, she always covered her face, never using a real identity. And *always* rotated her ring names like *Martha Madness, Candy the Krusher, Wicked Winona*... she made it impossible to be identified.

Maybe Yang knew. Maybe he didn't. But one thing was certain, she knew him.

Pulling at her jacket collar, she tried to give her neck some breathing room as she felt the perspiration dripping between her shoulder blades. She was walking to Yang Choo's place of business – the Palace.

A promise is a promise, right? Did a promise mean the same thing to a gangster as to the rest of the planet?

The Palace lights were just up ahead, blinking like Las Vegas, and just as dazzling as their owner. A mini city on a hill that was known as Yang Choo's place of operations. Or so she read in the police files.

Suddenly feeling insecure, she questioned herself, her motives, his promise... what if he refused to uphold it? He didn't need to help her. Shit, he owned her. And she owed him.

JoJo knew there was a strong probability that the leader of the LA Triads would be under some kind of surveillance by any number of government agencies and probably one or two rival gangs as well. It made sense to scrutinize his every move, analyzing any comings and goings. So when JoJo arrived in LA, she was careful, painstakingly careful, to take extreme measures to avoid anything that could tie Mr. Choo and herself together, including her car or a cab ride. And now, after all this effort, why was she suddenly... what? Reluctant?

Afraid.

It's too late to be afraid. She reasoned.

Too late to tell the Captain to cancel her LA orders. Too late to shove the white muddy envelope back into Mr. Choo's hand. And too late to place her hand over the bullet wound on her father's heart to stop the bleeding.

In the unbearable heat, wearing a baggy coat, hoodie, baggy clothes, a ball cap with a face smudged in shoe polish, JoJo stuck her chin out and walked right up to the Palace doors like she had a standing appointment. Live or die – it was too late to change her mind. The butterfly emerged.

Or maybe it was the snake.

##

She entered into the splash damage created by the streetlamp, watching as two guards mysteriously appeared from the shadows. It reminded JoJo of a video game when her character would hit a distance watch and trigger a monster... or sometimes a pot of gold.

She wondered which one it would be.

The guards approached her cautiously. And JoJo realized she had no idea how to convince them that she was a *friend* of Yang Choo, leader of the LA Triads.

Jesus, even she didn't believe the story.

The past three days and the entire walk through the valley was filled with ideas about what she *should* say when she arrived. She rehearsed a thousand monologues, explanations, and greetings, only to completely forget everything the moment it mattered. Instead all she could remember was the guard who painfully punched her in the gut when she tried to approach Mr. Choo at the graveyard. No one was ever going to punch her like that again.

Her body tensed in preparation to fight. In truth, she would almost welcome the explosion of effort required to take down these two men. Her ever growing anxiety was twisting into anticipation. It ran deep these days, and its claws were wide. It felt raw and combustible like gasoline waiting for the tiniest spark to set it off. Fighting was the great equalizer for her emotions. But she hadn't been in one for months.

JoJo stepped closer to the two guards, her fists balled tightly, ready to pounce, ready to defend, ready to attack.

Except...

Nothing. They did nothing. It was a complete letdown leaving her stuck in a surge of adrenaline. Her need for release was thwarted by their compliance while anticipation twisted right back into anxiety.

Without the slightest hint of curiosity, one of the guards slid their card through the access portal and punched in a passcode opening the Palace doors for her, just like that. No questions asked.

And if that wasn't enough to freak her out, they stepped aside bowing gracefully and respectfully giving her plenty of space to enter. Her mind was spiraling.

What the fuck just happened?

Suddenly all her reasons for coming no longer made any sense. After all, Yang Choo had a mole with the police, he said so himself. So of course he knew she was transferred. He probably arranged it. Watching the automatic doors slowly seal behind her, it was too late to change the direction of her little sailboat as she headed straight into the storm.

The hallway stayed silent and empty reminding her of the police station, until the boring colorless hallway led her right into the center of the Palace.

##

It was magnificent.

And rightly called *the Palace*. It took her breath away. The truly spectacular sight temporarily dissipated the anxiety she was fighting as her eyes feasted on hand carved statues of gold, jade, mahogany, and white granite speckled with shades of green. Hand painted pictures of dragons, tigers, and horses decorated the place while many of the walls were exquisitely designed pieces of stained glass. It was truly unlike anything she had ever seen before, built like the royal residences she heard about when they lived in China. It was a sanctuary befitting kings and queens, after all Yang Choo was a type of king in LA.

She rode up the escalator to the first floor where the elevators resided, knowing from the police reports exactly where to go. She read every report about Yang Choo's business, home, hideouts, and activities, assuming of course the reports were accurate.

Guards were stationed everywhere, and they casually and graciously moved aside as she passed by like she was some sort of royalty herself. Each one bowing, extending a hand in invitation, gesturing in the direction she needed to go, as if she didn't already know exactly where she was headed.

The longer she stayed inside this magnificent residential masterpiece, the more JoJo felt ridiculous in her crazy dirty holey outfit and shoe-polished skin. If her face wasn't already flushed from the heat, it was certainly turning bright red from the embarrassment she was feeling. Even the guards were dressed in fancy suits with shiny black shoes. By the time she entered the elevator, she couldn't stop preening herself like it made any difference at all.

Quieting her hands by putting them in her pockets, JoJo let her eyes roam the brilliant sophistication of the elevator. She covered every inch of the artwork surrounding her, mesmerized by the intricate details. It was even more elaborate than the main foyer, but what fascinated her the most was the painted ceiling of a jade lion chasing a red and gold dragon. And sitting at the mouth of the dragon was a small camera hiding in plain sight. She quickly looked back down, not knowing which parts of Yang's business were bugged or being monitored and which were secure. The only place she was fairly certain was safe was his personal space on the twelve floor – after all, there wasn't a police report in existence that mentioned it.

##

It's been three and half years since she talked with him.

Three.

Fucking.

Years.

The *what ifs* in her brain were beating her down, while her own heart was beating her up. It pounded so loudly in her ears that she almost missed the prompting from the guard behind her when he cleared his throat. But JoJo was frozen in front of the beautiful wooden doors to Mr. Choo's office. Her slightly shaking hand poised in mid-air above the gleaming golden doorknobs – the kind you might find at the entrance to a temple.

Jesus, everything about Yang Choo was intricate and elaborate! Even his fucking doorknobs. She cussed silently when the impatient guard reached past her arm and promptly opened the doors, shocking her back to reality as the bright lights from inside his office poured over her.

Feeling underdressed, unprepared, and utterly scatterbrained, JoJo's courage instantly melted and her two-timing, traitorous, double-crossing body decided to flee the scene. Taking one step backwards, she felt her foot hit the guard behind her, then felt his hand between her shoulder blades long enough for him to push her forward. On any normal day, in any normal circumstance she would've broken his hand, his nose, and his kneecaps for pushing her. But this wasn't any normal day and this certainly wasn't any normal circumstance. And JoJo's mind was totally blank. She forgot she was a warrior, a dragon, a martial artist with a black belt in ass-kicking.

But like every important moment of her life, it all left her when she needed it most. Just like it left her when she needed to save her dad.

Her mind went void of any thought at all.

Save one…

Or maybe it was just a feeling? Perhaps a moral instinct.

Because when the guard pushed her into the inner sanctum of LA's most notorious gangster, it was the very first time in over three years that JoJo actually felt like a dirty cop. Felt the full implications of the choices she made to get to this point. And the choices she still needed to make to keep going.

She couldn't change her mind now, the snake had already shed its skin.

Quickly burying her feelings, JoJo willed herself forward deeper into the lion's den, and deeper into the hole she dug for herself.

Dr. Joan M Savage

Chapter 7

Beauty and Ashes

Yang Choo's office was nothing like the traditional Chinese displays that shrouded the interior of the entire building. His office was shockingly beige and gray like any other basic office in the city, and the plain wooden floor was decorated with short white columns displaying the only thing interesting about the space – ancient antique weapons and armor. None of which were Chinese. In fact, they looked like British armaments and Roman chain mail.

Her eyes scanned the area quickly searching for the one thing that mattered most.

Maybe he wouldn't be so intimidating after all these years?

A small part of her hoped the lion had already feasted, and that she could get in and get out without losing anything valuable.

JoJo spotted him at the opposite end of the room behind a large mahogany desk. His nose was buried in a stack of paperwork which he held in one hand and in his other hand was a nearly empty glass of brown liquid on ice. His dress white shirt was rolled up to his elbows with the top two buttons undone. Even undone, Yang Choo looked put together. For a moment, JoJo paused just to breathe him in.

Goddamn it all!

Even after all these years he was just as intimidating as she remembered. Intimidating, intoxicating… and fucking beautiful. She was watching the lion in its natural habitat, and simultaneously hoping it noticed her and hoping it didn't.

This was going to end very badly if she didn't get a handle on the out of control freight trains running rampage through her brain. Why couldn't she think clearly? At least until the stupid guard pushed her forward again, forcing her all the way into his office. The intoxication turned into rage in the span of a heartbeat and she spun around to retaliate with every intention of beating the shit out of the man who dared to push her. Twice.

"Touch me again mother fucker and I'll kill you!" JoJo clamped her hand over her mouth, eyes wide. Apologetic. Her response was way out of line, and she knew it. They couldn't know who she was.

I mean how could they? I never identified myself.

And should she? Not after walking here in this heat and in this silly outfit just to protect her anonymity.

The two guards watched her reaction, both humored at her display of bravado more than intimidated, which only served to infuriate her further. And then they did the unthinkable, they shut the door in her face, sealing her fate. Her only way out was officially gone.

Behind her she could hear the lion stir.

JoJo slowly turned around keeping her eyes pinned to the floor. Afraid he would see all the fear, the worry, and the regret she was carrying. In her peripheral vision, she watched him move around his desk, and chanced a quick glance up. Her heart sinking when their eyes met. Nothing changed. If anything, he grew even more fucking intimidating than she remembered. His strength and power hitting her like hot steam in a sauna. Time had been very, very good to Mr. Choo.

His blank face and hard emerald eyes quickly flashed amusement as he studied her from head to toe. Sighing deeply, his humored expression served to lessen her anxiety and she was able to relax enough to fully lock eyes with him… once they made their way back up from her ludicrous outfit.

Needing a break from his stare, her eyes landed on the spectacular gold Rolex he was toting as it caught the light just right, flashing her.

The watch cost more than her fucking car.

Yang finally stopped about five feet from her, sliding his hands into the pockets of his shiny olive pants, taking the watch with them and leaving her confused about what to look at.

Still amused, he patiently watched her, letting her finish looking him over, and that's what she did. She didn't mean for her eyes to sweep over him so intimately, but she couldn't help it. And in that moment, she both loved and hated him. Loved him for being her saving grace and hated him because she knew she could never have him. He was forbidden fruit. He would always be forbidden fruit and isn't it the *forbidden* part that often looks the most appealing?

At least until it bites you back. Or poisons you.

JoJo had been traveling the world since before she could remember, and Yang Choo was by far the most intriguing creature she had ever met. It took a full minute to realize he was still waiting for her to finish admiring him, and she was suddenly very grateful for the ridiculous shoe polish that hid the bright burn of her cheeks. She dropped her eyes to control the crazy attraction she was feeling. At least the anxiety wasn't mastering her anymore, but then again, what was taking its place felt far more dangerous... and powerful.

"Like what you see?" he asked, making her face burn even hotter. And if the floor would open up and kill her, she'd celebrate it.

Did she *like* looking at him? *Fuck yes*. A thousand times, *yes*.

JoJo lowered her eyes respectfully. A heaviness resting right in the center of her chest as she remembered who she was, why she was there, and the whole goddamn fucked up situation that brought Yang Choo into her life. Blood returned to her frozen brain and the walls separating them returned too.

Abruptly, Yang snapped his fingers, shocking her from the reverie and leaving her a little more than confused by his actions.

"Leave us," he said.

She stepped back wondering what she did to offend him. Should she just leave without saying anything? She came so far... suddenly she noticed that they were not alone in the room.

How the fuck did she miss all his guards?

She watched in awe as several men appeared around the office space. One was seated in the far corner and another was in some side room she didn't even know existed. JoJo tried to keep her eyes lowered while they filed one by one past her and out of the office. So enamored with Yang Choo, she missed all eight guards.

If it was possible to be more embarrassed than she already was, this did it. A good cop would know her surroundings.

Who was she kidding? She never had any intention of being a *good* cop.

"I said leave us," he commanded again. There was still another guard seated on the couch. Frustrated, he slammed the newspaper down and came to stand right in front of JoJo. Eyes still lowered, she kept her face hidden. The guard grunted in distaste, then passive-aggressively slammed his shoulder against hers, knocking her back slightly as he walked out. Behind her the large doors closed with a final click, locking her inside. That final click resonated somewhere deep within her, and she exhaled loudly. She had been holding her breath.

It was official, her fears won. JoJo stood there staring at the ground and wringing her hands wondering what could possibly be next.

Listlessly Yang moved closer to her.

"It's my turn." His deep velvety voice interrupting her thoughts.

Reaching up, he lowered the hoodie off her head and then slowly removed her ball cap, freeing her shoulder length red curly tangles. They bubbled down into shiny strands dancing around her shoulders. He gripped the collar of her oversized dirty black parka and began unzipping it, dropping it to the floor.

JoJo's heart was pounding, trying to beat directly out of her chest. And she couldn't stop trembling, despite her attempts to stand perfectly still. She was holding her breath again.

It felt like a dream come true, and a nightmare all wrapped in one moment.

Underneath the parka was another puffer jacket that made her look twice her size. He snorted, humor igniting his eyes at the second layer he had to peel back. And as he grabbed the zipper, her heart literally stopped beating for a second when his knuckles lightly brushed against her throat. His closeness, his touch, left her weak-kneed and wobbly, wishing very much that she could fall to the floor right alongside the second jacket.

It was a miracle she stayed standing on her own. Feeling him undress her brought an excitement that was shooting down into her very toes.

Somewhere in her mind, somewhere sensible, she was wondering how far he would actually take it, and how far she'd let him.

Underneath the puffer was the hoodie, he snorted again and turning around, headed back to his desk.

"Are you going to make me do all the work?"

His voice was so fucking sensual. And the sensible part of her was still… *sensible*, ever reminding her that he was forbidden fruit.

Passing up his desk, he opened the liquor cabinet. And with his back to her, JoJo quickly stripped off layer after layer until she was down to a bright turquoise spandex workout outfit.

She was striking – even with black shoe polish smeared over her cheeks. Whether from the LA heat or being covered in so much clothing or the thrill of looking at Yang Choo, JoJo was sweating, making her skin radiant like it was covered in baby oil.

She couldn't have chosen a more flattering outfit if she tried, it hugged every curve, showing off every feature. Her hourglass body was stunning and despite the feminine curves, her toned muscles indicated she was very athletic. The color enhanced the deep amber highlights in her hair, and made her blue eyes shine brightly or maybe it was looking at Mr. Choo that made her eyes so bright.

He motioned for her to come over, and obediently she stepped out of the pile of clothes. She smiled when she caught his eyes sweeping over her in approval, giving her a strange kind of courage. And just for a second, before he turned away, JoJo thought she saw something in his eyes… something *more…*

Something.

But it was quickly gone.

Respecting his summon, she edged her way to his desk, keeping her arms wrapped around her waist in a girlish attempt to hide her figure. The sensible part reminding her to keep a healthy distance from him, especially since he was activating her fight, flight, freeze, and fawn modes – all fucking at once.

She was very grateful that he seemed preoccupied in making a couple of drinks. With a loud clang, he dropped large round ice cubes in each glass, followed by the pouring of a deep caramel liquid. Only periodically would he glance up as she approached him in a bizarre zigzag fashion like she was avoiding office landmines. When his eyes fell to her writhing hands, she quickly hid them behind her back.

Instead of handing her one of the drinks, he set them down, leaning his hip against the edge of the cabinet, watching her. She backed away, keeping her eyes ever on him, and keeping her invisible barrier between them. When he shifted, she moved further away, and when he straightened up, she stepped backwards. It was a weird sort of static stalemate between them.

And then something changed.

It happened so fast that JoJo wasn't exactly sure what really did occur. One second Mr. Choo was standing at the liquor cabinet, and the next he was breaking the invisible barrier.

He came at her Mach 1 holding something in his hand. When she couldn't see what it was, and couldn't move away fast enough, she did the only thing that made sense to her.

She attacked or maybe she blocked? It was defensive… and aggressive, forcing him away in what felt like hand to hand combat with LA's mafia king. But moving equally fast, Yang grabbed the wrist she was using to block with. The weird momentum they created from her attempt to block and run and his attempt to grab and hold, caused them both to lose their balance and fall hard against the wall.

Yang maneuvered himself to take the full brunt of the crash, while JoJo landed elbows first into his chest, knocking the air out of him. She barely opened her mouth to apologize when he suddenly flipped the situation, pinning her against the wall and twisting her wrist behind her back.

She froze, preferring the sting of a punch to the rising panic of feeling trapped. He was using his six foot plus height and two hundred pound plus weight to hold her five foot six body in place. Soaking wet she wouldn't be heavier than one hundred thirty pounds.

The pent up anxiety, unrequited lust, over-the-top fears, blaring doubts, and even her deep regrets were loudly demanding release. Begging for a catharsis in the form of violence. Insisting on hurting this man who had done nothing except to help her on the journey to fulfill her deepest desires.

She shook her head pushing the violent thoughts away. And Yang must've sensed the struggle in her because he started taunting her.

"Do it," he whispered, "Go ahead and try it." And then he tilted his head exposing the soft part of his neck, waiting to see if the snake would strike.

And JoJo *wanted* to strike, desperately. If for no other reason than his request for it.

Her whole body was vibrating with desire to scratch him, slap him, bite him...

Something.

It felt a little like...

Foreplay?

She found his eyes, silently begging him to release her before she really did hurt him... or worse.

JoJo was like fire and water. She ran fiercely hot and then turned freezing cold in an instant. She could turn everything she touched into ash. And with her violent and turbulent temper, she was like an angry, salty sea in the middle of a storm.

Yang Choo was like earth and wind. Solid, promising... uniquely beautiful. And just like the wind, one minute he was there and the next he was gone – like he never was.

Yang Choo left her alone for over three goddamn years.

He left her sitting alone in the mud and rain on her father's grave, buried in grief, loneliness, and pain without so much as a *fuck you* or a wave goodbye.

Dr. Joan M Savage

Chapter 8

Storm Chaser

JoJo had been alone for over three years. Even her sweet sixteenth birthday was celebrated with ghosts from her past. No one could know her true age, so she sat in a bar drinking root beer and toasting herself with a ketchup bottle.

And now, at this very moment in the arms of Yang Choo, she realized the depth of her resentment, and the profound loneliness that was consuming her. She was afraid to open her eyes and watch the wind disappear again. She wasn't a hostage, she surrendered – if only in her mind. And after all these years with only revenge as her companion, she desperately needed to be held. However twisted and sick it was.

Fawn mode gently trickled in and she found herself leaning deeper into him… yielding, like water on rock. She flowed and adapted, her body fitting perfectly against his. And as she gave in, she felt him pull back, releasing her altogether. It was just plain awkward now.

"Feel better?" The corners of his mouth tilted upward.

She did.

Jesus Christ did she ever.

JoJo gave an embarrassed nod, adjusting her outfit and hiding beneath her curls. She was attempting to look as self-controlled as possible, at least of her temper. All the other *feelings* he stirred within her were covered up and buried deep – even deeper than her regret.

Yang lifted his hand showing her what he was holding. It was a stack of wet wipes. Pulling one free, he started wiping a clean streak across her cheek making her feel like a child who was getting cleaned up after eating a bowl of spaghetti.

It was so goddamn sensual.

And equally disturbing.

She honestly didn't know what to do. Help him? Hit him? Run? Stay? Her big blue eyes opened wide with wonder as his fingers moved over her lips.

And just like that, he stopped, roughly shoving the wipes into her arms and knocking her back slightly.

"Are you going to make me do all the work?"

He was still standing uncomfortably close. Glancing up at him with an apologetic smile and a nervous laugh, she tried stepping past him to create some distance.

"No one showed you how to be a woman?" he asked. The intention behind the question didn't feel insulting or degrading. Even though it was. It seemed more like genuine curiosity, like he was checking on the numbers of his investment portfolio. But his intention didn't matter, the blush in her cheeks was steadily creeping down through her neck and arms. Turning her back to him, she took her sweet damn time cleaning off the polish until her face could recover... or her heart. She wanted to hurt him, and briefly considered throwing the stack of wet wipes at his head.

JoJo made a mental note to research *femininity* and *how to be a woman*. After all, she researched just about everything else to get to where she was. There actually *was no one* to show her. Suddenly, she felt the cruel, ugly, bitter resentment of loneliness again.

And then she was back on the edge. And everything he said felt threatening. And every move he made felt dangerous. And all she wanted was to get further away from him.

Without her permission, her body was unintentionally making its way closer to the exit until his voice interrupted her angry musing and lonely reminiscing.

"You've grown up."

"Yes," she croaked out her reply wishing she had just stayed silent rather than sound like a bullfrog. She wiped at her skin brusquely, trying to clean off all the years of pain, and scrape off all the goddamn blushing, all the while wondering how she could possibly be *grown up* and still not be a *woman.*

Even though they were no longer in hand to hand combat, she was certain they were still sparring. And he was winning, taking her apart, piece by fucking piece... slowly wearing her down.

"You've gotten strong."

She snapped, turning around abruptly.

"Yes. I've gotten very strong. Yes. I've grown up. And yes. Last time I checked I was a woman... whatever..."

When his eyebrows shot straight up, JoJo immediately regretted her tone. And lowering her head, she let her curls do their trick. Sweet Jesus! She felt like that fucking little girl he found in the graveyard all those years ago! Now she understood his question. *No one showed you how to be a woman?*

Clearly not.

Beneath her curls, she exhaled loudly, wondering to herself, *wasn't coming here enough? Showing herself and checking in?* Everything else could be done later and after she officially started her job. Years ago promises were made – unspoken promises. She will help his business using LAPD resources and he will help her find her father's killer. If cops were involved, if it was a police officer that murdered her father, then it will take hellfire and brimstone to bring the LAPD demons down.

It will take a monster to destroy a monster.

And Yang's organization was the perfect beast.

While she wrestled with her thoughts, JoJo realized it had grown too quiet between them. She glanced up, surprised to see that Yang had returned to his desk and was leaning back in his chair, hands clasped behind his head.

What a perfectly pure goddamn alpha move. He was keenly observing her... waiting for her to come back from wherever her mind had fled to. He only spoke when she finally made eye contact.

"Are you ready?" He rocked back in his chair further. She wondered if it would tip over.

Slowly she nodded, but stopped when he raised a questioning eyebrow.

"I... I was assigned to LAPD narcotics three days ago," she said, trying not to stutter.

"That's not what I asked." And as quick as lightning his hand pulled out a gun that was somehow attached beneath his desk. He aimed it at her for a half a beat.

JoJo went stone cold – blood rushing from her head, breath caught in her throat. She didn't blink. She didn't twitch.

After a few seconds, he began spinning the gun around his forefinger, toying with it like a gunslinger in an old western film. He was testing her, checking on his stock portfolio again. She hated him for it.

Once again, he aimed it at her, the hardened emerald eyes returning. JoJo was sick of this bullshit act. If he wanted her dead, she wouldn't have made it out of the graveyard, much less into the police academy where she had the power to report him and testify against him.

Lifting her chin defiantly, she marched right up to him and fearlessly stood over him, looking straight down her nose. The storm in her eyes heightened to a hurricane level event.

"There it is," he said as a cold lifeless grin spread evenly across his face. He spun the gun around his finger again. Playing with it. Playing with her. Chasing the storm away.

"You're going to need *that*... that right there..." he pointed at her eyes. "If you're joining the LAPD narcotics team." And then he stood straight up, towering over her and looking down at her, forcing her to lean backwards.

"Do you know the difference between an upstanding citizen and a criminal?" he asked. But JoJo didn't care anymore. She had enough. Turning away, she headed back toward her pile of clothes. She did what she came to do – show herself, say hello, give him the 411. *What else was there?*

Ignoring his question, she piled and stuffed the clothes into her arms until her face could barely see over the stack. Looking up to say goodbye, she saw that he had followed her and she didn't miss that he was still holding the gun. It laid loosely in his hand against his thigh. They stared at each other for what felt like an eternity. Her eyes constantly shifting downward toward the gun.

"Anyway... uhm... Mr. Choo, I wanted to let you know that I'm... I'm here. I mean, I'm back. Technically, I don't start work for another week... but... but I thought... I wanted to come by... and... I thought you should know," she stumbled over the words, despising herself for it.

"Uhm... thank you and goodbye." She practically ran for the door, planning to get dressed in the elevator.

Glancing over her shoulder one final time, she reached for the golden door handles only to see that Yang had already covered the distance between them, surprising her with his speed and agility. His hand shot out, wrapping his fingers around her neck in a choke hold. With no effort, he had her down to her knees and JoJo pretty much threw the clothes she was holding to claw and punch at his wrist.

Yang thrust the gun against her forehead, digging the barrel between her eyes and forcing her to freeze up again. She stopped hitting and resisting, choosing instead to glare daggers at him.

He pulled her forward until her head leaned against his thigh, and bending over he whispered in her ear.

"The difference between an upstanding citizen and a criminal?" he repeated the question from earlier.

A single tear slowly made its way down her cheek as she struggled for one breath. Maybe from the metal hurting her face, maybe from the loss of a schoolgirl's crush, or worse, the reality that maybe she really did sign a deal with the devil.

What did she expect?

For whatever reason, he suddenly loosened his choke hold letting her pull back to breathe. She bent over gasping for air, gagging and coughing.

JoJo fought the images flying through her brain of at least fifty terrible ways in which she could severely injure him, maim him, mar him, dismember him...

"Don't make me ask again."

"I don't know... nothing. Everyone's a criminal!" she spit out, still gagging and coughing. He smiled at her, releasing her neck completely, but keeping the gun pressed against her forehead. JoJo stayed on her knees, holding her neck protectively while mentally plotting his death.

"Betray me and I will end you. Understand?" His charm, his charisma, his seductiveness had all but disappeared. Right now he truly looked and acted like a mobster, a gangster, a criminal... a monster. And all she felt was disappointment for this man whom she had built up in her mind as some kind of savior.

Her hero worship became kryptonite.

"You think you have nothing to lose. No fear of death and no fear of pain… and why? Because you won a few underground fights. Everybody has a weakness, *June*. Never forget that and I know yours. I know everything." Tears brimming, she met his eyes, trying to hide the surprise she was feeling.

He didn't know her at all. She wasn't fearless. She was a fucking coward.

"We are born to fight, from the first moment we leave the womb. Fighting to breathe. Fighting to live." He glanced around the room at his collection of weapons standing like mini shrines throughout his office. "Look at all these weapons. From the beginning of time, we knew how to kill before we learned how to make fire."

Part of her was loathing him and another very small part was marveling. It felt like Alpha was showing something uncommon of himself yet working awfully hard to keep it hidden. They locked eyes. After a few moments, he took a deep breath shaking off her intense gaze as she stared up at him beneath the gun he still held against her forehead. She waited, listening, watching. His voice switched back to its sultry seductive charm, and she wondered what was real? The man or the monster?

"We're born to fight, to need, to read, to breed… we spend our lives in pursuit… never to succeed."

A monster and a poet, how fucking poetic. His words suddenly registered.

"To read?" Puzzled, her eyebrows lifted skyward taking the barrel of the gun with them. Amusement lit up his face and the dangerous power struggle between them ended.

"The dawn of reason," he answered.

Following the same hunch from the last time he aimed the gun at her, she grabbed the barrel and held it tightly against her forehead while standing up. Stepping toward him, she put enough pressure on the gun that it forced him to step back. His first retreat since she met him, and she never even blinked. The intensity of their locked gaze lasted an eternity and only ten seconds. And then he retreated yet again, surprising JoJo entirely.

"Don't play with fire," he warned, moving the gun away from her head but keeping it aimed at her. "And don't stir things up, you might just get what you want."

Stir things up? Confused, she plunged ahead anyway.

"And what *do* I want? Hmm? Tell me, what *do I want?*"

He shot another warning, immediately triggering feelings of apprehension like he busted her in the act of stealing a cookie. His look felt more dangerous than the gun to her head. She looked down to hide her blush.

"Don't pretend to know me, Mr. Choo," she whispered, searching for her courage. "And I *AM* ready. I've been ready." She slapped the gun away. "Are you?"

She waited to see what he would do next. The pause she let hang between them felt like the single most important moment of JoJo's entire life. Even more important than the first day she met him and asked for his help. It was do or die. She gave up everything to find her father's killer – everything.

Over the past three years, she became very good at reading the dynamics of any fight, and this felt very much like combat. From the first moment she entered this space, she was fighting herself or fighting him and right now she had no idea what this battle was about. The only thing she was certain of was that she was in the middle of one.

And JoJo couldn't read Yang, and she couldn't tell what his response would be next. So continuing in the do or die fashion, she carelessly pushed right on forward still ignoring all the warning signs and red flags.

"Are you done now, Mr. Choo? Is this fucked up interview over? Look, I thought... I just thought we should... establish some... *boundaries.* Conditions, maybe? I don't know. I'm not due to report to work for another five days. But feel free to keep wasting time and sizing me up. Would you like to check my teeth too?" She leaned toward his face and slammed her teeth shut a couple of times, exaggerating the show and watching the look of astonishment and disbelief flash across his face.

He seemed both offended and humored all at the same time, immediately followed by... *something else.*

In fact, JoJo surprised herself with her own audacious actions, leaving them both speechless. But she was quicker to recover, filling the silences and spaces and refusing to give him the chance to retaliate. Somewhere between getting choked or having a gun in her face, she grew a pair of balls.

73

Wiping her eyes, she put on her best poker face.

"And it's *JoJo… Jo-Jo.* You'll screw me if someone hears you call me *June.*" At that, she spun around to hide her faint, proud smile.

What more reassurance did he need?

She casually escaped to a different part of his office, hoping he would move, follow, or just leave the general area where her stuff lay at the door. She still had plans to exit as quickly as possible before losing anything truly valuable. Unfortunately, he wasn't budging, crippling any ideas she had of getting the hell out of that place as fast as humanly possible.

RED FEVER

Chapter 9

A Matter of Life and Debt

JoJo walked into her new apartment holding three extra keys and the stack of stupid clothes she felt compelled to disguise herself in. After a second of standing at her doorway, she violently threw everything in her arms into the center of her living room, followed by a small controlled frustrated scream.

Looking around the space, she searched for something she could kick or break, but her apartment was pretty stark naked. Except for the pre-furnished items that came with the place, it was filled only with a boxing stand, two suitcases, and the six boxes she brought with her to LA.

Yang had given her two burn cars, a burn phone, and a burn house.

An entire goddamn house.

Who the hell does that?

After all these years, she finally had a way to contact him – other than just showing up on his doorstep looking like the Michelin man. She stared at the phone in her hand, now *he* had a way to contact *her* too. What did that mean? She felt a chill run down her spine; everything was feeling too real now.

The burn house was going to be their meeting spot, and she would need unregistered cars for emergencies and any planned meetups. They were untraceable and hidden in areas protected from street cameras – including ATMs, gas stations, and mini-marts. No prying eyes.

Yang Choo created the perfect storm, and she just sailed right into it.

She memorized the addresses and phone numbers, deciding she would find the burn house and cars when out on official police business – a random coincidence. And the keys she would hide in plain sight, right alongside everything else in her life.

Letting out another frustrated scream, JoJo pitched the keys onto her empty counter, watching them slide down all seven feet of it, stopping just at the edge. It was exactly how she felt, on the edge. Pretending she had x-ray vision, JoJo searched the place with her eyes, scanning the boxes and suitcases as she rehashed every single item she packed.

Somewhere she fucked up, but where? Where did she go wrong? And how did Mr. Choo discover something that she didn't even know herself?

Hitting the rewind button in her brain, she thought back to the last moments in his office.

##

There was the man.

And there was the monster.

She didn't know which one was grabbing the two drinks he made earlier. Seeing that the ice had melted in them, Yang tossed the glasses loudly into the sink, completely shattering them. JoJo startled at the sound, positive now it was the monster making his entrance.

Without looking in his direction, she listened to the sounds of fresh ice cubes dropping into new glasses. The hard clang violating the uncomfortable silence that was slowly growing between them again. One minute the power struggle was over and now they were right back in it. His behavior was aggressive, almost hostile as he poured the brown liquid over the ice. He never did answer her question, they left it hanging.

"Don't play with fire," he warned her. *"And don't stir things up, you might just get what you want."*

"And what do I want?" she asked him.

To find her father's killer, of course.

Yang glanced up, beckoning her with his emerald fires, and within that one look she knew they were not done yet – at least he wasn't. She couldn't help the instinctual glance at her clothes, debating on making a run for it. At least until the aching bruise on her forehead changed her mind.

Holding both glasses, Yang extended the second glass toward her like a peace offering.

With strings attached.

"People are always fucking, and feeding, and…" he paused, taking a long sip from one of the glasses, "…and fighting."

The man was back – sounding sad and soulful, revealing that strange side of himself.

When she tried to take the glass from him, he moved it just beyond her reach.

"Some of us never learn to stop fighting. Tell me *JoJo,* has anyone ever taught you *when* to stop?"

Like a carrot on a stick, he dangled the drink. She hated when men did that. Her father dangled food and necessities like she ever really had a choice if she wanted to survive. Her Captain dangling the chance to stay in Indiana or come to LA like she had any other option than to go. And Yang dangled her future every chance he got like it was a goddamn carnival game. She was sick of it.

"It's okay to stop fighting," he said quietly, thoughtfully, staring right into her soul. His gentle warning breaking down the rage-fest brewing inside.

JoJo didn't know at what point she started staring at his mouth, mesmerized with watching the crystal glass as it touched what she imagined were very soft lips. Her eyes followed the liquid moving down his throat as he swallowed, while her brain was stuck wondering what that caramel liquid tasted like. Or maybe it was stuck on what Yang Choo tasted like.

"I'll make you this offer only once…" He waited until her eyes flicked back up to meet his.

"Stop."

She didn't understand. All she wanted was the thing he was holding just out of her reach.

"Stop now," he repeated. "Before it's too late. There's no shame if you choose to leave all this behind and… and walk away. *Just. Walk. Away.*" The last part felt more like a command. He held the drink out again, a pis aller and she knew it.

Didn't Charles Dickens warn that debt was a double-edged sword?

She stared at it considering all the implications of his words, her eyes rising from the drink back to his, and without her consent, she slowly and carefully took the glass from him. Their eyes stayed locked as they sipped in unison. A gentleman's agreement.

A promise.

A pact.

A pinky swear.

JoJo recited the words he left with her at the graveyard. Words that haunted her every day since.

"I have nothing left to lose. I don't even exist, remember? And you don't do anything for free." She watched disappointment flash in his beautiful eyes, easily replaced by the two cold stones that gripped her core. He studied her for a long moment, his face unreadable. Oddly, she didn't back down under his gaze, and it surprised her when he broke first.

"Then remove everything that connects you to me," he said pointedly. Her poker face immediately twisting into confusion, she began shaking her head.

"There's nothing... I have nothing. There's nothing left," she said desperately as her mind raced through everything she owned – every suitcase, every box, every pen. She thought through everything she did or said over the past few years. Text messages, emails, phone calls... even the papers he originally handed to her. She burned everything the day the Police Academy accepted her.

Certain now, JoJo repeated herself firmly.

"There's nothing, Mr. Choo."

One eyebrow went up as he casually sipped his drink. It took just one eyebrow to shake her world and collapse any confidence she thought she had, warning her that somewhere there *was* a thing. A mistake.

But where? Her mind struggled, fracturing into a hundred places and forty different timelines, reviewing a million conversations and revisiting a thousand events. There was nothing left of her past except her own memories.

June Shimmers was dead.

And JoJo Sparks killed her – burning all the evidence that she ever existed.

##

JoJo glanced around her apartment again looking for something to hit... or break, or fucking set on fire. She accidentally brought home all the frustration that built up in her from meeting Mr. Choo.

Where did she fuck up?

The only thing available to pour her anger into was the pile of clothes she tossed earlier, and their gentle compliance was completely unsatisfying when she finally kicked them. Jesus, since day one she was perfect in her secrecy, her performance, her training, and with every other goddamn thing in life. Yet somewhere and somehow there was a spot in her spotless record, and Yang Choo found it.

But where?

JoJo sat down on the step leading from her kitchen into her living space, staring at the boxes and mentally sifting through their contents.

Early on she quickly learned to minimize and pack light. The way her dad kept them on the move all the time left her feeling unsafe, unsatisfied, and always ill-at-ease. Those feelings were more real to her than any other feeling. So when she accepted Yang's offer, it was easy to live in a perpetual state of preparation, not only for LA but also for the possibility of leaving the country... if revenge came in the form of a dirty deed.

A small dust bunny rolled by reminding her that there wasn't much left of her life to sift through – not from her old life and even less in her new life. In a small sad way, she was reminded of her father. When he died, there wasn't much left of his life either.

Frustrated, JoJo sliced open the first box and dumped all its contents on the floor. Some random junk and a few new civilian outfits suitable for LA's *unique* style. The second box was shoes and boots. Nothing significant. The third box was heavy, filled with some books, notebooks, pens and a few stuffed animals that she often used to hide security cameras for her apartment.

She was about to move to the fourth box when she spotted something that made her stomach drop, her skin crawl, and her heart skip a beat. A wave of dizziness passed over her as she reached for the red journal she kept for the last ten years.

No. Fucking. Way.

As her hand wrapped around its old leather cover, she literally fell to her knees in humiliation. How the fuck did he know?

Even she forgot she still had it.

Clutching the book against her chest, she collapsed backwards into the pile of junk like it weighed a hundred pounds. JoJo laughed out loud at the ridiculous thought that he might have read it. Then she screamed in embarrassment at the ridiculous thought that he really might have read it.

It took a minute for the cussing spree to finally slow down as the details of what she included in that book of secrecy picturesquely unfolded before her eyes. Including first impressions of Yang Choo and details of a schoolgirl's crush.

How thrilling it was that someone like him would notice someone like her... and be willing to help. Memories bombarded her of that grieving, innocent, vulnerable, impressionable young teenager who was ready to be whatever he wanted and do whatever he wanted.

Poured onto every single page were the burning desires of an innocent girl who was crushing on LA's Triad king. A king with the power to awaken every single goddamn emotion possible for a human to experience – good and bad. They came fully alive whenever he was involved. Even just the thought of him set her on fire. It was awful, and she loved it. It was heaven, and she hated it.

Or maybe she hated herself? Her mind battering her as it filtered through the insanely intimate things she wrote down over the years. It suddenly felt as if the universe was conspiring to utterly humiliate her in front of Yang Choo.

Of course there were the typical sweet *Dear Diary* things, mundane things, school events, new friendships, hopes, dreams...

And then there were the terrible events she witnessed during their travels. Secretive things she was supposed to forget but wanted to remember anyway. Unsolved curiosities, memories, lingering questions about her past, and every awful nightmare since before she could remember. But worse, far worse were the descriptions of what she longed to do with the tall handsome gangster from LA. Things she read about in her dad's cloak and dagger collection of smut he kept hidden under his mattress. Things she saw in the adult movies he watched late at night when he thought she was sound asleep.

JoJo was entirely inexperienced when it came to actually doing any of those things. Yet every one of her fantasies and every secret desire was unabashedly and vividly laid out on those once pure white journal pages. Every intimate detail – including her only sexual encounter that had gone terribly awry.

"What if he read about *IT*?" *The one IT… the only It she ever did…*

The ugly thought rolled across her mind's eye like foreboding storm clouds moving across an empty plain.

After *IT* happened, JoJo scribbled down every goddamn detail. She documented the missteps, the lost innocence, and marked it like a warning for her soul – that should something like that ever happen again, she would know what to do.

And what not to do.

She flipped to the end of the journal.

It was the absolute last entry. The decade reign of worship in her red leather journal had come to its conclusion on the lowest possible note.

**

It happened. I did it. I had sex tonight. It was the worst night of my life. But at least I'm not a virgin and no one can make fun of me anymore for being one. Getting into the academy means I'm supposed to be different. Be someone else. Be someone stronger. Someone who knows how to use guns and knives, and how to get revenge. So maybe I should know other things too, like sex. Right? So… I did it. Even though mid-way I changed my mind. But I guess minds were already made up. I can't go back and fix things. But I never want to feel this way again. Never again.

**

JoJo shut the journal without finishing the last two pages that described what happens when you mix devils and spirits.

Instead of a beet red face, it was flushed ashen white. Her youthful features distorted momentarily, and her eyes stared blankly at the wall like she had just been sucked away into a different time and space. It took a long moment to find her way back into the apartment as each memory slowly released its talons. And when she did, she violently ripped out the ending of her book, shredding it to pieces until her fingers bled from the paper cuts.

JoJo's life was gifted with too much knowledge and cursed without practical application. In the end, writing it all down was her way of healing, of remembering, of living, and of tasting everything from bittersweet revenge to a heartbreaking crush.

She was afraid to let it go.

It was proof that an innocent girl once existed, that she was real, and whatever its worth, that she was part of a family too. It was a record of the price she paid, the hurt she endured to get here, and everything in between. Piece by piece and page by page her old identity was ripped apart while her new identity came alive, pen stroke by pen stroke, word by word, story by story. It was the demise of June Shimmers and the rise of JoJo Sparks. It was the end. It was the beginning.

Of all the fucking things to forget she still owned... of all the fucking things for Yang Choo to find. It had to be this?

That last horrible event in her journal was the same night she was utterly positive she burned everything that tied her to the past, yet somehow this twisted little book survived the culling.

JoJo threw it like it was a poisonous snake trying to bite her. Someone from the adjacent apartment began banging on her wall, launching a quick debate in her mind at who she wanted to kill more, Yang Choo or her neighbor.

It was a toss-up. She chose instead to quietly bury her face in her hands.

Surely there was something good? She randomly opened it and read the first thing her eyes landed on:

**

I decided I'm going to save myself for Yang Choo...

**

"WHAAAAT THE FUCK!?" She attacked the page, shredding it into as many pieces as her already sore fingers would allow. Shooting straight up, JoJo was ready to fight something... anything... anyone, but without an opponent she had only herself to beat up. Lately, that just wasn't enough, so she moved back to attack all the innocent books, shoes, and junk on the floor until she slipped, tripped, and fell right into the middle of everything. Releasing the last of her pent up frustration, she kicked and punched at the pile of junk creating a warped little snow angel right in the middle of it all.

Energy finally spent, she grabbed the little leather devil once again hoping for a better ending.

**

It's my birthday.

I saw a cat get hit by a car tonight. I almost missed her because she was as black as the evening sky and as dark as the asphalt she was laying on. She blended right into the shadow and darkness until I saw two shiny eyes light up in the middle of the road. It was dying. Its body was stuck to the pavement by its own feces and blood and it couldn't run away… even if it wanted to.

Happy-fucking-birthday to me. I spent it watching a cat suffer and die. I watched her fight for her last breath with every one of her nine lives. It was admirable, I think. I wonder if I could've saved it? I dunno, every time I got closer the harder her hissing and squawking and the more pain I could see she was in. I was doing more damage to her by trying to help. Instead I just watched. Like the people who watch two dogs rip each other apart and think it's entertainment. Like the people in the audience that cheer me on when I fight, waiting for that one moment when I finally draw blood – hungry and bloodthirsty. They jump to their feet in excitement like I just scored a winning goal.

A truly compassionate person could hit that cat over the head with a rock and relieve her agony.

Someone brave. Someone not afraid to do what needs to be done. Mr. Choo chose the wrong person. No matter how strong I make myself, I'm still a fucking coward.

I feel like I am that cat. One and the same. Our lives forever intertwined… because she made me realize how truly weak I am. I'll never vindicate my father if all I can do is watch when bad things happen.

What's worse? A good person doing something wrong for the right reasons? Or a bad person doing something right for the wrong reasons? And is it even worse to do nothing at all?

**

She read on. It was filled with hateful spurts, anger bashes, silly romantic antics and Yang Choo obsessions. It held special memories like winning Taekwondo fights and her feelings of both rage and power in the underground tournaments. Good grades and bad bullies. Her first kiss, and

84

her last kiss. Schools she adored and schools she abhorred.

Then there were the memories of her father. The constant disappointment she felt when he was never around. And just like that, it wasn't so special anymore.

✳✳

I wake up every day wondering about the man who killed my dad… and it motivates me. I haven't lost a tournament in three months now and I'm so close to graduating University. I've already applied to the Police Academy which is ironic because I hate all cops. Will I pass the lie detector test?

✳✳

JoJo shivered at the thought of someone finding this page and reading it.

Suddenly a very small part of her was immensely grateful that Yang warned her and she felt a little better about letting it go.

Closing the book one final time, she opened her apartment window. In the pile of stuff, she dug around and found her emergency kit, and freed the matchbook. Then taking her journal to the sink, she lit that mother fucker on fire.

"Now nothing ties us together," she whispered. "Sayonara June Shimmers, you never existed."

As if to cause one more problem before its departure, heavy smoke filled the space setting off the smoke alarms. She could hear her neighbors pounding on the walls again, and JoJo grabbed an old shirt, waving the thick gray fumes out into the darkness.

Dr. Joan M Savage

Chapter 10

It Smells Like Blood

Her first day on the job at the Los Angeles Police Department was filled with crazy dizzy paperwork, processing, and a million lessons in do's and don'ts. Her assigned digital to-do list was probably longer than a full forty hour work week and most of it was about which parts of the body were okay to touch and which were considered the red zones. It was a *go* or *no go* scenario. Each lesson leaving her wondering more and more what kind of morons she was working with.

It was a whirlwind of who's and what's, while document after document was piled on her new desk from insurance choices to the full background check requirements. The stack of files landed right next to the ancient obsolete computer, which she assumed was a practical joke considering LA had all the finest tech. She didn't bother giving them the satisfaction of trying to boot up the giant paperweight. Anyway, by the time it worked, her shift would probably be over.

She was passed from office to office and most introductions felt more like mini interrogations. By the time she reached her psych evals, she felt nothing short of a criminal. There were physical tests, gun safety and practices, and more introductions to other *good* cops that she'd most likely be working with from time to time. The term *good cop* felt like an oxymoron – and if someone used it one more time, she was seriously considering excusing herself to the bathroom to blow her head off.

As the day drudged on, she easily and quickly found the alphas of each group – male and female alike – with their constant pissing contests and side looks like JoJo was there to steal their lunch money. Once identified, it was a quick and simple task to see who laid claim to whom. Her plan required laying low and remaining invisible, so stealing someone's apple wasn't in the cards.

By the end of the month, she knew the *real* pecking order – regardless of anyone's actual rank. And this was the final key to staying innocuous while anonymously investigating her father's murder. Find the alphas at the top of the food chain, hide in their shadow, and feast off their leftovers. It worked in the animal kingdom, why not the police station? It felt like equal footing and filled with the same kind of creatures. Every beast she met that worked there longer than three years had a giant red target on their back. Hunting season started for JoJo Sparks, and nothing short of death itself was going to stop her from finding the predator that stole her life.

Indianapolis PD, Los Angeles PD… everybody owed somebody and it was strangely comforting to know that 'if you scratch my back, I'll scratch yours,' was a reoccurring theme among all cops. Some things never change.

A favor for a favor. Information for information.

An eye for an eye.

This was going to be slightly problematic since she had no connections right now – no favors were owed – and no one knew her from friend or foe. She had no vein to tap into if she needed something outside of her department, and last she checked, murder and violent crimes weren't necessarily associated with narcotics. Be it blackmail, bullets, knives, fists, fire… or beauty, in the end, it will come down to whatever works. Whatever she needs to do to find her answers… she'll do it.

JoJo peeked around her PC paperweight to view the other desks that were decked out with the latest and greatest systems.

Yang never prepared her for this high tech situation.

Fuck, he didn't prepare me for a goddamn thing.

Automatic body cams, mini drones, laser imaging… with each new enhancement she encountered, the tightening of her gut warned her that she was getting deeper and deeper into trouble.

So be it.

She'll learn it. She'll learn how to use everything. Until then, she planned on keeping her head down, paying full attention, and figuring out how to play well with others.

As if on cue, a pretty woman casually walked up to her desk. Both women sizing the other up. JoJo decided she was definitely someone who worked in admin.

"Welcome to hell," the girl smiled, extending her hand toward JoJo and sticking her left ass cheek on the edge of the desk. The woman flippantly tossing her long blond hair and laughing a short gunfire burst at the confused expression on JoJo's face when she called LAPD *hell*. This was new, someone else who loathed police officers and police stations. JoJo didn't miss that her confusion was clearly entertaining the woman.

"I'm Kaylee."

"JoJo."

"I know who you are. Everybody knows who you are. It's not everyday a female joins narcotics. I mean you are female, right?"

"Last I checked." JoJo's nose scrunched up.

"I mean what pronouns do you prefer?" It was obvious that Kaylee was on a fishing expedition, so JoJo decided to play along.

"I don't know… *they… you… ours…*"

"I mean personal pronouns," she corrected.

"Okay, how about *I… you… me?* Is this a hazing thing?" JoJo looked around the room to see a couple of guys pretending to look busy and none of them could hide their smiles worth a damn.

Kaylee was definitely from admin and on the prowl for information. And information was better than gold currency in this self-contained ecosystem. Too bad JoJo's personnel file was filled only with absolute necessities. It was a gossiper's nightmare, a blank slate giving nothing away.

Ignoring JoJo's response, Kaylee burst out with a million questions, never once slowing to receive any answers. Strangely, that's not what bothered her the most, it was that Kaylee's ass was planted on her desk. And it didn't look like she was planning to move anytime soon, missing all the *fuck off* signals JoJo was sending.

Standing up, she decided the only way to make her go away was to leave first… and headed over to the high tech espresso machine across the room. One great thing about LA was all the bells and whistles like fancy espresso machines probably capable of doing your laundry if you programmed it just right. Blondie followed right behind her, still chatting away.

"I like to call this place hell because it's so hot in LA – get it?" Kaylee snorted at her own awful joke, unintentionally forcing a small smile out of JoJo. Her loud piglike snort pleasantly surprised both of them.

Kaylee was ridiculous and for some reason JoJo didn't mind it. Still, the blonde woman wanted something. At first she thought it was just a fishing expedition on the new girl, except she wasn't listening to any answers. It took a couple of sentences for JoJo to realize this woman had an agenda, and she wished Kaylee would just get on with it. She tuned back in.

"...seriously though, with all this tech running day and night these rooms can get super-sweaty-hot sometimes. And if the air conditioning goes out... you're screwed." She made a slicing motion across her neck. "Certain death. Death by dehydration." She snorted again. "And then there's the days when we get rain... oh and if it's windy..."

On and on she goes and where she stops no one knows.

JoJo tuned out again, focusing on the hard copies she had to complete. Who on earth still uses actual paper these days? Even with all this high tech equipment, the police still manage to murder trees...

...and fathers.

Kaylee had stopped talking, her brown eyes staring curiously at JoJo, head tilted to the side like a cute puppy dog waiting for a treat. JoJo wanted to kick herself for missing her cue to tune back in.

"What? What was that?" she said while sipping her espresso. "Jesus, this is good."

"I said, are you from Indianapolis? What do you like to be called? Do you have a nickname yet? Why did you want to come to LA other than it's the best place to see the stars, if you're into that sort of stuff. Are you?" Once again JoJo didn't know which question to answer. She tried the shotgun approach.

"Yes."

"I can respect that." Kaylee patted the paper weight. "I hope you don't plan on using this oldie, the guys here can be such assholes... well, everyone except Tony. I should warn you though that he and I are... sorta a thing… an item. I mean we're together. I think. Anyway, us girls need to stick together."

And there it was.

All this goddamn chatter and pretense just to warn JoJo that *Tony* was off limits. Kaylee was pissing on her territory.

"Duly noted." JoJo tried to smile her absolute sweetest smile, leaning far back in her chair. The tension in Kaylee's shoulders noticeably relaxed and she let out a big sigh of relief. But JoJo wasn't done just yet.

"*Kay-lee?*" She tested the name. "If you can't tell that you and… *Tony*… are a thing, then dump his ass and find someone who isn't confused about what he wants. After all, *us girls need to stick together.*"

Blondie was shell-shocked into silence for the first time since putting her ass print on the desk. She could only stare, like JoJo just read her private email out loud. Her face turning slightly red while a thousand emotions and expressions ran across her face all at once. Again, as if on cue, a man walked up and put his arm over Kaylee's shoulders. If JoJo could say anything about this group so far, it's that they seemed to be well-oiled with perfect timing.

"Smells like blood. Fresh blood. Kaylee, who's the noob?" His hungry eyes moved brazenly and impertinently over JoJo's entire body, from head to toe. It was an obvious attempt to make her feel uncomfortable. But JoJo was learning the art of being comfortable being uncomfortable. Instead of shriveling down, she stoutly stood up, arms on her hips, giving him the full body tour. At least until she noticed blondie shifting awkwardly and glaring. Based on her reaction, JoJo took a wild guess.

"Ah, you must be Tony." He looked pleasantly surprised at her acknowledgment.

"Mass, man. Mass!" he said as he pulled up his pants and stuck out his chest.

"Mass? Or ass?" JoJo asked. They locked eyes.

"Massive. Big. Awesome. It's awesome that you heard about me."

"Actually, not at all," she said, plopping down in her chair and openly ignoring them now.

"Well can I just be the first to welcome you here and… damn girl, you got it going on. Are all Indiana girls as fine as you? We should definitely approve more transfers." He leaned over, visibly staring at her breasts.

"Hellooo, nice to meet you. You're *larger* than expected. I mean taller," he said as if he was talking to her chest. He wasn't even trying to be discreet now.

"Are you and Kaylee *bosom* buddies?" He glanced between Kaylee and JoJo, humoring himself.

From the corner of her eye, JoJo could see two of the other guys stand up and move closer like they might have to intervene, or worse, join in with the poking. Being teased was nothing new to her, and she knew just what to do with bullies.

JoJo turned her head to look at Tony, but instead of looking up at his face, she stared right at his crotch.

It was her turn.

Giving the once-over his full body, she started and stopped at his groin. Finally, extending her hand.

"It's nice to meet you, Tiny." The men behind her were snickering while Tony's face flushed.

"It's Tony…" JoJo looked down at his crotch again.

"Hmmm, ok? If you say so… it's just… well you're smaller than expected. Of course, I mean shorter."

For about a half of a second, JoJo was one hundred percent certain that Tony was going to grab her by the shirt but she gave him no opportunity. Abruptly standing up, she headed back to the espresso machine ignoring what she could imagine were death stares from hell.

All her senses were heightened, every hair standing on end.

Ready or not, here she comes. This wouldn't be the first battle she waged with other cops. Most of them usually happened during their mandatory physical training when a senior officer was attempting to show off and show up the rookies. They never saw it coming the moment she decided to kick their asses and pretend it was beginner's luck. She kept her martial arts background a tight secret. Usually.

Glancing back, she watched as Kaylee yanked on Tony's arm, pulling at him to leave.

"Let's go. Come on, Tony." She successfully wooed him away from

JoJo's desk while Tony continued whining.

"Tiny, my ass! I'll fucking show you *Tiny*." He kept grabbing his zipper and JoJo wondered if he really would pull it out in front of everyone. But Kaylee was relentless and clever in affirming him. She kept his hands out of his pants.

"I know the truth, Tony. She's just... she's new... and no manners yet. Come on."

They finally exited the area and JoJo felt safe enough to head back to her desk. Only this time, it was blocked by another guy – arms crossed, eyes narrowed, legs spread out like he owned the damn place.

She remembered meeting him earlier, actually she remembered meeting all of them at some point. It's just they became one giant blur of possible suspects. But this guy, this guy she knew well. He was going to be her partner, *and* their team leader.

Score.

By the way he was standing, her partner was definitely an alpha. It would be a perfect setup if she could manage to win him over. Because the way this week was going so far, she needed someone who wasn't afraid to take on the fucking world with her.

For one crazy brief insane moment, she had an overwhelming desire to call or text Mr. Choo. She quenched that fire faster than it could take form. She didn't realize she was still staring until he spoke.

"What's the problem?" he asked as she approached. JoJo's answer was to ignore him. Of course, he would *blame her* instead of the prick who picked the fight. When she didn't answer, he shook his head almost in disappointment.

"Trouble," he said, and the moment the nickname left his lips, JoJo was glaring at him. "Don't make an enemy out of Tony. Granted, he's an asshole but like all assholes, they serve a greater purpose. He's one of our best weapons specialists. Trust me when I say you'll want him on your side if things go wrong."

Things are already wrong. She mentally argued.

JoJo shook her head trying to fight the nasty reasonings that kept popping up these days. Lately it was getting harder and harder to silence the rage she painstakingly kept hidden. Fighting the dark thoughts, she failed to notice when her mouth jumped into the driver's seat.

"I doubt that," she whispered. Immediately regretting it and hoping he didn't hear, knowing full well that he did. Her gut twisted at the thought of having to make niceties with Tony and now this guy. She was trying to think of something to say to fix the damage.

"Fine."

Alpha was perfectly positioned to prevent her from sitting down. She had to stand there and be scolded like the new kid in front of the classroom. When she realized he wasn't budging, she budged instead. It was vital to win him over, best to start as soon as possible.

"I apologize. Okay? Is... there something I can help you with? Something you needed?" She tried not to glare at him, she tried to sound respectful and defaulted to pretending she didn't remember him.

"Is there something you needed... *sir*," he added. "Get your head on right, *Trouble*. You won't last long if you keep pissing people off. Teams work better when they... *act* like a team. Shocking, I know."

"Good to know. Good to know... and giving me a paperweight for a computer, sending over the blonde newsmonger, and letting Tiny, the group's *useful asshole*, welcome me is your way of... what?" She paused to let him fill in the blank, regretting every single word that left her lips but not really caring. It was his turn to glare at her. In for a penny in for a pound, she continued.

"Making me feel oh so warm and fuzzy? By the way, was that the team's welcoming committee? Am I pissing you off too? I wouldn't want to cause any *trouble*." She looked up and smiled sweetly, quickly adding.

"*Sir.*"

Bypassing him, she grabbed the stack of paperwork from her desk and headed to the police library.

"If you need me..." She pointed to the library sign. "Sir."

Jesus-fucking-Christ what are you thinking!? She mentally screamed. *Why would you treat him like that?* She wanted to kick herself as she made her way down the hall. Why was it getting harder and harder to put up with other people's shit? Looking up, JoJo spotted the signs to the Records and Evidence Locker, stopping mid-step, her heart skipping a beat. She would do anything right now to head there.

Anything.

Somewhere buried inside was her dad's evidence.

JoJo hadn't caught on yet that she was standing frozen in the middle of the hallway, itching to make one stop and take a quick peek. But she knew they would all be watching her right now, watching and waiting. It's the way things were. Watch the rookies and point out every mistake all the while pretending to be smug and superior.

And she would make a mistake all right, as soon as fucking possible so they would lay off her shit and stop *looking for one.* She learned during her first month at the academy it was better to make a calculated and controlled mistake than have a real one bite you in the ass.

Standing in the corridor, JoJo was trapped between her past and her present. Now wasn't a good time to go digging in random files involving a three year old murder case. She needed to wait a few weeks, maybe a few months, or at least have a damn good reason as soon as one presented itself. She shook herself free from the draw of her past, glancing back to see if anyone noticed her odd behavior.

Someone did.

Dylan McKay was standing down the hall keenly observing her. And when she glanced back at him, they ended up staring at each other for a few seconds too long – one waiting for an answer, the other waiting for a question.

In a weird way, he kinda reminded her of Yang Choo.

Another tall handsome alpha male. Except Dylan was ruggedly handsome in a boyish manner. He looked to be in his late twenties, with definite Asian influences in his dark hair and slightly slanted deep brown eyes.

Sticking her nose in the air, she spun around and marched toward the library, clutching her files and paperwork against her chest like they were schoolbooks. Dylan stayed standing in the middle of the hallway, legs spread, hands on his hips, taking up all the space while the people walking by had to shift their bodies and alter their routes to make their way around him.

Cocky son-of-a-bitch. He was going to be a handful.

JoJo shook her head remembering what her Indianapolis Captain once told her when she first put in her request to join LA narcotics.

Be overly cautious because nobody is your friend. Be overly cocky without being reckless. And whatever you do, don't let them know you're afraid.

Burlesque shrewdness and acting will save her life because drug dealers and gangsters smell fear and insecurity a mile away. Of course she didn't believe him until she saw Mr. Choo's behavior and his keen ability to sense her fear.

The gun against her forehead led to a very quick change of heart, and ever since that pissing contest, she had a new attitude and a very obvious chip on her shoulder. LAPD teammates may not like her now, but they will fucking respect her. She just needed a way in... including a major fuck up and a major win. It's the way things worked.

As she started to turn the corner, she glanced back to see Dylan still watching her. His eyes didn't shout attraction or lust, they spoke of mistrust and resentment.

If drug dealers could sense insecurities, what could cops sense?

Dylan's eyes were so full of suspicion that JoJo began questioning if her little act with Tony and Kaylee went a bit overboard. Maybe it was too much too soon...

Dylan's phone suddenly chimed, pulling his attention away from her. The minute he broke eye contact, it was the first time she realized she was shallow breathing. Almost holding her breath like a reckless driver with a near miss. And she was doing it again when he started heading over to her. Or at least was heading in her general direction.

By the pricking of my thumbs, something wicked this way comes.

"Hey Trouble, it's your lucky day. There was an anonymous tip about an abandoned warehouse, and I've decided we're going to take it... *partner.* So get your shit together and meet me ASAP."

His hand suddenly shot out, "Randall here..."

Dylan's hand wrapped around the collar of a squirrelly looking guy who just happened to be walking by them at that exact moment.

"...will show you where to go." Holding Randall's shirt, he guided him backwards, nearly tripping him while forcing him to face JoJo. The poor guy looked terrified, almost dropping the file and coffee mug he was holding.

JoJo felt the same way Randall looked. She wasn't ready. Her plan to either fuck up or win the day hadn't been thought through yet. She didn't have time to think of any ideas and still didn't know the team well enough to know who to impress and who to ignore.

She'll have to keep feigning fearlessness.

"Randall, this is Sparks, Sparks... Corporal Randall. He'll be your *personal guide* today. Corporal, show her the ropes, get her geared up, and get her to my cruiser... in..." Dylan flipped his wrist showcasing the sporty titanium Breitling watch he was wearing. Not something you can afford on a cop's salary. And just like that, Dylan McKay slid smoothly into suspect number one, *unless...*

Freight trains zoomed around her brain as she tried to simultaneously listen to both Dylan and her own crazy thoughts.

Unless Dylan was Yang's inside man?

"...twenty minutes. Got it?" Randall pushed his glasses up his nose, nodding profusely. JoJo found herself unconsciously nodding in unison until Dylan snapped his fingers commanding both their attention.

"Yes, Sergeant McKay. Absolutely, sir. I'd be happy to..."

"Now you have nineteen minutes, Corporal," he interrupted the groveling.

"Oh, sorry, uhm let me help... I can... should we put your papers down, maybe?" JoJo looked him over, sighed, and then met Dylan's humored eyes. One thing was certain, Dylan wasn't just AN alpha, he was THE Alpha around here. At least now she knew who needed to save her when she *accidentally* fucked up.

And who needed to see her when she chose to save the day.

JoJo's brain was burning with ideas while Dylan disappeared around the corner and Randall tried to talk and walk at the same time.

It seemed everything was finally coming together for JoJo Sparks.

Dr. Joan M Savage

Chapter 11

Ties That Bond

JoJo climbed into the passenger's seat of cruiser fifty one where an obviously annoyed Dylan McKay waited impatiently for her. To make his point clear, he loudly tapped his thumb on the steering wheel. JoJo didn't say a word as she buckled in. No apologies. No explanations.

She was mentally prepared for whatever came next. Fully anticipating doing something disgusting, like having to dig through trash bins for *evidence*, guarding a rotting corpse for a few hours, or take a drunken criminal who defecated on himself to jail. It was going to be something hideous for sure, and whatever the assignment, there would be no complaints from her.

She's been waiting what felt like a fucking eternity to get here. So she'll do it gladly, *and* she'll do it brilliantly.

As far as running late for her first assignment? Well that couldn't be helped. Corporal Ralf Fineous Randall was adamant that she be shown every-single-goddamn-detail of getting ready for her *first* assignment. Forty-five minutes later, she was positive Dylan set her up to look like an idiot in front of the whole team.

Yes, the *whole team* was waiting in the garage for her to clamber into the cruiser. Four squad cars, seven officers, and fourteen pairs of eyes watched her like it was an important moment in history and they all needed to be there to support her.

Part of her wanted to ask Dylan if they should all hold hands and braid each other's hair.

So be it.

An eye for an eye, and she was pretty sure that earlier she already gouged out one of Tony's eyes.

She didn't expect anything less from team leader Dylan McKay. And he'll most likely make an example out of her all day, maybe all week until Tony felt vindicated.

Round and round it goes, where it stops, nobody knows.

It was the same shit just a different city. JoJo unintentionally sighed loudly immediately triggering a reaction from her partner. His distrustful glances and wary behavior towards her gave her a nice heads up of what to expect from him. At least he wasn't hitting on her.

Too bad she couldn't reciprocate the warning that *he* was on *her* shit list too. After all, he had been an LA cop for almost 10 years now, which put him smack dab in the realm of possible suspects.

That... or he was Yang's bitch.

Yang Choo had someone on the inside, why not a team leader McKay? Is that what a fancy watch can buy these days? Still...

Something bothered JoJo about that.

She worked hard to remove all bonds that tied her to Yang Choo, and Mr. Choo was equally meticulous – even more so. So what kind of man would flaunt it? Surely there was another reason for Dylan's swanky watch, fancy leather shoes, and his hundred dollar haircut. She glanced sideways at him. Dylan *was* very handsome, perhaps somewhere there was a sugar momma involved? This is LA and not totally out of the realm of possibilities.

But something bothered her about that too. McKay didn't strike her as a man that could be *kept.*

She wasn't sure about anything concerning Dylan, only that he was working narcotics three years ago, and right now she didn't see any connection to her dad's case and the narcotics team. At least where her father's murder was concerned.

Honestly, she didn't know *what actually* concerned her father at all – like how he was friends with a gang leader? Or why cops showed up to his funeral?

Unanswered questions swirled around her brain until JoJo's sudden irritation grew to such an epic proportion that when she moved her leg to get comfortable, it shot across the floor and hit the door loudly, breaking the unofficial silent truce they were keeping.

"Spill it, Sparks."

"What?" She was so deep in thought that she almost forgot she wasn't alone.

"What's on your mind?" he said casually, making her wonder if it was even a question.

"Nothing."

"Oh it's something."

Damn right. What was on her mind was the one question she never got to ask Yang Choo, *'how did my father come to be friends with a mother fucker like you?'*

Dylan persisted.

"You like to shout without words."

"What? What're you talking about?" She finally turned to glare at him. Seeing her reaction, he let out a very loud obnoxious fake laugh.

Regardless if Dylan was involved in her father's murder, there was definitely something dirty about him – dirty as the garbage she fully anticipated digging into as penance for humiliating Tony. Or penance because she was female in the male dominated all-boy's-narcotics-club. Or because she was too sharp-tongued for this group. Or whatever the hell these guys come up with for picking on her.

"The Chief approved your transfer for your linguistic skills." Dylan interrupted her thoughts again.

"Is that a question?"

"...*sir.*" She added as spitefully as the first time he made her say it.

"Cut the *sir* crap. It doesn't suit you. I guess we needed to meet our diversity quota by hiring someone like you. What... did the entire police force not have someone old enough to know what the hell they're doing? How fresh out of the academy are you, anyway? Females don't exactly last long in narcotics, especially pussies without any real experience. Tell me Sparks, do you have any balls? Any experience in narcotics at all?" Feeling his stare, she chose to ignore him.

"Jesus, look at you, are you here to be an actress? I bet you were raised with a silver spoon in your mouth? Or at least offered a few silver spoons to suck. Is that how you got this assignment? Did you suck your way here? Planning to meet a movie star and retire young?"

JoJo stopped listening as he tried to poke any kind of reaction out of her like a dentist looking for the sore spots. Each question grew worse than the next. Occasionally, he would snort in frustration at her pensive and distant demeanor, finally slamming the steering wheel with his hand and demanding that she answer him – except, he didn't ask any more questions.

JoJo kept her mind preoccupied with thinking about the box she purposely left on her desk for the others to go through – it was filled with fake work items, fake family photos, and fake vacations she never took with fake people she never met. She even went so far as to buy a *'we will miss you'* coffee mug at a thrift store where strangers had illegibly signed it.

It was perfect.

And if that wasn't enough, she also left her personal laptop in the mix making it ridiculously easy to break into. Assuming one of them knew a damn about computers, all they would find is more pictures, to-do lists, and realistic ambitions: Write a book. Go skydiving. Meet Sylvester Stallone. Climb Mount Kilimanjaro…

Believable shit.

Her browser was loaded with funny Instagram reels and her search history contained 'fun events in LA,' 'upcoming concerts,' and 'cool local bars.' She left her email wide open – the same email assigned to her by the Indy police force. No matter how far back they went into her history, all they would find is unclassified work related stuff. Including a few emails inviting the team out for drinks.

She played the game well. Preparing for every contingency. Leaving no room for error.

So what if her whole life was a lie?

The thing she had going for her was that her DNA and fingerprints were not on file… until she joined the police force. Ben was never one for hospitals, and he faked everything during their overseas travels.

Her whole life was fucking fake.

Yang Choo was right, she really didn't exist.

##

Sirens blaring and lights flashing, they arrived at an abandoned warehouse with several other cop cars all pulling in together like an armada set to overtake a castle. Clearly this wasn't a real bust since the whole neighborhood could hear them coming.

Before Dylan pulled up to a full stop, JoJo already had one foot out the door.

Tony and his partner, Johnny, were first on site. And no matter how quickly she jumped out, Dylan was equally fast, lining up behind her as they made their way to where the team was gathering. Tony spotted her, immediately heading over, obviously still on the hunt – an eye for an eye. He was going after her other eye.

"Hey Sparks, don't start bleeding. You'll make the K-9's crazy."

Midstride, JoJo took a step at him like she would punch his face but both Dylan and Johnny stepped in front of their respective partners, blocking them. Unsanctioned cuss words flew at Tony while JoJo turned away to greet the third cruiser pulling up. Behind her, she could hear Tony whining.

"Jesus McKay, keep your bitch on a leash. She can't take a fucking joke."

He was throwing some kind of fit, and it almost sounded like her new partner was putting Tony in his place. For a moment she thought she heard Dylan reciting sexual harassment codes. Maybe there were official guidelines he needed to hear but she knew there were far greater unofficial rules of engagement when it came to bullies.

Bullies can sense every weakness. It's like they can smell it from a mile away.

Heart beating, face red, she knew she could never back down with Tony. No matter what. Not now. Not yet. Not if she was going to stay in narcotics. It was do or die. There was a clear and definite reason women didn't stick around and she was hellbent on beating those odds, even if she had to fight every single goddamn one of them. Fist to fist.

If she could handle Yang Choo sticking a gun in her face, then she could put up with their bullshit. Glancing back, she caught Dylan's eye as Tony continued to defend the size of his dick. Was Dylan really putting him in his place? It would be a first – someone coming to her rescue.

Fuck it, she would let him.

The closer she got to these assholes the more likely they would warm up to her and help her or at the very least, not hinder her while she started her own private investigation into her father's murder.

Three cruisers sat in front of the warehouse and JoJo watched as the fourth cruiser pulled around to the back, happily kicking up a sky full of dirt. She wondered what kind of anonymous tip would warrant such a response. The warehouse looked empty like it wasn't done being built yet, or whoever was building it stopped midway with internal and external scaffolds lining the walls.

As JoJo moved away from the drama, Tony's partner followed her, leaving Dylan and Tony to work things out. And one by one, the other teams walked off leaving her standing alone as she approached them. She was grateful that Johnny stayed beside her... that is until she looked up at him. She was met with hardened resentful blue eyes. So full of resentment, they almost seemed cruel as they peered down on her. He didn't say anything, just stood with his arms crossed waiting for the fit to end.

Johnny's eyes were even darker than Tony's. Jesus, they deserved to be partners.

Looking back again, JoJo watched as Dylan slapped Tony in the chest, knocking him back slightly. Although Tony was wider and broader, Dylan stood about two inches taller than him but both men were extremely well-built. In fact, her whole team looked like they could compete for ironman.

Dylan seemed driven and highly motivated – similar qualities that she possessed and appreciated. It meant he wouldn't stop even if all signs pointed to a *dead end*.

It suddenly occurred to JoJo that she was staring at her partner when he busted her. Eyes wide, she shook her head to break the spell, and turning away, asked Johnny what was going on. Johnny didn't bother looking at her when he answered.

"This building is suspected of being one of the Triad's warehouses. Maybe it's a big score. Probably nothing. But we had a legit anonymous tip... and our warrant came through."

JoJo's heart picked up the moment she heard *his* name.

Yang Choo? Her first real day on the job and she might end up fucking up his business. No, she'd protect him, but... if she gets caught, she'll lose access to all her father's records and any evidence.

A slow rise in her blood pressure made her slightly dizzy as she tried to think her way out of a million different possible scenarios. And not one of them gave her a way to warn Mr. Choo. She kept her burn phone in a secret pocket hidden in the glove compartment of her civilian car. Any outgoing communications from this area would be monitored right now so using another phone to warn him was out of the question. Surely he heard the sirens? This wasn't intended to be a bust, probably confiscation? Except, if there was something worth guarding, wouldn't there be... *guards?* No, Johnny was right. It was probably nothing.

Someone from another team suddenly grabbed the radio hanging from his bulletproof vest and started giving orders to search the place. Her mind was spinning with possible ideas to salvage the situation in case *nothing* turned out to be *something*. Although, Yang already had someone on the inside to warn him about stuff like this, right?

Worse case? Maybe this could be her *big* screw up. If this was Yang's warehouse, she could somehow fuck it all up and help Yang save his goods or whatever the hell they find inside. She would screw up so badly today that they would actually feel sorry for her and quit looking for an excuse to keep messing with her. Instead, they will pity her incompetence.

JoJo's seemingly perfect plan was slowly turning her dread into excitement when suddenly Dylan forcefully grabbed her vest, scaring the shit out of her. She nearly hit him when she took a protective half-assed swing.

"Keep your head in the game, Sparks."

But as quickly as he grabbed the vest he released it, causing her to stumble and almost fall backwards. Pissed as hell, she glared at Tony and Johnny as they laughed at her terrified expression and failed attempt to deck Dylan in the nose.

"Getting lost in thought on your first day will get you killed, Sparks. Or worse, get *me* killed. Keep your head in the game. Let's go, they need your skills."

##

Dylan and JoJo walked into the building side by side.

There were several Chinese people cleaning the floors and burning the junk they found by piling it in the center of the concrete space. They were curious about the cop cars even though it didn't stop or slow the pace of their cleaning. At the top of the unfinished roof was a small hole in the ceiling where the smoke exited in a steady black stream.

An old Chinese woman – far too old for manual labor – was dragging a large piece of wood across the floor. Dylan ran up to her and grabbed it, helping her put it into the fire. He spoke a standard Chinese greeting, bowing respectfully. And seeing his uniform, she began nervously rapid firing Chinese at him like she was explaining something important. Dylan raised his hands in utter surrender, shaking his head at the woman. He kept waving for JoJo to come closer, but she pretended not to notice.

"Slow down... slow down... I don't speak... wait... wait..." Dylan glared at JoJo, beckoning her to head over. Looking behind her, JoJo kept pretending he was calling for someone else. She silently prayed that the woman wasn't giving any details about Mr. Choo, and even if she was, JoJo could screw up the interpretation.

Hesitating a moment too long, Dylan finally started shouting for her.

"Sparks! You're up. Do your fucking job. What's she saying?"

Smiling at the woman, JoJo faced her, waiting patiently. Initially, the woman just stared back, giving her the once-over. And seemingly satisfied, she finally returned JoJo's smile and laid her hand gently on her shoulder like they were old friends or something. JoJo immediately proceeded to give her a proper respectful standard greeting for an elderly woman.

Seeing her respectful behavior, the woman began sharing while everyone piled in around them waiting in silent anticipation for the interpretation.

And JoJo just listened while the lady talked for a few moments, giving no expression as she droned on and on about a great many things. The boys grunted impatiently until Dylan finally bumped his shoulder against hers. But JoJo didn't want to interrupt the woman. She was sharing her adventures in leaving China. How she came to America. How she lost her children to the gang wars, and how they had no other place to stay warm and dry from the rain. She talked of the good and the bad and it all came out in a rush of emotion and pain.

As she neared the end of her story, the woman reached over and gently touched her cheek, clearly complimenting her. JoJo could feel her face burn as everyone's eyes followed. And if that wasn't enough, the woman pointed at Dylan, digging her finger into his chest causing JoJo's face to slowly turn a shade of red.

It wasn't until Dylan stomped his foot loudly and practically shouted her name that JoJo quieted the woman, putting her hands on her shoulders. The woman relaxed enough to take a breath, giving JoJo time to interpret.

"Well? For fuck's sake Sparks, by the time you interpret, we'll all be ready to retire. What did she say?"

"She gave me the history of how they came to America...and the...*problems* that followed. They were cold and saw this abandoned warehouse and decided to clean it up in exchange for a place to stay. I don't think she knows who owns it. And... well, that's pretty much it."

"Bullshit!" Tony piped in. "All that blabbering for one sentence? I'm calling you out."

"And everyone knows this place belongs to those Triad assholes," Johnny added. "It has their markings all over it. Do you really think they would let these... squatters... these... stray dogs stay here?"

JoJo couldn't stop the slow flush when he called them stray dogs. But she kept her head down and her mouth shut – her face turning red all over again. The old woman touched her cheek as if to give her strength while the boys whined and yelled at her and then at each other in a loud chaotic mess about how she wasted their time and was incompetent at interpreting.

Indianapolis was easy. There were barely any ties to Yang Choo. LA was a whole different ball game. She had to keep herself firmly guarded.

"Anything else you want to add?" Dylan silenced everyone with a flick of his hand.

Fucking alphas.

She shook her head, "Nothing *relevant*... sir."

"That was an awful lot of mumbo jumbo for nothing to be relevant," he said, not waiting for an explanation.

"All right, move out. You have your search parameters. Let's grind every spot of this facility. Technically we're here to make sure these people have their papers and... are safe. This is cut and dry, people. Cut and dry. So don't go making any messes!"

And they all scattered in pairs.

RED FEVER

Chapter 12

Diversion to Divergence

Without asking for permission, JoJo loudly announced to the squatters that the police were checking papers – giving intentional fair warning. In response, the elderly woman started pulling out her papers until JoJo shook her head, pushing them back into her pocket. Everyone had taken off in pairs, except Dylan who was clearly waiting for his partner, watching her every move. He finally interrupted the woman by loudly calling her name.

Bowing respectfully in farewell, she quickly fell in step behind Dylan.

"We're going high, Sparks. I hope you don't have any height phobias?" He glanced over his shoulder to read her expression, but her mind was elsewhere.

"We're going all the way up these internal catwalks, all the way to the ceiling… for a better perspective of course."

"Of course."

JoJo was certain he wanted to see if she was afraid of heights. Maybe she should be? While she pondered the idea of acting terrified of their climb, Dylan broke her concentration as they climbed to the second level.

"Why did that woman poke my chest?"

She was beneath him and was forced to stop or run into his ass. Looking down at her, he waited for his answer. JoJo couldn't stop the small smile that tugged on her lips nor the slow blush she could feel hitting her cheeks as she thought of all the crazy things the woman said to her.

And much to her distress, Dylan suddenly looked undeniably

enamored with her the moment he spotted the silly grin and girlish blushing. All the resentment, mistrust, and bitterness instantly disappeared from his eyes.

Jesus, and all she needed to do to win him over was to fucking look humiliated. JoJo hid her face by looking down. She couldn't possibly tell him what the woman really said…

Dylan was right, she *was* a goddamn pussy, and her face was a fucking traitor!

His sudden interest in her or his sudden *lack* of interest concerning their job could potentially get them both killed. Dylan didn't seem to care as he paused in between the two levels watching and waiting for her to answer. She had nowhere to run. JoJo would've preferred digging through shit and garbage looking for evidence rather than answer him. This was worse, far worse.

"What, Sparks?" he persisted, suddenly shocking the hell out of her with an unexpected smile now tugging at the corners of his mouth. The hard distrustful eyes were lit up with curiosity and excitement like a little boy on Christmas.

"Tell me," he demanded. "It's your fucking job."

JoJo sighed realizing they weren't going to move until she answered.

"She thinks… you are… nice looking. Now go. Please. Sir." He smiled a big lopsided boyish grin at her, nodded in satisfaction, and then started heading upward. They made it through two more steps when he suddenly stopped and looked down at her again.

"What else?"

Letting out an exasperated sigh, JoJo was fucking positive she had a real life Dr. Jekyll and Mr. Hyde on her hands with her new partner.

"Come on McKay!" She practically begged. "Nothing relevant *to this situation*. I swear it."

"What else?" Dr. Jekyll wasn't giving up. His lopsided grin was growing along with the brightness in his soulful humored brown eyes. Everything about his face softened as he watched and waited for her response. JoJo missed the Mr. Hyde who had been harassing her the entire day. At least that asshole was easy to ignore. Charismatic McKay made it impossible.

111

And he was right, it was her job to interpret everything, not just the stuff she deemed worthy of discussion. However, JoJo was just too embarrassed to repeat *everything.*

"She thinks… Jesus, it's really none of my business!"

"What's none of your business?"

"She wanted… she wanted to know if you were single. And…" The traitorous blush was slowly returning, "…she thinks you shouldn't be single at your age." JoJo readjusted the gun hanging off her hip debating on whether to pull it out and start shooting rather than endure anymore of this torture.

"Wait, how did she know I'm single? I mean what makes her assume that?" JoJo looked up and cocked her head like *are you fucking kidding me?*

"I dunno. Your ring finger is empty?" she answered too quickly like she spotted his ringless finger ages ago.

JoJo suddenly hated team leader Dylan McKay.

"I'm wearing gloves." He dangled his gloved hand in her face for effect.

"I don't… I don't fucking know! And I don't care." Her face was burning now, this time in frustration and anger. She was trapped on the ladder steps stuck between levels, head looking up Dylan's ass while he fucked around with her.

Finally, Dylan started climbing again until he reached the third floor and plopped down onto the metal grating. Resting his foot on the last step, he looked down at JoJo as she tried to finish climbing. His leg preventing her from reaching the third floor.

"All right, Sparks. I want all of it. No bullshit. And not just what you think is relevant." JoJo cussed at him, watching his eyebrows shoot up.

"Mother fucker! Jesus-fucking-Christ! She said I was… she thinks I'm… uhm… she thinks you're handsome and… you look at me… how you… *watch* me…" blush betrayer rising, "means you might… maybe *like* me… were attracted to me, and she wanted to know if we were… I should've said no-fucking-way! Then she wanted to know why we weren't… and uhm… *advised me* to… why such a… why a girl like me would wait for… marriage. I dunno, I could be wrong. It was all kind of jumbled. Can we go now? *Please.*" JoJo was pleading with her eyes.

112

Dylan seemed satisfied with her answer and removed his leg from the last step letting her come up.

"I know a little Mandarin too. And she called you *beautiful*. And she called me handsome and…"

"I know what she said!" JoJo hissed. "I told you it was all completely irrelevant and had *nothing* to do with anything other than to give your ass an ego boost."

"Well hell… *Trouble*, I appreciate you telling me the truth. Most of it anyway. But…" He copied her answer, "I dunno, I could be wrong. It was all kind of jumbled."

JoJo jumped onto the third level catwalk, glaring at him as she dusted off her gloves. Side by side, he stood at least half a foot taller than her. The woman was right about one thing, Dylan *was* incredibly handsome, especially when he turned into Dr. Jekyll with all his deviant charm.

"You're… not wrong. I just didn't think it was relevant," she answered. Dylan and JoJo stared at each other for a long moment. The tug-of-war between them finally seemed to end in a peaceful treaty. Turning away, JoJo squinted, staring further down into the dark catwalk spaces. The higher they climbed, the darker the spaces but JoJo was glad to finally focus on work.

"Relevant or not, you can't fight the truth." Dylan said from somewhere behind her. She spun around, staring at him with her mouth open.

Fucking cocky son-of-a-bitch.

"Too bad she didn't add *modesty* to your repertoire. Cocky-much?"

Dylan's eyebrows shot straight up.

"You thought I was talking about me?" His lopsided grin reappearing while his shoulders drew back a little further.

"What!? No. I mean… what?" JoJo blundered.

"I was talking about *her* description of *you*, Sparks, but… okay." It was clear that they were both embarrassed now. He immediately followed it up.

"Doesn't mean you aren't *Trouble* for that matter."

JoJo cracked a small smile and snorted at his comment. Dylan pointed at her like he was surprised to see her smile or maybe to hear her snort.

She echoed him. "Doesn't mean *YOU* aren't trouble for that matter. And truth and fact are hardly the same thing."

They were both trying not to laugh when suddenly JoJo spotted something moving in the distance, hidden in the shadows. She leaned over slightly to see past Dylan's broad shoulders. Someone in black shifted from behind one of the plastic pillars – JoJo marked a glint of metal.

"GUN!" she screamed, immediately dunking down while simultaneously spinning and hook kicking Dylan in the chest. She sent him flying backwards, flipping him right over the side of the railing, knocking him down to the second level. Bullets blazed past where their heads once stood only seconds before.

With a loud thud, Dylan landed on his back, one floor beneath and JoJo started running at the figure, dodging the gunfire – left and right like she was some kind of goddamn ninja.

Bullets were clanging and ricocheting off the railing and metal grating – some right next to JoJo's hand or foot. It was like she was flying as she quickly moved over the metal grating, using the rails to fling herself from one side to the other, jumping and rolling to avoid the spray of bullets.

When Dylan fell, he was already drawing his weapon, so when he toppled onto his back, his gun was out and pointing upwards. JoJo could see him through the grated holes beneath her, his gun following the dark figure. He let off two shots before the figure disappeared into the shadows. She could hear him running across the metal panels, and JoJo hurried to follow the phantom deeper into the darkness. The clanging of their feet against the flooring was the only thing announcing their position. Behind her and beneath her, JoJo watched Dylan running along the second floor, and further down Johnny and Tony were following from the ground level. Everyone was looking up for a clean shot. But it was so fucking dark and the shadows seemed to be growing the higher they went.

Just when she thought she lost him, she spied the stranger jumping off the side of the rail and swinging himself up to the fourth level like an Olympic gymnast. JoJo copied him, jumping up and off the side of the rail too, grabbing hold of metal grating on the fourth floor and flipping her legs upward. Her adversary was attempting to fly up the steps to reach the next level.

Planting her feet firmly, she pulled out her gun.

"Freeze! LAPD!"

He scrambled to get to the next scaffold, and for about three seconds, she had a perfectly clean shot. She hesitated.

Friend or foe?

What if it was one of Yang's men?

And just like that the opportunity was gone. Her mind rapt in a mental debate.

The figure bolted down the catwalk with JoJo close behind, still one floor below him.

Somewhere in the back of her mind was the very detailed lesson from Corporal Ralf Fineous Randall about the flashlight attached to her. But as she raced through the shadows, she decided to conveniently forget that lesson – the only reason her team wasn't open firing was because they couldn't be sure if they would hit JoJo. There were just too many shifting shadows.

She made her choice. She would put on a good show and in the end, the figure would unwittingly outwit her. She slowed her pace slightly squinting into the shadows.

More gunfire!

But who was firing? She could see her team beneath her and none of them were firing nor being fired at...

Like sliding into third base, JoJo hit the grated metal floor burying her head in her arms. Below her she could hear Dylan and the Captain calling her name.

When the fuck did the Captain arrive?

Now she really had to put on a good show! The moment the firing stopped, she was up and moving like someone possessed and obsessed with a mission.

Picking up speed as she ran, JoJo could hear Dylan clanging behind her and still beneath her while Johnny, Tony, and Captain Williams were racing her from the ground. Just as she neared another step ladder, this one segueing to all the levels, more gunfire exploded. Her hand wrapped around the metal pole to climb up as two more bullets zipped by. This time one of them ricocheting off the banister, striking her in the neck.

Painfully crying out, JoJo fell backwards almost hitting Dylan, who had just barely managed to climb up and land on his feet behind her. He nearly tripped over her when she crumbled to the ground. Gun out, he knelt down beside her, quickly checking for injuries and simultaneously trying to pull her down the ladder to safety. JoJo could feel her shirt getting wet beneath the sharp pain on her neck.

She was bleeding.

"I'm fine!" She pushed Dylan with such intensity that he fell straight back on his ass. It was too dark for him to see her wound anyway. He was yelling something at her. They all were. She could hear the Captain calling her name, except their words weren't registering.

Too many trains were zooming through her brain, and feeling the growing wetness down her shirt, she slapped her hand over the wound, and half jumped and half climbed to the next catwalk, leaving Dylan clambering. She was moving quicker than she had ever moved before. Adrenaline giving her fucking superpowers.

She was like a bloodhound that caught the scent of her prey, fully committed. A small frenzy overcame her as she spotted the phantom again, it almost looked like he was waiting for her. She pulled out her gun, firing three in his general direction – careful not to hit him. He fired one back and continued to run.

Suddenly, there was a loud pop like lightning struck or an exploding electric box, and the warehouse was thrust into complete darkness except the small hole in the ceiling venting smoke. Instinctively JoJo dove head first into the catwalk floor, hugging it tightly and waiting for her eyes to adjust.

Dylan caught up to her, activating his flashlight and unintentionally telegraphing their position. So JoJo slammed the light off, pulling him to the ground while Dylan wrestled her... until finally grabbing her by the bulletproof vest, he dragged her to the nearest floor ladder that connected the catwalks.

Her eyes finally adjusted to the dark at the exact moment she realized that the stranger was hurling himself straight down on them. Dylan was already sliding down the ladder steps, trying to pull her with him. It was too late for him to change his mind, Dylan was committed inside the metal ladder with JoJo's body blocking the top.

He left her to face the stranger alone, and she could feel him under her trying to push his way back up. She couldn't let him.

JoJo thrust her legs out to stop from going further down the hole.

Dylan jumped up to grab her vest and yank her down using his body weight, but the man in black had already reached JoJo and they entered into full hand to hand combat.

She was fighting from the floor, one leg keeping Dylan down the metal tube, and the other leg was busy trying to get off her ass, *and* block the stranger, *and* get in a kick or two, *and* keep him from getting on top of her.

With a well timed kick, JoJo nailed the man right in the knee, instantly collapsing him. She quickly used the pause to get off the ground. Dylan was scrambling back up to help her, except the moment his head popped through the hole in the metal floor, the stranger kicked JoJo smack in the chest, sending her flying backwards into Dylan. The force knocking him all the way back down the ladder along with a string of cuss words. Every time he made it to the top, he was knocked back down again.

Everybody was yelling bloody murder.

Between the shifting shadows dancing around them and the bright flashlights, no one could take a clean shot. JoJo and the stranger were practically on top of each other, right along with Dylan floundering beneath them.

The man in black was much larger, and easily maneuvered his way on top of her, straddling her hips. He kept aiming to punch her face, but she was quicker, blocking and moving her head to the point he would punch the metal floor instead of her face.

Her training in Krav Maga was blaring loudly in her brain, *hit, overwhelm, run!* But she couldn't land the *overwhelm* part to set herself up for the run and escape in the inferior position she was stuck in. Whoever he was, he was fucking good.

Suddenly, there was gunfire when someone beneath them fired a warning shot hitting the ceiling. It was too dark and while their flashlights helped, they also hindered everyone by creating massive moving shadows as the light passed through the grating on several levels of floors.

Between punches, JoJo was trying to get a good look at him through his black ski mask.

In a last ditch effort, she knocked him in the throat, gagging him and forcing him to sit back on her pelvic bone. His position allowed her to slide down further beneath his legs and lift her own legs from behind to wrap around his neck, yanking him backwards. With her thighs, she squeezed tightly, attempting to choke him. But with the blaring differences in size, he easily stood up like she was nothing more than a tiny monkey, and prying her off his neck, he threw her back into Dylan.

JoJo could see Dylan giving up climbing, instead he pulled out his gun, and standing directly beneath the man, he searched for a clear shot. An impossible situation given the tiny holes in the grating and the possibility of bullets ricocheting off the metal. She could hear him yelling for her to stand down and move away.

But JoJo had something to prove. Or nothing to lose. And she was on the dark figure as fast as her body allowed. They fought ferociously – obviously both highly skilled and professionally trained in several forms of martial arts as they faced off in the tiny space on the scaffolds. It was a sight to see and equally exhilarating as it reminded JoJo of her days in the underground fights. She felt alive. Free.

It wasn't long before she began sensing the way the phantom moved and shifted on the metal grates. She was on the verge of figuring him out when suddenly the lights popped back on, blowing the circuits, and showering the place with a spray of sparks. It sounded like a bomb went off or fireworks exploding and booming on the fourth of July. Everyone covered their heads from the sparkling shower, and just like that they were thrust back into darkness.

Thinking it was a bomb, JoJo face-planted into the metal grates, her eyes locking with Dylan as she covered her head. She could see his mouth moving… and hear him yelling something. But all she understood was the rage and the excitement and the power coursing through her veins. It wasn't until she watched drops of her own blood hit Dylan's face that she finally woke from the trance.

During the fireworks display, the man took off running across the metal plating using the shadows from the top level to stay away from any gunfire. He disappeared into the roof rafters.

Dylan finally managed to climb up to reach JoJo. But like a wild animal, she maneuvered her way around him and jumped up on the ladder to start climbing and chasing again. Only this time Dylan used his entire body weight to drag her down to the floor.

She was in fight mode, and crazy was all she could see.

But Dylan held on, grabbing her vest and forcing her back down the ladder while dodging the fist she tried planting in his face. Pulling his head back and ducking, Dylan evaded her second attack, grabbing her other arm as it came up to elbow him in the gut. He stopped one elbow mid swing, only to fall prey to her other elbow. She knew exactly where his bulletproof vest ended its protection.

He doubled over and JoJo was back to chasing her prey. Except this time Dylan threw his arms out, wrapping them around her waist in a giant bear hug, pulling her straight down to the floor, face first.

It was that final jarring slam to the metal floor from Dylan's body that seemed to break the frenzy. She didn't even realize she was attacking Dylan until he was standing over her with one foot on her back pinning her to the floor. He looked pissed as hell. Mr. Hyde returned. She knew she crossed the line by attacking him, so she resigned to just laying there and catching a painful breath.

His gun out, Dylan stood over her watching for the stranger to return but he had already disappeared into the roof along with the fading sounds of his boots hitting the metal grating. They grew further and fainter until it was quiet up top.

Still on the hunt, Johnny and Tony disappeared outside with weapons drawn and shouting at SWAT to surround the area.

Satisfied there wasn't another stranger or guard to contend with, Dylan holstered his weapon and knelt beside her. Apologetically – almost shamefully – she locked eyes with him, slowly sitting up. A small trickle of blood dripped down her chin. Using her arm, she wiped it, and spat on the ground.

It was Dylan's turn to lose it. And she could tell he was about to release his fury on her when his eyes shifted down to the Captain.

She followed his gaze. The Captain was on the ground floor looking up at them, listening. She watched as Dylan struggled with his temper, fighting to bite his tongue. Taking several deep shaking breaths, he ran his fingers through his hair and JoJo watched team leader Dylan McKay curb his desire to kill her. Or maybe just reprimand her.

For now.

At least in front of the Captain.

She sent him a quick grateful nod, not missing the warning he flashed her.

JoJo was so consumed with her own agenda, it was only at that moment she realized she had been fighting in the dark.

Dr. Joan M Savage

RED FEVER

Chapter 13

Two Shades of Blue

"Are you two all right? Did you get a good look at him, Sparks? Jesus, what the fuck were you thinking chasing him like that?" The Captain shot question after question at them. She just shook her head, peeling herself off the ground. Covered in sweat and blood, the adrenaline was melting away and taking with it all the natural painkillers. She had a debt to pay, and her body was already collecting.

JoJo made it about halfway to standing before collapsing, Dylan catching her and pulling her to her feet. Instinctively she pushed him away and unintentionally slammed her shoulder against his as she passed by. Up until now, she was moving on pure adrenaline alone... well maybe it was pure pride. Either way her body was seizing up fast.

She limped toward the exit, Dylan following close behind. And when he stopped to talk to the Captain, JoJo got side-tracked by the old Chinese woman. Grabbing JoJo's arm, she quickly whispered something in her ear, gently patting her back and causing JoJo's face to flush and her eyes to widen. She stared at the woman, unsure how to respond. For a long drawn out moment, all she could do was stare blankly until Dylan stepped up behind her.

"What?" he said when his eyes caught the expression plastered on her face. He repeated himself, leaning over trying to read her.

"What? What is it? What'd she say? Sparks! What'd she say?"

JoJo fumbled her words.

"Uh... she said... she said *thank you.*" Shaking her head and faking confusion. Dylan mirrored her.

"Why?"

She shrugged in response, continuing her trek to the exit.

Suddenly Dylan grabbed her, pulling her roughly against him and forcing their hard vests to collide, knocking the air out of an already painful side.

Her hands raised to defend herself, but it wasn't blood he was after. At least not the kind she was thinking. She forgot about her neck wound, and Dylan spotted it.

He pried her neck sideways, getting a good look at the injury like she was some kind of stretchy doll. She slapped his hand, trying to get free from him.

"What the fuck are you doing, McKay!?"

"Whoa! Calm down, Sparks. You're hurt... let's get you checked out. Calm down." She yanked her arm out of his grasp, angrily pushing him away.

"I'm fine," she mumbled, stumbling forward slightly. Dylan refused to let her go no matter how much she pushed and protested.

"I wasn't asking." He held on – almost dragging her toward the ambulance that was pulling up. It wasn't hard to do, she was too weak to struggle, making it easy to drag her and force her to sit on the tailgate of the truck. JoJo honestly didn't have the strength to resist anymore, and it felt good to finally sit and relax.

The EMTs started a standard work-up on her, until one of them noticed the blood on her neck, and then like an anthill she accidentally stepped on, they instantly came alive with energy, movement and flow – beginning with undressing her. Dylan was standing by while Tony, Johnny, and the Captain made their way over to her.

JoJo was in the process of pulling her black police issued sweater over her head, when two very disturbing things came to light. First, her light pink sleeveless undershirt was completely saturated in fresh blood, and if that wasn't enough to cause a stir, the exposed parts of her creamy white skin was shrouded with old scars. Head trapped inside the sweater, she missed their horrified expressions.

Her curly red hair was the last bit to pop out of the sweater hole, and it took a long minute to realize why all eyes were on her…

She forgot.

JoJo forgot who she really was and that she had too many scars for an average LEO, too many scars for someone so fresh out of the Academy, and too many scars for someone so young. It was after she saw Dylan's surprised expression, Tony's disgusted face, and the Captain's alarmed look that she remembered.

But it was too late. Everyone saw.

Trapped in the circle of silence, it was Tony's uncouth comment that brought light to reality.

"Jesus Sparks, what the fuck happened to you? Were you in an explosion?"

The Captain slapped the back of his head as soon as the comment left his mouth, following up with one of his own.

"Officer Sparks, did you get *shot!?* Holy hell! In the neck!?"

And then they started firing questions at her again. Embarrassed, JoJo was scuffling to quickly put her sweater back on and hide from all their intrusive inquiring eyes and questions. The EMT was fighting to keep it off and somehow they ended up in a stalemate. Eventually she stood up to make her escape, but both EMTs held onto her until she kicked one of them in the shin.

"Calm down." Dylan the diplomat broke the awkwardness by laying his hand on her shoulder, keeping her seated.

The idea of breaking his hand and making a run for it quickly flashed through her mind. But…she *did* owe him one. Dylan didn't sell her out in front of the Captain. Cussing, she plopped back down stewing in her humiliation, wishing the ground would just open up and fucking swallow her.

"Easy, Sparks. Take it easy. Guys, let's give them some privacy." And he began herding the group away from her, including the Captain, who seemed determined to get answers.

Jesus, Dylan really was *the* Alpha and he just happened to have a front row seat to her fuck up. Talk about timing.

She watched them leave and head over to the other two teams who had returned from a perimeter search around the warehouse, JoJo could tell they found nothing of significance.

Yang's man had escaped.

They were superficial – the gunshot wound on her neck, a small cut on her arm, and one across her ribs where the edge of her bulletproof vest stopped its coverage. Superficial or not, they hurt like hell. Actually *everything* hurt like hell.

JoJo glanced down at the cut on her ribs, wondering if it will fade or be added to her list of permanent scars. This one felt like a badge of *dishonor* received in the line of duty fighting against a team she admired, to protect a team she despised. Or was it the other way around?

Maybe *despise* was too strong a word for Dylan McKay and his little band of merry men. She was beginning to think that he might be an all right guy. An asshole, a cocky son-of-a-bitch, and a pain in her butt but... he wasn't *too* bad as a partner.

Glancing up, she watched as Dylan chatted with the other officers, and then make his way back over to her. She couldn't cover herself fast enough while the EMT was butterfly stitching her ribs. Anyway, she hurt too damn much to care.

"Another wound? Really Sparks? What the hell?"

She rolled her eyes at him. What could she say? Face red, she watched him bite his tongue again as he glanced back at the Captain. That's two she owed him. He started whispering in a rushed, forced manner.

"Why did you go after him like that? What were you thinking?" Dylan bent down to see the wound on her ribs, so she pulled her shirt down. They fought over her shirt as he tried to lift and look while she fought to keep it covered. Giving up from the pain, she chose instead to punch his hand away.

"That's the third time you hit me today."

"Instinct," she said apologetically.

"Is she okay?" The Captain walked up behind Dylan, startling them both.

Dylan and JoJo glanced at each other. They each knew what the other was thinking and they replied simultaneously.

"She's fine, sir."

"I'm fine, sir."

Their eyes asking the same question, *what was the Captain doing at the warehouse?* But the Captain was looking at the EMTs for a more truthful response about her condition.

"Actually she *is* fine, Captain. Surprisingly, they're all superficial," one of the EMT's stated. "They may smart for a bit... but all in all, you're extremely lucky."

"Sparks this is your first fucking day in the field and we nearly lose you? Is this how it's going to be? What happened up there? Where was your backup?"

"I'm fine. I'm fine, sir. And my backup was... backing me up," she said through clenched teeth as she struggled with pulling her sweater down.

"Officer Sparks, if you experience any fever, redness, swelling, sharp pain or numbness or anything out of the ordinary, make sure you get this looked at." He checked her lip and then her head and eyes one more time, giving her a clean bill of health.

Dylan and the Captain left her, returning to the group to finish up the conversation. She could hear them discussing their opinions on how the suspect managed to escape surrounded by SWAT. There was a motorcycle trail leading into the woods. The discussion then changed to, *why?*

Why only one man? Was he a scout? A watchman? A guard? And who the hell *conveniently* called in the anonymous tip?

They checked every space, crevice, and pothole for something of significance that would draw the Triads, anything. Everyone speculating why one gangbanger showed up to watch over some squatters, guilty of nothing more than cleaning up the space. It was nonsensical and it was making everyone uncomfortable. Something was off with the whole situation.

JoJo couldn't put her finger on the way she was feeling. It was like she entered a room where two people were arguing, she could cut the tension with a knife.

Sitting back, she ran the old woman's final words over and over in her mind. The woman didn't thank her… even though that's what she told Dylan. She warned her… at least… it felt like a warning.

Courtesy of Yang Choo. She whispered to JoJo.

Courtesy of Yang Choo? What the fuck does that mean?

JoJo's mind spiraled over the odd comment. She didn't trust herself enough nor Mr. Choo to call and ask him why? And what his intentions were.

Dylan's loud voice interrupted her thoughts.

"O'Leary's!? A round on me. The rookie has a clean bill of health." His eyes scanned and connected with each person as if he was making a mental note of the ones who agreed to go *and* the ones who said no.

JoJo knew she had to pay penance for their acceptance, and the price tonight was compliance – however fake or temporary. Maybe the beer would help with the pain?

Reluctantly, she nodded at Dylan. All cops seemed to bond this way, eating and drinking and…

Yang's words formed in her mind.

Feeding, fucking, and fighting.

Ties that bond. She shook her head trying to erase the words right along with his sultry voice. Whatever Yang Choo was or wasn't, he wasn't wrong about this. She needed to gain and maintain their trust and their acceptance, so she could crush the cop who killed her father. And in an iconic and ironic twist, she will use them to help her do it. Her heart began racing at the thought of burning through the whole fucking precinct if need be to find out the truth. And as her aching heart increased its beat, her rib began aching to the tune of it.

To hell with them all.

Or to O'Leary's. Which was a different kind of hell the way her body was protesting. She sighed, forcing herself to let go of the surging emotions. It was literally just too painful.

Dylan returned to escort her to the car. Her first day in the field had a rocky start but…

Mission-fucking-accomplished!

She screwed up enough to win them over without seeming too ridiculous. They thought she had something to prove by aggressively chasing the perp.

They couldn't be more wrong.

JoJo was protecting Yang, especially if the suspect was one of his main men. She intervened at every opportunity during that fight, removing any possibility of capturing the stranger and giving him the opportunity to double-cross or betray Mr. Choo. She wasn't sure of anything these days when it came to Yang – only that today was a very dangerous and deadly gamble.

The suspect was bigger and stronger, but she was faster and nimble, giving her the blaring advantage on the catwalks. JoJo had the gift of feeling the ebb and flow of any fight. It came as natural to her as walking, and during that entire fight, she never let go. She even *let* him hit her to look legit. A controlled hit. And a way to keep Dylan out of the fight every time he got too close.

The random ricocheting bullet couldn't be stopped with any amount of skill, and the knife to the ribs was the result of Dylan trying to push her out of the way so he could get up the ladder… *to help her.* He pushed her right into the blade.

She was trying to protect both her partner and the stranger by playing both sides of the board.

JoJo was playing chess with herself today.

She couldn't take the chance on Dylan's abilities. Every piece she moved and shifted across the board was a gamble. Keeping Dylan out of the game, keeping the suspect safe from the team by blocking him so they couldn't shoot him. And all the while she still had to protect herself from getting the shit beat out of her. It was exhausting.

It was exhilarating.

It was sheer dumb luck she didn't die.

There were too many unknown variables. And JoJo didn't know if the stranger was friend or foe. Fuck, she didn't even know if Dylan was friend or foe.

Suddenly, she felt very much alone.

It didn't matter anyway. She did what she set out to do. She showed her team a weakness. They needed to see it, and she delivered.

Dylan gently knocked on her forehead, startling her.

"Keep your head in the game. You're gonna be just fine. A few scratches."

But JoJo watched his face twist slightly and his worried eyes quickly scan her body. She wondered what was bothering him more, the old wounds or the fresh wounds? From what she could tell of team leader Dylan McKay, he wasn't one to keep things bottled up. He would reveal what was bothering him in his own time. She was sure of it.

And now she had time to make up some really good answers.

"Ya, you're fine. Nothing a couple of beers won't solve." he said, trying to force a half smile. "Once we get back to the station, Ca'pin wants you to head home…"

JoJo opened her mouth to protest while Dylan kept right on talking over her, never giving her the chance.

"There'll be an inquiry, but I was there the whole time, so it won't be a problem. Not too shabby for your first day, Trouble. Anyway, you need a shower and a change of clothes. By the time you do that, our shift will be over and we'll all be headed to O'Leary's. I'll text you the address. Just go and get cleaned up, especially your vest. Trust me, that shit will start stinking." He continued ignoring her, opening her car door like some kind of gentleman. She stopped mid stride, glaring. Without making eye contact, Dylan patiently waited like he had all goddamn day to stand there with the door open. When she didn't budge, he started humming and tapping his thumb on the roof, waiting and waiting… and waiting. Humming to the beat of his own tune.

JoJo couldn't take it anymore, frustrated she finally climbed in – angry and…

…something else.

##

It took six months in the Indianapolis PD before she got connected to the alphas. Today it took six hours. It felt like two shades of blue.

She decided to wear something non-feminine to the bar – an old t-shirt to fully show off the patched up neck wound.

Damn right! Instant respect!

She reached into her pocket to make sure she had her antacids – whatever she may have to drink tonight she wanted to be prepared. Some kind of hazing ritual? It might go another way, a pissing contest? Like darts or pool?

She sighed, feeling a growing sense of smugness at how easy it was to figure everyone out. And with the growing sense of smugness, something else was shriveling up and dying – something good. The *fake it till you make it* was starting to make it. It was one thing to *act* cocky while playing the game, but for a second, she started believing it… and pride most certainly had a way of fucking everything up at the most inconvenient time. Anyway, pride at what?

Being a good cop?

Fuck that shit.

Her mind was preoccupied with its own quarreling as JoJo entered the bar, pausing long enough to get the argument between pride and modesty to shut the hell up. This wasn't the time for a major meltdown, she was finally well on the way to being accepted as one of the guys. The old woman's words swirled around her brain.

Courtesy of Yang Choo.

Her mouth dropped open. Could he… did he… did that mother fucker set her up to be a hero? No fucking way.

There was no way Mr. Choo could've known she'd be at that warehouse today. Yet, the old woman was prepared for her. She looked around the bar and found the back of her partner's head. The group was sitting around a tall round table on tall bench stools as if any one of them needed to add height. JoJo was the only one who still needed a kiddie seat at the table.

Dylan was talking and laughing with Tony.

It was Dylan who decided she was going to the warehouse, and it was decided last minute. Dylan McKay with his expensive taste was the only one who knew she was going and that's because he assigned her to go with him. Maybe that's why Dylan was her partner? Yang Choo was keeping his people stacked.

She was lucky she hadn't been issued a body cam yet and lucky it wasn't recording every goddamn thing… or the *courtesy of Yang Choo* would get them both arrested.

One thing was certain, Yang used that woman to break her cover, possibly compromising everything. Was that the point? A reminder at how easy he could get to her if she fucked him over?

JoJo walked into full view of the table but she was so lost in thought that she missed Johnny approaching her. And when he slapped her back in welcome, she nearly pissed her pants.

"Hey Green, Trouble's here! This round's on you!" he said as if Dylan lost some bet.

Who the fuck is Green?

JoJo watched as Dylan just lifted his beer and nodded at the bartender who apparently could read drunk. Only one seat was open and it happened to be right next to her partner. The others got up and headed to the bar while the bartender started filling their mugs.

"Keep your head in the game, Trouble." Dylan greeted her, laughing. He took a long sip of the foamy amber liquid. She sighed and took off her jacket, hanging it on the back of her chair.

"Don't you want your *free* drink? Since apparently I'm paying, fucking again." He glanced over at her and smiled.

"Oh… and… uhm… good work today." He lifted his beer, pausing briefly in the air like he was toasting a ghost.

"Did Johnny just call you, *Green?*" she asked during the pause, ignoring his praise. He sighed and snickered a bit.

"Well, my last name is McKay. It's Irish. Green. Stupid, I know. But ten times better than my first rookie name." His nose scrunched up like something stinky drifted his way. JoJo's eyes were wide open, intrigued with his story. Dylan exhaled loudly and finished what he knew she was waiting for.

"*Leper.* It was fucking *Leper,* for leprechaun. Jesus Christ, am I glad *that one* didn't stick. Do I fucking look Irish to you?"

She shook her head.

"No, you look… Asian… uhmmm maybe Korean? And… something else," she said thoughtfully, studying his features.

"Irish. The *something else* is Irish. My dad was Irish… my mom, Chinese. They actually met in Chinatown if you can believe that. I guess *Green* works."

"So you speak Chinese?" she asked. He shook his head.

"Not like you. I can understand some. I lost most of it when she died – my mom." They grew silent, lost in their own thoughts for a minute, neither one wanting to pursue the topic.

Johnny and the boys returned to the table each holding two beers, except Johnny, he was carting three. He passed the extra one to JoJo.

"Man, that shit was awesome today. Never heard anyone speak gibberish so good." She looked at Johnny intensely

"Gibberish? I dunno Johnny, you seem to have mastered it." The table busted out laughing.

"Funny, real funny. Seriously Sparks, you kicked some ass today. Where'd you learn those moves?"

All eyes shifted her way.

She forgot to prepare. She never expected to be accepted so soon.

Damn it, where was her head these days?

Feeling herself start to panic slightly, JoJo paused and took a long sip of beer giving herself a minute to come up with something. Her mind raced and formulated different ideas while slowly gulping down the bitter liquid, painfully aware that all eyes were still on her. Through a small burp she answered.

"It's standard procedure in Indy. What? You don't have that here?" She smiled wryly. The whole table paused a second to think about it, and then busted out laughing again.

"Bullshit! I'm calling bullshit!" Yet they never asked her again. Instead they started on subjects they all seemed familiar and comfortable with and JoJo – the shiny new object on the playground – wasn't the main attraction anymore.

The boys talked well into the evening, finally winding down around midnight. She listened to all the station's gossip, suspicions, and issues… everything. The drunker they got, the louder they got and the more they talked, growing exceedingly obnoxious and acting as frothy as their beers.

And JoJo listened while they argued and spit and threatened to compare dick sizes. She literally had to stop them from unzipping their pants in the middle of the bar. Twice. She didn't need *indecent exposure* added to her list of ever growing misdemeanors and felonies.

Apparently blondie was a badge bunny and not just Tony's personal ego booster. She liked to hop from cop to cop or cock to cock as Johnny put it. JoJo got the rundown on just about everyone who was anyone at the station, and as midnight approached, they were flipping coins to see who got the wax and lube special from Kaylee tonight. The boys went up to the bar again arguing over who won the coin toss last week.

And team leader Dylan McKay never intervened.

He laughed and let them act as crazy as most of the criminals she knew – choosing to ignore their disorderly conduct. Or maybe revel in it.

Jesus, he was so goddamn good looking when he let his guard down. His boyish face matched his boyish charm and being at the bar with his tribe made him seem happy, content, and so very warm. Happy, content, and warm only managed to confuse JoJo.

So much for figuring everybody out.

Dylan and JoJo were sitting shoulder to shoulder watching the boys at the bar mock fight for Kaylee, when JoJo glanced at Dylan. Feeling her eyes on him, he faced her, their eyes locking. A semi-drunk lopsided smile slowly spread across his face. And JoJo was basking in his strength and soaking up his contentment. For just a second, the lonely hole in her soul seemed less empty with Dylan McKay beside her. He had a strange way of numbing her pain and filling her with a weird sense of comfort. Or safety.

Or something.

And the beer she was drinking was in the process of numbing everything else.

"What?" he whispered. Their faces only inches apart, Dylan's smile disappeared when JoJo suddenly leaned over and touched her lips to his. It wasn't a kiss really so much as a meeting of their lips. A soft touch.

His reaction was not so soft.

Dylan aggressively pushed her away, sliding his chair back. Shocked, he could only glare at her. JoJo was immensely relieved that the boys at the bar weren't paying attention because she was truly mortified by her own behavior... *and* Dylan's reaction. Her face slowly changed to a crazy shade of red. And JoJo chose to ignore the whole stinky situation. Anyway, she wasn't exactly sure what happened.

She decided to blame the beer. Or gravity.

Swallowing another long gulp, JoJo finished the last of it while trying to ignore Dylan. She turned away, hiding her face, watching the guys at the bar.

"What the fuck was that?" he demanded. She refused to look at him, instead letting her attention be pulled into the ambience of the bar. It was very interesting, and it occurred to her that the bar was ironically Irish. From the green and gold coloring to the Irish music playing in the background. She wondered if Dylan was leaning into his paternal roots or going all in with his nickname. You couldn't find a more Irish looking bar in LA unless it was St. Patrick's Day. All that was missing was the green beer. Dylan interrupted her thoughts, refusing to let up.

"Did you plan to fuck your way through the force? A regular badge bunny?"

JoJo didn't engage, refusing to acknowledge a word he said. Quite frankly, she was glad he wasn't interested in her. But men had a way of being protective of their lovers, *especially* the alphas.

Dylan noticed that she checked out, and gently knocked on her head.

"Anyone home? I said what the fuck was that?" He wiped his lips again, making a statement like she was a sloppy kisser.

Sighing in frustration, she finally answered with the truth.

"An accident."

"Your lips falling on mine was...?" he strung out the last word – inviting her to finish the sentence.

"An accident." And with that she moved away from him and joined the other guys at the bar. They were still arguing over who got blondie for the evening and Johnny waved down the bartender and pointed at JoJo. He poured her a shot. In one gulp she swallowed and despite her efforts to ignore Dylan, in her peripheral vision she could still see him in the mirror behind the bartender. He was staring or glaring at her back, waiting for her to turn around and come back to the table.

Instead, she leaned toward Johnny, whispering, "You wanna get outta here?" In response, Johnny gulped down the last of his beer and grabbed his coat while JoJo grabbed hers. Dylan stood up almost defiantly when they started walking out of the bar together. And for a moment, she thought Dylan was going to protest. But he just quietly watched them leave, all the while looking like the little kid who just had his Halloween candy stolen by the neighborhood bully.

Dr. Joan M Savage

Chapter 14

Truthful Lies

Dylan was annoyingly quiet.

He didn't even greet her when she arrived at her post the following day. Although he was responsible for getting her set up with the inquiry and all the other bullshit things she had to do after a shooting. He stayed cold and distant, kinda like the first day on the job. At least he wasn't asking any more aggravating questions.

But his silence was more annoying than his shotgun questions.

They were assigned light duty until a decision was made about the warehouse incident. Part of that temporary shit duty was to check out street cameras and ask around about the man they saw in the warehouse – busy work until she was cleared for active duty again.

Nobody was going to talk. And as predicted, nobody heard anything, nobody saw anything, and nobody knew anything. No motorcycles. No man in black. Nothing.

But this was Triad territory – of course nobody would talk.

And worse, nobody was talking inside the cruiser either. The blaring silence was getting on her nerves. Normally she would be thrilled for the quiet, except she wasn't. Dylan's distant manner and cold shoulder bothered her like an itch she couldn't scratch. Maybe because she felt she owed him for covering for her.

She couldn't take it anymore.

JoJo turned and stared at him.

By his sudden uncomfortable shifting and readjusting of his collar, she could tell he felt her gaze. Pulling a McKay move, she waited patiently until he finally had to acknowledge her. He was attempting to pay attention to driving while simultaneously glancing over to read her.

"What is it, Sparks?" The question was without tone. And it bothered her that it bothered her.

"What's wrong?" she asked, only to be met with blaring silence. Letting out an annoyed sigh she tried again, this time going straight for the pink elephant they were ignoring.

"Full disclosure… I didn't sleep with Johnny last night." She dropped the bomb to see if it made an impact. It did more than make an impact, it caused a cascading failure.

"Why the fuck would I care!?" he practically shouted, "I don't give a shit! I don't fucking give a shit! You can fuck the whole force for all it matters to me!" he responded too fast, with too much intensity, and with way too much emotion. Ignoring his outburst, she continued.

"We shared a cab to blondie's apartment. He went in and I went home. No kiss. No hug. No handshake. Nothing. We just shared a cab. That's all."

Dylan's eyes kept searching her face as if trying to read her, or find fault, and stay on the road at the same time.

"Bullshit," he said, his voice lowering an octave or two. His eyes continued moving back and forth from her face to the road, still searching for the truth. This time she looked away, her task was completed. The vibe in the vehicle had already changed. And suddenly, JoJo felt like she could breathe again next to Dylan McKay.

Dylan McKay who had a way of taking up all the space. The tension that was suffocating her only moments ago was finally gone.

In for a penny, in for a pound. She kept going.

"And full disclosure, I didn't like hearing you talk about blondie." Now she could feel his eyes on her. Neither one spoke again for a long while but the mood in the vehicle was definitely lighter and from the corner of her eye, she thought she saw Dylan crack a tiny smile to himself. She could hear him take in a deep long overdue breath, exhaling all the pressure with it.

It was done. She made her move on Alpha. Albeit too soon. But what the fuck, everything happened fast in LA. I guess that's how LA rolled.

Anyway, it's just a game, she reminded herself.

She had a mission, and she didn't care if she had to throw Dylan McKay under the bus to complete it. She sighed, feeling unsatisfied with her own conclusion.

Confusion was her nemesis, and McKay was... confusing. He had the power to influence the team, the power to make things happen, the power to cover for her. Just like he did in the warehouse with the Captain. When she eventually plays the '*my-dad-was-murdered*' card, he'll help her too. She was sure of it. Because that's what alphas do.

Dylan interrupted her thoughts, stopping the slow downward spiral.

"Where's your head, Sparks," he said through a boyish grin. All malice and tension dissolved.

And as far as talking went, Dylan and JoJo stayed silent after that, speaking only when necessary. They settled into a weird kind of professional and courteous partnership. Polite and awkward as she finished up training and all nonsensical paperwork. They found a safe professional groove which they flowed and operated in, however, everyone else in the narc department was an entirely different story.

JoJo went from zero to hero overnight.

Courtesy of Yang Choo

##

Lost in deep thought, she headed back to her desk – one hand holding a coffee mug filled with liquid goodness, the other holding a folder with her nose buried deep in its contents. She finally had preliminary reports from her warehouse *incident*. Witnesses, the anonymous tip, a footnote of the elderly woman's responses – courtesy of JoJo – and what SWAT found. Or in this case, did not find. SWAT, the fire department, and ambulances were called when the breaker exploded. Initially everyone assumed it was a bomb, but it was nothing more than an overload from faulty unfinished wiring. Even the fingerprints and blood samples came back with absolutely nothing of interest. The blood belonging to none other than yours truly – Officer JoJo Sparks.

It made no sense.

An anonymous tip that the warehouse belonged to Yang Choo, along with a picture of his train of black vehicles parked in front of it. She recognized Yang's license plate, so at some point he was there. There were no dates provided on the pictures. So why was this place special enough to warrant a search warrant?

A quick mental argument ensued as she struggled with the desire to contact Mr. Choo. Did she need to protect this place? But the real reason was lingering just below.

Why did he use that old woman to break my cover?

Especially after being so meticulous with erasing all connections between them. Was the woman a loose end now? On second thought, plausible deniability, she didn't want to know. She sighed, scratching her head.

And then there was another blaring problem – what if this was the *other* way around? What if it was a test to see if *she* was dirty? A test of her skills? And she didn't report what the old woman *really* said.

Jesus, she could go fucking crazy wondering which side of the chess board to play and what needed to be done to win. It was gnawing at her…

Which queen will she lose? And what is she willing to sacrifice? The black king or a white knight? She relented. It was an impossible situation, and no matter how cleverly JoJo played the game through and through in her head, in the end, she was still going to lose.

Lost in thought, she missed Tony coming out of nowhere and ramming into her causing her to drop the mug with a loud crash. Everyone looked at the perfect moment to see Tony reach out and *apologetically touch* the area where he *accidentally* slammed into her, which just happened to be her right breast. Cupping it, he apologized, simultaneously trying to hide a cheeky grin.

JoJo froze. And for the moment, her lack of response seemed like she was welcoming his advances. It really could've looked like a complete accident except the stupid cheesy grin growing wider on Tony's face as his lingering hand stayed too long where it didn't belong. It took a full minute for JoJo to finally catch up to the situation. And with a delayed overreaction of being frightened, she popped the file up to hide her fist from the hallway cameras as she strategically struck his face for maximum pain and minimal effort.

JoJo nailed him directly on the upper lip and nose. An excruciatingly painful area.

His eyes welled up with tears and he bent over in pain, blood gushing from his nose.

It was a bloodbath on the shiny white laminate floor and she was standing in the middle of it. JoJo started to mock apologize right back, but something very strange happened to the fearless and courageous JoJo Sparks... the moment her eyes fixated on the blood pooling around her feet, her body went rigid, her mind halted, and a wave of dizziness and weakness gripped at her soul. Dylan, Johnny, and a couple other officers came over to check on the loud crash. It was clear they knew the apologies passing between Tony and JoJo were all for show. Dylan was pissed as hell.

"Grow the fuck up Tony and lean your head back, you fucking sprung a leak."

Tony mumbled back,

"No way, I'm not swallowing." He coughed and gagged on his own blood, spraying JoJo's pants and shoes. Johnny grabbed him by the collar, dragging him toward the onsite infirmary. They started arguing as they walked away.

"Jesus, at least plug it! You're getting blood everywhere!" Johnny was hounding him.

"I'm not swallowing!" Tony grumbled back as they disappeared around the corner. The other two officers made themselves scarce not wanting to incur Dylan's wrath when he started yelling at JoJo.

"Goddamn it Sparks! You and Tony need to work your shit out! Look at this mess! What the hell are you thinking?"

But JoJo was unresponsive, paralyzed in the pool of blood while Dylan picked up the large pieces of her shattered mug. He was tossing them into the garbage can like an expert basketball player, yelling at one of the other officers who was trying desperately to quietly escape the scene of the crime.

"Hey, call maintenance for cleanup, would you?"

Standing up, Dylan had a look of pure disgust on his face from some blood that managed to get on his hand. JoJo tried to speak, respond – defend herself. Something. Anything. But nothing was happening, not even her mouth would move. All she could do was stare at the blood on her shoes and stand helplessly by while she was slowly sucked into her childhood nightmare. Her breathing growing increasingly erratic and her face flushed another shade of pale. She thought she might be having a heart attack or maybe her heart was attacking her by violently banging against her chest.

The tone of Dylan's voice changed to something jovial in nature as he tried joking with her.

Why did he sound so far away?

"Keep your head in the game," he said, and she could feel his hand fall on her shoulder, pressing her to move out of the blood. He only managed to rock her forward slightly.

Without her consent, JoJo's whole body began vibrating until she was violently shaking. For the life of her, she couldn't seem to catch her breath.

It was happening again. After three goddamn years of blessed freedom, the nightmare decided to return. And it returned with a vengeance.

It had the power to paralyze her.

Dylan leaned over placing his face directly in front of hers, attempting to read her. She was spinning out of control from so many emotions as her worst childhood nightmare somehow just crossed the line into reality, taking her hostage with it. Suddenly, JoJo was that pathetic little girl again trapped in blood and fire. The bodies around her were screaming bloody murder and she could smell the sickening stench of burnt hair and flesh.

What the fuck! She gasped for air.

Without warning, Dylan grabbed her arm and yanked her into the stairwell behind him, leaving a trail of bloody footprints.

"We need to talk, Trouble! Enough is enough! This bullshit between you and Tony needs to stop." Closing the stairwell door, he continued to drag her down the last set of stairs and into the basement boiler room.

Dylan pushed her up against the wall, quickly locking the door behind them.

It was all for show.

When JoJo locked eyes with him, she realized his anger and actions were all for show to get her into the quiet space and away from prying eyes. She leaned against the cold hard cement wall, trying to catch her breath, trying to absorb its coolness, trying to come back from oblivion. Dylan was standing by watching her quietly.

In the dark stillness of the basement, the screams from the burning bodies began to fade slightly. Her violent shaking was shifting back into soft trembling. But she still couldn't quite catch her breath... at least until Dylan instinctively pulled her into his chest, breaking whatever spell held her captive. The shocking jolt instantly calming her down.

"It's normal. This is normal after your first shooting, Sparks. You're going to be okay. Just breathe through it. Deep breaths. Keep breathing. It's just a panic attack. It happens to everyone." He tried to sound soothing except she could hear the worry crack his voice.

Why did it return after all these years? And how could it have so much power over her?

JoJo didn't have the heart to tell Dylan that this wasn't her first shooting... instead she collapsed against him, feeling too unstable to stand on her own. She held him in a death grip like her very life depended on it. And Dylan didn't say another word, choosing instead to wrap his arms tightly around her. There was something warm and wonderful about being in the arms of team leader Dylan McKay. She felt some relief.

Fuck, she actually felt *safe*.

The nightmare faded into the nothingness from which it came. Her trembling subsided, and her heart and breathing finally came under control. The moment she had some inkling of self-control, JoJo quite suddenly and aggressively pushed Dylan off her. Turning her back to him, she hid her reddening cheeks, and quickly put herself back together again. It was like nothing even happened. Shirt tucked in and hair slicked back, she reached to unlock the boiler room door to get as far away as possible. Only Dylan had other plans it seemed. He cleared his throat, stopping her.

"Sparks... wait." He sounded harsh, giving her pause. When she turned to look at him, he was the one struggling now. She watched him take a deep uncomfortable breath, nervously running his hand through his hair.

"JoJo, I'm married."

Her stomach dropped.

Another wave of dizziness hit her and she didn't have the strength yet to force a poker face. All she could manage was a stiff back and erect shoulders. She meant to leave, instead she glared at him, unable to hide the disappointment she was feeling. When she didn't run away and she didn't respond, Dylan started stuttering.

"I mean... I'm not really... it's over... unofficially but... officially though... I am technically... still married."

Jesus, what the fuck?

She had enough, not bothering to let him finish and without another word, JoJo quickly flung the boiler room door wide open with a loud bang. The door hit a very shocked Johnny as he watched JoJo flee the room. His shock changing to amusement when he spotted Dylan coming out of the same dark room, chasing her. Dylan accidentally ramming right into Johnny and knocking him straight on his ass. He quickly stopped to help him back up while JoJo flew past them and headed up to the second floor ladies room.

Was everything a lie? It felt like it was all merging into one truthful lie.

And the thing that was bothering her the most in this whole goddamn fucked up situation was that her fake *'we will miss you'* mug was shattered.

Talk about perspective.

Chapter 15

Black King. White Knight.

Despite the boiler room incident with all its awkwardness, JoJo mustered the last bit of courage she had to show up to O'Leary's. She had to, especially after Johnny busted them in the boiler room. It was the only way to cut the head off the gossip snake. And despite the earlier tensions with Tony, everyone else showed up too, most likely because it was JoJo's turn to buy. Anyway, going home without a buzz meant she would have to face two ugly truths... first, the nightmare returned – and far worse this time. Why? Did the shootout really trigger it? JoJo was involved in several gun related incidents in Indianapolis, so what? Just because she looked like a fresh inexperienced rookie didn't make her one.

Her nightmares died with Ben, and she just as soon leave them buried. A befitting end considering they were usually triggered by him in the first place.

And second...

Dylan McKay.

He was fucking up all her plans.

And speak of the devil, Dylan and the guys were at their usual table, so she headed over trying to look as cool and casual as possible. Tony had two black eyes with his nose taped up.

Locking eyes with her, he made instant peace by *thanking her* for the drink that she would eventually be paying for with an ashamed nod and a slight lift of his beer. She assumed it was an apology anyway. But just to be sure, she walked right up to him in a ballsy attempt to confront the beast.

The group leaned in a bit closer as she approached like another fight was about to ensue.

Instead, JoJo let rip a huge smile, surprising everyone. She affectionately patted Tony on the back.

"Hey Tiny, you should uhm... bump into Kaylee and not me. Less hazardous and all that. Blondie would... like that... I believe."

Tony smiled sheepishly. "You think so?"

She nodded, hanging her coat on the only available chair, which happened to be sitting right next to Dylan McKay. Again.

The worst and most uncomfortable place she could possibly think of right now.

Determined not to be moved, she pushed forward with all pretenses that everything was well in JoJo-Sparks-land.

"I'm positive, Tiny. You know, she mentioned you on my first day. Yep, she made it crystal clear that you are off limits."

"I'm not off limits," he argued, looking like a little puppy eagerly waiting for a treat.

"But you *could* be off limits, right?" JoJo hinted, winking at him.

Tony missing the point entirely, plunged ahead. "I'm not off limits Sparks, so if you want to..."

"A girl doesn't do that unless she knows what she wants, and Kaylee *knows* what she wants. What I'm saying is you could be off limits... if you get your shit together." She smiled again hoping this time he got it. The rest of the group was tangibly relaxing as they realized JoJo was negotiating a peace treaty instead of a call to arms.

Shrugging his shoulders, Tony's confidence returned right along with a side dish of cockiness, and before her very eyes, he transformed right back into an asshole.

"FYI Sparks, anytime, anyway, anyhow, I'll check out the boiler room with you."

And there it was. Time to cut the head off the snake.

"The boiler room? Let's see... McKay threatened my job. Threatened to fire me. And threatened to report me. Is that what you had in mind? I mean if you're gonna start a rumor like that at least let me get some foreplay out of it. Fucking Johnny…" She glared at Johnny, shaking her head. He was gulping down his beer pretending to hear nothing and see nothing.

"So is that what you want, Tiny? You want me to report you?"

Tony glanced back and forth between Dylan and JoJo trying to decide what to believe. Finally, he looked at Johnny who shrugged his shoulders and started gulping again.

"I thought… I thought…" he stuttered.

"You thought wrong. Anyway, *thinking* really isn't your strong suit now is it?" And with that, they all started laughing. The war ended and JoJo could hear Dylan chuckling. When she glanced over at him, he looked both amused and impressed.

"She's right, man. You and Kaylee make a great… *team*. Snag that girl before someone else does." Dylan said, following JoJo's lead. And she realized that the war between them was over too.

Johnny slammed the table with his empty glass scaring her back to reality.

"Sparks! Thanks for the beer!" The other guys grunting in agreement.

"Another round!" Johnny shouted and like cattle they headed to the bar for their refill while Dylan and JoJo stayed behind. It started feeling a little deja vu-ish.

Johnny turned his back to the bartender as he waited, staring at JoJo and Dylan with a cheesy grin on his face. They sat quietly not even looking at each other, both fully aware of their audience. Finally Dylan waved for the waitress to come over.

"Can we get two shots of cinnamon schnapps and two shots of the Cop's Special? My tab please." JoJo glanced at Dylan wondering if she was going to have to drag him or any of their asses home tonight. There wasn't a chance in hell she could carry any one of them.

They quietly watched the boys argue over who won the coin toss and the right to visit Kaylee tonight. Tony seemed unusually aggressive about it and Johnny became preoccupied with backing up his partner, finally ignoring Dylan and JoJo. Anyway, it felt like Dylan wanted her alone, like he had something to say… needed to say. But there was nothing to say.

The waitress arrived with the four shots.

JoJo was resting her chin on the edge of her beer glass like she was already drunk. She was just so damn tired. Revenge was tiring. Or maybe it was the return of the nightmare that stole her strength. Or Tony's unwelcome advances. Or her wounds trying to heal. Or her mind spiraling over the cryptic message the old woman gave her. A gift and a warning? Or maybe it had something to do with her partner being unofficially officially *married*.

Who the fuck cares?

They were still sitting shoulder to shoulder despite having the whole table to themselves. JoJo liked feeling the warmth of his shoulder pressed against hers. She liked feeling his strength. His peace.

And she liked that Dylan covered for her three times now.

The beer was hitting all the right spots and the aches and pains felt further away. In her peripheral vision, she could feel Dylan's eyes piercing into her soul. Glancing sideways, she gave him her full attention. He placed one shot of the Cop's Special in front of her and took the other one for himself, raising the glass to toast.

"Peace," he said, and JoJo's eyes widened, suddenly wondering if Dylan McKay had the power to read her mind. Leaving his toast hanging in the air, he waited for her to join him. It reminded her of the car door and every other time they had a conflict of interest. What Dylan wanted, Dylan got... because he had the power of patience, and she did not.

He made the toast *personal* and made it so she couldn't refuse. Of all the toasts to toast and all the words to use... he chose *peace*.

Fuck it.

She picked up the milky looking fluid and they struck a deal. Deep in her heart she hoped it wasn't another deal with a devil. She hoped that Dylan really wasn't Yang's inside man and that he wasn't a dirty cop, and she hoped beyond hope that he had no part in her father's murder. So far Dylan was the one good thing in this shitty fake job and she couldn't take it if he ended up biting her on the ass instead of covering it.

When the liquid hit her tongue, JoJo unexpectedly gagged as she swallowed the hideous thick substance. It was chunky and sour and utterly disgusting.

Dylan's booming laughter suddenly filled the bar. It was such a loud genuine hearty laugh, that JoJo found herself unintentionally smiling back. It made the taste worth it.

"They don't like cops here, what can I say? But we get it for a buck so it kinda became a thing." Still laughing, he shrugged. "You had to at least try it once. And that's why you follow it with..." He picked up the cinnamon schnapps. "*This*... it chases away the bitter."

JoJo didn't argue and didn't wait, grabbing the second shot she tried downing it as fast as humanly possible.

But Dylan quickly made another toast, so JoJo held the spicy liquid in her mouth, her cheeks puffed out like a chipmunk as the cinnamon burned her.

"Partners," he said, and they took their time swallowing, locking eyes and slowly enjoying the cool burn down their throats. On cue, the group returned to the table with their mugs overflowing with foam. And as the shots slowly made their way to her head, JoJo suddenly found everybody fucking hilarious. For a few minutes, she didn't think about revenge or hatred or dishonor or dirty cops.

Or maybe it was a few hours.

Instead she laughed until she cried, and even peed her pants a little when Tony shot a pretzel out of his taped up nose, landing it in Dylan's beer.

Peace indeed.

Nobody said goodbye.

They were too busy fighting for cabs, and over who won the coin toss. And like a bad omen, the moment Dylan and JoJo stepped outside it started to rain.

"Come here," he said, grabbing her arm gently and pulling her until they were both standing under the tiny awning of the doorway. They had to huddle together to enjoy its protection from the rain. Dylan positioned JoJo's back against his front, his hands resting on her shoulders.

It was for survival's sake.

Unintentionally leaning a little deeper against him, she was soaking up his heat instead of the cold rain. She loved the smell of rain, but there was something else in the air, a pleasant musky aftershave mixed with cinnamon that made JoJo want just a little bit more. And like another warning, lightning flashed and the heavens opened up into a heavy torrential downpour. JoJo started counting the seconds before the thunder replied.

A storm was coming. You would be a fool not to notice the signs.

Dylan shifted her further away from the rain, forcing their bodies to touch. She could feel his warmth against her back and she basked in it, just like a snake that crawls onto the road to steal some sunshine.

Unofficially officially married.

JoJo couldn't stop herself from stealing some of Dylan. He interrupted her basking.

"Jesus, what's a guy gotta do to catch a cab around here?" And like they were magic words, a cab pulled up before he even finished the sentence.

Fucking alphas.

"Come on Sparks, or you'll be here all night."

"Me? I was here first. You're the one who'll end up waiting."

"Exactly, so we should share. Come on." Dylan managed to swindle her into sharing, adding a new level to the warning already brewing within her like the storm brewing around her.

Warning? They were partners. Professionals. Two purely professional partners just sharing an innocent cab ride to their respective homes. Which was true… mixed with the tiniest white lie. It was the tiny white lie that was keeping the cab ride uncomfortably silent.

Dylan slipped into an unusually pensive mood or maybe he had too much to drink to notice the thick heavy awkward silence that filled up the entire space. So much so that even the cab driver was casting glances back at them. Like he was waiting for a fight to break out.

Or something else.

When Dylan finally spoke, JoJo caught herself jumping slightly.

"I hate the rain," he muttered.

He turned to face her as he finished his thought. Simultaneously, she looked away to stare out her own window.

"I love the rain," she countered. An afterthought followed that she didn't mean to say out loud.

"It washes away the blood."

"What?" he said, his worried eyes returning.

Fuck. She could only imagine what he was thinking now, especially after what happened at the station. She chided herself for opening her mouth. It was as if he was reading her mind again.

"What happened today?" he asked gently.

What did happen?

She was asking herself the same question… all fucking day.

It's been a long time since the nightmares haunted her and even longer since getting squeamish around blood. Fuck, she saw more blood in one underground fight than most people will see in their lifetime. So…

JoJo shook her head and shrugged her shoulders, refusing to meet Dylan's curious stare.

…so why now? A shiver ran through her whole body. You can't have reactions like that and stay in this business. And she was so close to the truth.

A red flag went up.

Maybe her timeline needed to change. After all, wasn't it already screwed up? She planned for at least six months getting her foot in the door.

It took six hours.

She planned at least one year before she made friends and it took one week. And hooking up with an alpha? Well…

She glanced over at Dylan.

…well that took no time at all.

Goosebumps shot across her arms. It was cold in the cab. Cold in her heart. Everything felt so goddamn cold when answers were elusive. She wrapped her arms around her body for warmth as she thought about what that might mean for her future.

Maybe she needed to make a bold move now, and fuck everybody.

Yes, it might destroy her, ruin her, rob her future but in the end, it will ultimately save her. She was in too deep now and there was no going back. JoJo needed the truth and the thought of spending one more day not knowing was slowly killing her.

If everything was happening fast in LA then why fight it? Why not catch that wave and ride it all the way to shore?

May fortune truly favor the bold.

Closing her eyes, she could still feel Dylan boring a hole into her head. He was waiting for more than a shrug and all she had to offer him was silence – except for the rain hitting the windows and an occasional tire plunging into a puddle. JoJo had her own questions too. They ran through her like subway trains that kept picking up more passengers with more questions and it was getting crowded in her head.

Was Dylan dirty? She needed to know if she was going to successfully keep their relationship in perspective.

Fuck, what difference does it make anyway? Would he even admit to anything? Or worse, what if he confronted her right back? And *she* actually *was* dirty.

It was an endless cycle of mental bullshit without any answers. At the very least she needed to ask him. It was an itch she couldn't scratch. A splinter throbbing in her finger. Every cell in her body demanded an answer from team leader Dylan McKay who was married but not married and wore Armanie and used a Gucci wallet when he paid for everyone's drinks. The one and only cop who ever covered her ass when she actually faltered. Her sanity demanded it.

But…

There was one little problem with this new plot forming in her head and its potentially new timeline.

Yang Choo.

He invested too much to get her here. She was his fail-safe.

JoJo sighed deeply, rubbing the space on her forehead. Her reaction today was… unacceptable.

What happens if your fail-safe starts failing?

Like the beer she drank, it was supposed to be her fail-safe. And it failed. It flopped. It didn't do fucking shit to help her with the pain, or her obsessive thinking, and it certainly didn't hold up to the promise to be liquid courage. JoJo felt anything but courageous right now. In fact, for the first time since she was a small child, JoJo Sparks was feeling straight up terror.

If...

No, when...

...when she made a bold move to find her father's killer, she had to keep it a secret from Mr. Choo and his informant. Any move right now was a risk to her job, ergo, a risk to the Triads. She was a blaring link to the meticulous Mr. Choo himself.

The same red flag that went up earlier was actually a red bullseye – right in the center of her back should she fuck anything up. And having a panic attack in the middle of the police station might be the shovel that digs her grave.

If Mr. Choo ever found out.

So whose side was Dylan on? Black king or white knight? The splinter throbbing in her finger just became a stake poised over her heart. The trains in her brain got fuller and more crowded as she struggled not to ask herself any more internal questions. Or external ones.

Out of nowhere, Dylan chipped away at the walls she was keeping tightly around her.

"My mother was murdered right... *there,*" he said, pointing to some place on the street only he could see. And her walls came tumbling down. The trains in her head halted and everything grew quiet.

She searched his profile for the punchline, for the lie, for anything that would keep him at a distance, and keep him from getting any closer to her own pain. But his face was blank, he stared out the window with his forehead plopped against the glass like some small child saying goodbye. He laid one finger against the window as he pointed to the hell he was reliving. Outside was nothing but empty streets and sidewalks and rain. Feeling eyes on her, she glanced up catching the nosey cabby again. Tilting her head, she narrowed her eyes dangerously, silently threatening him. Instantly he shifted back to focusing on the road.

Dylan was lost in his past, staring out the window struggling with something dark and terrible, something she knew only too well.

Suddenly the whole fucked up situation she was immersed in was

154

feeling too real.

Tit-for-tat. It was her turn to pull him into the boiler room hot seat.

"I'm sorry," she said.

It came out flat. Like a bad joke. Unpracticed. Inexperienced. And somehow it must've sounded like an invitation because Dylan continued with his story.

"It was senseless," he whispered.

Lifting his head off the window, his gaze easily shifted to her.

"She was just walking home from work... like she did a thousand times before. That one fucking night... she walked right into the middle of a fight. A goddamn gang fight and who the hell knows what it was about. Some idiot insulting another idiot... drugs, money, sex... fucking senseless pointless shit."

His voice cracked. Swallowing and clearing his throat, he broke free from JoJo's intense gaze and fixed his eyes on the back of the seat in front of him. There was an advertisement for an Amber Alert – a missing person's report and a picture of a lost, kidnapped, sex-trafficked, or probably murdered little girl. The picture showed what she might look like today if she were still alive. Dylan reached up and touched the girl's cheek. When JoJo looked at it just right, it could easily have been a picture of herself. It's inevitable, at some point everyone sees themselves as the missing person. Dylan continued.

"Just like that she was gone. Ah hell..." he snorted. "I was seven. I don't even remember it anyway."

JoJo accidentally forgot to shut her mouth.

"I think you remember everything."

Again, their eyes met. Dylan's lips pursed together making him look like a tortured little kid.

Jesus, weren't they a pair? She was back to being that frightened little girl with bad nightmares and Dylan was a tortured little boy and neither of them had any resolution. Maybe that was life? No resolution until the final resolution. No wonder they became police officers in this fucked up shitty world. If they couldn't get any resolution, they could help other people get theirs.

I had no choice. JoJo reminded herself. It was the price of admission.

The fee to join the game. And resolution was expensive these days.

After a beat she could hear him whisper.

"I remember it was raining. I remember it still feels shitty." He forced his boyish lopsided grin but despite his efforts he couldn't quite cover the sadness she saw brimming in his eyes. For the first time during this entire day of hellish bonding, she didn't stop herself from giving a genuine response and wholly smiled back. It was more about comforting him the way he comforted her in the boiler room. Somehow their smiles turned to chuckling, and chuckling into laughter.

It was a *fuck you* laugh, and it heightened until they were crying. Only when the cabbie suddenly pulled to the side of the road, hitting a hard bump in the process, did their senses turn back on. The laughter ending right along with their ride.

The driver turned to look back at them, leaning over his passenger seat to point to a building.

"Here," he said through a thick accent. She looked around investigating where Dylan lived. Dylan already had a handful of money out and was stuffing it into the cabbie's hand

"Keep the change, man, and stay safe out there."

"Thank you very much sir, thank you very much."

He kept repeating his gratitude as he counted the immensely large tip.

RED FEVER

Chapter 16

Dirty Lies and Filthy Ties

JoJo planned to take the cab home.

Yet found herself standing at the entrance of Dylan's apartment like a goddamn vampire needing some kind of formal invitation to cross the barrier.

Unofficially officially married. She was palling from curiosity.

"You should wait the storm out." Dylan said. "I'll call you a cab as soon as it lightens up." He was leaning against the door panel, arms crossed over his chest like a cowboy in an old western film. A tiny hint of a smile pulling at his lips as he watched JoJo struggle with coming or going. She stared down at her hands – it was the storm building inside her that really had her on edge. And the longer she stalled, the more awkward the situation felt.

Lightning flashed.

One thousand one, one thousand two, one thousand three…

Thunder rolled and Dylan interrupted her count with his knack for stating the obvious.

"It's getting worse." It was an invitation.

The storm inside her was getting worse too.

Wouldn't this be the perfect time to question him? Why not use this time?

Her reasoning was sound.

And fuck the repercussions. She needed the truth.

Lightning flashed again.

One thousand one, one thousand two…

The thunder answered and JoJo stepped into his apartment leaving a puddle of mud where she once stood.

##

The only time Dylan stopped staring at her was the moment she finally entered his place, and then he suddenly seemed fascinated with his wet squishy shoes. It was her turn to stare at him with a *what-the-fuck-now* look. She realized too late he was going to kill her with small talk.

"You know the weatherman said we had a forty percent chance of rain. How the hell are we in a storm?" he said as he shook his head like a wet dog, scattering water everywhere.

JoJo drifted further inside, half listening to Dylan rant about the inaccuracies of weather reports and how it could be considered an obstruction of justice. He would throw out a question or two but she didn't bother answering, and he didn't care.

It wasn't as dark as expected when the door closed behind her. Surprisingly, the entire south and west walls were made of beautiful long windows. The streetlights pooled in giving enough light that she could see everything clearly. Although it was sparse, it was shiny. One leather lazy boy and a giant 52 inch TV sat in the middle of his living room. In the corner was a beat up boxing stand with his gloves and wraps thrown loosely on the floor.

One chair… only one. And not a single picture of a family.

Or a wife.

He was a man who was very alone. Or wanted to be alone.

The decor was not what you would expect from a cop. Or maybe it was exactly what you'd expect – just missing a table full of half-eaten Chinese takeout, used coffee mugs, squished beer cans, and an empty box of donuts. There wasn't a feminine touch in sight.

While she was busy stereotyping him, Dylan grabbed a hoodie off the coat rack on his way in, not bothering to turn the lights on. It didn't feel right to have them on anyway, like somehow that would be inviting the neighbors over. She scanned the entire empty space, making a complete visual round until her eyes landed back on Dylan.

She barely had enough time to react when his hoodie came flying at her. The zipper hitting her lip, giving it a sting. She glared at him.

"I thought you'd be faster," he said, like it was an apology.

And before she could send a few cuss words his way, Dylan was pulling off his wet jacket and t-shirt, dropping them straight to the floor like a little kid who just came home from school.

Mouth open, JoJo caught a glimpse of the six-pack he was hiding under his clothes. The well aimed cuss words immediately stopping short the moment her eyes fell on his naked chest.

She couldn't stop staring.

Instead of scanning Dylan's apartment, she was scanning Dylan. Her eyes slowly moving from his chest, to his abs, down to where his jeans barely hung just off the edge of his thigh bones. She found herself wondering how they stayed on without slipping down, certain it was the only thing he was wearing.

Busting her stare, his boyish lopsided grin made an appearance and JoJo's face turned red. She could only lower her eyes to the floor. A floor that was made of wood – the real kind and not the fake laminate. An apartment like this was rather costly in LA, and suddenly JoJo remembered why she was there. Moving deeper into his space, she followed Dylan into the kitchen, fighting the urge to pick up his wet clothes and throw them at him.

Still chatting away about non-essentials, Dylan opened the refrigerator, bathing his wet naked chest in its white light, mesmerizing JoJo again. Jesus, she didn't mean to look at him but her eyes kept finding an excuse to land on his beautiful skin. For all she knew, he might as well have been lathered in baby oil.

He grabbed two bottles of beer, and all JoJo had the power to do was watch how every movement caused ripples throughout his muscles.

Lightning flashed again, flooding the whole apartment in bright white light.

Her heart thundered in response.

She was fucked.

##

"Put your shirt on!" She didn't mean to say it out loud, nor with so much gusto. She hadn't spoken at all since they arrived.

"No. It's cold. And you should take yours off," he said.

"Then put a dry one on."

"I'm soaking wet."

"Use a fucking towel and dry yourself off!" Her voice was rising again. Dylan had a funny way of pissing her off. She grabbed the roll of paper towels sitting on his kitchen island and threw them at him. They bounced off his perfectly chiseled back causing her face to darken an even deeper shade of red despite her efforts to remain a purely non-partial objective professional partner.

Ignoring her, Dylan easily popped the top off one of the bottles, holding the beer out for her to take. The goddamn waiting game of Dylan McKay. This time she let him wait while her eyes crawled over every inch of every muscle on his chest, gradually making their way down to his abs.

A chill shot down her spine when a slight warning went off in the back of her mind as Dylan patiently held out the beer for her to take. She felt this same sensation with Yang Choo when he offered her a drink. It felt more like an invitation, or an agreement, like she was about to sign a contract.

Fuck it, maybe a drink is just a drink.

She moved closer to him, silencing the warnings, reminding herself that she still had questions. Questions that would be easier to ask – and answer – over drinks. And just as JoJo reached for the beer, she spotted a deep scar that ran along Dylan's arm. Something she never noticed before... something they both had in common. It ran from his wrist to his elbow. Her hand passed up the beer to lightly touch it, following it up his arm.

Dylan inhaled deeply the moment her cold finger began tracing the scar all the way up to the elbow. She watched his jaw clench tightly and all his muscles tensed up. His inviting smile faded but Dylan didn't move.

The lights emanating from the open refrigerator and the windows were enough to see that this scar had been deep. The condensation on the beer hit the floor, getting lost somewhere in the puddle of rain beneath their bodies. Somehow their puddles had merged into one.

This time Dylan didn't jump or push her away like she was some kind of snake. He stood as still as possible, his eyes glued on her, studying her... waiting.

And JoJo's hand continued past the scar, following the muscle in his forearm, up to his biceps, then to his shoulder. Her fingers stopping at the base of his neck – another scar. It almost looked like someone tried to slit his throat. And somewhere in the back of her mind the same warning went off again as she remembered another tall handsome Asian man who owned half of LA and would have no problem slitting Dylan's throat. The thought broke the trance she was in and JoJo quickly withdrew, grabbing the beer on the way back to her own personal space.

Turning her back to him, she was reminding herself about perspective when she felt Dylan grab her arm. He wasn't ready to stop what she started, and he wasn't letting her retreat either. But she didn't mean to start *this*... and she was quite certain Dylan wouldn't be satisfied with just *this*.

She was right.

He slammed his beer on the granite island, the top foaming up and spitting over. The loud clang made JoJo glance back in time to see Dylan coming for her, reminding her of the man in black at the warehouse.

It was going to be another fight.

She knew what she did... and why. In a way, Dylan was like the foaming beer that poured over. Holding her arm tightly, JoJo caught his thumb and twisted it painfully forcing him to let go. She easily stepped out of his grasp and quickly put her beer on the counter preparing to outmaneuver the wild fire she saw growing in his eyes.

It was chaotic. The unstoppable force came at her again, pulling her hard against his chest with her hands landing on bare skin. She could feel every muscle in his body tense up with uncontrolled desire.

"I'm not yours," she whispered breathlessly. It came out before she thought it through. Closing her eyes, she tilted her head in anticipation of his kiss.

Except none came, his soft voice interrupting her expectations.

"Then whose?" he whispered back. His breath brushing against her cheek. But JoJo was too swept away to remember what she knew better than to forget. It's just he was so fucking close.

And then Dylan kissed her.

Although her lips accepted him, her hands lay flat against his chest pushing him away. Her willpower was diminishing, especially when Dylan wrapped both arms tightly around her and pulled her inside his warmth.

His kiss deepened, and against the better voices shouting in her brain, JoJo received it.

For a moment, it felt like she mattered. It had been so long since she mattered to someone. And so long since someone just held her. Not because she was having a panic attack or because she was sick or wounded... but because JoJo was somebody special and she was somebody's special somebody. And there was no good and no evil to contend with. No dirty lies and no filthy ties. No dirty cops, and JoJo Sparks wasn't a figment of Mr. Choo's imagination.

If only...

The moment the Triad king showed up in her thoughts, JoJo cooled off, coming back to reality.

Dylan slowly, almost begrudgingly, released the tight hold he had on her, laying his head on her shoulder. It was painful for both of them. He wasn't pulling anymore and she wasn't pushing. Another truce, perhaps? Still loosely surrounded by his arms, JoJo's fingers began a curious adventure following his strong chest muscles. His strength utterly fascinating her. And when her thumb gently passed over his nipple, he shuttered, whispering her name and laying his forehead against hers.

It sounded agonizing, almost like an explanation. Ignoring the warning sirens, JoJo continued exploring all that made up Dylan McKay. She was truly captivated by him as her fingers started tracing different parts of his body. They ran up his arms, over his back, across his chest, and down his abs. When her fingers lightly glided over his hips just at the edge of his jeans, his whole body shuddered, sending his hand up her back, and disappearing somewhere in her red tangles. But when he tried to kiss her, JoJo retreated, burying her face in his chest.

"I don't belong to you." If she could keep a rational thought in her mind she would've kicked herself for saying such an obvious thing – a thing that easily starts flaming curiosities in someone. But JoJo was too hypnotized when her fingers found another scar that ran across his collarbone, she traced it lovingly, brushing her lips over it. His scars making her feel connected somehow. And Dylan let her.

"People don't own each other," he murmured.

"You're right. And you're wrong." Came her muffled reply from beneath his chin as her lips explored his throat. She was so enamored with Dylan that she forgot to disguise the pain in her voice. It wasn't until she felt him pull back slightly to look at her that she remembered everything. Who she was. *What* she was. And why she was there. Silently, she answered the questions forming in his eyes.

If only…

When…

As soon as…

Tantamount to… *never.* JoJo already sold her soul to get here. The real question was did Dylan do the same? She could see his sincere attempt to read her until she carefully slipped back into her resting poker face, forcing her stormy blue eyes into clear blue skies so that all looked well on the home front.

Dylan reached up and wiped a few raindrops from her cheek, brushing away a strand of stubborn red curl with it.

She knew he wouldn't push her for answers while she was folded in his arms, but she also knew he wouldn't leave it alone either. The intimacy they were wrapped up in was ripe for truth-telling.

Now or never.

Looking up, JoJo smiled sweetly at him, watching his boyish lopsided grin forming.

"Dylan?"

He kissed her forehead.

"Hmmm?"

"Are you dirty?"

"What!? What the fuck!?"

"Are you a dirty cop?" she asked as innocently and sweetly as possible.

164

He pushed away sharply, glaring at her. Offended. Angry. About a thousand emotions crossing his face all at once along with one obvious and blaring truth.

He didn't say no. She had her answer.

"Dylan please…"

He released her completely, moving away and turning his back on her. He grabbed the beer he slammed down earlier.

"Why the hell would you ask that? Who the fuck asks something like that?" He chugged his beer, then grabbed another one and began chugging that one too.

Pulling a Dylan-move, she decided to just wait patiently for him to stop being so pissed. Eyes locked on him, her blank face in order, JoJo watched Dylan load up on liquid courage. Despite having her answer, she knew… she absolutely knew there was more to it. She was sure of it.

When he finished his second beer, he leaned over, both hands on the counter, head bowed.

Dylan had a story to tell.

And JoJo listened, secretly hoping and praying that whatever he was trying not to say didn't involve a tall handsome gang leader.

Dr. Joan M Savage

Chapter 17

The Devil You Know

Dylan didn't say no when she asked him if he was dirty.

Except...

It was unsatisfying. It was more to it than a simple *yes* or *no*.

"Dylan please, are you dirty?" No matter how many times she tried to shut her mouth, the question still came out. And each time she asked, Dylan responded by guzzling another beer.

He was building up his confidence to tell on himself. So she just waited, feeling empty and sick at herself for asking. But worse, far worse was the hypocrisy of it, and the simple fact that she didn't really want to know anymore. She didn't fucking care. But JoJo learned long ago that you can't reseal a bottle of fine wine once you pierce the cork, no matter how costly. It was already destroyed, the only way to save it was to savor it.

It took a few minutes when Dylan did the unthinkable...

He came clean.

"Once," he answered softly, even the rain and thunder quieted down for his moment of truth. JoJo's heart and mind weren't so respectful. They were too busy screaming profanities at her for being such a hypocritical ass.

Fuck it. She would savor it.

Dylan leaned over the kitchen island struggling with his emotions while JoJo was fighting with her own too. Fighting the desire to wrap her arms around his naked back and kiss the muscles pinched between his shoulder blades. She wanted to comfort him, and she almost fell victim to her own desires when Dylan's hollow voice stopped her.

"Just once," he repeated again. "Judge me… don't judge me. I don't fucking care. I'd do it again." He laughed a cold heartless laugh, turning his head to watch her reaction.

"He was a serial rapist, one sick mother fucker. The guy fucking confessed. He confessed JoJo…" Dylan straightened up to his full six feet plus to face her. His muscles tensing up again, biceps bulging – it looked like he wanted to punch something, or someone.

"That mother fucker told me where he put the bodies… where he threw them away like… like they were nothing but garbage. Right to my goddamn face. I swear to god it was turning him on or something. He told me the details. Sick twisted details about every girl he… *raped… murdered.* The bastard was so… *proud…* of his work. And I could stomach it… Jesus… I could fucking stomach it… until… when… when he got to the little girls…"

Dylan looked sick, choking up. Going back to the refrigerator, he pulled out several beers, quickly finishing one after another. She couldn't help imagining the words he spoke, reliving atrocities of her own past. So when he tossed the first empty bottle into his sink, she nearly jumped right out of her skin as it bounced around the hollow stainless steel hole.

He laid his hands back on the island counter again, showing only his profile. JoJo didn't know what to do. What to say. How to help. How to fix what she just broke.

A tear rolled down his cheek as he fought to blink them back. Or maybe it was the rain from his hair.

"He fucking… he… uhm… he… there were these two little girls… one was only three fucking years old." He took a shaking breath or maybe it was more like he was struggling to breath.

"I fucked up. A dumbass rookie move about reading him his Miranda Rights and just like that…"

Dylan snapped his fingers, standing his full height.

"That mother fucker walked because of me. Because I fucked up. Goddamn it! He confessed everything! I screw up and he gets a *get-out-of-jail-free* card? So ya, I planted evidence on him. One of the… the little… the three year old, Hannah, I planted a hair on his coat and some dirt. The same dirt he tossed over her fucking body after he…" Dylan paused for a long moment. Remembering. Reliving. "Anyway, it was enough to look like a mistake. No more. No less."

The darkness lingering in his eyes was painful to watch. He had buried it, just like the rapist did to those girls and JoJo was digging up the dirt. To what end? To satisfy her curiosity? To ensure his loyalty? Or because he was the one person she actually respected and needed to know if he was working for the Triad king. It mattered. For some reason it mattered.

Even though Dylan was staring right at her, she could tell he wasn't really seeing her, he was trapped in darkness somewhere. Bowing his head, he whispered.

"I've never told a soul. Judge me, don't judge me. I don't regret it. I'll never regret it. It's my secret… my sin… my pain to carry."

All she cared about was that Dylan wasn't working for Yang Choo. She shifted uncomfortably, wondering what happens now. What does one say to a fucking hero who just happened to commit a terrible crime in the process?

They both stayed quiet. It was a long time before Dylan seemed to return to his apartment and notice JoJo was still there.

She was shivering, suddenly remembering the dry hoodie in her hand, and without thinking, she pulled off her wet shirt, exposing her creamy white skin, her scars, and a light pink lacy bra. And just like that, Dylan was back.

JoJo slowly put on the dry oversized sweater, zipping up the front while Dylan's eyes were devouring her from head to toe. She missed his transition from despair to desire. Anger to hunger. Zero to sixty in three seconds.

The zipper stuck about halfway up. Although her skin was beautiful, she had more scars than he did. And when the malfunctioning zipper wouldn't budge, she quickly glanced up making sure Dylan wasn't planning on helping get it unstuck.

They were too far to touch, and too close to ignore. Face to face, both bare and bathed in the white light of the refrigerator. Dylan's expression shot a quiver straight through her making her heart flutter. He was mesmerized by her and she was grateful for a way to help him back to sanity.

Finally winning the fight with the zipper, JoJo broke the intensity building between them. His eyes followed the zipper up until they found hers. She shivered, this time from the excitement he was causing. Suddenly, JoJo understood what she had been doing to Dylan every time she let her eyes devour him. It was unfair. It was...

...*something*.

He cleared his throat.

"Who?" he asked.

"What?"

"You said you belonged to someone... you know what, never mind."

"And you're married." She immediately regretted the words, watching his face darken. She just brought him into the light only to toss him back into darkness.

Zipping the hoodie to the very top of her neck was her way of shutting down all the sexual tension. The invitation for him to share wasn't an indication that she planned on being equally candid. Unfair as it seemed, any more conversation could put everyone's life at risk. She cleverly copied his answer.

"It's my secret... my sin... my pain to carry." Her cold tone warning him away. "Thanks for the hoodie."

"I like seeing my clothes on you." He smiled briefly. "So, am I dirty, JoJo? Am I?" He was looking for something, searching her face and eyes for absolution. She took a minute to answer, thinking very carefully about her response.

"No, Dylan. No. You're a goddamn hero. You gave me the right to judge you, and I do. You're a fucking hero, now let that bullshit lie go that you're dirty. Let it go."

"A hero, huh? Don't I get a hero's welcome then?" She hid her smile, and he kept going. "If I'm a hero, why're you acting like I'm the villain?"

But he had it wrong. He had it backwards. There was only one villain in his apartment and it wasn't Dylan McKay.

Before another word was spoken, she was already heading out the apartment and down the hall.

JoJo felt like she was in a haze, trying to wake herself from a weird dream. It was the elevator ding that brought her back to reality, only to realize Dylan was quietly calling her name, trying not to disturb his neighbors. Holding the elevator open, she peeked slightly around it, using it like a shield in the middle of a gunfight.

When their eyes met, he smiled a lopsided apologetic grin and gently tossed her an umbrella. Dylan made it impossible to hate all police officers.

And she desperately wanted to hate him for that.

Stepping outside into the cold, the haze of Dylan McKay lifted when the icy rain started pelting her face. But fuck, it felt good. It was mother nature's equivalence to a cold shower.

The streets were empty, the day was empty, and what she just walked away from left her soul empty. A part of her was happy to be away from Dylan, but this was always the worst part of any day... the ending of it. No matter how good or bad the day went, she clung to it for fear of what tomorrow would bring. The devil you know – she preferred the devil she knew and not the unexpected new hell waiting around the next corner.

And that's when she spotted something moving in the shadows directly across the street from her. The midnight darkness and cold rain almost guaranteed no visitors. Yet, in the alley someone was lurking. And at the furthest point of her eyesight, JoJo was sure she could see the tail end of a black SUV.

No fucking way.

Everything was quiet, even the thunder had moved on leaving just a gentle rumble in the distance. JoJo stepped out of the building and glanced up to where she knew Dylan's apartment overlooked. Even though his lights were on now, he was nowhere to be seen.

Satisfied she was alone, she popped open the umbrella and ran toward the black SUV.

Toward the devil she knew.

Dr. Joan M Savage

Chapter 18

"Red Rover, Red Rover..."

"What the fuck?" she whispered to herself, edging her way into the alley where she spotted the shadow. She darted in and out like a cat trying not to get caught, stretching herself to see clearly through the rain. The further down the alley she went, the more black cars she spotted. They were like big dark shadows decorating the cement around the apartment buildings, as if the Triads had tagged the road with their train of vehicles.

Could it be him?

It couldn't. Why would *he* be here? She slipped behind a trash container, peering over the side, wanting to be seen and not wanting to be seen at the same time. A hint of a smile formed on her lips at the thought of the Triad king waiting for her to leave another man's apartment. She would be lying if she denied the small part of her that wanted it to be true.

Jesus, am I really so pathetically hung up on Yang Choo?

It was infuriating. He was infuriating.

I have Dylan now. As if that explained away her rapid heartbeat and feelings of excitement rising up at the thought of who might be in that black SUV. Her heart was thundering worse than the distant storm.

You don't have Dylan.

And on and on the slow torment and deep argument continued in her soul from the moment he announced his marital status in the boiler room.

JoJo recognized Mr. Choo's unique license plate.

That mother fucker!

And after another quick debate with herself, she decided the safest option was to check in.

Just in case.

JoJo stepped out from behind the dumpster, and beelined it toward the back door of the SUV. About two steps into her flight, Yang Choo simultaneously stepped out of the shadows, bringing her to a sliding, abrupt halt.

He was drenched. His expression, unreadable.

"What the fuck!? What're you doing here?" she said, nearly skidding to her ass to stop from crashing into him. Despite her best efforts to stay standing, she simply plopped down on her backside right in the middle of a puddle. Cringing at the thought of having to put her hand down to push herself off the ground. It *was* an alley after all – for all she knew, she was sitting in blood and piss and god knows what else.

"How… did you find me?" She wasn't sure if she was disgusted or impressed.

The thought of sitting in someone else's feces didn't compare to the rush of emotion that instantly filled her at the magnificent sight of Yang Choo. Her fascination with Dylan instantly washing away with the rain. She wanted to hate her fickle feelings, if only she could.

How long does it take to stop crushing on a gangster? He was no doubt waiting to torture her, scold her, or generally be of some sort of nuisance to her. But she didn't fucking care, he was wet and beautiful and looked like he stepped straight out of a romance novel or the cover of GQ. Her heart dropped right alongside her ass hitting the pavement. Even though she was sitting, she half expected to be kneeling at some point with a gun planted against her forehead.

He wasn't saying anything.

Excitement shot through her body only to quickly dissolve into fear. She was positive now that there was such a thing as fight, flight, freeze, and *fuck you* mode. She was living proof they can exist simultaneously inside one person.

It was mother nature to the rescue again. The cold rain bringing back some of her common sense.

"Is something wrong, Mr. Choo?" She tried again. His silence was becoming more and more frightening.

What if Yang heard about her meltdown at the police station? Was that worthy of a personal visit from the king himself? How did he even know where to find her tonight? Dylan's patience and persistence got the best of her curiosity or she would already be home in bed. Being here was a last minute decision, sort of. She looked over her shoulder into Dylan's all windowed apartment. It was easy to see inside, especially with the lights on. How fucking convenient.

It's possible this is just a weird coincidence.

Another theory starting to form, *what if this is about the warehouse incident?* Maybe she should've texted Mr. Choo to explain that she had no warning about the raid.

Except...

He knew she'd be at that warehouse, right? Or the old woman knew, anyway.

Maybe there's an emergency?

The burn phone was locked in her glove compartment, and she didn't check it before heading to the bar. JoJo was slowly losing her sanity sitting on the cement while her mind and gut twisted into all the *what ifs* she was creating. And the longer Yang stood there staring down at her with his poker face intact, the worse it twisted and turned.

Shaking her head to ward off confusion, JoJo circled back to her original questions.

"Mr. Choo, what're you doing here? How did you find me?" Still hoping for the coincidence theory. The questions just popped out of her mouth.

Surprising her, Yang held out his hand for her to take. It took a minute to register what he was doing, and blinking back the raindrops, she cautiously slid her hand into his strong, warm one. Part of her was waiting for another storm to hit or for the other shoe to drop.

He pulled her up gently, and when she leaned over to grab the umbrella accumulating water in the upside down bowl it created, she noticed Yang's eyes dropped downward to the hoodie she was wearing. Although it was fully zipped up, its oversize pulled the front down revealing enough cleavage to make a good man wonder.

Following his gaze, JoJo gripped the front to close off any exposure like she was suddenly shy. She lifted the umbrella, shifting closer to him and covering them both in its shelter. It reminded her of the first time she met Yang Choo, only this time *she* was covering *him*.

JoJo searched for some sort of explanation, finding instead a fire in his eyes warning her that he was pissed as hell regardless of what showed on his face. So she waited quietly, watching him stare at her like he was planning on saying something important or like he was conflicted about his words.

It wasn't long before her lips began to tremble, followed by her body shaking. Even with his closeness, her teeth were chattering loudly. Yang finally turned away, releasing her from the spell his eyes were holding her under. Exhaling loudly, JoJo hugged herself to stay warm, still waiting for an explanation, a reason, something, anything.

When he started speaking, she moved around to face him, listening through the noise of the rain.

"Jesus, JoJo! I thought... fuck! There was a shootout tonight with the Yakuzas. Six dead. Two were cops."

Glaring at her, the intensity in his eyes was growing.

"Why the fuck didn't you answer your goddamn phone? And what the fuck are you doing *here*?" he demanded.

She simply nodded through chattering teeth.

"I gave you that fucking phone for a reason. And why is your other phone turned off too?"

JoJo didn't know what to address first, hand shaking from the cold, she reached into her pocket to check her phone. It was dead, so she smacked it against her thigh a few times for effect then tucked it away hoping that explained everything.

This wasn't like him at all. It was confusing. It was frightening. It was messy. It was *something*. She had a million questions, but right now, she was just too damn cold to give a shit. Glancing longingly at his SUV, she motioned toward it with her chin, pleading with her eyes.

And just like that, the strange situation came to its strange conclusion, and the Yang she knew reemerged, grabbing her arm roughly and pulling her against his side. He wrapped his arm around her waist and took the umbrella from her. Holding it over them, he almost dragged her toward his

SUV.

The moment he shifted back into his ruthless, self-controlled nature, his minions suddenly drifted out of the darkness like shifting shadows in the alleyway – blending perfectly with the night and the trash. She never would've noticed them.

Maybe the first shadow wanted to be found?

JoJo leaned closer and deeper into Yang solely for warmth, absorbing the heat radiating from his body. She knew he was angry, it felt like a fever. Tonight it was healing her, even though it burned her on any other day. But tonight… tonight she fucking reveled in it, relishing in the heat he was providing. A special by-product of Yang Choo's rage.

JoJo watched five more men emerge from other parts of the alley – appearing suddenly out of nowhere like ninjas and then disappearing into their vehicles. She was still so shocked at how many men she missed. And then her mind went blank as Yang slid into the back seat next to her. He reached over and easily dragged her ass across the leather seat to bring her right up against him, tucking her under his arm. JoJo didn't fight it, in fact she melted like butter on hot toast.

This definitely wasn't like him at all.

His energy filled the space and was filling her too. This was purely for survival purposes only, she convinced herself. So what if he smells nice?

Nice?

It was a fucking aphrodisiac. Or maybe Yang Choo was the aphrodisiac? She clutched her hoodie tighter around her neck, and decided to hold her nose before she lost control and ended up straddling him right there in the back seat. Turning away, she looked out the window like it was no big deal that her first crush just put his arm around her, or that he smelled like a goddamn angel. She just hoped he couldn't feel her pounding heart.

Outside and through the rain, JoJo spotted another man lurking in the alley, and much to her dismay, she realized it was Johnny. Half in the shadows and half out, Johnny was standing against the building, holding a six pack of beer. Their eyes locked and the moment it registered what was happening, she quickly dunked down to hide, forgetting the widows were darker than the night.

What did Johnny see?

The moment the panic started to hit her was the moment it dawned on her that Johnny was Yang's inside man. Of course, he fit the profile perfectly and he seemed extra interested in the activities of one JoJo Sparks and one Dylan McKay. It all made sense now.

"What's wrong? You're safe." Yang interrupted her sudden desire to hide.

Maybe she shouldn't know about Johnny? Or Yang would've already told her who was working for him. She decided to forget what she saw.

"Oh, uhm… nothing. I didn't want Dylan to see us, I forgot your windows are shaded."

Yang looked up at Dylan's apartment as they passed it, his knuckles gently tapping against the window like he was planning on punching it.

One by one the train of black cars drove off looking like a funeral procession.

JoJo started worrying.

How many men saw her face tonight? At least two of them for sure, maybe more. This was careless. And way too reckless for the Triad leader.

If only she had minded her own goddamn business when it came to Dylan McKay, she would already be home and in a hot bath.

For some reason, Yang took her to the burn house. Clearly he wasn't done addressing whatever brought him out tonight. What foul and delicious thing *could* bring a king out in the rain?

While Yang unlocked the door, JoJo was snuggling up against his back and internally practicing her apology for not checking her burn phone. And for her regular phone being dead. And for the warehouse. And for her breakdown at work, and for whatever the hell else he took issue with. A childhood nursery rhyme played over and over in her head,

Red Rover. Red Rover, send JoJo right over.

Except the kids never called on her. As a cruel joke, she was always the last one standing in the game. What was a joke to those nasty bullies, was a constant reminder that she would always be the last one standing. Whatever it takes. Let Mr. Choo bring his hellfire and brimstone, she would find a way to stay standing.

JoJo hurried into the house while Yang and his bodyguard, a man she recognized as Lee Chin, headed to the driveway. She could hear their raised voices as they argued about something, so JoJo moved out of eavesdropping distance. What she didn't know will probably keep her alive.

JoJo had only been to the burn house once to get a feel for its location and make sure it was equipped with a first aid kit, water, and survival necessities should the need arise for her to disappear. It's where she kept her run bag – one of them anyway. She was smart enough to know that there might come a day she would be running from a gangster lord too.

Ben taught her well.

Shivering violently now, she practically ran to the linen closet for some towels. And as she dried off, the arguing grew louder until Lee Chin got into one of the other vehicles and peeled out of the driveway leaving Yang Choo and his big fancy SUV.

Yang entered the house loudly slamming the door behind him, startling JoJo.

This whole day felt like one giant clusterfuck, including the Triad leader's personal bodyguard driving off and leaving their leader unprotected. And with a police officer no less… albeit, a dirty one.

Deep in thought, JoJo slowly towel dried her hair, studying Mr. Choo. At least until they locked eyes, he looked pissed as hell and like a lion about to pounce on his next meal.

Pissed at who? Me? Lee Chin? Or both?

The closer he got, the more pressure she felt to drop eye contact and focus on drying off. It wasn't long before her eyes snapped back up desperately trying to read him. It was difficult to focus when his dress shirt clung to every single goddamn muscle on his chest and arms. Even his pants hugged his exceptional body, every single part of it.

She was doing it again, just like the first day she came into his office. Filling herself up with him. Taking as much as she could before it became obvious.

Except obvious came and went already.

Turning her back on him, she cut off her view cold turkey. And all her unanswered questions came flooding in along with a side dish of guilt. It occurred to her that her feelings for Yang Choo were a direct violation of her feelings for Dylan McKay.

Feelings? No-fucking-way.

Her *only* feelings should be anger.

Mr. Choo was careless showing up at Dylan's apartment tonight. And then there was Johnny. At least now she knew how Yang found her. If Johnny is the inside man then Yang would know everything.

Everything.

JoJo could feel him behind her, feel his heat again. His voice sending a wave of chills down her spine.

"You were in his apartment," he said as if that explained everything. She spun around to glare at him.

"So what?" It came out like a sudden sneeze you can't stop. His expressionless face twisted slightly before returning to its default poker face, followed by his hand very slowly and very carefully wrapping around her neck like he was planning on choking her.

"So?" she repeated with less force, very much aware of his tightening fingers.

"Maybe I was in his bed too," she whispered the last part, wondering why she was poking the lion and wondering what he was going to do about it.

It gave her an inordinate amount of pleasure teasing and toying with the boys at work, but Yang Choo was on a whole new level. It was the difference between sparring with friends in a dojo and fighting for survival in the underground fights. The scars on her body were testament to the extreme differences in the games she played. The bigger the risk, the greater the reward, and the deeper the scars when things go wrong.

This game would either ignite his simmering rage or make him forget it.

She had her answer when his hand squeezed her neck a bit tighter like he really wanted to choke her. Placing both hands against his chest, she used the wall as leverage to push him back. And instantly he pulled forth a dagger from the back of his belt. His reaction felt more instinctual than threatening. That is until he took one of her hands, and flipping the dagger, slid its hilt into her palm.

"You want to fucking play? Then let's play."

Guiding her hand, he pointed the blade against his chest. The knife was the only thing separating their bodies. JoJo's back was to the wall and the pressure she felt on the hilt made her wonder if it was cutting into his fancy shirt... or worse.

"Do it," he whispered. "And you can be free." He was so close, she could feel his breath tickle her hair, and JoJo lost all sense of direction. It occurred to her that *he* was toying with *her* now.

"Do what?" She tried to sound brave. "You're crazy."

Or something. Is this another loyalty test?

Even if she wanted to turn on him she had no information, saw nothing, knew nothing of his organization. He kept her separate from him in every possible way. She closed her eyes.

"I don't want to be free. We have a deal and I won't break it on my end," she whispered breathlessly.

In response, his hand tightened around her fingers while slowly leaning his body deeper into hers. He was daring her. Dazzling her. And all she could do was stay frozen lest she act on the impulses her body was sending.

"I won't betray you," she reiterated, hiding in her curls. The hand he was squishing started throbbing now but she needed that pain to keep her grounded.

As quick as their game started, it ended. Yang released her, returning the dagger back to its sheath. While JoJo lowered herself slightly, planning to dunk down under his arm and escape. But before she could bolt, Yang lightly brushed a red curl behind her ear causing her face to darken a deeper shade of red.

"Two cops died tonight, Officer Sparks. Don't make me... *wonder* about you again. Keep your phone on, and I'll keep my dagger... off, deal?"

Eyes wide, she nodded slowly. She wasn't on her knees with a gun to her forehead but it sure felt the same.

JoJo held herself plastered up against the wall as hard as she could. Part of her preferred the gun to her forehead instead of *this*. *This* felt way more dangerous than the gun. He was being far too civil and far too messy.

Eyes still wide, JoJo was silently waiting for the other shoe to drop. He wasn't the type of man to make deals. Dealmaking and diplomacy was something Dylan would do.

Sensing that now might be a good time to disappear, she quickly made a mad dash to get away but his hand caught a handful of red curls, stopping her short. It wasn't necessarily painful.

It was… *something.*

Yang gently tugged her hair forcing her head to tilt upward, exposing her neck. He wasn't letting her hide behind any curls like she did whenever things felt *uncomfortable.* His expressionless face transformed into slightly amused.

Damn, he ran so fucking hot and so fucking cold in the span of a heartbeat.

And JoJo couldn't hide her rapid heartbeat, her shallow breathing, her shaky weak knees, and the ever growing scarlet mess spreading and spilling from her traitorous cheeks into her goddamn neck and shoulders.

Fight, flight, freeze, and *fuck you* kicked on, and against her better judgment, she tried another tactic. Reaching up, she gently laid her hand on his wrist, smiling sweetly.

"You *enjoy* holding me captive, don't you?" she asked, lowering her voice seductively. "I'll make sure to keep my phone on, *just* for you. *All* for you. I promise." She blinked her eyes the way the actresses did in the videos she'd been watching ever since Yang asked if anyone taught her how to be a woman.

She followed it up with a small nervous sensual smile.

Yang Choo stood almost a foot taller than her so when he started leaning down, her knees buckled slightly thinking he was really going to kiss her this time. JoJo slammed her eyes shut, expectantly.

But it was a warning.

"I'm not a game. Understand?" he whispered dangerously. Or was it seductively? The lines between them blurred when it came to Yang Choo.

Eyes popping open, JoJo nodded her head against the hand buried in her hair. The blinking and the smiling, abandoned. His eyes shifted down to her lips causing a cascading failure in her brain while his other hand slid up her back, landing on her nape and drifting over to her collarbone. He began gently caressing her Adam's apple until JoJo softened into him, finally releasing her vice grip on the front of the hoodie.

His fingers followed her neck downward until they reached the hoodie zipper that JoJo had been meticulously guarding. And when he started unzipping it, instinctively both her hands shot up to hold the zipper in place.

"It smells like him," he said.

His soft low voice was just another titillating aphrodisiac. Feeling his hand wrapped up in her hair, the other one trying to undress her, his breath on her cheek, and the heat from his body... something dangerous and primal woke deep inside JoJo. It felt unhindered with abandon, like when she competed in the underground fights. Vicious and relentless. JoJo came unglued.

She let go.

Arms shooting up around his neck, and one leg draping around the back of his thigh, she forced their bodies to collide. JoJo pulled herself into him, her body forming around his.

"Fuck..." was all he managed to say before she started clawing at him, ripping through his dress shirt buttons. One hand disappearing inside it while the other was making its way down his pants.

"Goddamn it, JoJo..."

Yang pulled harder on her hair each time she tried to close the distance between them. His other hand unzipping the hoodie until the two sides fell open. When he yanked it off her body, he accidentally yanked her off him right along with it. She landed flat on her ass.

Glaring down at her, it occurred to JoJo that he wasn't reciprocating any of her *affection*.

She wanted to die.

Feeling the full brunt of his rejection, humiliation rushed over her and she silently begged the ground to crack open and swallow her.

"What's your problem?" she whispered, fighting back the wave of tears threatening to humiliate her further.

Yang was holding the hoodie in some sort of weird victory fashion, while JoJo shriveled up even further, wrapping her arms around her chest to cover herself.

"Oh *now* you show some fucking decency?" He lifted the hoodie high up. "I told you, it smells like him."

Pulling his dagger out, he thrust it into the hoodie over and over, shredding it.

Completely destroyed, he threw the pieces across the room, and JoJo and Yang locked eyes and locked horns. She was glaring daggers at him until she noticed the blazing inferno in his eyes and his shaking hand.

Standing up, she attempted to calm herself down and regain some of her dignity, watching carefully as the dagger quickly disappeared and his shaking hand slid into his pocket.

His eyes drifted downward, lingering too long on her chest, and all JoJo wanted to do was kill him, or at least gouge his eyes out.

So when he turned around like he was giving her some privacy, his sudden display of chivalry pissed her off even more, if that was possible. She wanted to grab the dagger sheathed at the back of his belt and finish what he started when he had it against his chest.

And just like that, he was heading for the door. The wind was blowing away again.

"If you need anything… let me… let Lee Chin know."

If I need anything? If I need anything! Are you fucking kidding me!?

JoJo had too many questions, despite everything.

She followed him, not wanting things to end this way. And maneuvering herself, she blocked the exit forcing him to face her. He met her eyes briefly, then shifted downward. She forgot she was still shirtless.

"What… why? Tonight you… why did… what happened… why were you even…" Bullet trains sped through her brain not giving her a fully formed thought. Only one thought was crystal clear.

Why don't you want me?

He answered at least one unspoken question.

"I didn't like seeing his hoodie on you. I didn't like you in his apartment. And I didn't know which two cops were killed. I invested… in you… it would be… a fucking shame."

Shame?

She shook her head, still feeling confused, watching his eyes fall on her chest again. He cleared his throat.

"It's my secret... my sin... my pain to carry," he repeated the very words she and Dylan spoke to each another.

JoJo's face melted into one of sheer horror. Backing away, mortified, she finally covered herself.

"You were listening!? His apartment is bugged? Are you fucking crazy!? What's wrong with you!" She screamed, and JoJo practically ran to the closet, grabbing another hoodie to put on. He followed her.

"I told you, I will... we will... the Organization will protect you! We keep tabs on all the cops you come in contact with. Especially right now. I know you see why... I had to make sure you were... *integrating.*"

"*Integrating?* Integrating!? I was inta-fucking-grating just fine tonight, without your goddamn help!" She couldn't stop screaming at him.

"JoJo, I always have eyes on you... until you get situated! Or settled!"

Angrily she fought to zip up the pink hoodie she had stashed there.

"I didn't hear from you in years! YEARS! You didn't give a shit about me! And now suddenly you want to make sure I'm... I'm... INTEGRATING!?" Glaring at him, she bit her lip begging the tears to go away.

"You want me to apologize for protecting you? You said you belonged to someone else. Who JoJo? Who goddamn it!?" He quickly crossed the distance between them, roughly grabbing her wrists and forcing her to look at him.

She pushed him away with all her frustration and this time he tripped over the end table, falling backwards. He stayed down, bent over, holding the back of his head with his hand.

"Fuck!!" he yelled, slamming his fist into the floor. But he looked beaten. He didn't look like the monster she created in her head. He didn't look like her tower of strength. And he certainly didn't look like a king.

JoJo stared at him for a long hard minute feeling slightly remorseful, embarrassed... *something.* She read the reports on him and studied his profile and in all of them he is never considered anything less than self-controlled and meticulous. In fact, the way the reports were written by different officers, spanning over a decade, there was almost a tone of... *admiration* for LA's mafia king.

She never knew him to be so chaotic, uncontrolled... messy.

Until tonight.

The mighty king was sitting on the floor looking more ashamed than she felt.

Curbing her appetite for revenge and her desire to cause further damage, JoJo slid to the ground beside him. They sat there quietly for a long time. Neither one moving nor speaking and in its own way, it was healing to say nothing.

"You all right?" She gently touched his hand, drawing his attention. From beneath his fingers, she could hear a muffled threat.

"First McKay and now me? How thorough of you. I'm not interested in McKay's sloppy seconds." His green eyes glared at her through his fingers, gleaning her reaction.

He lit the fucking fuse. And JoJo exploded again.

She couldn't stop the detonation even if she wanted to. Her hands, developing a mind of their own, started punching and slapping at the parts of his face still showing. By the third swing, he caught her fist mid air.

"Don't fucking stir things up again," he said, pushing himself off the ground and away from her. "I need to leave."

In her childish fantasy, LA was meant to bring them closer together since they shared a common goal. She romanticized it – being united in purpose and deed where Yang was seeking revenge for his best friend, and JoJo was seeking revenge for her father. It was meant to be a special bond between them, but it evolved into something else altogether.

She felt further from him then in all the years he ignored her.

"I don't understand?" she whispered, not even trying to disguise the pain. She couldn't bring herself to ask him what he wanted in the first place. What was his point? Was it really just to make sure she was alive? And if that was the case, wouldn't hearing her and Dylan talking be enough proof she was fine? So why stick around? Why bring her here?

As he was leaving the house, Yang paused for half a second, almost like he was going to fire one last shot at her... or apologize. Instead he punched the wall, leaving a hole with a bloody streak, and leaving her sitting alone on the floor with more emotions than possible for one human to carry.

He didn't even look back.

Dr. Joan M Savage

Chapter 19

Remnants

JoJo pulled into the police station. Her mind had only one objective today...

Coffee. Please let there be a fresh pot of coffee.

The night-shifters weren't exactly known for their kindness in keeping the pot full and warm. But there was always the espresso machine. She loved LA, the city of espressos. And after last night, she barely pulled in two hours of sleep. The way things were left with Yang Choo made sleep nearly impossible and robbed her of any rest in her soul. Humiliation does that.

It was a straight up miracle she pulled off a couple of hours of sleep after pouring herself a warm glass of milk. Two hours left her feeling worse than if she had stayed up all night overdosing on caffeine and boxing.

She was sitting in her SUV, checking herself in the car mirror one more time before heading in for her shift when she spotted the Captain and Johnny walking into the parking lot. It was still way too early for any of her team to be at work. Her heart skipped a beat and then dropped into her gut.

If Johnny is working for Yang, then she's safe. If she miscalculated that and if he just happened to be at the wrong place at the right time last night...

Oh Jesus, was he... *reporting* her?

"It's his word against mine and Dylan is your alibi for last night." She reassured herself.

I hope. A small voice added.

The Captain was dressed for work, and Johnny was dressed like a street thug or undercover vice or like he just got off from an all night stakeout.

Changing her mind about going into work early, JoJo started her SUV. She was just about to back up when the most absurd thing happened.

Johnny slapped the Captain across the face.

Dunking beneath her dashboard, she couldn't help but watch the scene unfold.

What the fuck was happening?

Nobody was behaving normally, including Yang Choo, including herself. The humiliation of last night needed very little prompting to return. She thought of Yang sitting on the floor after she pushed him, suddenly feeling very grateful that Yang sent all his men home or there would be hell to pay.

The argument was brief, ending with the Captain retreating back into the station. Were they lovers? She shook her head. *Impossible.* The way the narc boys drooled over Kaylee like eye candy, JoJo was positive of their sexual orientation.

Johnny ran across the parking lot, getting into an old beat up car that didn't belong to him.

Another Yang Choo burn car?

She thought about Johnny slapping the Captain. Who does that? Somebody fearless, somebody with nothing to lose, somebody who has the power of a gang leader to back him up if he were to get in trouble.

Shit.

She decided to follow him, right into Yang Choo's territory. She had enough proof now that Johnny was Yang's bitch. Then why did she still feel so compelled to keep following him? Maybe because Yang shut her out of every part of his life, and no matter what happened last night, Yang was the only person on the planet who knew the real JoJo.

She couldn't take that lightly.

JoJo stayed at least a block away as she followed Johnny, arguing with herself the entire time, when suddenly he spun his car into a one-eighty, skidding it against the curb in an impressively perfect parallel parked position. Instantly his POS was facing the opposite direction, giving JoJo only a millisecond to hide her face as she passed by.

The abandoned building he parked in front of was a remnant of Yang's earlier empire – a nightclub that never launched. Now just an eyesore and a canvas for little gangs to paint their graffiti. It was a tagger's paradise and an unofficial homeless shelter.

Maybe Johnny wouldn't notice her personal vehicle or that it was miraculously driving itself after she ducked down!

She cussed at herself for being so careless and quickly decided to pick up one of Yang's burn vehicles.

There was nothing around this neighborhood, so whatever Johnny was up to, she hoped there was enough time to make the switch and return to investigate.

But JoJo couldn't shake the feeling that something was off. Her internal senses were blaring louder than a tornado warning.

It took a little longer to change cars and her outfit. But Johnny's car was still sitting right where she left it, in front of Yang Choo's old abandoned nightclub.

Dressed head to toe in one of her baggy outfits, she picked the entrance closest to where she parked in the alley. It was like any other abandoned building.

Moving deeper into it, she stepped over broken wooden beams, glass, and piles of trash left behind by squatters and vigilantes. It was a rusty, dusty, dirty mess. And in spite of it, JoJo could tell this place was once something extraordinary with faint colors of red and gold, decorated with beautiful Chinese designs hidden under the cobwebs and dirt. There was no question who this place belonged to, his signature was all over it and no amount of tagging could hide it.

Looking behind her, JoJo accidentally left her own signature on the dusty floor. Which meant that Johnny couldn't have come this way or she would see his footprints. Circling back, she found another trail. If caution were an outfit, JoJo got dressed in it fast. Nothing felt right, and nothing felt safe. The longer she followed the trail the louder the warning screamed in her head. But JoJo just kept following the breadcrumbs until she ended up in front of a metal door. The door was much newer, cleaner and made of an entirely different material than the building itself. There weren't any handles or visible locks, it was just a sheet of solid metal.

She pushed… and leaned… and fingered the edges but it didn't budge. It was an entrance of some sort because the footprints ended there. Frustrated, JoJo looked around and much to her chagrin, spotted a high-tech camera at the far edge of the corridor. Pulling her ball cap further over her face, she backed up into the same tracks she came in on, erasing each one with a sweep of her shoe to hide the size of her small feet. Feet that clearly didn't belong among the larger, wider prints. No evidence was good evidence.

JoJo wondered how much the camera caught. To be honest, it felt like the inner workings of another government agency. Circling back again, she decided to come from behind the building. JoJo peeked around the corner checking for people or more cameras. There was a low-tech sweeping camera, and at the moment it was facing the opposite direction. Before she could stop herself, JoJo made a mad dash to stand directly beneath it. About three feet from her was a small cement staircase leading up to another metal door.

And no fucking windows.

She looked up. She'd have to climb higher to find a window, and without any certainty that it wasn't sealed off. She was sitting beneath the camera where the two walls merged, wondering if she could rebound her way up the wall when suddenly the metal door swung open. The heavy steel opening right up to her cheekbone and stopping just shy of touching her. Her eyes squinting and face turned sideways, she was pushing her backside up against the brick wall as tight as possible.

Letting out a breath of relief, her body tensed again when she heard footsteps on the cement stairs. She was fully expecting a gun in her face or some kind of attack, but nothing came. And JoJo was trapped behind the metal monster.

Or maybe…

She lowered herself slowly and quietly until she was squatting. The door was three feet above the ground, and three feet was all she needed. Looking under it, she spotted a man dressed in blue overalls stretching his back. He stayed on the stairs, standing at the edge of the first step, his back to her.

JoJo positioned herself next to the cement stairs, peering into the building. She could see other people in blue overalls sitting in front of different monitors.

It was impossible to get a good look without risking being seen. Especially if the man outside turned around. So far he seemed content where he was and it wasn't long before she could smell cigarette smoke. What could she do? Her brain was scrambling for answers.

Pulling out her phone, JoJo lifted it just enough for her camera to get a good look. She hit record, moving it slowly back and forth, hoping to catch anything, something.

After a few seconds of recording, she switched to the photo option and started snapping random pictures, zooming in and out, feverishly clicking. And then immediately sent everything to her Google Drive for safe keeping.

She couldn't help but see some of the pictures.

It wasn't as high tech inside as she imagined.

One of the first things she caught was three heavily decorated investigation whiteboards. They were very similar to her own with clippings, pictures and hand drawn lines. She was clicking so fast she couldn't quite catch what was on them... until she zoomed in.

It was her father's picture. She smiled, of course Yang Choo was investigating his murder. So why not involve her? At least she was certain now that Johnny was Yang's inside man and quite possibly the Captain too.

Clicking and zooming, she could barely make out some of the other faces.

JoJo spotted an old picture of herself with a large red question mark over her head. Yang wouldn't give her identity away, not without perjuring himself. There were pictures of all the power players in LA, and in a small way it reminded JoJo of Ben's collection. He liked to know who was who in each new city.

Yang's caravan was included on one of the boards, but it was tilted too much for her to capture anything of real value from it. Jesus, all she wanted to do was run into that room and shout that they were on the same team.

There were several computer screens of streaming cameras and she didn't recognize most of the places, except... the front of the Palace and the police station.

Her mind circled all the way back to this operation belonging to another law enforcement agency. Why would Yang have pictures of his own men? Unless he was weeding out the moles. She was going nowhere trying to figure it out from the other side of the camera.

In her final few snaps, she zoomed in as far as it would let her. JoJo saw images of Dylan and the narc team – her eyes opening wide – and her. They were at the bar together.

What the fuck? This was last night.

Her final picture included a very private view of Kaylee and Tony on a couch in what JoJo could only guess was Kaylee's apartment... and they weren't watching TV.

This was definitely Yang Choo's style.

JoJo plastered herself against the cement base, unsuccessfully talking herself out of one more look.

She peeked up, searching the room for Johnny. He was standing in front of one of the monitors watching people go in and out of a busy building somewhere downtown.

JoJo sighed deeply. Despite everything – she trusted Yang Choo. At least, she trusted their amalgamated resolve for revenge, and he was just too fucking brilliant to deserve anything less.

And too self-controlled. Her mind reminding her about last night.

JoJo was about to duck back down when she realized the man at the top of the stairs had turned around.

Keep your head in the game, Sparks. Dylan's voice cautioned her but it was too late. One puff of smoke later, his eyes were looking right at her. And she watched in horror as they slowly opened wider and wider, finally registering her presence.

JoJo sprung to life... and then about three things happened simultaneously – using the rail, she thrust herself past the stairs and the man, giving herself momentum to take off running.

The man instantly slammed his hand on what looked like a button just inside the doorway, setting off an alarm, and like a speed demon his other hand grabbed the back of her jacket, mercilessly yanking her straight backwards into the ground with a hollow thud. The impact forcing all the air from her lungs in a loud grunt.

Two men dressed as security guards poured out of the building. And right before it hit her face, JoJo saw a gun – from who the hell knows where the man had stashed it in a pair of overalls – and began wildly beating her with it.

Her one advantage was the size of the alley. It was too small for all of them to fit on the ground around her. As the man beat her over and over, she stopped only defending herself and started on offense. Her arms and hands protecting her face, she brought up her knee and nailed him in the head. Surprisingly he was still holding the cigarette in his mouth.

Adrenaline coursed through her body like a double shot of espresso, bringing every muscle to life at exactly the same moment. Catching the man's hand as he retracted from a well-aimed attack, she twisted it, forcing his fingers to release their hold on the gun. It was easy sliding it from his hand and right into hers.

The two guards were screaming at her in a language she didn't recognize.

JoJo managed to kick them away enough to aim the gun over their heads and fire a warning shot. The sound scaring them back into the building, giving her enough time to land on her feet and take off running.

Suddenly Johnny came charging out of the building, jumping high off the cement stairs just as JoJo fired another warning. To her horror, she watched Johnny collapse to the ground from her second bullet. Alarms were blaring louder in her head than from the building, and if she had the means to concentrate in the middle of the chaos, they were screaming something like, *you just fucking shot a cop!*

And quite possibly Yang Choo's inside man.

If anyone was fucked right now it was JoJo Sparks. There wouldn't be a person alive *not* looking for her if she shot both a police officer and the mafia king's bitch.

Yang would fucking kill her. She was certain of it.

At least they weren't following her as she bolted for safety around the corner of the building, but Karma was a bitch and JoJo heard someone fire their weapon again as she was rounding the corner. One bullet hitting the brick near her face, sending a spray of red clay, and the other...

Her side exploded with pain, flinging her against the far wall like a dog running too fast on slippery tile. She mindlessly fired back, keeping them stuck inside their doorway as she pressed on.

And looking back one final time before disappearing, JoJo watched them dragging Johnny's body into the building.

##

The bullet passed between two ribs, and barely nicked the soft side of her arm. It was a clean hit through and through – no doctor required, but will definitely be a new addition to her collection of ever growing scars. She gave a deep sigh of relief that her baggy outfit gave them no clear target. No one could anticipate how tiny she really was beneath all those layers.

Now she just needed to get cleaned up and get her ass to work before anyone suspected her.

Popping the trunk, she grabbed her work clothes and the white plastic container with a big red cross plastered on the front of it.

RED FEVER

Chapter 20

Not Another One

JoJo was desperately trying *not* to think about what just happened as she put herself back together pretty much using duct tape and lunch baggies. The baggies controlled any leakage. The duct tape for everything else. She learned long ago how to patch herself up after the more brutal underground fights. Blood and bruises led to concerns, and concerns led to questions.

And JoJo didn't have any answers. Not when she first started fighting, and certainly not now.

She had four scratches across her neck, a bruised collarbone, and the back on her right hand felt like there was definitely something broken. These were only the spots people could see...

JoJo entered the police station, spotting Dylan and Tony engaged in a conversation near the entrance. Dylan sent a small nod her way, his eyes lighting up the moment he saw her, and she quickly returned it, beelining for their department. She couldn't afford anyone getting too close, and seeing. Her hand instinctively covering the scratches on her neck.

It was all working out. No one can know it was her this morning. Or that she shot Johnny. No one can put her at the scene, and as long as she appeared healthy, there *was nothing* to figure out.

Nothing, she repeated to herself in an effort to control the ever increasing panic. *And Mr. Choo won't suspect I'm the intruder.* Her future depended on it.

Except...

JoJo felt guilty. And if she felt guilty for shooting Johnny, then how the hell was she going to kill the cop who murdered her father?

Or cops?

Another thought popping into her mind almost stopping her mid stride.

What if the man who murdered her father... was a father?

Years of planning, years of plotting, years of preparation in the name of revenge just fell to the ground and shattered into a million little pieces because JoJo's moral compass suddenly decided to give a shit.

Jesus-fucking-Christ. Really? But what happened this morning is different? Isn't it?

Concerns and questions continued plaguing her, and she couldn't do a damn thing. If she inquired about... *Johnny*, it will only raise red flags... unless... unless his body was found.

JoJo felt sick.

And just as she was passing the men's restroom, a hand shot out from behind the door, yanking her in.

It was Johnny.

Pushing back the pain from her rib and from the back of her head slamming against the tiles, she had to top herself from throwing her arms around his neck and hugging him! Feelings of relief flooding her in wave after wave. He was not only alive but clearly unencumbered – at least that was her impression from the effort he needed to throw her against the wall. *And* somehow beat her to the police station.

"Johnny... what... why..." JoJo quickly changed her tone. "What the fuck! You freaked me out! You lucky son-of-a-bitch! Lucky I didn't beat your ass!"

She couldn't afford to show weakness.

Glancing down, JoJo checked to see if her make-shift covering wasn't leaking.

"JoJo Sparks…" he said, watching her closely and looking very conflicted about something.

She wondered why she wasn't breaking his nose or at the very least busting a kneecap. Maybe because she wasn't a murderer. They stared at each other – it was anything but sexual. In fact, what she saw in Johnny's eyes started frightening her. It was… *loathing*.

What did he know? She chose to remain silent, studying him carefully, waiting.

JoJo watched as the loathing in his eyes deepened, suddenly wondering if he was going to hit her the way he hit the Captain. It was loathing and…

Lust.

For fuck's sake, not another one. Not another goddamn Tony.

The longer they stood there, the faster the joys of being innocent of murder mutated into anxiety. JoJo started coming up with plausible explanations for whatever came out of his mouth next. The warehouse? The shooting? Yang Choo? All she knew was that she wasn't arrested this morning. Johnny didn't report her. Or he didn't see her.

Oh shit, is this… is this another courtesy of Yang Choo?

"What's going on?" she finally said, feigning innocence and trying to sound pissed at the same time. When he didn't answer, JoJo tried to move away, pushing his hand off her, but he literally slammed her back into the wall again. He was grip locking the front of her shirt like he was really planning to punch her. His force and aggression were uncharacteristic, like she was dealing with someone other than the coworker she shared a cab ride from O'Leary's or the compassionate man who half carried his partner after JoJo punched him.

She had enough.

"Let go, asshole," she warned, feeling the hostility still growing in him. Her hands wrapped around his wrist, accidentally exposing the bruise that was slowly transitioning into an ugly shade of blue. Johnny seemed to be admiring it when JoJo squirmed trying to pry his fingers off her collar. The scratch marks on her neck were clear as day, fresh from when the guard grabbed her jacket and pulled her to the ground. His fingernails caught some flesh too, leaving four perfect red streaks. She needed to escape from under his scrutiny before he figured everything out.

But she had to wait to see what he knew, oddly, he was way too

200

interested in checking out her wounds.

"Seriously, I'm not in the mood for games today. I had a rough night last night." She winked, playing it off, attempting to lighten the mood only to watch it fall flat. JoJo finally stopped squirming, resigning herself to glaring.

Johnny's other hand reached over her body and locked the bathroom door, her eyes following him. She realized shit was about to get real and a warning as loud as a tornado siren blared in her head that Johnny knew something and he was about to lay it on her.

Releasing her slightly, he started poking at the bruise, digging his finger into the reddest part of it like a dentist looking for a cavity.

"What the fuck!?" She slapped his hand. "Yes, mother fucker it hurts. Now let go before *I* hurt *you*."

It was when Johnny started caressing the scratches on her neck that she finally lost it. Twisting her head sharply, she forced his hand away. But before she could really hurt him, what he said next turned her blood cold, stopping her in place.

"Choo's handiwork I see," he said arrogantly, self-assured. JoJo's eyes widened, followed by her face changing to a paler shade of gray. There were too many things she was covering up. Too many lies she had to keep in place. Too much emotional drama and pain to be able to stay in complete control, and at the very moment she needed it most, her poker face failed. It took a second to recover.

A second too late.

"What're you talking about? I picked up some guy last night. Ya, it was a bit rough but, no pain, no gain, right?" She feigned confusion.

They both knew it was too late, JoJo already showed her cards. And Johnny seemed less interested in her words now and more interested in her reactions. He smiled a wicked grin.

"I already know everything, and I gotta say, you two looked so... *cozy*," he said as his eyes made their way down to her chest, across her lips, landing on her neck again.

One bright spot was that Johnny was assuming her scratches and bruises were from last night and not from this morning's fuck up. While her mind had a hundred trains rushing in and out, it was slowly dawning on her what was happening. Johnny was pushing his body against hers.

As tired as she was, JoJo pushed back, forcing his hand off her shirt and finally knocking him away. She used the wall for support, feeling utterly spent. The adrenaline from being shot had long since abandoned her. Leaning over her knees with her butt to the wall, JoJo was catching her breath while hiding the fear lingering on her face and hiding her body from his errant eyes.

She warned him again.

"Fuck you, Johnny, you're crazy. And as far as *who* I was with last night, it's none of your goddamn business. I had a rough night. That's it. That's all you need to know. Damn, I need some coffee."

Ignoring him, JoJo straightened up and fixed her shirt by tucking it neatly in her pants. She was leaving.

In a truly spectacularly evil fashion by her own teammate, Johnny kneed her in the gut with all his height and weight. The sucker *punch* collapsed her straight to the ground, leaving her gasping for air. The whole world changed between them in an instant, especially when she looked up and saw the immense pleasure her pain was giving him.

She curled around herself, her diaphragm refusing to let her breathe, and Johnny knelt down over her, whispering against her ear.

"Our sexy new recruit is Yang Choo's pleasure pussy. Did *NOT* see that one coming." He laughed a disgusting fake laugh that made her skin crawl. It sounded like a mix between a hyena and a madman. They both knew if she wanted to kick his ass right now, she could.

And that was her mistake. She didn't. Her lack of response confirmed everything without saying anything.

"This isn't like you," she said, gasping and coughing. "Why?"

JoJo was giving him the space to admit his own dealings with Yang Choo.

"No, *Sparks*, this isn't like *you?*" he immediately spit back, and he was right. She should've broken his nose by now.

Johnny was kneeling in front of her and using his finger, he forced her face upward to look at him.

"Jesus, this is just too good to be true. I'm your fucking guardian angel."

And that did it.

The moment he said *guardian angel,* it confirmed everything. Only Yang knew about her journal and all the intimate notes calling him a *guardian angel.*

Johnny *was* Yang's bitch, and now she was Johnny's.

Courtesy of Yang Choo.

I guess I'm not integrating well enough. Her thoughts blasted. And suddenly she really did feel like someone's sloppy seconds.

She couldn't even look up anymore.

Was last night really just about her loyalty? And this morning she accidentally destroyed it. A purely innocent mistake following Johnny to Yang's abandoned building. But who would believe her? There was no one left to tell. JoJo's nausea grew right alongside her feelings of isolation and aloneness. And while she rehashed her crazy encounter with Yang last night, trying to remember any forgotten details, she could feel Johnny's fingers tracing the scratches that ran across her neck again.

He was grinning at her, his grin growing bigger and bigger.

"I see your little mind working Sparks." He spun his finger around and round in front of her nose. "Don't forget what I know." He seemed to answer one of the questions in her head. "And what I know, in comparison to what you know, would leave your head spinning." His face gleaming with a sick mixture of loathing, desire… and victory. She moved away from him, finally sitting up and getting off the disgusting stinky floor.

JoJo couldn't stop questioning why Yang would punish her like this. If he didn't want her a simple *no* would suffice. Maybe last night was supposed to be *punishment,* except she was enjoying it too much. Way too much.

But not today.

No matter how she analyzed the situation, hurting Johnny right now would jeopardize every avenue to finding her father's murderer.

All this time, JoJo couldn't quite shake her first crush… until now. After this, she wanted nothing more to do with Yang Choo. He was a gangster. A drug dealer. An asshole. He represented everything ugly and terrible in this world.

He was the fucking leader of it.

Johnny abruptly broke her concentration by punching the wall next to her head to get her attention.

Just like Yang. Johnny even acted like him.

She didn't flinch. Her mind quieting and focusing on him because it was clear that he still had some message to relay like the old woman.

Courtesy of Yang Choo.

"Dylan will be so heartbroken," he said with mock concern, shaking his head and caressing her cheek while her mind was screaming obscenities at him. And at Yang. She suddenly felt like Dylan's hoodie. Stabbed in the back and shredded.

What Johnny said next, sent her over the edge.

"I'm going to have fun with you, Sparks. Over and over and over… and over." His hand slowly slid from her cheek down to her breast, very carefully as if he half expected her to rise up and kill him. But JoJo was frozen in her own thoughts, rantings, and double-crossing nightmares. She was barely even breathing.

Johnny rubbed around the outside of her shirt, and finding her nipple, he circled it with his thumb. Groaning, he slammed his teeth together like he wanted to bite her. She still didn't flinch – if she did, she was afraid she would kill him. And this time check to make sure he was dead.

Johnny's mischievous grin was growing like an advance warning that something sick and twisted was about to follow. His fingers began unbuttoning one spot on her dress shirt, slipping his hand inside. It still felt like another test, like he was watching her every move… waiting for her to respond.

Johnny found her breast and began playing with it for a moment. She could see him getting aroused since he was squatting directly in front of her. His other hand slipped down between his legs to rub himself.

"Fuck Sparks, I can't take it. You make me so fucking horny!" He grabbed her hair roughly and pushed her face between his legs, rubbing his dick against her forehead. She was bent over with very little leverage to move, so instead of pushing Johnny away, she thrust her head forward forcing him to fall on his ass.

He started laughing.

"We have some *unfinished business* to discuss tonight," he said.

When he jumped up, he tried to dry hump her face against the wall, his badge bouncing off his hip. She couldn't help but memorize the numbers,

6620, burning them into her brain.

Readjusting his dick in his pants, he headed toward the bathroom exit. Just before unlocking the door, he spread two fingers into a peace sign, and started flicking his tongue in and out of them.

Disgusted, JoJo shut her eyes until she could hear the door unlock, open, and shut again. Still sitting on the floor, she let out a long sigh, and slowly pulled herself together. Starting with buttoning her shirt and ending with scrubbing her hands raw until she felt clean again.

Dr. Joan M Savage

Chapter 21

Pussy Politics

JoJo reread the tampered report of her father's murder. It was the only thing that would occupy her mind after the incident in the men's bathroom.

She was suddenly very grateful that she printed it out before logging out of Corporal Randall's access yesterday.

She knew four things about the report. First, it was falsified or somehow tampered with and somewhere there was a signature or a digital record of the person who did it. Someone had to sign off on it. Second, there was physical evidence in a locker – worst case, whoever fucked with his records removed the evidence too but at this point any kind of hope was still hope. Third, the name *Ben Shimmers* was synonymous with *Mercy Angel Warehouse*, which meant she at least had one new topic to research. And fourth, when she exited out of Corporal Randall's login, she couldn't get back into her dad's file. It was classified, and for whatever reason, above her paygrade. She would need Ralf's help again if she kept digging digitally.

JoJo took a deep breath, the stench of the men's bathroom stuck in her nose, stale urine, bleach, and Johnny's cheap aftershave. No matter how many times she blew it and rinsed it, the smell just lingered. Her deep breath triggered her rib, causing JoJo's face to twist in pain and her hand to instinctively protect it.

She glanced around the office to see if anyone noticed.

She was invisible. If only it would stay that way. If only it started that way.

Slowly rising to her feet, JoJo made sure everyone was preoccupied, everything was getting too complicated, her plans were backfiring, her timeline was all fucked up, and the one thing she had going – her anonymity – was compromised.

Suddenly she was incredibly grateful that Dylan and she were still on desk duty from the shooting. There is no way in hell she could function like this. Grabbing a slip of paper, she wrote *Mercy Angel Warehouse*, and headed toward Records. She was rushing without looking rushed and doing her damnedest not to draw any attention to herself. But no matter what she did, there seemed to be a goddamn spotlight shining down on her. She didn't know who was watching now nor whom to trust.

JoJo was alone.

##

Handing in her request for any available hard copies of the warehouse, JoJo decided to wait even though there was no guarantee they would work on it today. At least she was away from her desk. And that felt good. Safe.

Well saf-er.

She slipped into an empty desk with a public computer, unwilling to risk anyone accidentally looking over her shoulder as she keyworded *Mercy Angel Warehouse* and *Ben Shimmers*. She got one word over and over again.

Classified.

It made no sense. The few things she did have access to included something about a fire at that warehouse. So she pulled any file with *warehouse, fire,* and *Mercy Angel*.

What did her dad have to do with a warehouse fire?

Should anyone check her digital trail, she left a very distinguishable path. JoJo rubbed her head, trying to get rid of the dull ache forming between her eyes. She was being paranoid. No one would look over her shoulder and no one would care to research her search history.

It didn't matter if she was being paranoid, she couldn't stop covering her ass.

Too many people were trying to fuck it.

Dragging her recent warehouse incident into the fold, she felt it might make more sense to include keywords like 'warehouses' and 'Triads.' Yang Choo and Ben Shimmers were friends, if there was even one connection, she had a solid reason to request access to Ben Shimmers classified material.

JoJo pulled everything, including irrelevant reports, and in the mix came another two words.

Red Fever.

As she read the name, a flash flood of memories poured into her with such enormity and intensity that her body literally started shaking. JoJo wrestled back the tears. It was the first time she saw Yang Choo – wrapped under her dad's arm in the picture she stole, and the day she saw the file on *Red Fever 5L.*

Or was it SL? She couldn't remember. She was forgetting things. Forgetting her dad.

There was so much fucking regret in JoJo, that it took everything in her not to drive to her father's grave and finish what she started before Yang Choo walked into her life. Yang Choo – her guardian angel turned into a soul-sucking devil with Johnny as his devoted minion.

The feelings of regret were merciless, reminding her that she never really knew her dad. She never pushed him for information in fear that Ben would leave and not come back if she asked too much. And that's exactly what he did anyway.

At least JoJo had the next step to take, *Red Fever.* The news was covering the ten year anniversary the day he died. And of all the things to remember, the only thing that stuck with her was making fun of the name because it sounded like a porno.

When she typed in the keyword *Red Fever,* the same word popped up.

Goddamn-mother-fucking-classified!

She'll have to wait until they give her access, and she'll have to complete her full training as a goddamn police officer.

No matter how hard she tried, JoJo just kept hitting a metaphorical wall called *Classified.* There had to be another way. Lowering her head in her hands, she tried remembering what her dad looked like from the picture she saw hanging on the whiteboard.

Was he ever happy? Was she? Why couldn't she think of any happy memories?

Did he need her the day he was killed? Maybe if she was with him, she could've been his wingman. Looking back at the word *Classified,* JoJo noticed the date. It was her fake birthday today. Yang Choo's assigned day of her birth. The day she came to life and the same day she died.

Death and rebirth.

Happy-fucking-Birthday, JoJo Sparks. Time for more pussy politics.

She would figure out who could access this stuff and make friends. Very good friends. Her mind floated to Dylan. Team leader Dylan McKay, dirty but not dirty. Guilty without regret. He did something illegal to save a hundred little girls.

Maybe he'll do it again to save one more.

It had to be handled with care since Yang Choo was listening that night. And if Yang, then why not Johnny? They could easily twist Dylan into something ugly—into their own personal gofer.

The image of Johnny slapping the Captain took over her mental space. Followed by the image of Yang Choo shredding Dylan's hoodie.

Why did Dylan share his secret? Now Yang Choo owned them both.

And it was all her fucking fault.

JoJo suddenly felt very motivated to get out of this place as quickly as humanly possible. On one of the few available records that included the name *Ben Shimmers*, a number popped up beside his name – 6516. It reminded her of Johnny's badge popping her in the face. Maybe the numbers were in reference to a specific police officer investigating the case? The reporting officer? It could even be referencing another case altogether. Perhaps it will lead her to the person who erased his history?

There were too many fucking possibilities.

If only she could focus. Maybe it was time to start investigating the old-fashioned way. Starting with hard copies of the photos that were available to her. She couldn't make any digital copies logged in under her own ID, especially if she wanted to avoid any digital trails. She settled back in the chair adjusting her body to hide the smartphone she pulled from her pocket. She was already itching to get home to review the details she captured from this morning.

One step at a time. One breath at a time.

Inhaling deeply, she calmed herself and pressed the *record* button on her phone.

JoJo started capturing every piece of information that loaded up on the screen.

She zipped through all the files, all the witnesses, the reports, the photos, collecting everything she could access. Who was Ben Shimmers that he had so many classified files on him? And who did that make her?

JoJo had been a blank slate for far too long. An unmarked grave. Maybe that's one of the reasons she found Yang so alluring, he never shared anything. She flew to him like a moth to a flame, never once considering what happens to the moth.

Dr. Joan M Savage

Chapter 22

Figments

A million questions were rolling around in her brain as JoJo Sparks walked through the halls of the Los Angeles Police Department. She needed answers. Answers that gang leader Yang Choo could provide. But fuck it all, every time she got near him, her mind went blank and she forgot everything she planned to say. It was becoming annoying.

As she rehashed her awkward encounters with the Triad king, JoJo turned the corner and slammed right into Dylan McKay's bulletproof vest, bouncing off like he was made of rubber. The files and folders she was carrying exploded everywhere.

Goddamn it! She was already bruised and beaten and hurting so badly she couldn't stand it.

JoJo gasped loudly when she attempted to bend over and pick up her paperwork. Her body was just not a willing participant yet.

"Jesus, Dylan... what the fuck!"

The concern was growing on his face as he watched her unsuccessfully attempt to stand up straight. She changed her attitude real quick.

"Uhm, sorry 'bout that... what can I do... do you need something?" She smiled sweetly, hiding the sharp pains shooting throughout her body.

Dylan's face was raging with questions, and understandably so considering it had only been a few hours since she left his apartment. Her whole fucking life just flipped in a few hours.

He'd want to know why she looked like hell. And what could she possibly say at this point? Especially when his hand lightly pulled down her shirt collar that was covering the scratches on her neck. She didn't want to be touched, not by him, not by anyone. And certainly not right now while the stench of the men's bathroom was still stuck in her brain. She turned her back to him.

"Were you... at training this morning?" he asked casually. Too casually.

Training? That would explain the bruises.

"Yes," she lied.

The files lay scattered on the floor between them, neither one making an effort to pick them up. JoJo couldn't. And Dylan wouldn't. It was obvious he was testing her.

"I just talked to both instructors, they haven't seen you since the shooting."

"It was at a different training... place."

She leaned over to make another attempt at grabbing the files. It felt like Dylan was about to go into full investigation mode and she learned day one to recognize, and avoid, his obsessive expression.

"A different training place? Huh? And where would that be?" he asked, studying her as she made another attempt to bend over. It was truly pathetic. In fact, the whole situation was just pathetic, and what made it worse was that they both knew she was full of shit.

Fuck it. She might as well own it.

"None-yo..." she answered. And finally, and successfully, and painfully bent over to pick up her mess.

"*None-yo?* Never heard of it. What kind of training is that? Where is it located?" He pulled out his phone to do some good 'ol Googling.

"None-yo-business," she said as she nearly landed on her ass trying to pick everything up. Looking up from his phone, Dylan glared at her, his lip twitching. What was she thinking!? Telling Dylan *it's none of your business* was tantamount to a private invitation into all her affairs.

"Are you going to help me or not?" she asked. But when she looked up into his face, she saw his deep worry and genuine concern.

"Dylan, I hit your metal vest a little too hard. That's all. It's okay. I'm

214

okay."

He wasn't buying.

"And how exactly did it cause four scratches?" JoJo was just about to blow up at him when he very suddenly and very quickly knelt down beside her and started helping.

"Sparks, whatever else we are or... are not, we're partners. Everything else aside, I'll stand with you. So don't make me force the answers out of you." He flashed his boyish lopsided grin. "You know how annoying I can be when I want something." Dylan the diplomat was calling for a truce before their war even started.

She followed his eyes as they scanned her body, watching them stop at the points she knew were damaged.

"JoJo..." he whispered her name.

"Dylan, I'm fine," she interrupted. "Thanks for helping." Holding eye contact for a brief moment, she had to stop herself from curling up in a ball and crying. Her eyes told the whole truth and nothing but the truth. It was her mouth that was the big fat liar.

Just as she was about to break, Dylan interrupted her downward spiral.

"Lunch," he said, breaking her weird train of thought and curbing her desire to land in his arms and weep uncontrollably.

"We're going to lunch, Sparks. Let's go."

JoJo shook her head, answering too quickly.

"I can't. Something's come up." She faltered with an excuse as she picked up the last of her files. Her usual cocky demeanor was failing her. No, it fucking just flew out the window leaving behind an awkward childish girl.

And why the fuck not?

Just because Yang Choo made her older didn't mean a damn thing. She was allowed to have a childish meltdown every now and then. She smiled at the thought of how many times Dylan had contributed to a minor. Talk about being a dirty cop.

When she looked up, she caught a deep shadow of worry slowly creeping into his eyes. One thing was certain, Dylan wasn't going to let it go. They started something... no, she started something. She fucked herself by playing pussy politics with Dylan McKay. And it's nearly impossible to get off a bullet train once it leaves port.

She would need one hell-of-a-good cover story, and soon.

##

Throughout the rest of the day she avoided Dylan, feeling his unintentional silent interrogation and critical judgment every time she glanced up and caught him staring. As long as no details were required, JoJo had an epic cover story. Something about a wild one night stand…

Her phone was burning a hole in her pocket as she thought about the pictures and information she captured, and time was ticking so goddamn slowly it was practically standing still. Twice she thought about sneaking into the bathroom with her phone and taking a few peeks at what she captured and twice she stopped herself because Johnny was sitting at his desk watching everything. Then there was the Captain, who never left his office and Dylan who never came into his office but liked to walk by it.

She was feeling more and more trapped, and just when JoJo thought she couldn't take sitting at her desk for one more minute, Dylan was standing right in front of it. She couldn't tell how long he'd been there, only that he looked like he'd been standing there for some time. Arms crossed, furrowed brow… nosey.

Purely instinctual, JoJo looked back to see if Johnny was watching. And with a big sigh of relief, he was nowhere to be seen. She was certain Dylan caught the whole three second emotional rollercoaster she just went on.

"Lunch. And I'm not asking this time, Trouble. You had plenty of time to do whatever the hell you needed to do. I'm hungry. Let's go. And you can explain why you have the files from our first case."

He caught her off-guard and she accidentally showed him her genuine reaction. She really *did* want to have lunch with him. She needed to get out of this place.

Taking a deep painful breath, she found herself half-smiling back and half-relaxing just feeling him near. She gave him a big genuine smile and he seemed to relax too, his smile turning genuine.

"It's just business, Sparks. I wanna hear your take on any new research from the warehouse. I saw the photos you dropped earlier. So? What did everyone overlook? Cause you clearly found something to be this engaged. And we might as well grab a bite too." He turned and walked away, not waiting for an answer. And JoJo unconsciously started following – until she remembered the real reason he wanted her alone.

JoJo will have to explain her bruises and scratches – the training story was blown. And if she really did tell Dylan she had a wild one night stand, there would be hell to pay. She just barely got him to trust her again.

Will I really have the guts to tell him I fucked a stranger last night?

For a brief second, she thought about mentioning Johnny.

Dylan would kill him.

Maybe not *kill*, but he would find a way to fire him. That's the thing about alphas, you don't fuck with their shit.

And Johnny…

She saw the vengeful spirit within him. It takes one to know one. Johnny would retaliate, calling upon the powers that be, which very likely included the Captain… or worse.

Yang Choo.

And Yang would easily kill Dylan without a single drop of remorse. She thought of Dylan's poor unsuspecting hoodie. Saying anything right now will only start a goddamn war.

Suddenly, she felt like a very small little girl. Confused. Trapped in a nightmare. Lost. Wishing more than anything that her father was around to fix things.

What do I do? Oh daddy, what the do I do?

Dylan glanced back to see why she wasn't following because JoJo stopped right in the middle of the hallway. The whole situation with Dylan both taunted and invited her. But truth is truth. And JoJo had to let him go or watch a good man burn.

She squeezed the files hidden in her jacket for support and courage. They were the only things left of her father, and she was done pretending her whole world wasn't hiding in her jacket waiting for the fucking day to end.

It was time to cut the cord. JoJo stammered, still caught between desire and reality.

"I… can't… I have… I'm… I'm taking some personal time."

Personal time? She was embarrassed just to hear the words leave her mouth.

"I mean medical leave… now… today. Like right now. I was just about to head there." JoJo's ass had been plastered in her chair since first running into Dylan. And who the fuck takes *personal time* when there was only a few hours left of a workday? But it was all she could think of.

Doing an about-face, she headed toward HR and away from Dylan… and his lopsided grin, his endless questions, and the ever growing concern she saw in his eyes. There's a reason camping grounds have clear signs, *Don't Feed the Wildlife.* Well she fucking fed him, and now he refused to leave.

Dylan was watching her walk away, his mouth wide open.

"I'm sorry, Dylan."

Sorry for screwing up your life, sorry for unintentionally involving you with that asshole Yang Choo, and sorry for most likely destroying your career, your livelihood, and your future.

"I really am… about everything," she said, half expecting him to throw a fit. Instead, he cocked his head, flashing her his boyish grin.

Feeling guilty as hell, JoJo practically ran to HR.

##

It was easy to get the next two days for medical leave.

On the condition she produce a medical note when returning, they put her on two days paid leave just before the weekend. That gave her four full days. It seems everyone already knew about the warehouse shooting, so it took nothing at all but a small mention of some *side effects* and they wanted to give her a whole goddamn week.

Four days will do.

JoJo already had plans. She wanted nothing more than to spend some time remembering her father, and hopefully, learn more about him. It's been so long. Maybe she'll find some answers to all the swirling questions, without all the fucked up interruptions. Her mind suddenly wandering to Johnny.

JoJo quickly shook her head to clear it.

Her plan was to lose herself in rediscovering her father's life. Putting the puzzle together like what she saw in Yang's abandoned building, adding in the bits and pieces of unclassified material she's been collecting.

She sighed deeply, it will be nice to finally get her shit together and let her body heal. But more importantly, come up with a viable plan to get her hands on the physical evidence sitting in a locker and the classified paperwork she requested. Assuming it still existed.

She may have *requested* the paperwork but only someone with the proper clearance could pick it up.

She'll save that problem for another day.

The moment JoJo exited HR, it was like a weight lifted off her shoulders. She could almost bring herself to smile, except for the noxious odor still dawdling in her nose from Johnny's cheap aftershave. It was the first time any of her plans were actually starting to work out, and it felt like she was standing behind the starter's gate, excited and stomping her feet, tossing her mane and waiting for the goddamn horn to blow. It was simple, get to her desk for her car keys and personal shit, and then to team leader McKay's desk to drop off this paperwork – simple. Then she was home free.

She touched her pocket making sure her phone was still there like it was a security blanket.

Nothing to worry about. So why did her heart pound like she just snorted a line of coke? Just because it felt like the roof was about to collapse on her didn't mean it would. And she definitely didn't need to worry about Dylan holding her up at his desk. Dylan frequented his desk about six percent of every day since it was like kryptonite to him. She had a ninety four percent chance of a successful hit and run without facing him again.

But it really wasn't Dylan she was worried about.

It didn't matter anyway, she was going home.

She was tired, hurt, and stretched beyond her limits, and lately the terrible, horrible nightmares were visiting her even during waking hours.

What was real?

Only her father had the power to make them disappear, and she could barely remember his face. She couldn't remember his voice. Like a thief in the night, memory by memory of him was being stolen away. Her childhood, her family, her life… it was slowly disappearing.

Yang's voice popped up in her head, *June Shimmers never existed.*

And JoJo Sparks was nothing more than a figment of his imagination – badge and all. She took off down the hall as fast as she could without actually running. This figment was home free, or at least free to go home.

And hide for a little while.

And maybe, just maybe, she could think clearly again.

RED FEVER

Chapter 23

The Dark Things

Quickly and quietly, JoJo moved down the long hallway back to the narc division to get her shit and hightail it out of there as fast as humanly possible. All the while hoping to whatever Higher Power was listening that she ran into no one.

It was working…

…for about five feet. When suddenly Johnny appeared, peeking his head out from inside a janitor's closet. Stepping just outside the door, he held it open for her like a gentleman holding open a door for his lady.

"I have something to show you," he said with a wicked grin fast spreading across his face. The glint in his eye was a pathetic mixture of cockiness and gloating.

"I'm leaving," she stated, like it was enough to hold Johnny at bay.

Flight or fight?

She glanced past him wondering what her chances would be to make a run for it. Or beat the shit out of him right here in the middle of the police station. But the files she had hiding in her jacket were starting to itch. Anyway, it didn't matter, there wasn't a place she could hide without Yang Choo finding her. She sold her soul to the devil and Johnny Smith was collecting.

While she rationalized between fleeing or fighting, JoJo froze when he opened the door a little wider forcing her without force and threatening her without threat. The trapped feeling hitting so hard that her stomach dropped and JoJo felt a warm rush between her legs when she pissed her pants a little. She tried summoning some courage to stand her ground.

"I said I'm leaving. I have work to do." She pretended to be reading her leave paperwork as she passed by, watching Johnny from the corner of her eye.

"That's cute you think I'm asking."

In the midst of her irrational thoughts and the slow rising panic, JoJo wished very much that Dylan McKay would show up.

And tell him what? No, this was her own mess of her own making and no one could clean it up but her.

Ignoring Johnny, JoJo kept walking.

She only made it a few feet before he grabbed her shirt, throwing her inside the closet like a rag doll. She slammed loudly into the metal shelves, and spinning around, fists raised in defense, JoJo was ready to fight this time.

"Did you think you could just sneak off without me knowing? I know everything," he hissed.

The door shut behind them, sending her into darkness.

JoJo tried to breathe normally knowing she still didn't have enough information to make a move against Johnny. And she was so close to figuring things out about who murdered Ben – like trying to remember the name of a song that keeps repeating in her head. She had the words and the tune, she just needed a name. She needed time.

Glaring at him, JoJo stayed silent, guarding the files hidden in her coat and guarding the knowledge that somewhere just down the hall might be a box of evidence.

Evidence!? Her mind unlocked from its frozen state, and her heart sped up. Johnny had been here long enough to have clearance. Her eyes shifted down to the dangling access card attached to his hip.

It took less than a second to decide to play along.

This would be pussy politics in its finest moment, she lied to herself.

Johnny was saying something crude about her tits while trying to land a sloppy kiss on her lips but she kept her face turned away, now hyper-focused on finding the perfect opportunity to swipe his card. When he pulled back, she was envisioning different scenarios on how to steal it, and how to play along without losing too much of herself in the process. At least until she knew the reason why Yang felt the need to send him. Everything needed to be subtle.

Tuning back in, JoJo glanced down at his key card again. Johnny was grinning wildly when she finally noticed his dick hanging out of his pants. He was stroking himself and whispering all his perverted desires.

"What the fuck are you doing?" She wanted to kick him right between the legs, especially while they were spread so wide open to match JoJo's height. He was too preoccupied with watching himself get hard. And when JoJo began backing away, he grabbed her shoulders and started rubbing himself on her thighs.

How much of herself will she lose trying to win this war?

"I can't wait until tonight," he whispered, begging her like she was a willing participant.

"There is no *tonight*, asshole." She pushed away with nowhere to go. Her back was up against the shelves.

"Keep talking. Come on baby... keep talking... you're making me so fucking hard." Using his knee, he rammed it between her legs, forcing them open like a cop about to do a pat down.

Then gripping her ass cheeks, he started pushing and rubbing himself against her.

Hearing Johnny moan made JoJo want to vomit. Instead she groaned as his belt buckle was scaping her ribs. The tighter he pulled on her and the harder he pushed against her, she was certain her rib would break this time.

JoJo held the files of her father between them like they were a shield, giving her side some relief from his buckle. At least until Johnny reached up and grip locked her wrist with all the strength of a full grown man. She had a choice, fight him or...

She opened her fist.

Guiding her hand downward, he compelled her fingers to encircle his dick. And holding her hand in place, began masterfully masturbating with it. Each time she let go, he painfully squeezed until she complied.

And then something strange happened.

JoJo disconnected, like she was having an out-of-body experience.

One minute she was feeling rage, and the next a type of euphoria, like she and her body decided to part ways. It was like watching a movie of someone else's life. Someone else was holding Johnny's dick while he thrusted in and out of her hand. And it wasn't *her* breasts Johnny face was buried in. She was just a Silent Observer. An alien in her own body.

Her hands were so sweaty from the stress of the day, from the heat in the closet, and from the pain in her rib that it was easy to accommodate his thrusting. The Silent Observer stared up at the lights in the closet – wishing they were on. Even though her eyes had adjusted to the dark, she wished there was light. Everything seems better in the light.

Feeling him twitch, Johnny was yanking and jerking himself harder and harder, grabbing her shoulders and forcing her body to bend into his. He was getting close to cumming, his pace quickening, his moaning lengthening. And after a few more seconds, he shuddered and convulsed, and her hand was wet from him.

She immediately wiped it on his shirt, triggering him to half slap and half push her, giving her the distraction she needed to unlatch his key card from his belt and pocket it. This time she was ready for that push, protecting her ribs.

"Fucking cunt!"

But it was over, and all he could do was stare at the thick wet mess she wiped on him. He quickly regained his composure, smiling his wicked grin, and keeping her trapped in front of him with one arm resting against the shelf to cut off any escape. The other hand zipped himself up.

"If you keep your mouth shut... so will I..." he said, reaching down deep between her legs, massaging her pussy. And JoJo let him. She was too afraid of the dark things she felt awakening and spreading inside her.

"Damn, I'm gonna have fun tonight." His massaging grew harsher and rougher and deeper like he was purposefully trying to hurt her and provoke a reaction.

"You and I have an open door policy now... hmmmm, I mean an open door pussy." He laughed as if it was funny, then taking some of his cum on his fingertip, he brought it up to her face.

"Now, show me how grateful you are, I want some of me inside you. I prefer women who swallow." He brought the finger holding his semen up to her mouth.

The Silent Observer disappeared and something else returned.

Smacking his hand away, the dark and twisted thing erupted inside JoJo. Maybe she finally had enough of people trying to fuck her, kiss her, touch her, grab her, fight her, hurt her, change her, or kill her and what burst forth felt nothing short of a psychotic beast.

A monster truly capable of murder.

All the doubts she once had about her character and aversion to killing dissipated in an instant. After all these years of mentally avenging her father's death, JoJo never fully played the story out to its natural conclusion – the death of another human being.

Until now.

The monster was out for blood and JoJo knew she either needed to leave the closet immediately or kill Johnny. Using the momentum she created by smacking his hand and releasing resistance, she headbutted his lips.

Johnny cussed, and drawing back he smacked her hard across the face – this time her eyes watering from the hit. He held his mouth painfully.

"I'm gonna play with you all night, bitch."

Before he could finish the sentence, JoJo violently kicked him, sending him flying into the wall of chemicals and the murder monster high-tailed it out of the janitor's closet barely caring when she caught sight of Dylan McKay standing at the end of the corridor. He was leaning against the wall, staring at the HR door.

Goddamn nosey mother fucker.

Yet, she wished Dylan there. Needed him there… at least until she saw the shocked and disappointed expression on his face as she bolted out of the closet instead of HR. And worse, far worse was Johnny exiting right behind her, too busy fiddling with the belt on his pants to notice who was watching.

She wasn't stupid. Shit was going to hit the fan.

But fuck Dylan if he thinks she was closet whoring. And fuck Yang if he thinks she was Dylan whoring. And fuck Johnny for making her feel like one.

She wasn't herself anymore. And if she could breathe fire, JoJo wanted nothing more than to burn the whole fucking building down…

…with Johnny still inside.

RED FEVER

Dr. Joan M Savage

Chapter 24

The Girl Who Never Existed

One good thing about the beast was that it had a great set of steel balls.

JoJo looked at the burn phone, the number she dialed by heart was already fading off its screen. Yang Choo sounded cold and distant when she asked for a meeting.

But she did it. And he agreed to meet at the burn house tomorrow morning at 8am. She would confront that mother fucker about Johnny.

She'll apologize.

Beg.

Ask for forgiveness for whatever fucked up thing he thinks she did to deserve this. She'll promise him anything, do anything.

Correction, she'll do anything *except* Johnny.

But after hearing his voice, JoJo suddenly felt deeply insecure. When she first met Yang, it felt *exciting*. Maybe not *fun*-exciting... but *thrilling*, like a terrifying roller coaster.

There was something electrifying about teaming up with one of LA's most powerful men. He was handsome, powerful, rich, generous, *and* he noticed her when no one else did. He found her before anyone even knew she existed.

She was impressionable and desperate. How could she not be excited? And... grateful? And the best part, the part that made it all worthwhile, was their common secret goal.

Revenge.

As soon as she dropped off her leave paperwork, JoJo headed straight home, never giving Dylan or anyone else the chance to talk to her. She was too afraid she might seriously lose it and start shooting people after the way she felt. How ironic that they would give her a gun but not clearance.

She wanted nothing more than to get into the shower and scrub the smell of Johnny off her. And then find something valuable in those files to give Yang Choo as a peace offering. There must be something concerning his Organization that he might find useful, and maybe, just maybe she could negotiate a ceasefire concerning Johnny. She'll barter with indispensable information. Something. Any-fucking-thing.

She would even sign over her soul – if he didn't already own it.

And the very first place to start was handing over all the recordings and pictures, and everything she took from his abandoned building. That alone should be enough to get Johnny off her back... *literally.* A shiver ran through her as she thought about the janitor's closet, and then the aftermath...

...*the fallout...* Dylan's expression when she exited the room. For some reason it was bothering her, and it was worse that she couldn't just push it out of her mind.

Still distracted by the smell of chemicals and cheap aftershave, JoJo started her vehicle and pointed it in the right direction. Despite all her sound reasoning, logical conclusions, and mental distress, JoJo still felt the sting of disappointment that Yang Choo refused her even after throwing herself at him. And then sending Johnny to finish up? What a brilliant lesson in sloppy seconds.

She pulled up to a stoplight waiting for the light to turn green, suddenly feeling like the stoplight was somehow metaphorical.

Maybe she wasn't cut out for this life? And right there at the corner of Somewhere and Nowhere, JoJo started thinking about what it would feel like to join her dad.

After all, that *was* her goal before she met Yang Choo.

He changed everything showing up in his double-breasted pinstripe handmade Italian suit. And when he covered her with his umbrella, and invited her into his life, she thought she finally found a friend – a home – a family of sorts. And to what end? To live a hell on earth serving him?

No thank you. JoJo was done.

With her eyes closed, she tried to remember what Ben looked like. And the nights he'd come waltzing into their apartment carrying a McDonald's Happy Meal for her. She was so goddamn happy to see that little box of pleasure.

Oh daddy, why did you leave me?

The first few hot tears slipped down her cheeks.

I can't do this anymore. I can't keep pretending.

The tears quickly turning into deep soul-crushing despair.

"Why didn't you tell me anything?" she sobbed. "Why? Why didn't you warn me about the police and the mafia? And... and... why were we always running?"

I miss you. I can't even remember you anymore.

"Why did you leave me like this?"

Her thoughts continued into a darker spiral as she picked through the different creative ways she could easily join him instead of avenging him. The world would go on and not a goddamn person would miss the girl who never existed.

The price of revenge. She heard Yang Choo's warning echo through her thoughts. She was nothing more than a worm on Yang Choo's hook wiggling to be free, and all the while dying a slow painful death.

No one showed you how to be a woman? He asked her when she arrived in LA. Is this how he wanted her to grow up? Act like one of his prostitutes? She slammed the steering wheel over and over again as she thought of holding Johnny's dick in her hand.

The thrill of partnering with the Triad leader was shot when Johnny shot his load on her.

She felt sick.

The moment her despair hit its peak, a car horn honked, startling her, followed by several other honking horns. She looked up, realizing she was sitting at a green light and the cars behind her were either honking or yelling. One guy was giving her the finger. Slamming down the gas pedal, she burned rubber, flying like a bat out of hell as the light turned red again. A very small part of her hoping the oncoming traffic didn't stop to let her pass.

Wouldn't that be the perfect answer to everyone's problem?

Jesus, when did I become a problem instead of an asset?

JoJo slammed the steering wheel again, rehashing how Yang Choo held a gun to her head threatening her – warning her – never to screw with him. She cussed him out until her rib was cussing back at her.

Looking down, she could feel the wetness against her skin, her clothing starting to show the first signs of blood seeping through it. After all Johnny did today, it was her own goddamn anger that broke the tape and reopened the wound. She stopped beating up her SUV and decided to just fucking drive it.

##

JoJo had the records and pictures scattered all over her living room floor, wearing nothing but a small t-shirt and panties, having showered repeatedly to wash off the stink of Johnny, the men's bathroom, and the janitor's closet. And it still wasn't enough. So much for dinner and roses at a five-star hotel.

Her wound was cleaned and tended again, this time wrapping them lightly and gently with tape, which made it significantly less painful. After all that happened, she wasn't entirely sure the rib didn't fracture. All she could do now was to let it heal, and let herself heal too.

JoJo sighed. She had four days to forget how shitty things turned out.

And it felt so damn good to build her own investigation board again – putting the pieces together with all the times and dates tossing and turning in her brain. Her phone lay open as she watched the video she recorded earlier of the files and the warehouse incident, screen capturing each significant page and then wirelessly sending it to her printer.

The printer was buzzing softly in the corner pushing out page after page. So far, she had to change the ink cartridges three times already. And every time she thought of Johnny, she had to shower and change her clothes again.

If only she could shower and change her life. She focused on the task at hand.

Unanswered questions and confusions were still mixing up in her brain, like sorting out a smoothie after running it through a blender. Every file kept bringing her back to a warehouse fire. There was just a small description – like a footnote – of the *Mercy Angel Warehouse* fire. Witnesses around the area described smoke and flames. Every piece of information added another piece to the brain smoothie.

But what happened? Where's the original case? And what does this warehouse have to do with my dad?

She closed her eyes remembering the day he was murdered. The one good thing about so much information, it was triggering the memories of her dad again. It was the one bad thing too… bringing her back to that lost little girl watching the police take photos of his body while he laid in the street like somebody's trash.

The chalk outline burned bright in her memory.

No weapon was found.

Gunshot wound to the heart.

She could still hear the EMT's pronouncing him dead, then covering him up with a plastic sheet.

It was pouring back into her, all the things she wanted to forget. Like how they pulled her off him and left her standing in the crowd like she was nothing. She hid the blood that soaked into her clothes, and she hid her face. And now after all these years, she had no idea why. Why did she feel so compelled to hide from the cops that day? Why didn't she just tell them who she was? Would a home be worse than working for Yang Choo? Would a home be worse than Johnny? What was so wrong with letting the system take her?

She shook her head, quickly stopping that line of thinking. It probably saved her life if a dirty cop was involved. And running was all she knew… every instinct kicked into overdrive that day, forcing her to disappear, forcing her to run… and hide. Right or wrong, she couldn't have done anything different. Her soul was demanding it.

Sitting bent over the pictures for such a long time, a slow throb of complaint was starting with her rib. So JoJo laid flat on the floor, trying to stop the flood of memories. At first she hoped the pictures would trigger her memory, and that's exactly what they did. Now she couldn't turn it off.

JoJo closed her eyes for one second.

##

She was dreaming. It was half sleeping and half waking one. But this dream was different, it wasn't full of blood and fire and people screaming. In fact, the home she was in made her heart ache for a house of her own. She didn't recognize it, only that she knew the place because she was in the middle of doing laundry. Her phone vibrating, she answered it, holding the laundry basket against her hip.

"Hello?"

"JoJo, where's the paperwork?"

She froze. It was Ben.

"Dad?"

"Where's the paperwork?" he asked again.

"Dad, I tried," she said and went back to doing laundry like it was a normal occurrence that her dad just called her from the afterlife.

"What are you going to do about it?" his voice demanded through the line. JoJo shrugged her shoulders, shaking her head.

"I don't know. I'll call the DA's office, press charges." she answered, confused. The other end stayed silent, the feeling of deep disappointment from him lingered.

Finally, JoJo screamed into the phone, "You're fucking dead. You're FUCKING DEAD!" Then she hung up.

Behind her someone came into the house. Somehow she knew who it was.

"Hello brother," she said, never looking up. And laying her phone down on the washing machine, she headed toward the bedroom with the basket of fresh laundry against her hip. The clothes were so clean and white and fragrant that she didn't want to wrinkle them. Everything was clean.

The voice behind her asked, "What're you going to do?"

Looking down at her pocket, she realized that she left the phone on the washer, and a small wave of concern rushed through her that he would steal it.

"Well if my phone is still there when I get back, I'll call the DA's office." And she started heading into the darkness.

##

JoJo popped straight up, forgetting her rib was trying to mend. Groaning, she started peeling off the photos that were sticking to her face and arms. She shivered from being on the cold floor, rubbing her arms and thighs to wake up and warm up.

She turned up the thermostat a couple of degrees. Grabbing a bottle of water, she walked back to the living room and stared at the garbled mess. But her mind wandered right back to the weird dream.

What did it mean? Was it a message?

She wasn't sure what she believed spiritually, only that there was *something*. If she did believe in *something*, then this dream was the first dream she ever had that didn't involve her burning to death or drowning in blood... so maybe... just maybe...

Could Ben be trying to tell her something? She didn't have a brother so who did he represent to her? Dylan?

Whatever its meaning, it felt significant.

Or it's just a fucking stupid dream.

One thing was certain, JoJo was getting all her wishes. She wished Dylan would show up at the janitor's closet and he did – worst wish ever. She wished the photos would help her remember her dad, and they did – second worst wish ever.

Maybe forgetting wasn't so bad, maybe it was part of healing? And letting go was part of moving on.

Except...

If she forgot, then who would remember? It's like Ben was erased.

The thought caused a ripple through her soul – like father, like daughter.

The dream wasn't wrong, where *was* all the paperwork? She hoped Records came back with a hard copy, something, anything, and if not Records...

JoJo grabbed Johnny's badge off the floor, swinging it back and forth.

Then maybe the Evidence Locker. She would need to move quickly though, before Johnny reported his badge missing. Tonight? Or early tomorrow morning before she met with Mr. Choo?

The beast in her definitely had a set of steel balls. Doesn't fortune favor the bold? She would need fortune all right and lots of it. Because only someone extremely powerful could go around erasing entire cases without raising any red flags. Imagine the chaos if an officer could doctor a case at will? It could potentially fuck up decade long investigations. It's impossible. There were too many fail-safes to prevent just that.

So why did all the fail-safes... *fail?*

Now she understood why Yang Choo recruited her so young, and cleverly placed her among the wolves. He knew it would need to be someone without a background and without a history.

Standing over the unorganized mess and sipping her water. She was creating a flowchart in her head, building a timeline, building a case that wasn't nonsensical. And so deeply lost deep in thought that when she heard a knock on her door, the sip of water she took shot right out of her mouth. Her heart rate skyrocketing.

There's no fucking way Johnny would show up here. She was positive he wouldn't dare show his face once she contacted Mr. Choo for a meeting.

Unless...

Yang really didn't give a fuck one way or the other.

Despite the pain, she moved swiftly, shoving everything under her couch. JoJo grabbed her old dirty holey thick pink bathrobe. It had seen too many days but it covered her entire body and was the least attractive thing she owned.

When he started pounding on the door, JoJo quickly thought through what she was going to say and do. She still had one ace in her hand – she was meeting Mr. Choo tomorrow. That should be enough to stop a goddamn freight train.

Taking a deep breath, she decided to let the beast come out to play.

She would go toe to toe with Johnny if need be, and she would stop that fucking freight train – whatever the cost.

Aggressively tying her robe closed, JoJo grit her teeth and wildly and angrily flung open her front door, fully intending to get in the first punch. But she accidentally yanked the door so hard that the sheer force of its momentum easily slid her into the wall with it when her fuzzy socks provided no traction. All she could do was brace herself while the wall painfully broke her fall. That was four times today she got slammed into a wall.

Her robe flung open showcasing her naked legs, pink panties, and a white see through t-shirt that barely made it past her belly button. Of all the fucking things to be wearing...

For half a second, her face twisted in agony, then surged red with adrenaline as she prepared to fucking beat the shit out of Johnny.

Except...

It wasn't Johnny.

Dr. Joan M Savage

Chapter 25

Don't Bite the Hand that Feels You

"Dylan…" She couldn't keep the relief from flooding her voice. Not this time. Her poker face temporarily displaced.

"Dylan…" JoJo was fighting back a strange sensation of tears, and Dylan was fighting very hard to not look at what was showing under her open robe. She was relieved he was so focused on her body that he missed her mini meltdown and momentary emotional vulnerability. It took a second to put her poker face back into place. Dylan was looking rather sheepish holding a six pack of beer. Shrugging his shoulders, he lifted the cans like they were a peace offering.

"Wanna drink?"

JoJo smiled and nodded. He could look all he wanted, she didn't fucking care. He could have anything he wanted and do whatever the hell he wanted. She didn't give a damn, only that he was here and Johnny wasn't.

She visibly released the tension she had been carrying all day, and purposefully fell back against the wall, letting it hold her up. The relief so intense, she found herself fighting stupid childish tears again,

What the fuck's wrong with me?

"Hey I think I saw Johnny downstairs…" JoJo didn't let him finish, instead she grabbed his arm and pulled him into her apartment.

"Nosey neighbors." She lied when his eyebrows shot up.

She knew Dylan was fishing, knew he saw her and Johnny in the closet, knew why he came over tonight. He was *the* Alpha at the station, what else should she expect?

When she pulled him into her apartment, she nearly pulled him up against her and they ended up standing too close. Dylan broke the awkwardness by repeating himself.

"Wanna drink?" he repeated, clearly struggling to hold eye contact. JoJo smiled and closed her robe, nodding again when words failed her. Or maybe it was because of the knot in her throat choking her.

Dylan walked past her looking around her place and doing exactly what she did at his place, sizing her up and stereotyping her. The blaring difference – her place was a crappy hole in the wall, and Dylan's place was something you'd see a famous actor living in. For a second, she fought back a quick wave of insecurity.

It devoid of all décor, pretty much empty. A few boxes stacked in the corner, a punching bag along with some dumbbells, and an old three seater couch that sat in the middle of her apartment. It was the cheap ugly green and yellow striped one that usually comes in pre-furnished places. The only surprising thing was a stack of plants sitting at her far window. They looked like they'd seen better days. Watching his eyes fall on the plants and then back to her, he cocked his head questioningly.

"They're rescues. People throw them out and I *save* them." It was her turn to smile sheepishly now. "They just need a little love. Maybe they need to know someone wants them." She shrugged her shoulders. "Eventually they'll decide if they want to keep living or not."

Watching his face, something about the way she described her plants caused a worry line to form between his eyes. There was no way he could suspect anything being wrong. She was meticulous with her lies and every other part of her life.

JoJo was a rescue too, she needed a little love, and eventually she needed to decide… well… a great many other things.

She shivered at her own dark thoughts lately.

Dylan was heading for her couch when JoJo suddenly remembered… *everything*. Stepping in front of him, she stopped any further entry. Her robe opening again forcing Dylan's eyes on the four scratches that ran down her neck, and the big blue bruise building color on her collarbone. She distracted his stare.

"Wait. Wait here, please." She disappeared into her bedroom, yanked the comforter off her bed, put on her slippers, and grabbed her keychain.

"Come on." She headed out the door in her robe and slippers with the giant white down comforter shoved over her back.

"Uhm… I hope we aren't going out like this… and when I say *we*, I mean *you*." Dylan smiled his lopsided grin. "I do like those green slippers though… you have a funky grandma vibe thing going…"

She giggled, "Just shut up and come on… *please*," she said, heading down the exit stairs and periodically glancing back to make sure Dylan was following. Although she struggled with the steps, she thought she was making good time until Dylan grabbed the oversized comforter from her. His six-foot plus frame easily carrying it without dragging it over every step.

Every time JoJo looked back to see if Dylan was still there, she could see the questions forming in his eyes. She knew they were building, creating momentum, and would eventually start coming her way. Dylan wasn't the type to let sleeping dogs lie. His visit was a fishing expedition. But goddamn it… she really didn't give a shit. Not tonight. He was here. And Johnny wasn't. And fuck everything else.

Descending deeper into the dark basement, they entered a small laundry room. It was empty and quiet with no windows.

And no listening devices.

She took the comforter from him, spreading it on the rectangular table used for folding clothes. Watching her curiously, Dylan stood at the doorway, hesitating to go in all the way. His confusion was apparent with all the questions lingering in his eyes. So JoJo waited, watching him fight whatever he was fighting, watching him make peace with his moral compass. One step led to two, and finally he passed through the entryway.

Immediately JoJo shut the door behind him, locking it and sticking the doorstop underneath like a double layer of security. She kicked the rubber stopper harder and harder until it began to split. Nobody was getting in.

When she spun around, she saw the worry line sitting right between his eyes.

"Are we doing laundry?" It was rhetorical, and even though he was smiling, it never touched his eyes.

JoJo slipped around him and slowly, grudgingly, pulled herself up on the table, letting out a long deep sigh. Her legs dangling over the edge, her robe opened again with her skimpy t-shirt barely touching the top of her thighs.

"Dylan…" she whispered, her head hanging low. "Someday I'll explain everything."

"Someday?" He sounded disappointed. They both knew that *someday* was code for *never*.

Suddenly JoJo had no idea what to do next, defaulting to picking at her hangnail, and it was clear that Dylan didn't know what to do next either. He stood at the doorway like an awkward schoolboy. And the fact that the room was deathly quiet made everything seem much worse.

Finally JoJo chanced a quick look up, busting him staring at the scratches and bruises. Not asking her anything was probably killing him, and *someday* was about to turn into *now*, so JoJo stared at the six pack he was holding, beckoning him with her eyes to make do on his earlier invitation.

And he did. Smiling his lopsided grin, he freed a can, popping it open and handing it to her while still managing to keep his feet at the doorway. He grabbed another for himself, and they sipped in silence for several minutes.

JoJo was just enjoying the peace and quiet, swinging her legs off the table like a little kid sitting at the edge of a swimming pool.

Without meaning to, Dylan was investigating the little laundry room, getting caught up in a fascinating dust bunny, and JoJo couldn't help but smile at the sincerity in which he examined the furry thing. Eventually, he ended up leaning his hip against the table right next to her knee.

There was nothing subtle about Dylan McKay, and she enjoyed listening to the pleasurable sounds he made when he gulped his beer. But the silence between them had gone on for too long and she could sense Dylan's darker thoughts brewing.

Without looking up, JoJo smiled when she felt his eyes studying her, possibly confronting her in his head. She knew the exact moment he gave in to whatever the hell he was thinking. And she waited, sitting there as unassuming as possible. Head hung low, beer in her hands, she barely even moved to breathe.

Dylan was hunting. So she let him.

"You took medical leave, not personal leave. Is your… *neck* hurting?" He was terrible at subtext. Keeping her eyes down, she shook her head *no*. Why lie? He already knew something wasn't right. Dylan let out a loud frustrated sigh.

For some reason all JoJo could think about was that her knee was touching his thigh. He only had to shift his body three inches to be standing between her legs. By the way she was sitting, they were already open and inviting. Just three inches of separation. She would wait, listening to Dylan drink.

It wasn't long before he shifted a bit closer to her, reaching up, he lowered the collar of the robe to look at the bruises and scratches on her neck.

Oh... why not?

JoJo let him. She even helped him by dropping the robe off her shoulders, freeing her arms and tilting her head to the side giving him the best view possible to satisfy his curiosity. She didn't want to fight anymore, or argue, or make excuses. She didn't want to be alone.

His eyes accidentally dropped to her exposed thighs.

Quickly averting his gaze, Dylan gulped the rest of his beer, then grabbed another one. And JoJo stared at his profile, wondering why he wasn't making eye contact and wondering why he felt so far away despite his closeness. Where was the Dylan from their stormy night in his apartment? The Dr. Jekyll who thought she was beautiful? Perhaps it was Mr. Hyde tonight? And Mr. Hyde didn't want Johnny's sloppy seconds.

"I thought I saw Johnny outside."

At the mention of his name, JoJo started gulping her beer too. Sometimes it seemed like Dylan had the power to read her mind. Or maybe she was reading his...

Watching her curiously, he gave her a fresh one and kept right on poking.

"I thought I saw you come out of the janitor's closet today."

She remained silent knowing everything could be used against her in Dylan's personal court of law. Until the silence was so damn deafening that even JoJo couldn't take it. His questions were making her feel dirty, like the dust bunny he was examining earlier.

Feeling his frustration growing, she glanced up to see him glaring at her, his smile fled the scene of the crime.

"Jesus, why don't you ever answer my questions!?" He was pressuring her to be as forthcoming as he was the other night. He was trying to connect emotionally by demanding it, but JoJo was incapable. At least until she could find a way to clean off the stink of Johnny and break free from her Yang Choo obsession.

Sighing sadly at her useless dysfunctional feelings, JoJo held the beer between her knees, allowing the coolness of the can to keep her grounded, *and* keep her mind off the janitor's closet.

Her robe lay in a pile curled around her backside, and when she looked up, she found Dylan's eyes exploring her body. Reaching over again, he gently caressed the bruise on her wrist. Even though she flinched at his touch, she didn't pull away. So he wrapped his fingers around it, forming the perfect bruise of someone holding her too tight. She extended her hand giving him full access to her wrist, her hand, her arm…

His hand slid up to her neck again, following the four perfect scratches with his fingers. And JoJo remained open to his touch, inviting him with her body, creating no resistance between them. Offering him everything in exchange for his silence.

And he knew it. But he just had to take it. And so he did.

"Fuck it," he said, shifting around the three inches of separation, and moving his body to stand directly in front of hers. Her beer was still sitting between her knees. When Dylan set it aside, JoJo held her breath.

His hand was promising something intensely pleasurable as it moved over her bare skin. Gripping the blanket, he pulled it into him bringing JoJo with it, sliding her to the edge of the table and forcing her knees to open around him. His lips landed on her neck, deeply drinking her in until his body laid over hers. One hand disappeared underneath her t-shirt, lifting it over her head, giving himself an all access pass. JoJo arched her back to bring his mouth even closer. His other hand slid south, dipping lower and lower, gently tugging at her panties. And JoJo helped him. Pulling one leg free from their confinement and offering Dylan everything he wanted.

Dylan hesitated only once.

When his hand skimmed over the make-shift bandage that covered her rib, he took a small pause. At least until JoJo cried out loudly in pleasure and desire. She leaned into Dylan's touch, letting her soul go free.

It was JoJo's turn to go hunting.

Both her hands were tied up in his shirt and down his pants, pulling and forcing him to collide against her on the table. She lost all sensibility, gripping and grabbing and wrestling him to come inside and play. Until Dylan grabbed both her hands, stopping the craziness and slowing her way down. She was burning too hot, too fast, and at both ends. And Dylan was just getting started. No matter how wild JoJo got, Dylan was steady and gentle and so goddamn tender she thought she might scream.

Dylan the fucking diplomat.

But in the end, her rib thanked the better angels of Dylan against the inner demons of JoJo... no matter how hard she fought to mindlessly fuck him, he managed to keep the beast at bay, forcing her to make passionate love instead.

JoJo was resting her head on Dylan's chest, feeling his even breathing, his steady heartbeat, wondering if he had fallen asleep. He was so warm, so strong, so still. She snuggled deeper, pulling herself closer to him.

He wasn't asleep.

"Who hurt you?" His voice breaking their quiet truce.

She tensed. JoJo was positive she bought and paid for her freedom tonight. Freedom from his questions. Sex doesn't cover as much as it used to these days, but she knew better than to bite the hand that was feeling her.

Dylan must have felt the sudden tautness in her back because he began gently stroking her. From the moment he removed her t-shirt, she was planning on claiming her wound was from the knife fight at the warehouse. It all seemed pointless now. He interrupted her stray thoughts.

"I saw your personnel file when you transferred to my team. It doesn't mention anything that would explain... the scars. Were you in an accident?" His hand moved up to her red curls.

"Your ribs weren't that bad last week, were they?"

Shifting uncomfortably against him, Dylan exhaled loudly, clearly exasperated and went right for her jugular.

"Why was Johnny outside?" he demanded, pulling her closer against him at the same time, and she was grateful he was not making his question an *'or else.'*

JoJo wasn't resisting him, but she wasn't sharing either.

"And why're we in the laundry room? Jesus, you're so goddamn frustrating! You don't answer anything I ask. Look, if you and Johnny are… just fucking tell me the truth."

Her response was so over-the-top that she even scared herself.

"No! Never! Don't fucking ever say that again. Don't ever fucking say that! Never say that to me…" Her whole body twitching, she painfully popped up to glare at him. Seeing his wide, surprised eyes, she winced and slowly lowered herself back down onto his chest.

"Not intentionally, anyway," she whispered, feeling him holding his breath. When he exhaled his voice lost its tenderness.

"You're not going to fucking elaborate on that are you?" Another rhetorical question. A shiver ran through her body, and JoJo was hoping Dylan didn't feel it. Except his arms wrapped tighter around her until she finally relaxed. After a beat, he shifted himself to his elbow, studying her.

"I'll stay the night with you… *if* we go back to your apartment. That is… if you want me to…"

She didn't let him finish.

"Yes. Okay. Yes… yes if you want to… I mean. Yes." She couldn't hide the desperation in her tone nor the joy on her face that she wasn't going to be alone tonight.

Dylan easily picked her up off the laundry table along with the oversized comforter and JoJo's legs wrapped around his waist. He carried her into the elevator and into her bedroom. Before they even reached her apartment, he was ready for more.

It was different this time. Something changed in Dylan McKay. Instead of being cautious, hesitant, and incredibly gentle, Dylan came unhinged, devouring her all night long like he was making up for lost time. So they made love again and again… and again. This time in her queen-sized bed without the impending fear of falling off the table or the table breaking beneath them or worse, that someone might actually need to do laundry.

It was JoJo that needed to take a break. Her rib screaming bloody murder, and she had to excuse herself to the bathroom twice to rewrap it, afraid Dylan would spot the fresh blood and his questions would start all over. It wasn't easy figuring out interesting ways to maneuver around her ribs. And following his lead, they continued well into the early morning hours.

##

It was around 3am when Dylan finally crawled off her. They were tangled up in the sheets, the covers, and each other. And as sure as the sun rises in the east and sets in the west, Dylan was back to being Dylan.

"What happened to you?" he whispered. She stirred, kissing his neck. Laying her head on his chest, she could feel his heartbeat, and the soothing up and down motion of his breathing.

"Seriously JoJo, it's fucking making me crazy. Answer me. Say something. Say anything. Lie to me, goddamn it!" Dylan came unhinged during sex and now it was too late to put him back in the bottle.

"Like... this one?" His hand traced a long scar that ran across her back. "How did you get this scar?"

JoJo sighed deeply, and when she finally answered, her voice was so soft, sultry and tender that what she said almost sounded like an oxymoron.

"I ran in some pretty dangerous circles before LA."

Dylan snorted, causing her face to bump up off his chest. She giggled.

"Really? So... you're not even going to *try* to make up something believable? Just... just go straight for the fucking lie. Is that it?" His chest vibrated as he laughed again. Painfully, she lifted herself up, and rested her chin on her folded arms across his chest. Meeting his eyes, she couldn't stop her smile in response to his cheesy grinning. His head was laying on one arm, the other still caressing her back. When she popped up to look at him, he readjusted himself on the pillow to see her better.

JoJo shook her head, inhaling how masculine Dylan smelled after sex.

It was making her high. And goddamn he was handsome too. She never really appreciated how handsome and strong he really was until his pecs and biceps engaged to support his head. JoJo gave a sheepish grin at getting busted admiring his body.

He waited patiently for more, his small lopsided grin slowly growing on his boyish face as he waited to hear whatever she was inventing.

"Believe it or not but have you ever heard about underground fighting?" she asked. He nodded slightly.

"I was one of their regular fighters."

Eyes wide, he pushed himself up on his elbows, accidentally sliding her off.

"Bullshit! No way. I watch those fights, I would've remembered you."

She bit her lip, smiling coyly.

"Do you remember Martha Madness? Wicked Winona? Candy the Krusher?"

"No shit!? Wicked Winona!? Candy the Krusher!? She is epic. *You* are epic! CK was my favorite. But she... you..." His hand traced the long scar that ran across her back again. It was dawning on him.

"I remember how you got this. But why did you stop? Why switch names? You could've gone pro."

JoJo momentarily forgot who she was. Or maybe she remembered, and the truth slipped out.

"Well I was underage..." She stopped short, catching herself.

"Underage? Jesus, how old are you?" Her mind was spinning trying to come up with something plausible now.

"Don't you know it's impolite to ask a lady her age?" She deflected, grinning sweetly and hoping he would stop being Dylan for five seconds to let that slip up, slide. But he didn't catch it and he didn't put two and two together. Eyes bright with excitement, he was too enamored with her to hear what she really said.

"After you got this *injury*... you disappeared. Now that I think about it, they all disappeared, Wicked Winona, Martha Madness... CK.... Why? Why'd you quit? You were awesome?"

"I got into the police academy and those fights, well, some of them anyway, aren't always exactly on the up and up, if you know what I mean."

His face was covered ear to ear with a genuine grin. Seeing his joy and excitement made her giggle, until they both started laughing.

JoJo groaned, grabbing her ribs.

"Don't make me laugh." She whined playfully.

Suddenly, he grabbed her roughly, gently pinning her beneath him. Dylan wrestled her passionately, and she was only too eager to play as her legs wrapped around his waist.

"Welcome to LA's premium underground bedroom tournament! On top we have Dylan the Daring and beneath him…"

"Dylan the daring?" she teased, giggling loudly when an obtrusive knock at the front door interrupted them.

JoJo jumped straight up like a scared rabbit bolting for safety, immediately hitting the floor running in search of her clothes. It was slowly dawning on her what she just did… and with whom… in her possibly bugged apartment.

Was it Johnny Smith or Yang Choo at the door? She really didn't know.

"Shit! Shit! Shit!" She panicked, ripping through the covers and sheets for her PJs. And then like a sweet soothing balm, she felt Dylan's hand rest on her shoulder – a gentle reminder that she wasn't alone.

She never did answer his questions and whoever was at the door, after this, it was going to be Dylan times ten. He'll never let it rest.

"Dylan, stay here. Don't leave the bedroom, okay? Please." Crying out to the Universe, JoJo quickly prayed that the mafia king wasn't standing on the other side of that door.

Fuck! Fuck! Fuck!

"Who's calling on you at…" Looking at his watch. "Almost three thirty in the morning? Really?"

"Please Dylan. Please just stay in this room. Please." She couldn't stop her voice from cracking, she should've known better than to try and control Dylan McKay.

Calmly taking her hand, he managed to stop the frenzy. Then putting on his boxers, he pulled her close and charged forward to open the door.

Fucking alphas.

Dr. Joan M Savage

Chapter 26

What You Don't Know

Johnny Smith stood at her door leaning against the ledge, eye fucking JoJo.

He snorted when he saw Dylan in his boxers, shaking his head when his eyes landed on their interlocked fingers.

Instinctively JoJo withdrew her hand, bringing it to her neck as Johnny laughed his hyena laugh. He was clearly wasted, eyes bloodshot and bulging red, swaying slightly as he tried to focus on JoJo. He smelled like he hadn't bathed in days, reeking of stale beer.

Without warning, Johnny leaned further into the apartment, or maybe it was more like falling towards JoJo. He reached out to touch her face, completely ignoring Dylan and the pissed expression he was harboring. So JoJo stepped back, slapping his hand away and giving Dylan clear affirmation that Johnny wasn't welcome.

That's all it took for Dylan to step between them, blocking Johnny's view.

"Hey buddy, what the hell you doing? It's after three. Do you need a ride home?"

Dylan the fucking diplomat.

Still ignoring him, Johnny tried touching JoJo again. His hungry eyes devouring every inch of her. JoJo wanted to vomit.

"Johnny, you're drunk. Why're you here? Come on, let me take you home." Dylan stayed between them, and reaching out his hand, he laid it on

Johnny's shoulder. The gesture looked more like Dylan was helping him stay upright. But any sane person would've caught the warning.

This time Johnny knocked his hand away, finally acknowledging him.

"*You* go home, McKay. It's *my* turn." And licking his lips, he continued eye fucking JoJo until Dylan snapped his fingers in front of his face, drawing his attention.

"Let's get you home, Johnny. I'll call you a cab."

JoJo felt the sting of disappointment in Dylan, wishing he would just break his nose or his knee. Or his fucking face.

She'll take just one finger. The finger he used trying to feed her cum.

Everyone lost in their own thoughts, Johnny suddenly grabbed Dylan's hand off his shoulder and yanked him right out of the apartment, tripping him forward. Johnny slammed the door.

Sighing loudly, JoJo glared. She was no longer bound by the laws of location – the police station. And she had a trump card with her meeting tomorrow. She could kick his ass right now and blame it on the rain.

Dylan was banging on the door to get back in.

"Goddamn it Johnny, open the fucking door!"

She could hear the panic in his voice and feel the panic in herself as Johnny's eyes locked on her breasts with hurricane level intensity. But despite Dylan being on the other side of the door, JoJo felt her confidence returning. She stepped closer to her front door, saying loud enough for Dylan to hear.

"Dylan, give us a minute, okay? Just a minute."

The banging stopped. She could hear his muffled reply from the other side.

"Fine. Sixty seconds."

"I'm gonna need more than a minute," Johnny whispered, moving in closer to JoJo and slipping his arms around her waist.

Sniffing her hair he whispered, "Should I tell McKay who you're really fucking?" His hand slowly untied her robe and he buried himself face first between her breasts.

Something ugly woke in JoJo, grabbing his ear, she twisted it, quickly kicking his knee out from under him and dropping him hard. He barely had a second to scream when she brought her knee straight into his nose, listening to the crunch of it breaking.

Still holding his ear, she whispered, "Tell him whatever the fuck you want. In the end, it's your word against mine and you're the bigger dick. Don't ever touch me again, asshole or I'll fucking break every bone in your body. Do you know what that feels like? Huh? It's excruciating. I got the message. Now you guys can go fuck yourselves!"

She threw him to the floor, her face distorting from her own pain. High on all the adrenaline, she temporarily forgot her rib.

JoJo wasted no time opening the door just as Dylan kicked it wide open, almost hitting JoJo in the process. He looked mad as hell until he saw Johnny writhing on the floor. Grabbing his shoulder, Dylan tried helping him stand.

"Walk it off, buddy."

Angrily, Johnny pushed him away, removing his hands from holding his nose. Blood gushed down his face forming a puddle in her entryway. Seems only fair that both Johnny and Tony deserve a broken nose.

Like a dumb drunk, Johnny took a swing at Dylan who easily avoided it causing Johnny to fall back on his ass. His face burned red with anger, embarrassment... and blood. If it was possible, Dylan looked even more pissed.

"Get the fuck outta here, Johnny," he said much to JoJo's satisfaction. Finally Dylan lost his diplomacy. "I'll call you a cab. JoJo, get your phone." He stayed planted in front of Johnny.

Ignoring him again, Johnny stood up in a drunken bloody mess and slid his way down the hall toward the elevators, leaving a bloody trail. In more ways than one.

"Ask her who she's fucking, McKay! Ask her! Look at her! Look at her neck! You know whose handiwork that belongs to? Ask her, asshole! What you don't know! *You* get the fuck outta here if you know what's good for you!" Dylan followed him, making sure he actually got into the elevator.

Johnny slammed the down button and it immediately opened like it had been waiting for him, he practically fell into it.

"Do you need a cab?" The fucking diplomat returning.

"Fuck you, McKay." And leaning slightly out of the elevator, Johnny glared at Dylan and JoJo one last time.

"This is bigger than you mother fuckers!" He pointed at JoJo. "Even bigger than your dick on the side, Sparks."

Dylan charged the doors threateningly forcing Johnny to step back in. He laughed as they closed, shouting out one last warning.

"You don't know whose pussy that belongs to McKay. Watch your back, *dickhead*." The elevator doors shut leaving a confused and pissed Dylan standing in his boxers in the long hallway. He seemed to come out of his stupor when some of JoJo's neighbors started peeking out their apartment doors.

Dylan hurried back down the hall, and JoJo knew what was coming. She knew what was about to happen and dropped her eyes, afraid to see this side of McKay. Afraid of the truth. It was then JoJo realized she was standing in a pool of Johnny's blood. Her feet were covered in it.

Suddenly JoJo could feel the slow pull back into her nightmare.

Not again. Stop.

She fought to hang on, hearing Dylan slam her apartment door. She closed her eyes, and tried to stay grounded but the sounds of people screaming were everywhere and getting stronger and louder. Hands were grabbing at her, or was it Dylan?

She could hear him interrogating her, calling her – someone was calling her.

Why wasn't her mouth working? She couldn't answer, her lips wouldn't obey. Her heart was pounding loudly, as loud as the screams. JoJo slammed her hands over her ears trying to push out all the cries for help and the people calling her name.

There's so much blood. Why is there so much fucking blood?

Squeezing her eyes shut, JoJo held her ears even tighter. But the screaming only got louder and louder until JoJo fell to the floor. She could smell his blood, smell flesh burning, or maybe she was burning? She couldn't take it. It was too real. Too painful. JoJo cried out, curling up over her knees.

When the pain in her rib grew louder than the screams in her head, she found herself coming back from hell. Dylan was kneeling in front of her, prying her hands off her ears and whispering something. Something about blood. Something about being clean.

JoJo blinked.

She was on the floor, kneeling in front of her apartment door. And Dylan was next to her with several bloody towels, and two rolls of paper towels. He had cleaned up all the blood, except what she was sitting in.

Their eyes met, her body violently shaking, JoJo didn't know what to tell him. What to say... maybe the fear of Dylan's wrath and Johnny's sick attacks finally made her lose her mind. She took a deep breath, giving Dylan a small smile.

But he looked truly terrified.

One minute she was having an out of body experience, and the next she was back to herself. It reminded her of the janitor's closet and becoming the strange Silent Observer. Dylan was holding her shaking hands in his, and just like that, she didn't feel separated from herself anymore. Almost as if he was holding her together, holding her into one piece.

Saying nothing, he helped her stand and using an entire roll of paper towels, he cleaned her legs and feet. When he finished, he had a large garbage bag of bloody products.

He sealed it up and washed his hands. Watching him carefully, JoJo backed up until she was leaning against the wall, exhausted, and wondering what the hell was coming next. The screams were slowly leaving, just like nightmares do once you wake up.

Dylan stared at her for a long moment, and they shared an endless amount of information during those few seconds. Reading each other's mind, knowing without sharing and sharing without saying a thing. He smiled, releasing her from his interrogation, and leaning against the wall next to her, he crossed his arms and ankles, waiting... thinking.

Like a magnet pulling at her, JoJo slid sideways falling against his shoulder, her own body feeling too heavy to carry. She was absorbing his strength, and her heartbeat was finding its way back to normal.

JoJo inappropriately broke their truce with the only weapon she had left.

"Shall we finish what we started before we were so rudely interrupted? *Dylan the Daring* was about to..." She left it hanging, smiling flirtatiously at him like the last 10 minutes never happened.

It was clear Dylan was fighting with himself, staring at her apartment door like Johnny was about to bust through again. She heard everything Johnny told Dylan. Everything.

What could she say at this point? Johnny and Yang got reckless and careless and for what? She only had a few more hours left before she could ask Mr. Choo *why*.

JoJo's invitation finally won the fight with Dylan because he took her hand and pulled her into his arms. It was a *fuck everything* move.

She knew them well.

Sweeping her up into his arms, he carried her back to bed. JoJo hid her grimace when her rib protested but she never lost her smile. When Dylan laid her on the bed, she could see his mind working again, pausing, thinking…

Laying on her back, she began seductively swaying one knee back and forth, back and forth, opening her legs, closing them, opening, closing…

Dylan surrendered, slowly crawling up her, kissing her knee, her thigh, her abdomen, her breast, until he covered her. His lips accidentally touching the four scratches on her neck. Dylan was harder to handle then every other man she ever met, except Yang. Feeling his withdrawal again, she found the familiar worry wrinkle forming between his eyes.

"JoJo…" he whispered but she leaned up and caught his mouth with hers, kissing him hard and passionately while her other hand disappeared downward between their bodies to stroke him through his boxers. He broke the kiss, moaning softly, his head falling on her shoulder as her hand performed a different kind of magic.

"JoJo…"

"Shhhhh we can talk about what happened another day, I promise," she whispered, and he gave up. She was buying his silence again, and they both knew it.

RED FEVER

Chapter 27

All the King's Horses and All the King's Men

"Shit, I have to be at work in a few hours. Maybe I'll take leave too." JoJo was hoping Dylan was just joking. Staying still and silent, she kept her head on his chest and away from his prying eyes.

"Are you awake?" he whispered, stroking her hair tenderly.

Of course she was fucking awake. She was meeting Mr. Choo in a few hours. And after what they did to Johnny, she wasn't entirely sure what the consequences would be. She nodded her head, afraid to open her mouth, afraid of listening ears.

If Yang *was* listening, he'll get an earful of Dylan's sloppy seconds. Over and over and over...

And over again.

Dylan groaned, "I have to get up. I need to head home and get my shit for work."

JoJo squeezed him tighter. Refusing to let go, refusing to let the day start. And if she had the power to wrestle the sun, she would bind that mother fucker in place and keep the moon as the rightful heir in the sky.

The events of the last 24 hours were bearing down on her like a two ton steel trap crushing her soul.

All the king's horses and all the king's men, couldn't put her back together again.

Will Johnny be at work? Will Dylan talk to him?

Of course he will! Because that's what Dylan does. Dylan the Daring was nothing more than a politically correct attaché. The perfect diplomat.

Anyway, it was over for JoJo. She blew it.

She thought she had all the time in the world to fit into this new life and slither into the files belonging to her dad, and then in a truly epic old fashioned cloak and dagger way, find her dad's killer. And just like the day she magically showed up in LA in masks and baggy clothes, she would magically disappear the exact same way. No one would be the wiser. She was playing the long game.

But it was happening too fast now like an out of control freight train. Whatever the plan, it had to be done now... like right now. Before Johnny realized she took his access card, before Yang Choo *warns* her or worse, before Dylan discovered all her dirty little secrets. Since Johnny's untimely visit and irresponsible confession, Dylan already had all the information he needed to bury her, *if* he only knew in what order the pieces fit.

It was now or never. She sighed loudly, triggering Dylan to sharply glance back at her.

"Hey, I'll be back. Just get better? Or whatever the hell you need to do to come back to work, cool?" He misunderstood her sigh. Pulling the covers over her body, JoJo hid her bandage in case it was leaking again.

Dylan became a different machine once Johnny left. His tenderness was replaced with an intensity she could only describe as rage. And her body paid the price.

While Dylan dressed, JoJo was forming a plan in her mind, hoping beyond hope that her body wouldn't fail her. It still felt tense and awkward between them and when he leaned over to kiss her goodbye, he kissed her forehead even though she offered her lips.

"We'll talk when I get off work."

JoJo wondered if it was a warning, a preemptive strike, or an assurance that what he did was more than a hit and run.

It was around 4am when Dylan left. And the moment she heard her front door close, JoJo jumped into action, well, she *imagined* jumping into action until her body protested.

"Come on, you got this. It was worse in the underground fights, and you survived. Now get up." She commanded her rib to silence and her exhausted body to move.

Pushing past the pain and the fatigue, JoJo put her *unplanned* plan into action.

##

It was the perfect time at the police station. The in between moments where one shift ends and another begins. With Dylan McKay still all over her, JoJo arrived before any co-workers or people who could recognize her face. She had no time to shower or rest or eat.

Wearing a ballcap, her baggy clothes, and toting Johnny's access card, she walked into the station, hanging onto the small bit of hope that there was evidence in that Evidence Locker. And whoever was erasing her dad, somehow missed it.

She was impatient and she knew that patience only comes with trial by fire. JoJo was smack-dab in the middle of the trial and when fire is involved there's a high probability of getting scorched.

Patient or not – time was imperative. Dylan was already suspicious, and she was meeting Yang in a few hours. And if Johnny was a warning, who the fuck knows how bad, *bad* could get from a gangster. It was unthinkable. But *unthinkable* was preferable to not knowing the truth about her dad.

Moving swiftly through the hallways, she was careful. Careful to avoid looking up at the cameras because even a partial view was all their facial recognition software needed. Careful to use her left hand for things like opening doors and signing in, and careful to change her gait... perhaps each thing alone was seemingly insignificant but when put together could make it easy to implicate her. A person's gait was like a fingerprint, and she was equally careful to leave none of those behind too. She wanted nothing to tie her to what she was about to do next.

##

Exhausted and lightheaded, she arrived, taking a quick break to catch her breath and attempt to slow her heart down from the excitement. It should be *terror* but all she felt was excitement. It was an internal wrestling match with her emotions. The wiser part of her knew to prepare for disappointment if the evidence was missing, but fuck it all, her emotions were all over the goddamn place. It was like a tidal wave meets a tornado and she was in the middle of it trying to decide which way to steer her little boat.

Clearing her throat, she felt at least semi-ready to grab the attention of the person manning the locker. They were hidden behind an actual oversized newspaper. Flipping the top of the paper down, a slightly overweight gray haired elderly cop was stationing the place. And scrutinizing JoJo.

Nonchalantly, she lifted Johnny's badge, then buried her nose in a case file pretending she needed to read him the case number as if she didn't have that mother fucker memorized. And burying her nose in the file was her way of hiding her face as she read off each number slowly. All the while hoping he failed to notice she wasn't tall and male. He was more interested in helping her than playing security.

"Well hello there," he said cheerfully, his body fighting him as he tried to stand up.

"Whatcha reading?" she asked, lifting her chin toward the paper, and getting his attention off her.

"Oh nothing new, yesterday's news. Just trying to catch up. This job makes it easy to catch up on my reading." He handed her the sign in sheet. "I imagine you're caught up on the news, I've just started reading... hell, you're probably living it." He chuckled.

She had been overly cautious with every aspect of this adventure, even in the midst of the last minute planning. Until it came time to sign her name...

...and nearly fucked it all up by signing her own name.

She was so grateful that it only took one swipe to quickly correct it since *Johnny* and *JoJo* were close in letters.

"I doubt that," she answered, "And I haven't read, or watched for that matter, any news since last week. Pretty pathetic?" She didn't look up from the sign in sheet, taking her time filling in the date and time. She could feel her mind and body slowly sinking as the adrenaline started wearing off.

The cop checked over the case number and with a few cracks and pops from his knees, he disappeared somewhere in the back room.

The dizziness was worsening. She was losing her ability to hold it together, and desperately trying *not* to get excited.

Trying and failing.

She was so fucking close that her heart kept skipping a beat, threatening to expose her. And her emotions might as well be blackmailing her as she fought for control. Still holding the pen from signing in, even her hand was shaking. The whole situation was surreal.

All the fluctuations in her heart and body were causing the dizziness to get worse. It wasn't just the pain, her body was weakening too quickly like she was losing blood. JoJo lifted up her shirt and checked the rib. It wasn't leaking.

And then it occurred to her that she hadn't eaten in two days and the only liquid she had was a few sips from a bottle of water and the two beers Dylan gave her. Her body was shutting down, at the worst possible moment. She already gave her all to Dylan last night, and right now she was standing on straight willpower and adrenaline alone.

JoJo sat down, closed her eyes, and began some deep breathing exercises. Patiently waiting.

Patience – the thing created with trial by fire.

And JoJo was fucking burning.

The man returned and plopped down an old beat up box on the counter, scratching his head, looking a bit confused. And not a moment too soon. Her body was breaking out in a sweat with the first few drops slowly crawling down her back. She desperately needed some water but truthfully, the only thing that mattered to JoJo was that something remained of her father – the existence of evidence.

"Well this is interesting," he said, still looking confused. "It looks like this was repeatedly checked out... by your boss."

JoJo was grateful she was sitting down, the ups and downs of this case were making her crazy. Maybe it was going to be an empty box, just like the report. Erased. But by whom?

The department boss? The Captain? Dylan?

He responded as if reading her mind.

"Williams never did have any patience. I moved out of narcs years ago, before Williams became Captain. How the hell he got that job, lord only knows." He was chatting away as he looked over the sign in sheet, not really seeing it, but making sure she filled it out correctly.

Captain Williams?

JoJo couldn't help picturing Johnny slapping him across the face, wondering which asshole really was the boss.

"Well Captain Williams did say he wanted it first thing in the morning *again*... so... he must not be done with it." She grabbed her file, avoiding eye contact with him. She had to stop herself from just taking the box and running out the door. It was her weak body that made her a wiser person today.

JoJo strategically took a minute to put her file back together as some of the sheets had fallen at odd angles. There were some questions rolling around her head.

"You knew the Captain?" she asked.

"Sure did. He was an ass then, I bet he's still an ass now." He chuckled, sitting back down, he picked up his newspaper and licking his fingers, began searching for the place he stopped reading. JoJo tried to control the shaking of her hands as her arms went around the box of evidence that belonged to her dad.

It was all she had left of him – whatever fit inside this small box. It could be a fucking pen and she'd be happy. The box was light enough.

Holding it tightly against her chest, JoJo opened the door feeling like she had just pulled a Hail Mary with Johnny's access card. She couldn't stop the big cheesy grin spreading over her face. Suddenly it was all worth it. All of it.

Until...

"I can't believe he's still on about that dirty cop," he said as he buried his face back in the newspaper.

JoJo paused, holding the door open with her foot.

Dirty cop?

"I thought he let it go by now. I guess that's why he's Captain. Don't let things go so easy. Not much for a life outside work but I guess makes one hell-of-a-detective." He snapped the paper down, startling her and glaring. "Don't tell him I said that. He's still an ass!"

Eyes wide, JoJo nodded. She couldn't move, letting another wave of dizziness pass.

"Dirty cop?" she said, trying to sound as disinterested and nonchalant as possible but failing miserably.

"Ya, your case involved a dirty cop. Haven't you read it?" The shaking moved outward, spreading into the rest of her body. She fought to keep it out of her voice.

"Not yet. I'm a bit behind. But the man who killed... *him...* was definitely a cop, right?"

He snorted at her question.

"He wishes. And the case you're holding is a *them*. So many goddamn people, a fucking tragedy really."

What the fuck? She didn't understand. Nothing made sense.

"I thought you said he was dirty."

The old man dropped his newspaper, a bit agitated now at her ignorance, studying her carefully. It was like they were speaking two different languages.

"Ya, and Williams was obsessed with finding him," he stated as if that explained everything. JoJo finally turned around, looking right at him, no longer caring if he saw her face. She needed answers.

"So Captain Williams wants to find the cop who killed Shimmers?" she tried repeating.

"What?" He was clearly confused by her question.

"I'm sorry, what?" she shot back, staring at him and waiting for more. JoJo was burning inside with trial by fire.

"No, *Shimmers.* Anyway, last I heard, he got what he deserved." He went back to reading his paper. JoJo's lip twitched.

She stood there too long, pausing and staring at nothing. Trying to put the pieces together. And all she could come up with was that this man believed her daddy deserved to die. She was fighting between rage and grief and both were equally powerful forces wreaking havoc in her body.

He flipped his paper down again, watching her over the corner's edge.

She turned her back to him hiding the emotional roller coaster she accidentally jumped on. She had to say something.

"You must think I'm an idiot, but I really don't know the history, like... like *why* did he deserve what he got?" She bit off each word, controlling her desire to jump over the counter and choke him. Or grab the bright yellow pencil sitting on his desk and *stab him*.

"Then I recommend reading the whole report and not just the cliff notes, honey. *Everybody* knows *this* case, if you've been around longer than a few years, that is. It was the talk of the city. Still is in some circles. It was a massacre. A real tragedy."

When her heart rate shot up, the dizziness returned in wave after wave, this time bringing with it her own nightmare. Bloody floors, burning bodies, people screaming. Instinctively she tried to put her hands over her ears, nearly dropping the box of evidence. The cop was still droning on and on about a fire but he sounded like distant chatter on a TV in another room.

"...he burned the whole damn warehouse down with everyone trapped inside. I tell you it was right out of a horror movie. I'm surprised Hollywood hasn't made a movie out of it yet."

JoJo was getting sucked deeper into her own nightmare. She needed to leave or end up blowing her cover if she passed out. Opening the door, she walked away as fast as she could, with the old cop yelling behind her.

"Hey! Hey! Well good luck with Williams. Still can't believe he made Captain!"

The door closed behind her and she hurried toward the exit, playing tug-of-war with her brain. Pushing and pulling to hang onto the last few threads of reality instead of falling on the floor in a fetal position. Each thread she pulled only served to unravel herself instead of the mystery.

Ben Shimmers started the *Mercy Angel Warehouse* fire.

Ben Shimmers got what he deserved.

And everybody knows the story.

Dr. Joan M Savage

Chapter 28

Bloody Trails and Tales

JoJo left everything in the burn car.

She could still taste Dylan on her lips, smell his aftershave on her skin and she was meeting Mr. Choo in less than two hours. There wasn't a moment of reprieve in over two days and she had long since passed physical and mental exhaustion. Her four day resting weekend was turning into a whole different kind of nightmare – as if she didn't have enough of those to contend with. It was a miracle she was still standing, functioning on straight willpower and orneriness.

All she wanted to do was dive into her dad's evidence... remember him... remember something more than the look in his eyes as he lay bleeding out. And forget what she just learned. Surely it wasn't true. She misunderstood, that's all. Right now she had other issues to consider, like if Yang Choo shredded a hoodie for smelling like Dylan McKay, what would he do with a person?

Stepping out of the shower, a bloody trail traveled down her side and leg. The wound needed to be cleaned and closed up after her crazy night, and butterfly stitches weren't going to cut it this time.

Gritting her teeth, JoJo poured the 70% alcohol over the fleshy mess, biting down on a towel as she silently screamed into it, letting herself fall against the back of the toilet. She was openly crying now, there wasn't any reason to hide it anymore, even from herself.

Ben deserved what he got.

Was that why they were always on the run? She wanted to kick herself for not listening to the whole story, but truth be told, she didn't want to hear it. Couldn't hear it. It was another tale told by cops who have nothing better to do than create gossip and hype. Her father couldn't have committed those crimes against humanity. He wouldn't do that.

Would he?

As the sting subsided, JoJo cringed at what was coming next. It was going to hurt far far worse than anything she experienced up to this point. She had more than a physical wound that needed tending to and closure.

She pulled out the staple gun from her stolen medical kit. This kit brought her through many illegal fights – until Candy the Krusher got crushed by Damien the Demon.

She was feeling the same way she felt the night her back was ripped open by the steel edge of the metal cage she was fighting in when Damien the Demon took a cheap shot.

Why did the cop's words feel like another cheap shot? Instead of ripping through her flesh, it ripped through her soul leaving another bloody trail. Every glimpse into her past turned out to be just another bloody trail. What was real?

JoJo focused on the fact she had evidence waiting for her. It was part of her father and she held onto that thought as she tried to grip enough of the skin on her ribs to staple the hole closed.

Staples were quick. Fucking painful but quick.

JoJo clamped down putting in the first staple, and screaming into the towel she was crushing between her teeth, fighting to stay conscious. She couldn't afford to faint now, so she pulled out an epi-pen and jammed it into her thigh. The rush flew through her instantly like the high from jumping off a building or skydiving. Her heart racing wildly, she used the fake strength to put the next two staples in. It still hurt like fucking hell.

But the old cop's words hurt worse.

She poured more alcohol on the wound. This time a wail escaped her lips and this time it wasn't silent. Using the towel, she thrust her face into it, drowning out the intensity, and beating her fist into the cabinet until she collapsed against the back of the toilet again. Aching and stewing in the agony of betrayal.

Because everybody knows the story.

Everybody.

##

Sitting on the floor in the burn house, JoJo didn't dare bring in her father's evidence. Instead she brought all the pictures and videos she took when she followed Johnny. She would give everything to Yang Choo as a peace offering since she didn't have time to find anything specific. She wanted to regret Dylan's arrival last night because he took the time she needed to scour the reports to find something of value.

But she couldn't bring herself to regret Dylan. She only felt gratitude.

She was looking over the pictures when she heard Yang's motorcycle coming down the road. Quickly hiding the paperwork under the couch cushion, she couldn't stop her face from turning red.

Jesus, even after everything she discovered, she still couldn't stop the excitement his visit was stirring. That is until she rehashed the mental images of what Johnny did to her in the closet.

Excitement terminated.

The blushing disappeared into flushing, leaving her a paler shade of white. She was operating solely now on the half a stick of butter she found in her refrigerator and some sketchy leftover yogurt that turned her stomach sour. Or maybe it was her feelings toward Mr. Choo that turned it sour.

Whatever it was, she needed to keep peace with the Triad king until the matter with her father was settled. A deal's a deal. And JoJo will play the hand dealt to her – at least until she carefully and cleverly stacks the deck in her favor.

Yang was parking his motorcycle. It was as loud as the thoughts racing through her brain, especially the thought that Johnny might have already spoken to him. But maybe not, he was pretty drunk. JoJo was hoping very much that Johnny kept his mouth shut for everyone's sake.

Standing up, she turned her back to the door, mentally preparing everything she was planning to say. She certainly didn't want to be glaring at the Triad leader when he entered. She'll be tactful, careful, wise, and she resolved to negotiate a peace treaty, not start a war.

If only she had listened to the better part of her brain.

Behind her, the door opened, bringing all thoughts of peace and harmony to a skidding halt. Cleverness and carefulness abandoned her the moment she heard his deep sultry voice.

"Well, you've got me all to yourself," he said with his usual sensual charm. "Now what?"

Now what indeed.

RED FEVER

Chapter 29

Quid Pro Quo

Refusing to turn around and look at him, JoJo didn't even flinch. Mostly in an effort to keep from passing out from the cursed excitement he was causing. She gripped the back of the couch for support in case her knees buckled whether from exhaustion or his sultry voice – it was a toss up.

"Do you hate me?" she asked softly. It just slipped out, totally against her will. She was met with nothing but a wall of silence.

"I understand why. I do. You feel responsible to help your friend's kid. Left to clean up a mess you didn't ask for. I really do get it, Mr. Choo. It's a burden. But my intention was always to help you. In every way. I swear it. Quid pro quo." She turned around quickly to catch a very worried look on the face of the man who was once her hero. Immediately followed by his solid poker face.

JoJo took a step forward, still using the couch for support, swaying slightly. Yang did not miss her instability.

"What's wrong with you?" he demanded. But she ignored him, not out of spite. In truth, she was barely holding it together.

Waiting for another wave of dizziness to pass, JoJo promised herself that once she was done confronting Yang, she'll take the next two days to recover.

"I want to clear things up with you, Mr. Choo. I didn't know about your warehouse, that first week I started working? I didn't know it was a raid until I was standing in the middle of it. There was no way to warn you." She laid her whole body against the back of the couch, standing up was getting too hard. And she was so tired. So goddamn tired that her voice sounded frail and weak even to her own ears.

"You got my message?" he asked, stepping around the couch to stand in front of her. Suddenly his eyes shifted down to her neck. Reaching up, he lowered her collar for a better look, just like nosey-ass-Dylan.

"Don't touch me." She pushed his hand away, hugging her ribcage protectively. She followed his eyes when they snapped to the hand nursing her gut, the back of it had turned into an ugly blue and purple thing.

Grabbing her arm roughly, he drew her closer to him for inspection. And JoJo fought to pull away as his gaze swept over her entire body searching for more injuries. When they landed on her wrist, she tried to withdraw and hide herself before shit really hit the fan. But it was too late. The Triad king spotted the growing blue and red handprint of Johnny Smith.

"What the fuck?" He glared like she was somehow to blame. "What the fuck happened!?"

In a pathetic fit of anger, JoJo yanked her arm away only to rebound right back into him. It was like he was helping to hold her up by one arm, until she finally wrestled herself free. But JoJo couldn't take it anymore, she doubled over in pain.

Moving as far away from Yang as the room would allow, she tried to hide her feelings of disgust and something else. Something worse.

Betrayal.

Leaning her back on the wall, she wiped the beads of sweat forming on her forehead.

"I got your *message,* Mr. Choo. And I said I'm sorry. Sorry for the warehouse. Sorry for Dylan. Sorry for making a pass at you. Sorry for fucking with your shit. I'm just so goddamn sorry for whatever I did to make you hate me. And I got your message loud and clear. Now please call off your dog. Please."

"What the hell are you talking about? That's a highly trusted friend of the family. I have more faith in that *dog* than anyone else I know," he shot back.

Putting *Johnny* and *highly trusted friend* together in the same sentence felt like a terrible faux pas. It only took half a second to realize she was getting nowhere with him. Her peace offering would have to wait another day. At least she knew where she stood now. It was over. She tried. It was time to cut her losses and run.

"Never mind. Forget it. I'm leaving."

JoJo pushed herself off the wall and beelined for the front door in case Yang Choo had any other *messages* for her – abandoning everything she planned to say and do. It was too much and she wasn't sure she could remain standing much longer or even remain conscious for that matter.

Skidding into the front door, JoJo meant to plow through it but Yang beat her there. He caught hold of her arm again, stopping her mid stride. That simple act and short yanking motion hurt more than if he had just punched her. Falling forward, she dropped straight to the floor like he shot her in the gut. She groaned loudly, her side throbbing something fierce now.

With what little strength she had left, JoJo scrambled to get away from him like a crab caught outside the tide, racing to get back in. Somewhere between the couch and the front door, breathing became laborious as the staples ripped her flesh with each inhale. That's the problem with staples, they don't allow any give, and unless she surrenders to them, they can do more damage than good.

Just like Yang Choo. Fucking relentless.

He followed her as she crawled away, watching until she finally collapsed against the back wall, surrendering to the staples…

All she could do was glare while he slowly kneeled in front of her, his demeanor instantly changing to something resembling *compassion*.

"It was just a message, JoJo," he said gently. "I thought it would… benefit you. Get you through things. Help you acclimate with your peers." Taking her chin between his thumb and forefinger, he tilted her neck sideways to look at the scratches. JoJo let him.

But she never surrendered to him.

"Help me? Help me?" she hissed while he investigated her neck. "You fucking asshole. Just because you didn't want me, doesn't give you the right to send someone else."

She slapped at his hand. Another truly pathetic attempt by Candy the Krusher. There was no life, no energy, and no strength left in her. Dylan already took it.

And Yang wasn't letting go.

He just held on until the pain forced her to stop beating him, until her whole body was shaking, and her tears poured down like the rain on the first night they met in this house. Her plan to make peace with Yang Choo failed. And she no longer had any intention of salvaging the situation. Her breathing grew more and more labored right alongside her anger, and JoJo's face flushed another shade of pale. Giving up, she relented to rest her chin in his hand, using it to help her sit up.

"*Want* you? JoJo, I roughed you up a bit. Why does it matter now?"

"Mother fucker," she whispered, still fighting to shut her mouth. "I hate you. I fucking hate you." She didn't sound genuinely hateful, she sounded genuinely hurt. And like a giant pendulum swinging back, she took a swing at him with her free hand. But he caught it midair. She tried scratching at the other hand holding her, then punching it, then slapping at his face to force him to let go.

Exhaling loudly, Yang pushed her back a little too hard, accidentally slamming her back into the wall. The shock of it instantly calming and silencing her.

He looked truly apologetic.

"Jesus, JoJo! I saw your fucking chart, the EMT's documented you were fine. So what if you're grounded for a couple of weeks. Is that why you're so pissed?"

"What?" JoJo was having trouble understanding him. He wasn't making any sense and the pain spreading through her made it impossible to focus. Twisting her body at an odd angle, she turned her back to him, one hand holding her torso up while the other protected her ribs. Every breath came with a groan – the staples in her side felt like they were ripping her in two. What was supposed to be an easy fix was turning into a different kind of nightmare altogether and JoJo deeply regretted putting them in. She deeply regretted a great many things.

Yang never looked so off his kilter. Maybe once, the night she tried to fuck him.

He fidgeted with his motorcycle gloves, staring blankly. And JoJo stayed as still and silent as possible, watching him carefully, and all the while hoping he would just fucking leave.

They were standing at an impasse.

Finally, ever so carefully and ever so slowly, the mafia king squatted down next to her again. The expression on his face was hard, and she felt a twinge of fear that perhaps this time she pushed him too far. When he spoke, it sounded like he was biting off every single word.

"I'm going to ask you one more time, JoJo Sparks. What the fuck happened to you? And if you don't tell me, I will fucking burn through every person you know until I get an answer... starting with Dylan McKay."

JoJo's eyes widened, terrified he'll make good on his threat, remembering what he did to Dylan's hoodie. She stared at him as confused as when she started this shitty day.

How could he not know? Didn't he orchestrate it?

"Didn't you... I thought you... did you send Johnny Smith... to..." She couldn't finish the thought, too embarrassed to think she might have things all wrong.

Yang's eyebrows shot up, instantly going silent. He studied her... thinking... plotting...

Maybe everything she believed *was* wrong. What if Johnny wasn't working for Yang Choo? And what if her father wasn't a saint? Maybe Captain Williams was dirty, and Dylan wasn't.

And finally, Yang Choo. Fucking Yang Choo. A gangster, a mobster, a drug dealer, a monster... her fucking guardian angel.

She had her answer.

Suddenly JoJo fell forward and right into his arms, nearly knocking him on his ass. She was gripping him tighter than if she was sitting at the peak of a roller coaster about to barrel downward.

And she let herself cry.

JoJo cried deep and hard and unabashedly in the arms of the only person who ever truly knew her.

Dawning and reasoning were winning out as she held onto him like he was her lifeline out of hell. She couldn't break her addiction to him.

And she didn't want to.

Then something crazy beautiful happened, Yang Choo, leader of the LA Triads, lifted his arms around her and held her tightly. Digging his fingers into her back, he squeezed her against him until JoJo yelped from the pain of her protesting rib and sadistic staples. Quickly releasing her, he gently shifted her away from him.

They were both surprised and equally confused as they stared at each other. JoJo sniffed, wiping her nose on her sleeve as her weeping came to its natural conclusion. And Yang stood up, instantly creating distance and unconsciously putting the couch between them.

Even though JoJo's face was slowly turning red, it was Yang Choo who looked most embarrassed. For a moment, she was in a sort of heaven on earth, at least until he opened his mouth.

"Look, I don't have time for this shit. As far as the warehouse situation, I gave you a way in and you took it. Which, by the way, worked. It worked so goddamn well that you got to fuck your partner as a consolation prize. Last chance JoJo, when I walk out that door, I *will* find out what happened to you, one way or another."

"You left me no choice with Dylan. I mean, I *thought* you left me no choice. Everything is a mess, Yang. And I don't know how to fix it." She closed her eyes for a second, resting her head on the wall and letting the whole situation have space in her to make some sense. JoJo was afraid to mention the building and the pictures, and she was definitely too afraid to admit what she stole from the police station.

"And fucking your partner is how you fix it!" His inexorable anger sucked her back into the conversation.

A terrible thought suddenly crossed her mind – maybe she was a glorified *prostitute*. Exchanging sex for protection?

"I had no choice," she defended quietly. "I thought you sent Johnny. I thought... I thought it was revenge and that *he* was your message... for... I dunno..." She looked up at him with wide innocent trusting eyes, totally open and vulnerable. He could tell her anything right now and she'd believe it. Anything.

"Do you swear it? Promise me that you didn't send Johnny. Swear to me that he's not working for you. Swear it, Yang. Promise."

"Johnny... Johnny Smith..." Yang said his name like it was a disease. "I can't promise, JoJo. There's a shit-ton of people who work for me, but I didn't *send* anyone to hurt you. Jesus Christ! I have people watching over you... every goddamn day. Every-fucking-minute, starting the moment I took you from the graveyard."

As she considered his words, the atmosphere around them seemed to lighten up, and their energy seemed to change into... *something*... a small smile crept over her lips. And suddenly the world wasn't such a hellhole filled with devils and demons and darkness. There was life and light and... love.

And angels.

"*Every day?* Really?" She mocked. Her smile grew as she watched Yang magnetically being drawn toward her.

"Because I don't recall any help when I got my ass kicked by Damien the Demon. That was the worst fight I've ever experienced. Brutal recovery. And the first time I actually needed a hospital, and the last time I'll ever go... so... who was watching me then? Who watched me get my ass handed to me?"

"Me."

"Bullshit! I would've known."

"When I heard who you were fighting, I flew in... and warned that mother fucker..."

"What? You didn't! What did you do!? That's cheating!" She tried to stand, only to painfully slither back down the wall. Seeing her struggle, Yang protectively moved in a bit closer like he was ready to take a bullet if needed. And for the first time since meeting him, she saw his instinct toward her. It wasn't threatening or angry or hateful like she believed. She was seeing him in a whole new light.

"That whole fucking system is for cheaters! Everybody cheats. And I warned Damien. He didn't listen. Have you seen him fight?" His hardened emeralds returning.

"What... is he... where... what did you..." She wanted to sound angry, but all she could feel was impressed. Yang answered her unspoken question.

"What he did to you."

JoJo decided she didn't want to know anything else about it and didn't realize she was staring up at him admirably until he started uncharacteristically fidgeting again.

"Was any of it real?" she whispered thoughtfully, reevaluating her time as a fighter. Reevaluating everything. "Did I actually win any of those fights?" Suddenly JoJo was rethinking her whole life since meeting Yang.

"Some."

"I thought I was invincible."

"You are." His tone had an edge of finality. The ending of a conversation. And she knew it. But somehow his words were... *something*.

She was so deep in thought that when he cleared his throat, she found herself jumping slightly. The pendulum swinging back with a vengeance.

"What?" she asked gently, still reeling from the new light she was seeing him in.

"You didn't fucking answer me and I want an answer now! Why did you *need* protection? Did... did he... did Johnny..." Yang slammed his fist into the couch. "Goddamn it! Why the fuck would I send someone to hurt you? Have I not done *everything* to protect you? Watch over you? Help you? Why did you fuck your partner!? Why did you need *his* protection? Answer me! Why the fuck do you have scratches on your neck... and bruises and..." He stopped abruptly, eyes widening, mouth gaping open.

Yang was staring at JoJo's chest. She followed his gaze and to her utter horror discovered her wound was leaking, leaving a fast growing bloody stain spreading out over her shirt.

Worst-fucking-possible-timing.

She quickly lifted her knees to hide it, cussing silently at herself. He saw the neck scratches and the bruises, but he had no idea about her side. Until now. She watched his lip twitch and his eyes turn dark. And something she never noticed before, a vein throbbing on the side of his temple.

"What. The. Fuck. Why're you bleeding? Goddamn it, you fucking tell me everything right now."

JoJo bit her lip. Should she tell him about his building? About following Johnny? He wasn't sure if Johnny was working for him, but at least he didn't send him. It was getting harder and harder to keep thinking clearly. If she could just get an hour of sleep, perhaps a small nap.

She switched subjects.

"I wasn't ready… to… *be* with Dylan last night. I mean I can barely fucking move. It was him or Johnny."

"Or me." Yang added too quickly, immediately correcting. "You could've come to me."

"What do you think I'm doing here, Yang?" She let her head fall back against the wall.

"So Johnny did this?"

She shook her head.

"Then that mother fucker McKay? I'm going to kill him."

"No! It's… complicated. It doesn't even matter. He owns me now." JoJo didn't have the energy to fight or explain anymore, big tears rolled off her cheeks. She could barely keep her eyes open.

"McKay doesn't own shit!" Yang sounded so far away.

"Johnny. It's Johnny. He knows about us. And he's making me… he's blackmailing me." She closed her eyes for just a second. When she opened them, Yang had magically appeared next to her with his fingers checking the pulse on her neck. She moved away.

"I'm fine. I just need some sleep."

"You need a doctor," he said and she could feel him lifting up her shirt to see the bandage.

"No! No hospitals!" JoJo pushed him away, trying to stand up, while Yang fought to keep her seated.

"Goddamn it JoJo…"

"Just leave Yang. Go. You said you didn't have time for this. So go. Leave. Just get out!"

He was clenching his fists, his face twisting in anger. He was accustomed to controlling everyone and everything and JoJo was sick of it. She knew the dangers of going to the hospital right now. They would write a report, and if Johnny discovered it, he would easily put two and two together. And she just made peace with Yang. She could almost feel another level of blackmail starting.

"Please go. I just need some rest. Please. I'll be fine. The situation with Johnny is… handled. Dylan handled it." Regretting everything the second it left her lips. Dropping her eyes, she didn't want to witness the fuse she lit, especially when she had barely finished disarming the last one.

Painfully drawing her knees up and hugging them, JoJo buried her face.

"You're so good at leaving me alone," she whispered. A deep sadness filling her at the realization of how much she believed was really just twisted truth.

"What?" His voice cracked like he hit puberty. She shook her head, refusing to look up, letting her hair hide the rest of her face. She didn't know what to say anymore. Too much had happened for words, and she needed a minute to breathe. JoJo was suffocating in her own feelings.

"I'll fucking kill him," he whispered a promise. And tired of fighting, JoJo kept her face hidden between her knees, whispering her own promise.

"You don't need to Yang. It's always been you. It will always be you." She peeked at him through some of her curls.

Bowing his head and closing his eyes, Yang rubbed the throbbing vein on his temple.

"What do I do now, JoJo? What can I do? What do you want from me?" He looked as broken as she felt. It was such a strange thing to witness in the Triad leader.

She never meant to crumble a king.

Gently laying her cheek on her knee, she watched him withdraw. He picked up his helmet and jacket and disappeared out the door.

Listening to him start his motorcycle, it was the first moment she truly felt free. And laying her head on her arms, JoJo was afraid to move because if she moved, then the world would pick up right where it left off. And where it left off was terrible and dirty and painful.

Maybe she found peace with the Triad leader but she didn't have peace within herself. And she didn't feel clean after what Johnny did. He stole her self-worth, ruined her self-image, ripped a hole in her courage, and then twisted her into a woman who uses sex like a commodity.

But worse, far worse than any of those things, was the profound shame she felt in herself for doing nothing to stop it. That shame rolled over and over in her, filling everything with its deep remorse and penetrating humiliation.

JoJo was drifting, falling into a fitful sleep and without her permission her brain started rehashing all things Johnny.

Every.

Single.

Detail.

Over and over like a bad movie stuck on repeat. Her brain looping through all the would-haves, could-haves, should-haves, what-ifs, and if onlys. It was becoming a kind of madness she couldn't escape from. Another nightmare to add to her repertoire.

Yang Choo wasn't afraid to do what she only dreamed about doing. She already murdered Johnny several hundred times in her mind, and twice before breakfast. She just didn't have the courage to do it in reality.

But Yang did.

As sick as it sounded, she admired him. He was courageous, strong, beautiful, and everything she wanted to be. He wasn't afraid of war, battling, fighting, and killing. He wasn't afraid of anything or anyone. And magically, JoJo began resting in the thought that his presence in her life made her invincible.

Yang Choo wasn't afraid of anyone. And he was watching over her.

After a few moments of letting her mind wander aimlessly, it occurred to her that the sound of the motorcycle never grew distant. She could hear the loud muffler still in the driveway. Weakly lifting her head, she looked up, and standing in front of her was Yang Choo.

He came back.

For the first time she actually looked right at him, met his eyes and held them unencumbered. Relief washing over her, erasing all the shame as his very presence forced every demon to flee.

In one swift motion, he bent over and scooped her carefully into his arms. She didn't resist, and even helped by sliding her arms around his neck, letting her head fall onto his shoulder.

This was her dream come true if she wasn't already dozing off against the warmth of his strong body. Inhaling him, she filled herself with his musky cologne and leather jacket. Filling herself with all things Yang Choo.

Taking her into the bedroom, he laid her gently on the bed and pulled the covers over her, tucking her away. She sighed, relaxing and melting deeply into the mattress. Leaning over her, Yang paused directly above her face, trying to hold her eyes with his. It felt like he was apologizing or maybe he was asking for forgiveness or maybe he was forgiving her? Whatever it was, it wasn't sexual. It was fucking beautiful.

But it didn't last. She was too tired and warm and safe. And her eyes refused to stay open no matter how hard she commanded them. She was drifting again. Until she twitched awake, briefly opening her eyes. Yang shifted closer, burying his face in her hair.

Cheek to cheek, he whispered. "Stop facing things alone. Stop hurting alone. You're not alone anymore."

His healing words were giving her the right to breathe. She sighed again and let her cheek rest against his. He was so soft, so gentle... surely she was dreaming, reality was never this good.

"JoJo, I pushed you away because... fuck..." His breath tickling her ear. "I just... I'm here for you. No matter what. No matter... *who* you want."

Sleep was pulling on her, beckoning her until she felt his hands cupping her face, forcing their eyes to meet again.

"You were just a kid when I first met you." He was whispering so softly. "I only ever saw a kid..." He shook his head, smiling. "And then you... strut into my office... wearing fucking twelve layers of clothes. I... something changed. You were... *you*... and I wasn't prepared for that."

His light was pushing away all the darkness festering in her soul.

"I'll take care of everything," he promised. And pulling away, he adjusted his leather jacket, his eyes turning hard and cold as he prepared to leave. JoJo forced her mouth to move.

"Don't take Dylan from me." Goddamn it why couldn't she keep her mouth shut?

Yang paused at the door, his back to her. He stood motionless for a very long time and then without a word, disappeared into the other room.

JoJo snuggled deeper into the soft mattress, relaxing everything, all at once, entirely.

##

It felt like she had just barely closed her eyes when Yang was gently tapping on her shoulder. He was sitting next to her on the bed.

"Drink," he commanded.

Holding a glass of orange juice, he lifted it to her lips. But JoJo couldn't break the chains of exhaustion holding her in a state of helplessness. Shaking her head *no*, she kept her eyes closed until she felt his soft lips on her forehead, eyes popping open wide. That got her attention. He pulled back.

"Drink," he repeated. And held it against her mouth. The cold hard glass, a stark comparison to his warm soft lips. She struggled to sit up, and absolutely could not do it. It was like she had been drugged with a powerful sedative and not even his kiss could break the spell.

Yang readjusted his body, placing his knee behind her back to help her sit up. The moment the sweet tangy liquid touched her lips, she gulped hungrily, pushing on his hand and further tipping the glass. She took the whole thing in a few gulps, wasting only the tiny bit that dribbled down the sides of her chin. Yang was smiling tenderly as he watched her feed on his provision.

As soon as she took the last of it, she collapsed.

She meant to say thank you.

"We should talk," she murmured, wondering why everything felt so heavy.

Moving a strand of hair from her forehead, Yang's voice was a soothing balm on her wounds.

"We will. Later."

She briefly forced her weighted eyelids open, searching his, but he was looking at the wounds on her neck, her collarbone, her wrist, and finally she felt him removing the tape on her rib. She tried to fight him before the darkness sucked her back under. It was impossible.

"Jesus… did you… did you fucking *staple* yourself?"

It was too late. She was already drifting again, and despite the angry tone, his voice was still healing her soul.

"You need a doctor."

If JoJo had even an ounce of willpower left, this was the moment she needed to rise and object. The room was spinning, the heaviness refusing to let go, and sleep was pulling her deeper and deeper into its wide open welcoming arms.

As she lay trapped between sleep and wakefulness, she could hear Yang talking, and then another deep voice responding.

The only thing she understood before succumbing to the alluring pull of unconsciousness was that Yang Choo, leader of the LA Triads, was ordering an attack on the LAPD!

Dr. Joan M Savage

Chapter 30

Haven and Hell

There was a bothersome beeping.

It was pulling her out of a peaceful sleep. As her brain started coming back online, the heaviness was lifting and causing the beeps to grow louder. Eyes still closed, JoJo knew she was in a hospital.

The smell. She hated that fucking smell.

The day she gave up underground fighting was the day they had to stitch up her back. If one memory stuck out the most from that traumatic event, it was the lingering sterile hospital smells. She held her breath for a moment, hoping the nasty stink would disappear.

She could even taste it.

Holding her breath suddenly prompted the heart monitor to beep abnormally, triggering an irritating alarm. The closer she came to being fully awake, the faster the beeps sounded.

And then a cool hand touched her face making her jump, pushing away the exhaustion. Eyes fluttering open, she whispered.

"Yang…"

"Sparks, it's okay. You're safe. Whoa! Calm down. You're safe!" She beat at the hands touching her.

Sparks?

The voice was too soft, the tone too gentle. Her eyes adjusted to the bright lights to see her partner sitting next to her – hands raised in surrender.

The last moments before passing out came flooding to her mind. Yang had called an attack on her team!

But Dylan was safe.

Her face turned red as she remembered her plea. It all seemed like a bad nightmare.

How the fuck did I end up here? Where is Yang? Did the police know it was me who took the evidence?

Lifting her arms up, JoJo checked to see if she was handcuffed to the bed. So maybe the old cop never reported her for using Johnny's access card.

Question after question beat mercilessly at her like waves crashing on the shore, and her blood pressure kept spiking while the heart monitor was blaring and sharing all her secrets.

Dylan was freaking out, desperately trying to sooth her.

"You're safe. It's okay. You're okay. Uhm, Jesus Sparks, what the hell? What happened to you? You said *Yang.* Do you mean Yang Choo? Did the Triads do this? Johnny said something last night…" At the mention of his name, her heart rate spiked again. This time she yanked off all the sensors, generating a steady flat line and sending the system into a full red alert.

Trying to quiet the machine, Dylan unplugged it, only to discover the four hour battery backup. He started pressing random buttons, setting off every alarm possible.

Finally, he found the button which at least silenced the noise even though it was still blinking red. It wasn't even sixty seconds when a nurse came bolting into the room half expecting a dead patient. As soon as she entered, Dylan flashed his badge and pointed to the exit.

Fucking alphas.

Blatantly ignoring him, the nurse quickly checked on JoJo, and seemingly satisfied she wasn't dead, punched her code into the machine to shut it down. JoJo had to stifle a laugh when the nurse stuck her nose in the air at Dylan's display of bravado, and walked out without so much as a *hello.* Surprised and a little impressed, Dylan shook his head and snorted, focusing back on JoJo.

"So what happened? Do you think it was Yang Choo? The Captain, you, Johnny, and Crumb from vice were all hit last night. You've been out cold for... almost..." He checked his watch. "Fourteen hours now."

JoJo shot straight up in bed, her mind reeling as she tried putting it all together.

"Johnny's dead?" Her lack of disappointment was *almost* apparent.

And the Captain?

Dylan shook his head, "No, everyone's alive. I think you got the worst of it."

Yang didn't kill anyone. Should she be disappointed? She still wasn't certain if the Captain killed her father.

"Ya know, I think I was being followed too... but fuck it all, I was already headed back when the calls came in. Fuckin' Johnny got his car smashed pretty good. That son-of-a-bitch was lucky he was literally right down the street from the station."

Spying on us.

If Johnny is still alive then he really is Yang's bitch.

While JoJo was filtering through the events of the past 48 hours, she suddenly took notice of Dylan for the first time since waking up. He looked like a complete wreck. Actually, he looked terrified.

His hands were shaking like an old drunk and his eyes were bloodshot and wide. Every time he looked at JoJo, his worry line returned and he obsessively ran his hand through his hair. He rambled on and on about nothing.

"Everyone's fine. We're all fine... fuck! Johnny's car... totaled... Jesus... surprisingly he's fine... the station's on high alert, families are alerted. Leave is canceled. Fuck. Fuck. Fuck. What the fuck pissed the gangbangers off this much to attack? It's *Red Fever* all over again. It doesn't fucking make sense..." JoJo laid her hand gently on his arm, silencing him.

"Dylan, everyone's fine. Right? We're all fine."

Taking a deep shaky breath, he smiled, nodding at her and intertwining his fingers with hers, Dylan finally started calming down.

JoJo had a few seconds to think.

Red Fever? She knew that name. The title on her father's file. And it came up again in her search at the station. She was planning on asking the journalists who were reporting the story the day her father died. It was one more thing to add to her list of ever growing things she didn't understand or needed to research.

She glanced up at Dylan who was pinching the bridge of his nose with his free hand.

Yang needed a cover story to bring her to the hospital. He was hiding her in plain sight as one of the victims from the attack. And from Dylan's description, not a one was seriously hurt. She smiled to herself, Yang left Dylan completely alone.

"Dylan, what's *Red Fever?*"

"It's... it's... Jesus, I hope it's not happening again. It's a fucking shitshow. They call it *Red Fever* because it was like... like a goddamn fever broke out making people crazy. It was an all out street war among gangs... and the cops were stuck right in the middle. Gangs were tagging neighborhoods in blood, can you believe that shit? It was a goddamn blood bath. Neighbor against neighbor, kids killing kids... innocent families gunned down. It was a nightmare, Sparks. A fucking nightmare..."

She closed her eyes to ward off the first images of her own nightmare trying to break in. *No. Not tonight.*

Not.

Fucking.

Tonight.

She quickly interrupted its hostile takeover.

"How did I get here?"

But he looked as confused as she felt.

"You drove yourself Jo. They found you sitting in your car in front of the ER. Thing is they said it was impossible for you to drive... and if that EMT guy hadn't found you and started putting you back together, doc said you might've bled out."

He kissed her hand, but JoJo withdrew it.

"Where is he?"

"Who? The EMT guy? I dunno. No one can find him. We searched the cameras and the one in front was just too blurry. He literally could be anyone. I wanted to question him, see if you said anything, had anything on you. Anything that would help us to figure out what the hell is going on." He stood up and stretched, popping and adjusting his neck.

"So you think it's Yang Choo?" she repeated his question.

Dylan seemed back to normal, he was playing with her TV remote, changing the channel to a boxing event.

"No," he said, putting the remote down. "It doesn't fit his style. This isn't his MO. He doesn't attack cops. And he doesn't dabble in explosives. This feels more like the Italians. Shit, it could be anybody. Don't worry about that right now. I better check on the Captain. I'll be back later, okay?" JoJo closed her eyes and nodded. Despite feeling Dylan's hand on her arm, she kept her eyes closed. She could hear him call for the nurse as he shut the door to her room.

It wasn't even a minute when her door opened again and an attractive woman entered carrying a tray full of medicinal goodies – including a couple of syringes and some colorful pills in cups.

She was different from the nurse who Dylan unofficially kicked out. This woman had pink streaks in her hair, a tiger tattoo on her forearm, and her name tag read *Candy*. She reminded JoJo of Skittles.

Watching her carefully, JoJo was considering who covered up the fact that she put in her own staples. Dylan had a crappy poker face and if he knew, she would never hear the end of it. Feeling her rib, the staples were gone. Someone cleaned them up too.

Yang?

No, he was too stressed over seeing them. JoJo decided it was best to exercise her right to remain silent.

"Interesting wound on your rib." The nurse interrupted her musings.

Was that a question? JoJo averted her eyes when she realized she had been staring at her pink hair.

"Interesting marks on your neck too," she said and JoJo decided to feign surprise.

"There's a mark on my neck? No kidding." She laid her hands over her neck like she was protecting it from vampires.

"Your hand is turning an interesting color."

JoJo glared at Candy now, she didn't like people who spoke in subtext. It reminded her too much of Ben.

"I was thinking the same thing about your hair," JoJo piped back, not bothering to be subtle. Candy finally glanced up and they locked eyes. Or was it horns?

"I'm easier to find." She smiled a humorless smile, one that was practiced and insincere.

Fucking subtexter.

"Do you get lost often?" JoJo didn't mean to pipe back.

Candy worked quietly, choosing not to answer.

As if someone could sense the mounting tension between them, a phone started vibrating loudly. Candy lifted her leg and pulled out a cell phone from a leather pouch attached to her ankle. For a minute, JoJo thought it was an ankle cuff that housebound criminals wear.

"Yes, sir." Candy took a quick peek at JoJo, then turned her back on her. "Yes sir, I did. She's awake… and…" Candy snuck another look at her. "And *perky.*"

Perky? She wanted to be pissed at Candy. No, she wanted to be pissed at Yang for bringing her here! But she was too busy trying not to smile as she realized Yang Choo was checking up on her and that Candy was his inside mule. His promises from last night rolled over her like a warm breeze blowing away the stink of the hospital.

"Yes sir, it's all taken care of. And thank you again, sir." She hung up and shoved the phone back into its pouch, all the while pretending to ignore JoJo.

"That was a hell-of-a-lotta *sirs.* Why do you help them?" It just slipped out. For some reason she felt like poking the tiger with a stick.

"*Them* who?" she responded. And JoJo answered by lifting one eyebrow high in the air like, *you gotta be kidding me.*

"It's hard to explain," she sighed.

"I'll do my best to keep up."

"O-k-a-y. Well, I was working for the *Organization* as… uhm… one of their... I was a... oh fuck it, I was a working girl. And it was my night off."

"You get a night off?"

Candy rose to her full height, hands on her hips, glaring at JoJo. She immediately bowed her head apologetically.

"Sorry. Continue."

"I was out with some friends... and my boyfriend," she said sadly. "We were just trying to have a good night. Dancing, dinner... a normal everyday evening." She smiled her insincere smile.

"And then... we were at the wrong place at the wrong time. Some stupid kids in a gang trying to prove themselves... they... uhm... they... they took everything." She paused for moment, clearing her throat, struggling with every word.

"They attacked me and then... and then... uhm... killed my boyfriend. Just like that." She snapped her fingers. "They killed him. His only crime was loving me." Candy suddenly stopped moving, trapped in the memories of some horror only she could see. Her hand frozen midair over the medication she was putting together. It was like someone hit the pause button in the middle of a movie.

Mortified at herself, JoJo was trying to muster another apology but Candy never gave her the chance.

"Needless to say, I didn't handle... *life*... very well, and I ended up... well, I was in an alley one night, strung out on some new junk they were selling... and the strangest thing happened." For the first time since she entered the room, Candy really looked at JoJo, even though it felt like she wasn't really seeing her at all. But JoJo was already completely invested in the story.

"I found a note shoved into an empty tequila bottle. Literally, a message in a bottle, if you can believe that. I'm not sure why I cared what was on it. Boredom? Curiosity? The drugs? Who knows. Anyway, I broke the glass and read it." She paused.

Completely enthralled, eyes wide, JoJo was waiting for the rest of the story.

"What did it say?" she whispered like an eager little kid whose mother stopped reading at the best part of a bedtime story.

"It said, *overcome evil with good.*"

"What!? What the fuck?" JoJo crossed her arms in frustration, Candy was clearly toying with her.

"I'm not kidding. That's what it said."

"What does that even mean?"

"I can't explain it but I understood. I just completely understood what it meant." Candy was smiling now as she finished loading the syringes full of clear liquid.

Exhaling loudly, JoJo prompted her to finish.

"Well? What does it mean?" It *was* a fairly decent story after all.

"For me, it meant doing something good toward the men who might be responsible for... for taking *everything* from me. That's why I *help them*. Every gangbanger I save here could be the one who murdered my man. Every gunshot wound I treat, or favor I do, might be helping one of the men who hurt me."

"Why? That makes no sense. I would fucking hunt them down and kill those mother fuckers! No, I would cut off their... I would... I..." JoJo grew silent realizing she would do nothing. Because she did nothing with Johnny. A strange and heartbreaking disappointment filled her soul until Candy's warm and gentle voice brought her back.

"I can't imagine doing anything more... *good*... to overcome what they did. I really can overcome evil with good. And I do it here every time I help someone like you."

Someone like me?

JoJo stared at her long and hard. No matter how she thought it through, she *was* working for Yang Choo and that meant she was part of it. She was part of his gang by default. And part of the problem by association.

Candy grew pensive, lost in her forbidden memories. And JoJo was wondering if Candy actually overcame anything at all. She looked heartbroken, even haunted. How's that for overcoming? She decided not to push it, keeping the silence between them while Candy injected the medication into her IV.

When she started cleaning up, Candy spoke again.

"Later on I found other quotes that were more appealing. Let's see, my favorite one is, *do good to your enemies and it will be like pouring hot coals on their heads.* Ya, I like that one." She smiled at JoJo who was wondering

294

which part to take seriously, if any of it.

However, she did relate to the *hot coals*. Now *that* quote she could get behind, except, it wouldn't be metaphorical coals hidden in the folds of some random act of kindness. No, it would straight up be hot embers… on their heads. Candy interrupted her.

"I would appreciate your discretion in this matter, Officer Sparks. Mr. Choo went out of his way to get me this new life. What school… what hospital for that matter, would ever consider hiring a junkie? Mr. Choo gave me a miracle. I'm happy to serve him."

She knew all about the miracles of Yang Choo.

"And I enjoy nursing. I enjoy helping people. If you think about it, without those bad things happening, I never would've found my true calling. I love this job. I absolutely love it. This is my haven."

"It's my hell," JoJo whispered, utterly confused by the entire conversation. Mostly because there was a little green devil screaming on her shoulder and throwing accusations at Candy. Accusations that sounded strangely like *jealousy*.

Why did Yang help you? Were you his girlfriend?

Did you date him?

Fuck him?

Candy was beautiful, bright, and probably knew how to do things that JoJo only read about in books. The little green devil wouldn't stop drawing up images of Yang and Candy together.

To make matters worse, Candy started whistling like she was suddenly in a very good mood. And JoJo started scowling like she was suddenly in a very bad mood.

They didn't speak again, leaving JoJo to count the seconds until Candy finally left her room.

She needed to think about more important things other than who Yang Choo was banging. She needed to ask him what he knew concerning the warehouse fire involving her dad. But that's not what came out of her mouth today. Somehow that's never what comes out of her mouth when she's with Yang Choo.

Every fucking time.

What she plans to say and what she actually says are miles apart. It was frustrating.

By faking an attack on the LAPD, Yang bought her some time to keep using Johnny's access card. He may have been covering for her injuries, but he just might have given her the perfect opportunity to find out everything the old cop from the Evidence Locker knew. She needed to return and talk to the only person who seemed to know anything about Ben Shimmers.

Even if he wasn't working tonight, according to him, *everyone* knew.

Maybe she was using it as an excuse to leave the hospital, or maybe she really believed it was the only way, but JoJo unplugged herself, grabbed her shit and disappeared into the corridor and out of the hospital without a single person of interest ever noticing.

Chapter 31

Stab and Twist

She was careful. Even though LEOs were on high alert, it felt like life itself was unfolding everywhere to help her get answers.

She opened the door to the Evidence Locker, relief instantly flooding her when she saw the man's gray hair barely visible over the newspaper he was reading. It's like she never even left.

"Captain Williams was hit tonight," she said.

He flopped the paper down, staring at her in a bizarre kind of surprise.

"Not surprising. Is he…?" He left the question hanging, searching her face.

She shook her head. Although the man professed to dislike Williams, his grunt and relieved laugh told a different story.

"Hello *Johnny*," he said with a sardonic twist, one bushy gray eyebrow lifting upwards.

"My dad wanted a boy, what can I say…" And JoJo plowed right into her question, never giving him time to read her for inconsistencies. All the while hoping he didn't really check up on her after that last visit.

"You said *everyone* knew about the murder and about the dirty cop. But no one knows. Am I asking the wrong questions? You seem to be the only person who knows all the details." She tried to sound as nonchalant as possible even though the need for the truth felt like it was killing her.

His smile indicated he saw through her facade. And leaning in closer, he was acting like he had some confidential gossip to share.

"Or nobody *wants* to talk about it." The ugly grin grew on his face as he watched her interest peak. Her attention was making him feel important. So-fucking-be-it.

"Why? I don't understand why? If a dirty cop is involved, why not talk about it?" She could hear the agitation in her own voice, laced with desperation and resentment. Maybe he'll think she's seeking a promotion and mistake her desperation for ambition. He lifted his paper, licking his fingers, searching for a particular page.

"Because it's an embarrassing and shameful thing, *Johnny*."

He knew. Fuck it. She pressed on.

"Doesn't anyone care about the truth?"

"Truth? Like… why you're not male and about five inches taller? Ya, I looked you up," he said, puffing his chest out.

"Okay, how about truth *for* truth?" she responded very carefully, watching his reaction. He didn't need to bargain, all he had to do was press a button and rain fire and brimstone on her. Full precinct lockdown. But she could tell he was enjoying their little game, he liked the company, the attention, the control…

"I'm new, *obviously*, and since I can't access all this stuff yet, my friend loans me his badge. I know it's not *technically* authorized but people do it all the time. I watched the Captain do it when he wanted Tony to grab something from his office."

She assumed it had to be true. It made sense that this stuff happens as people hop through different divisions doing favors. She hoped it was true.

The corner of the newspaper bent down as he peered over it to watch her. And she focused on having as blank a face as possible. It was a good thing he couldn't see her beating heart.

"Look, if it was stolen, alarms would be blaring right now. I was given an extra day because the Captain was attacked. Maybe… maybe it's connected. Shit, I dunno. Maybe I'm just ambitious and you're the only cop who seems to have his head on straight." She would try flattery.

The old man continued to stare at her, unconvinced.

"I'm not exactly asking for information that could ruin a current case, especially if everyone already knows. And… not to be indelicate, but from what you said, everyone died. I want to see if there's a connection to another case involving Yang Choo and the warehouse that we hit a couple of weeks ago. It just feels like there's some connection. I could be wrong, then again, I think the Captain came to the same conclusion. Why else would he check out the evidence?"

Her story became stronger the longer she spoke, as if she was weaving it into reality. Even she started believing it.

And so did he.

"What do you want to know?" he finally said.

"Why a dirty cop can murder someone and no one is doing anything about it?" It came out all wrong, angry, and raw. It's not what she planned to ask, but it's what she really wanted to know.

"I think you got your facts wrong, sweetheart."

She stiffened, biting her lip to keep her mouth shut.

"Then fix my facts," she said, biting off each word. "The files are classified and I can't make heads or tails of anything."

"Maybe they're covering it up. Of course they would. Wouldn't you cover for your partner?"

She nodded, sighing loudly. Of course she would… and will.

"You seem to be more invested than simple curiosity," he stated.

Was that a question? JoJo shrugged her shoulders. It felt like a question. And he kept right on going, right through the stoplight.

"How badly do you want this information, *Johnny*? Wanna show me your tits?" he said, repeatedly lifting his eyebrows in the air. Now that was a question. What a fucking cliché.

Smiling sheepishly, he motioned toward her chest.

"Want me to break your face?" It was a knee-jerk response, but damn it if her face wasn't turning bright red.

"Just wanted to see how far you'd go for that *ambition* of yours." He went back to reading.

"I think it's happening again," she said softly, trying to pull his attention back.

"Never. That would never happen."

"How do you know? How can you be so sure?" She wasn't.

"Because nobody will ever be that naive to gather in one warehouse again. Yang Choo would never allow it."

It was a good thing that he was preoccupied with his paper or he would've seen her poor poker face at the mention of her guardian angel. She was about to blow everything she was trying to accomplish.

But JoJo couldn't control the frustration building.

"What!? What the fuck does that have to do with Ben Shimmers being murdered and no one investigating? And how do you know what Yang Choo will allow? He's a fucking criminal!"

The old man looked surprised, caught off guard by her level of intensity and frustration. He mirrored it, slamming the paper down.

"Ben Shimmers deserved to be murdered a thousand times over for what he did!"

Her blood felt like it was beginning to boil, and she had to hold her hands to control the shaking.

"Do you get that, sweetheart? Nobody *wants* to investigate because he deserved it!"

No matter what she did, the shaking just kept spreading. Hate had a way of taking over – taking over everything and taking charge of everything.

JoJo was using all her willpower to not grab the stupid yellow pencil and weaponizing it. Anyway, stabbing him would be too easy, and not nearly painful enough.

Finally, she found the strength to look at him – to really look at him. He must've seen something in her eyes that scared him. She was scaring herself.

"Who are you?" he asked.

"I told you I'm new to narcotics, and I'm just trying to make a good impression which is why I'm working these stupid long hours, dealing with assholes, and nobody will give me the fucking help or information I need. So could you please, please just answer my fucking questions without being a dick?"

And before I cut you.

"I should call somebody." He started reaching for the landline on his desk.

"Yes. You should! Do that! Because asking to see my tits was way over the line."

His eyebrows shot straight up. JoJo took the power back, unwilling to lose it again.

"One more question? Please?" She gentled herself, quickly turning the charm back on and the anger off. It was working. He responded, nodding and folding his paper away.

"Why cover up Ben's murder? I understand you think he *deserved* to be murdered, which is, a whole other discussion, but if there's a dirty cop running around murdering people, don't you want to know? A dirty cop is a dirty cop."

The old man stared at her for a long time, scrutinizing, perhaps debating on whether to talk or call security. Her patient endurance won out, or maybe he was too afraid of having to attend another sexual harassment seminar on his day off.

"Ben Shimmers *was* the dirty cop. He murdered over a hundred people in cold blood. MURDERED. Including an innocent family, cops, gangsters, kids. He burned them alive. Every. Last. One of them. That psychopath locked them all in a warehouse and lit that mother fucker on fire. What kind of person does that? So yes, nobody wanted to investigate his *murder*. Nobody cared. All that mattered was bringing him to justice, in LA! He was right under our noses. Yang Choo did us all a favor by finally killing that rat-bastard Ben Shimmers."

JoJo's heart fell two stories, shattering as it hit rock bottom.

"Yang Choo? No... no... that's not possible," she whispered.

"Choo sent out funeral invitations announcing Shimmers *forced retirement*. There wasn't a single soul who didn't show up to witness what he did *and* to pay their respects to the Triads. Cops, gangs, families, city officials... everybody. We were all there. And there wasn't any fighting, it's been a while but the city finally united over the death of that psychopath. What a great day."

As he talked, a numbness was spreading over her body like novocaine.

"You asked why nobody was investigating his murder? Because we know who killed Ben Shimmers. And if you think there's a cop in this precinct... in this state who will seriously go after Mr. Choo, then you're just crazy. We owe him. We *all* owe him. We should've thrown him a goddamn parade." He turned his back to her, hiding his emotional breakdown.

But JoJo couldn't hide hers. There was a knife in her back and it was painfully twisting around and around. It hurt worse than when Damien the Demon took a cheap shot and ended her career in the underground fights. It hurt worse than holding her father's bloody body in her arms.

The old cop plunged the knife in one more time for good measure. It was a stab and twist. The twisting makes sure the wound will never close.

"Had Shimmers lived and gone to trial, every case he ever worked on was open season for appeal. His death was the best damn thing that ever happened to this city."

The old cop spun around just in time to watch the exit door slowly closing.

JoJo did it again.

Dr. Joan M Savage

Chapter 32

Unturned Stones

JoJo's burn clothes lay shredded and strewn across the burn car looking like a wild animal had mauled her. She lay back in her seat holding her ribs, breathing in and breathing out, and in between she just kept screaming. She couldn't stop screaming, even after her voice was cracking and threatening to fail. Sweat poured from her and each breath felt like she was slowly suffocating.

Yang Choo did us all a favor by finally killing that rat-bastard…

Her face and arms were puffy and red from beating up the car and losing. But it wasn't the car she wanted to hurt.

Yang Choo.

Her mind was feeding on his name. Taking it apart like pulling pieces of bread from a dinner roll. Taking apart every single day of her life since meeting him, piece by piece, day by day. Every moment she spent thinking of him, every kiss, every touch, every ache.

A fucking sick lie.

JoJo slapped the part of her face where he whispered his promises last night, promises that she wasn't alone, promises that he would take care of… *everything…*

Lies.

Burying her face in her hands, she let humiliation and betrayal completely take her. Ben Shimmers… Yang Choo…

Were they even fucking friends?

She hated the old cop for polluting her dad's name. His crooked voice playing over and over accusing everyone she ever loved.

He murdered over a hundred people, burned them alive. Nobody wanted to investigate his murder. Nobody cared.

JoJo cared. She gave up her youth, her hopes, and all her dreams to avenge Ben.

And everything else she gave to Yang Choo.

Gagging loudly, she quickly slammed her hand over her mouth to avoid vomiting, forcing herself to swallow it back down. She was on fire, burning up inside – aflame – like the people her father murdered, every cell combusting and exploding.

Still…

A very small part of her hoped that maybe, just maybe, this was some sort of elaborate untruth and tall tale the cops were using to blame Yang as their scapegoat so they wouldn't have to go digging in their own backyard.

And her father really wasn't a fucking psycho, an arsonist, a murderer… *a dirty cop.*

She gagged again as all her own terrible choices slammed into her in wave after wave, biting, ripping, terrorizing. Including the choice to ignore all the clues over the years by pretending to be a happy family. And all the while she was living and eating with a mass-fucking-murderer. Daughter of a serial killer. Daughter of a psychopath. She should include that on her resume.

But…

Was it even true? A small part of her desperately trying to justify. *It wouldn't be the first time cops lied to cover their asses.*

It didn't take long to convince herself that it had to be a misunderstanding, and JoJo made a quick and fast decision to dig into the evidence she stole. It didn't matter if the whole goddamn world was looking for her and Yang's piece-of-shit burn car. She needed to find something, anything, to clear up this bullshit. Her sanity depended on it. No, it fucking demanded it. No more dancing on the edges, no more one-foot-in and one-foot-out scenarios, JoJo was jumping straight into the deep end by breaking and entering into the sealed bags of evidence. Of all the laws she broke to get here, this is the one that could potentially hang her.

Fuck it, this evidence belonged to June Shimmers anyway.

If JoJo wasn't already shaking from the rage coursing through her veins, she most certainly would be shaking now from the sheer excitement of what she was about to do. She had been fighting tooth and nail for the opportunity to hold her dad's evidence... waiting and waiting and goddamn waiting. It was the moment where truth and lies collided. The moment of the big reveal. The very thing that poked and prodded her in the morning to get up and keep going. And it was finally here.

Too bad the price of admission cost more than she ever dreamed possible.

One by one JoJo breached the seal of every piece of evidence concerning her dad.

The first piece of evidence slipped out and landed in the palm of her hand. It was a gold cross necklace with a misshapen base, chiseled into what appeared to be the bottom half of a key.

If it really was a key, it would be fucking impossible to figure out where it fit.

JoJo was tempted to throw it out the window before she let one more disappointment cut into her. It was utterly impossible to imagine what it opened considering the hundreds of different countries and cities they lived in over the years. Scouring her memories, JoJo struggled to recollect a gold necklace in their travels. But just like everything else in Ben's life and just like the police reports and the evidence bags – there was nothing.

JoJo hung it around her own neck, hiding it under her shirt.

The accompanying report stated his hand was holding it when he died but that wasn't true. JoJo was clutching his hands, his chest, his body, his shirt as they took him away. Suddenly a rush of hope returned that what she heard and read about her father and Yang Choo was nothing more than pure unadulterated *bullshit*.

Fucking cops! If they lied about the necklace... then maybe...

Years ago the evidence was screened for DNA, blood, and fingerprints, and according to the reports it belonged only to Ben Shimmers. Another fucking lie! Where was JoJo's DNA? It should've been all over Ben when they whisked him away. Why didn't the record show that? Or at least list it as an unknown variable?

She picked up the next bag of evidence, her hope returning in the tiniest of increments.

It was a beige rubber band bracelet that was *allegedly* found on his wrist. JoJo had no memory of Ben ever wearing any bracelet, *ever*. Then again, she hardly saw him after they arrived in LA. In fact, the longest stretch they spent together was when she was holding him as he lay dying.

Flipping the bracelet inside out, she read the wording etched inside,

God grant me the serenity to accept the things I cannot change. – St. Jude's Catholic Center AA.

She slid it on her wrist.

The last two bags contained his clothing and wallet. Picking up his shirt, JoJo buried her nose in it, wishing to God she could just smell him and remember something good.

Except…

She couldn't remember anything good. Not really. Every good memory involved other people, none of which included Ben. Why? But the deeper she dove looking for the light and love in their relationship, the worse her memories became. Each one darker than the next until she had no choice but to close her eyes and calm her mind.

Her heart couldn't bear the load anymore. Drowning in the surge of disappointment, JoJo opened the final piece of evidence – his wallet. The most fucked up disappointing thing of all.

It was empty.

Every year JoJo faithfully gave him wallet-sized pictures of her achievements – winning Taekwondo tournaments, school pictures, eighth grade graduation. But there was nothing. Nothing of her at all. The only thing Ben Shimmers had in his wallet was cash, license, some faded receipts, and a phone number handwritten on a piece of paper. The report stating the number was untraceable and no longer in service.

How typical. Ben was never in service for JoJo when he was alive –

what did she expect after death?

Collapsing over her steering wheel, she released the floodgate holding back her painful sobs. Anger mutated into intense grief. It was the first time in a long time that she allowed herself to grieve over her father. After all this time and pressure to get to LA, she felt truly abandoned and colossally alone. What a fucking waste. It was all just a fucking waste.

Her mind circling back to the beginning of this mess.

Why did Yang save me? Why?

She couldn't bear the thought of life without him. No matter what Yang Choo did, she couldn't rid herself of her need for him. And if he just explains he didn't do it, she'll believe him. She'll forgive him.

And if he did it?

It was too late. Doubt already took root and seeded in her heart. It was Occam's razor – the most likely solution is the simplest one because there were less guesses and less speculations. Sometimes truth is just truth. And the simplest answer to Yang's behavior toward a wayward fifteen year old girl?

Guilt.

His affection made sense because it wasn't affection at all. It was fucking guilt.

Somehow she hoped the evidence would absolve them and point to another dirty cop.

Another? In her heart, she already condemned Ben.

And Yang Choo? She was never more certain now that he killed Ben. It explained their entire relationship. It explained everything. Guilty until proven innocent.

JoJo sat up, wiping her nose on her sleeve.

But it's over now, isn't it? She did what she set out to do and solved the mystery.

Another voice piped in reminding her of the mission. And gripping her chest, JoJo felt the truth stab at her. Finding the murderer wasn't *all* she set out to do. She made a promise… took an oath… a pinky swear…

…to kill.

Him or me?

Leaning over and opening the glove compartment, JoJo pulled out a gun. Holding it somehow gave her strength, and she relished the cold hard steel against the dull ache in her hand. This small metal object possessed all the power in the world to stop her grief, and JoJo wanted nothing more than the freedom it was promising – freedom from thinking, feeling, hurting. Freedom from memory, from pain…

…*from killing.*

She would do anything to escape the foul thoughts plaguing her – thoughts involving first degree murder. Premeditated and burdensome. Dark reflections returned in wave after wave, tormenting her until all she could imagine was a violent ending.

"Dad," she whispered through the tears. "What do I do now?"

Her sobs slowly transformed into heart-wrenching wails.

Like a magnet pulling at the metal weapon, she mechanically lifted the gun to her head. But halfway between her lap and her temple, two very strange things happened almost at the exact same moment like divine synchronicity. First, the hand holding the gun paused when JoJo caught sight of her dad's beige bracelet hanging out of her sleeve. It had flipped to display the name of the center, almost like it was advertising. Was it too much to hope that whoever worked there would remember Ben?

There was nothing left *but* hope.

Second, her eyes looked past the bracelet, noticing the garage wall directly in front of her. It was tagged with the Triad gang symbol. There wasn't a better spot in the entire space for the artwork to be so *in her face*.

It was a fucking sign. A stone left unturned.

And the invisible chain that seemed to be forcing the gun to her head finally released its malicious hold. Out of sight, out of mind. JoJo jammed the gun into her pocket, quickly pulling herself together. Somewhere between the pain and the anger, she forgot that she ran out of the police station with stolen evidence. Time was of the essence, and *right now* wasn't conducive for a downward mental spiral. Honestly, she had no idea how long it would take them to find this car, and she still wasn't entirely sure that the hospital didn't report her missing or if the Skittles bitch was covering for her. Regardless, it would only be a matter of time before the police figured out which area she disappeared to after leaving the police station. The car was a liability now with too much blood and too much of her DNA to leave it to be discovered.

She had her next steps.

Digging around her run bag, JoJo grabbed the lighter fluid and matches she kept on hand. Something Ben pounded into her to always have handy in case they needed to quickly close a wound… or start a fire.

How goddamn fucking poetic.

She squirted the fluid over the seats, the steering wheel, the evidence bags, covering every spot she touched or bled on.

Saturating the entire car and all its contents in the flammable fluid, JoJo stood back to admire her handiwork. A cold heartless grin slowly spread over her face as she thought of the great pleasure it would give her to burn Yang Choo's vehicle. Disappointed only that it wasn't his entire Palace.

Like father, like daughter.

It was a very dark night of the soul.

Folding up an old piece of paper, JoJo origamied that mother fucker into an airplane and lit the back end on fire. Then standing one-foot-in and one-foot-out of the stairwell, she sent the burning airplane on its way.

It flew round and round like a smoking F/A-18 aircraft that was shot down and spiraling out of control. For a second, she wasn't sure it would make its destination. But somehow the flaming fighter flew right into the combustible solvent instantly igniting it and wreaking a small explosion. All at once, the entire area was a giant ball of flame just as she slammed the exit door shut.

JoJo could feel the heat rush under the door from where she was hiding in the stairwell. The explosion shook the whole building, sending dust particles raining down around her. Holding tightly to the banister, she wondered if the building would hold up, with part of her hoping it didn't.

It was Yang Choo's fucking garage.

Dr. Joan M Savage

Chapter 33

Innocence and Guilt

From the distance, JoJo could hear the fire trucks honking and blaring as they raced toward the garage.

It was a *burn* car after all.

JoJo paid the cabbie to park down the street from the *St. Jude's Catholic Center* just in case she ended up a suspect. If the cops *somehow* put it all together, and if the cabbie *somehow* could be traced back to her, well, fuck it. He can tell them everything because he knows nothing, except he dropped a tall blonde woman off in an alley.

Tall and blonde. It was her very last burn outfit. JoJo dressed in a long blond wig, short skirt, a red leather jacket, and shiny red knee-high boots with three inch heels. An outfit no one would ever catch her wearing. It was perfect.

It will be hell trying to figure out where she really went. There were too many addresses, buildings, businesses, and apartments to search. Her whole life has been about covering her ass, and today wasn't any different.

Her phone suddenly vibrated in her back pocket. It was the devil.

Where r u?

She started typing, ~~go fuck yourself asshole~~. Quickly deleting it.

She tried again, ~~I never want to see u again, mother fucker~~. And deleted that too.

What could she say right now? Nothing. She had nothing left to say.

Her notifications popped up with four missed calls from Dylan. She switched to messaging him.

~~I'm fine. Following up on a call~~ then stopped. Dylan couldn't know she left the hospital yet. Instead she texted.

Running tests. Chat later.

Her phone instantly chiming back.

Ok. Somthin happnd @ station. I'm stuck here. Will call u later. Text when ur done.

Deleting everything, she stuck her phone away. As far as anyone was concerned, she *was* still at the hospital. Only Yang would know the truth *if* Candy was still working. And if she wasn't covering for her? Well, she was fucked anyway.

JoJo made her way through several different alleyways before she arrived at the backside of the church. And cutting through their finely cared for lawn, she followed a small brick path to the front doors. From a quick glance, the colors reminded her of the Palace but picturesquely, it looked like any other Catholic church with its thick wooden doors and colorful stained glass windows.

It felt like the Universe Itself was opening doors for JoJo Sparks and making a way where none existed because *St. Jude's Catholic Center* was open for sunrise prayer and confession.

Another fucking sign.

And the best part? Priests are like lawyers, JoJo can admit all her shit and they can't say anything to anyone. What is said in confession stays in confession. It's a sacramental seal… inviolable, and exactly what she needed to ask about the bracelet.

And all things related to Ben Shimmers.

It was beautiful inside like an old art museum detailed with paintings of saints and historical events and a wide red carpet that ran right down the center of several wooden pews. Sitting at the front of the church was a podium, a table with a million burning candles on it, and a large obscene cross with a bloody dead guy hanging on it.

JoJo got chills looking at the crucifixion of the naked man, wondering what he did to deserve such treatment. Did he betray a friend? Was he betrayed? She tried remembering the details from the catholic confirmation classes she was forced to take as a child.

It was a weird sort of deja vu.

Tearing her gaze away from the gruesome scene, JoJo wrestled with intrusive vengeful thoughts wreaking havoc in her heart and mind. One thing JoJo Sparks knew well was how to confess. She spent many a night confessing her sins to the poor priests stuck with babysitting her.

Sliding into the confessional booth, JoJo peeked through the screen into the attached adjacent booth hoping someone was available and ready. A priest was sitting on the other side, his head bowed while his lips were silently moving in prayer.

"Bless me father for I have sinned... it's been... it's been... Jesus-fucking-Christ, it's been forever since my last confession." JoJo could hear a small cough of surprise from the other side of the booth.

"What ails you, my child?" A soft voice drifted through the lace covered wooden screen that separated them. It smelled old and musty, with a faint hint of mothballs and some lingering cheap musky perfume from the person who came before. Something the priest said didn't sit well with her.

"*Child?* I'm no one's child. I'm an orphan. No. I'm a fucking lie. I don't exist." For some reason she was fighting back stupid tears.

Stop it! I'm not here to confess.

She needed answers. She came for answers... despite the soul-wrenching anguish that clung just onto the edge of consciousness, demanding to be heard. Suddenly the reality was too heavy to bear alone.

Yang Choo did us all a favor by killing Ben Shimmers... a dirty cop...

The harder she tried to hold back her tears the stronger they became, as if they were feeding off her willpower and gaining momentum. In a last ditch effort, JoJo punched herself in the thigh a few times hoping the pain would force her tears back into hiding. The priest immediately interrupting the attack on herself.

"Stop this! It's a sin to harm yourself!" he hissed at her from the other side.

"Then bless me father for I'm about to sin! The ultimate fucking sin."

"Suicide is not the answer, child."

JoJo didn't mean to shout, her voice echoing through the entire church.

"I'm nobody's child! I'm a goddamn lie! My whole life is one giant fucking lie! Even my name!" She desperately fought to calm herself, not wanting to make an enemy of him.

"I'm sorry. I'm sorry, priest. It's not... *suicide*. It's survival. It's war. Revenge. I made a promise to kill him. It's him or me. And I just... I can't. I can't do it. I won't hurt him." She lowered her head, the blond wig catching on the back of her collar and pulling. In a crazy violent frenzy, she ripped the wig off her head and beat it against the wall as if she were killing a small animal, her red curls popping out wildly like they couldn't wait for their freedom.

Once the wig was thoroughly dead, she ran her shaking fingers through her sweaty untamed hair.

"Vengeance is the Lord's." His voice interrupted her mini meltdown.

"I have no choice." Shaking her head, JoJo collapsed against the back wall like she was suddenly too tired to speak. And too tired to move. Reality was exhausting.

"Help me understand, child... daughter..." He cleared his throat uncomfortably.

Smiling dully at him, JoJo leaned her head forward to look through one of the holes.

"JoJo. Just call me JoJo. Do you want to hear something funny, priest? I'm... I'm..." She couldn't say it. Burying her head in her hands, she let the anguish return in droves as she admitted her guilt.

"I'm a dirty cop," she whispered. "I'm a fucking dirty cop... and my dad was a dirty cop too." As soon as it left her mouth, JoJo was surprised. It was all making sense now. She really is her father's daughter. How befitting that Yang Choo should finish off the Shimmers family line. It was fate.

"Forgiveness is available..." The priest started saying until JoJo punched the wooden laced window separating them.

"I don't *want* forgiveness! I was hired to be dirty! Hired by the very man who killed... *who murdered* my father. Yang *murdered* him... for... for... Jesus Christ! For being a goddamn dirty cop. Why not kill me years ago? What was his plan? Be another hero? Maybe this time the city will actually throw him a parade. He *must* kill me, priest. Or I *will* kill him," she barely whispered the last part.

"Why would Mr. Choo want to kill you, child... daughter... *JoJo?*" He tested out the name.

"I told you... if he..." Suddenly her head popped up. "Wait a minute!"

She glared at him through one of the holes.

"I never said it was Yang *Choo*. Yang is a very common name." JoJo kicked open her little booth door, and standing outside the priest's door, she yanked it open, almost tearing it off its hinges.

"Don't. Fucking. Lie." She warned, watching him carefully.

The priest seemed beaten down by life and the parts of his skin that were still visible looked like melted wax. Whoever he was, he'd been through hell and back.

"I wasn't planning to..." he said, carefully standing up.

"Then answer me!"

"You never asked a question." He cocked his head giving her a small lopsided grin suddenly reminding her of Dylan. Without meaning to, she found herself relaxing, struggling with feelings of compassion for this man with so many scars. But despite his hard appearance, he remained gentle, kind, and fiercely passionate. Everything about him was nonthreatening, yet JoJo sensed he could be extremely dangerous if cornered.

Sniffing, she wiped her nose on her sleeve, never looking so young as when she did that. The priest noticed.

"Are you even old enough to be a cop?" He shocked her with his question, causing her to stumble over her words a bit.

"What? I... of course... I..."

"Don't. Lie." He copied her tone for tone. Impressed, she smiled slightly in defeat. Whoever he was, he had the gift of disarming even the most powerful nuclear weapon – her temper. Of all the places to come clean, this was the worst place for honesty and the best place for fibbing.

As far as JoJo was concerned it was the best of times, it was the worst of times.

She finally answered him, shaking her head *no*. And dropping her eyes, she fell into her characteristic panache of hiding beneath her red curls. They were sticking out everywhere from the weight of her sweat and being trapped under the wig too long.

Suddenly the priest leaned over, very interested in her appearance. He tried unsuccessfully to study her hidden face, and quite out of nowhere, grabbed her wrist, forcing her to look up at him.

"Who are you?" he whispered in both shock and awe with a thousand different emotions crossing his features.

"Let go. Stop it! I'm JoJo Sparks! Maybe once upon a time, I was... I was June Shimmers." It felt like she was really sinning by admitting her name.

"Shimmers? Oh dear God..." He reached out to touch her hair, and she slapped his hand, pulling her wrist out of his calloused melted fingers.

"Get off! What the fuck is your problem?"

But he wasn't looking at her with lust, fear, hunger, or disappointment. It was something else altogether... it was...

Familiarity? Recognition?

She couldn't put her finger on it. Fuck it, what difference did it make, anyway? They were strangers, and she wasn't planning on having a future much longer.

"Look, Yang Choo *will* have to kill me... or I *will* kill him. Understand?"

But he wasn't paying attention, he was too busy staring at her like he had just won the lottery.

"Did you hear me?" She stomped her foot on the ground like a ten year old throwing a tantrum. Her act of defiance seemed to break the spell he had fallen under, releasing JoJo from his scrutiny. If *everyone* knew what Ben did, then he was probably labeling her as the psycho's daughter.

JoJo collapsed, her head falling into her hands.

"Shit. Shit. Shit. I can't. I won't kill him. I can't do it."

"Are you in love with him?"

"Yes. What!? No! I mean no! Of course not. NO! No fucking way!" She glared up at him, her hand covering her mouth, eyes wide open, face turning bright red.

"I am NOT in love with him. He's... he's... a liar. A murderer. A criminal. A fucking liar. He made me into a dirty cop."

The priest's face had her second guessing everything, and JoJo felt very small under his long hard look.

"What?" She crossed her arms defiantly.

"I think I understand now. So, Yang Choo lied to you, correct?"

"YES! Uhm... no... not exactly."

"Then he bribed you?"

"Not really."

"Oh I see. He *persuaded* you, maybe? Seduced you? He is a rather handsome man." The priest was studying her face carefully. She shook her head feeling the red rising again in her cheeks.

"Got it, got it. Then of course he threatened you! Forced you to become dirty!?" he said, slamming his fist in his hand for emphasis. And a very strange thing happened deep inside JoJo, she suddenly felt very protective of her guardian angel.

"He wouldn't do that!" she defended.

The priest's eyebrows shot up, and she quickly turned her back on him.

"I don't know. He said he didn't do favors for free. How else do I interpret that?" She felt ridiculous, and so fucking small. JoJo almost had to stop herself from sticking her hand behind her back and crossing her fingers. What's the point? The priest would know it anyway.

Beckoning her to follow him, he sat in one of the pews, inviting her to sit across from him. She watched him limp pitifully to the seats, feeling terribly sorry for him and she didn't even know why.

"So let me get this straight, Yang Choo convinced you? Maybe even blackmailed you?" JoJo glared at him now. Agitated and desperately confused.

"I'm not sure. He wanted to help me catch my father's murderer. The fucking cops weren't doing anything. And I was too young to do anything." She got lost in thought, remembering the angel who showed up at her father's grave with his umbrella and double-breasted pin-striped suit, smelling so goddamn good she never had a chance except to fall in love with him.

Love?

The priest brought her back from the civil war waging between her head and heart.

"He was helping you?"

She turned away, the weight of his questions were fucking drowning her. They were grating and annoying, and she was certain he was feigning innocence despite being guilty as hell.

"How do *you* know Yang Choo?" she finally asked, deciding the best course of action was to simply ignore the question.

"I imagine just about everyone in LA knows of him."

For a brief moment, they were both whisked away in their own thoughts about Triad king.

"The day my father was buried, Yang gave me a package. It gave me a new identity, making me older, sending me to college, and eventually into the police academy." She was growing more and more confused as she thought through the gangsters actions, and her own choices.

"When did he ask you to become a dirty cop?"

"He didn't," she surprised herself. "Oh my god, he didn't. I mean… it was implied. Wasn't it? He's… he's a fucking drug lord, a fucking gangster, a goddamn mobster!" She crossed her arms and plopped down on the seat in front of him. His eyes were wide and innocent, curious and nonjudgmental.

JoJo let out an exasperated sigh, looking away. Her stern erect shoulders and back buckled under his gentleness and she crunched down making herself smaller, as if the chair could somehow suck her up. As soon as she buckled, her rib screamed at her and she cried out in pain, leaning over to one side.

"Are you all right, my dear?" He reached for her, quickly stopping himself.

"I'm fine," she said through gritted teeth, and he let her be. At that same time her phone began to vibrate loudly and JoJo was suddenly very grateful for the reprieve. Slowly, studiously, and very rudely, she pulled the phone out in front of him.

Where r u! Why'd u leave the hospital? I have ur GPS. I'll send an fkng army.

Unconsciously, JoJo shot straight up like Yang Choo was right behind her, calling her name. She didn't want him to find this place. This needed to be her secret for now, her solace, her hideout, her sanctuary.

"I have to go," she said, grabbing her wig and pulling it down over her wild curls.

"Have to? Choose to? Want to?" The priest asked while he slowly pulled himself up. JoJo didn't mean to watch him struggle.

"I have to. I *choose* to. And I *want* to." JoJo headed toward the exit, texting and walking.

OMW

The priest called to her, interrupting the panic that started slamming her heart against her chest. Stopping at the door, she waited, giving him a minute to catch up. It hurt to watch him hobble but it would be a greater insult to cover the distance for him. Looking down, she pretended to adjust her backpack until she felt his hands gently rest on her shoulders.

"Don't do anything irrational, *please*. And tomorrow I'll explain a great many things to you."

"Like what? Fifty two ways not to sin? I'd rather kill myself." JoJo stuck her nose in the air.

"Don't joke about that," he chided. Then gently pulling on her shoulders, he forced her to look at him.

"Who's joking?"

"JoJo, what brought you to church today?"

Looking around the building, it took her a second to remember why she was there and lifting up her hand, she let the bracelet jiggle around her wrist.

"This belonged to my dad. I just... I wanted to know the truth about Ben Shimmers."

He smiled a lifeless smile. It was a mixture of sweet and sour.

"Come back tomorrow."

"Why?"

"I'll tell you about your dad… and your mom." Her jaw dropped and her hand unconsciously wrapped around the cross hidden under her shirt.

"You knew them? Do you know me? Did they come here? Were you friends? What happened to my mother? Is she alive? Does she live here? Did he… did my dad… did he really murder people?"

The priest raised his hands, silencing her.

"I'll tell you everything tomorrow. Come back tomorrow," he said and JoJo released one giant deep long heavy sigh.

"Priest, I can't be sure *he* won't kill *me*."

He smiled his lopsided grin forcing her to return it.

"He won't. And please call me *Father* or *Father Jason*. Whichever." He let her shoulders go.

Head down, JoJo was still lost in thought. Did she really want to die never knowing the truth about Ben Shimmers? Or her mother? Did she have a choice? Jason knew exactly what kind of bait to throw in her pond to keep her hooked.

"You know, I came here to see if you knew Ben Shimmers. And now, I don't give a shit anymore. Look, I'll drop by if… if I'm still alive."

Doing an about-face, the priest started hobbling down the red carpet toward the front of the church.

"You will. And when you come back, I'll also explain where you got your red curly hair." JoJo's eyes widened and her jaw dropped again. She had too many questions. So many things were going through her mind, freight trains speeding by and she couldn't catch any one of them.

Her phone vibrated loudly, startling them both.

10 min b4 I cum looking 4 u

"It's now or never, priest."

"I'm fine with never," he answered.

"I'm fine with now." And with that, she walked out, ready to face her destiny.

Or death.

Dr. Joan M Savage

RED FEVER

Chapter 34

Page Forty Six

JoJo aggressively pushed open the double doors to the Palace entrance, walking into Yang's office like she owned the goddamn place – his eyebrows shooting straight up when both doors slammed loudly against their opposing walls. He was already on his way to her, relief covering his face.

That is until he noticed her expression.

The dark haunted look and puffy red eyes stopped him dead in his tracks.

"Why are you roaming around? I gave you plenty of time to heal without any fucking suspicion!"

Ignoring him, she sauntered further into his office.

"How the hell did you sneak out of that hospital? I have people watching you... and where the fuck did you go? And what... what're you wearing?" He sounded like he was coming undone.

Looking down at her clothes, JoJo realized she looked like a prostitute. Unfortunately, it was the last burn outfit she owned.

They locked their eyes, and then horns again. It had the same feel as two cowboys facing off in an old western showdown.

JoJo drew first.

"You know, I was thinking, I never got to go to prom," she said out of nowhere. Her voice, soft and sweet. She began curiously investigating his

325

office like she had never been there before.

"Why did you leave the hospital?" he demanded, biting off each word, clearly holding back his temper.

But JoJo wasn't in any condition to go round and round with him today. A wicked grin spread over her face making Yang's eyebrows shoot up suspiciously. Or maybe it was the impious glint in her eye. He shifted uncomfortably, quieting down… waiting. She continued.

"I never got to play on a sports team or… shit! Be on the debate team! I would've been good at that."

He took a few steps, stopping halfway between JoJo and the exit.

"I never got a cap and gown, or to walk the red carpet for my diploma." Her hands disappeared inside her jacket pockets.

"I didn't think you'd mind," he said much too calmly, despite his agitation.

He returned fire.

"Where were you? Your burn car… is fucking burnt! Why?" Frustrated with her lack of responses, he exhaled loudly.

"What the fuck, JoJo! Are you all right? What happened? Why did you leave the hospital? What happened to your car?"

JoJo stared at him with a blank face, ignoring his warnings. She continued on as if she didn't hear him.

"I never got to play any high school games. Three Minutes in the Closet, Spin the Bottle, Truth or Dare," her voice shifting to sultry and seductive.

"We should play a game. What do you think, Yang Choo, leader of the LA Triads? Do you want to play with me? You seem to enjoy playing with me."

His eyes narrowed slightly, his patience nearing its end.

Yang broke free of her intense gaze, taking a shot in the dark at why she was behaving so strangely.

"JoJo, I had to take you to the hospital. You needed medical attention. One of my guys dressed as an EMT and dropped you off at the ER. That's it. That's all. Nothing else. And… I didn't take Dylan from you," he said bitterly.

Now her eyebrows lifted, and they locked horns again.

"You swear it, truth teller?" she mocked.

It was Yang's turn to respond with a blank face, obviously knowing better than to answer.

"How about we make our own little game and call it... Absolute Truth? What do you think, Yang Choo fucking king of LA? How about some absolute truth between us?"

"What the fuck happened, JoJo? We left you at the hospital. Then I hear you fucking snuck out. And now your car is destroyed. I am... was... concerned." He turned to head back to his desk, her tone stopping him.

"You concerned? About me? Ha! A little late, don't you think?" Her laugh was too forced and fake. He glared at her, his lip twitching. And JoJo smiled. She was getting to him. Maybe it was enough to make him angry. Angry enough to do what she couldn't... wouldn't do.

Yang fired a final warning shot, "I don't want to play any games. I don't want to play, period. Grow up."

"But I wanna play Absolute Truth." And JoJo pulled out the gun.

Yang's face lost its color, his hard emerald eyes narrowing carefully. She finally had his full attention. And right there on his gorgeous shiny wooden floor, JoJo emptied out all the bullets, save one. They bounced around his floor, rolling loudly in different directions. For a moment, it looked like Yang was going to pounce on her, but she was too far out of his reach. He inched his way closer and closer. And when JoJo shut the gun chamber and spun it, his eyes grew to saucers.

She aimed the gun at him.

"You humiliated me. Used me. Stole my life. My future. You broke me... you should be so proud that you accomplished the ultimate revenge. I'm actually jealous."

"What're you talking about, JoJo?"

"Absolute Truth, Yang Choo, guardian angel. Do you know who killed my father?"

Yang held his breath, staring at her in disbelief, his eyes opening wider and wider.

"Ahhht, times up." And JoJo pulled the trigger.

Grabbing his chest and grunting loudly, Yang bent slightly forward as if the gun had actually fired on him.

"Are you fucking crazy!?"

JoJo exhaled, feeling nothing but desperate relief. She had been holding her breath too. And as quickly as the relief came, it went. Replaced by the cold hard glint of someone who lost everything and had nothing left to lose. She spun the barrel again.

This time she aimed it at her own temple. Yang quickly lunged forward, only to have the gun pointing at him. He stopped.

JoJo lightly lifted one finger at him, moving it back and forth while mouthing the words, *no-no.* Eyes glued on him, she put the gun to her own temple again, her voice weak, tortured, and pained. It cracked when she spoke.

"Absolute Truth. Did you kill my father?"

Eyes wide, he stared blankly at her.

"It's complicated."

JoJo smiled.

"Ahhht," she whispered sadly. "Times up." And closed her eyes as she pulled the trigger.

Simultaneously, Yang dove for her, knocking the gun slightly off kilter. And much to both of their surprise, as he was tackling her the gun fired slightly past her head. The bullet whizzed by barely missing her skull, taking instead the life of some red curls. They floated to the floor while Yang tore the gun from her hand, throwing it across the room.

"What the fuck!? Are you crazy!?" He held her tightly, pinning her to the floor while JoJo's face twisted in pain from both the physical weight of Yang Choo sitting on her chest and the emotional weight of Yang Choo sitting in her heart. Staring vacantly at him as he held her to the ground, his expression was more telling than hers, switching between perplexed and enraged. She knew all about confusion and anger and relished the fact that he was finally experiencing a smidgen of her agony.

Finally crawling off her, side by side they sat quietly on the floor until JoJo stood up like nothing out of the ordinary happened. She casually straightened her clothes and her hair, hiding the sharp jabbing pain in her side.

Yang stayed on the floor, his hands massaging his temples.

"You killed my father," she whispered coolly and unconcerned as if she were commenting on the weather. Or maybe she was in a state of shock.

Yang punched the floor and standing up, he headed to his desk, grabbing the drink already waiting for him. He glanced back at her, quickly gulping down the entire glass of brandy in one swig. JoJo wasn't moving. She wasn't impatient or agitated. She was deathly pale, eerily still, and utterly too quiet.

Neither reaction matched the seriousness of the situation.

She stared at him, waiting for his answer... or his retaliation. She gave him no choice now.

JoJo looked like she had died, leaving nothing more than a shell – a shell patiently waiting for the truth.

Yang sat at his desk, studying her for a moment. Finally he sighed deeply, his shoulders slumping forward slightly.

"Yes. And no."

JoJo listened. Her eyes unintentionally drifting just past his head like she meant to be looking at him but wasn't, unaware where they pointed. She was facing all the years that he had lied to her.

She broke the long grueling silence.

"Why?" she whispered. Her lack of emotion was frightening, her eyes shifting back to him.

It was too goddamn quiet.

"Page forty six," he finally responded.

Yang made his way over to the safe in the wall, and tapping in some numbers, popped it open. It was filled with guns, passports, a knife, cash and other things she could easily arrest him for. There were several manila envelopes he was searching through, finally dragging one of them free.

He tossed it, gently sliding it across the floor until it stopped at the edge of her shoe. JoJo picked up the envelope, it was her childhood fantasies and nightmares. The envelope contained copies of her journal, the journal he made her destroy.

"My journal? You said to destroy it. You said you wanted nothing to tie us together," she whispered as she continued reading page forty six. He numbered each page with a marker like they were evidence from a crime scene.

She didn't understand.

Page forty six was one of the more detailed descriptions of her nightmare – standing in blood and fire, people screaming, her body burning...

Before she made it through the first paragraph, JoJo started shaking when fragments from her nightmare rushed to the surface. Crumpling the page in her fist, she closed her eyes again, refusing to remember. She didn't want to remember anything anymore, she just wanted to forget. All of it – every moment up until now.

"My nightmare." Keeping her eyes closed, she was fighting to stay in the present. Her hand instinctively coming up to protect her rib. When Yang tackled her, he didn't pull any punches and her ribs were voicing their agony since the adrenaline was no longer masking it. Anyway, she should be dead. She heard it – clear as day. The gun fired. That bullet was meant for her. And she came today with every intention of dying. It was an act of mercy, sparing herself the promise to kill her father's murderer. At the very least, sparing Yang the responsibility of finishing off Ben's daughter. The gun spoke the truth. She should be dead.

But Yang.

JoJo found her way back into the room.

What does my nightmare have to do with my dad?

When she finally opened her eyes, she startled slightly to see that Yang had strategically positioned himself right next to her, his default expression returning, right along with the hardened emeralds. His eyes staying fixed on her.

Holding page forty six out to him, she demanded an explanation without asking for one.

In the end, she wished more than anything he had just kept the truth to himself.

RED FEVER

Chapter 35

Fantasies and Nightmares

"I was there." His voice cracked. Clearing his throat, he tried again. Suddenly, he looked nothing like the man she believed him to be. Where was the toughened thug? The hardened mobster? The impenetrable outlaw? Where the fuck was the rugged, sturdy, steely man? Instead he looked very much like a child being scolded. And for whatever reason this made her even more furious, her compassion distorting and melting away.

"What... what the fuck are you talking about?" She threw the pages at him, and they scattered in the air, drifting downward in all directions.

"It's just... fantasies and nightmares, you son-of-a-bitch!"

"No, I was there! I was fucking there! I saw the whole thing! It wasn't just a goddamn nightmare! It was a massacre! A fucking massacre! Including your parents! Your father... my friend. How's that for *absolute truth*?"

He bit off the last part like it was the final word in an argument. Her eyes wide, she was getting sucked back into the hell that drug her down most nights. The memories ripped at her, tearing her apart, and clawing their way into reality.

Turning her back to him, she tried hiding the private civil war waging inside, while Yang marched back to the empty glass at his desk. With shaking hands, he poured himself another drink, and gulped it down. Half of it missing his mouth and pouring down his neck, saturating his dress shirt.

"Does that help?" she barely muttered.

"Yes. I'm unapologetically me." He sounded unconvinced. Slamming his empty glass on the desk, he beelined to her so fast that she had no time to react. Yang grabbed her shirt and practically lifted her off the ground.

"Get this into your head, Ben Shimmers was a fucking murderer! He burned... innocent... people... alive... in that warehouse." His voice breaking again, and she could feel his body shaking. Yang looked crazy from the memories of an atrocity she only dreamt about. And she knew if she said anything right now that he could easily kill her – his desperation demanding it.

Unguarded and dangerous, he laid it all out for JoJo, all the pain he'd been carrying, the lies, the sick memories of Ben. And what he must've seen every time he looked at her knowing her father caused so much damage, destruction, and death.

So much for it being an accident or a misunderstanding.

According to the man she loved and admired most in the world, the nightmare was real. No wonder Yang Choo didn't want to be with her, couldn't be with her – no... actually ran from her. He would never see her as anything more than a psychopath's daughter. She wouldn't blame him if he hated her too.

Impossible love.

JoJo forced her mind to tune back into his rantings, barely listening as she bore witness to the hate in his eyes and the grief in his voice. Yang Choo was showing her everything, the hurt, the guilt, the grief, the shame, and most surprising, the fear. He looked almost craven.

Shutting her eyes, she hoped he would just end things quickly. What a better way to avenge that massacre than to kill his only child? Yang needed revenge for what Ben did far more than she needed it. It was excruciating to witness his agony, and it was her fault he was reliving it.

"Why make me a cop?" It slipped out. "Why bring me to LA? I don't understand."

"I didn't! I wanted you to live a goddamn normal life. But you went and fucking applied to the police academy. The fucking *police academy*! I couldn't believe it. And YOU requested the goddamn transfer to LA. There's only so much I can do to babysit your ass and run my city."

Her eyes widened. His words felt like a two ton brick landing on her head.

"It was me?" she whispered. "Everything... was me?" It was a terrible moment of truth. But despite her terrible choices and bad decisions, nothing pained her more than the thought of who her father really was and who she was as a result. Absolute truth was killing her.

She preferred the burning sharp jab in her rib to the broken emptiness filling her soul.

JoJo failed her mission.

And there was no longer any reason for the existence of JoJo Sparks. There never was. Suddenly she wished Yang would just put an end to everyone's suffering and kill her now. But he was too busy venting.

"...and then we spotted Ben back in LA. And I saw you, I saw you journaling. I had to be sure it was him, so when you left the apartment I returned and read your journal. That's when I knew."

It was becoming unbearable now that he admitted it was her very own journal that killed Ben. Was everything her fault?

His words were coming at her faster and more furiously.

"He probably took you as a fucking bargaining chip, keeping you around in case he got caught. Who the fuck knows? Maybe he came to care for you... or..." He looked her whole body up and down, shaking his head hard like he was trying to erase an image. Finally, he slammed his fist into his temple.

"Don't tell me... just don't fucking tell me! I don't want to know!" His voice raised an octave, threatening, like she just fucked up all his plans. His hands wrapped around the front of her shirt again and this time he lifted her straight off the ground.

"Don't fucking tell me if that mother fucker... if he... FUCK! Don't tell me goddamn it!"

"I won't," she whispered softly, unable to stop the very large tears that spilled over and down her cheeks. JoJo Sparks was done playing Absolute Truth, but Yang Choo was just getting started.

"Ben knew the cops would hunt him down like the shithole he was. He was a piece of shit! Do you hear me!? Ben Shimmers was nothing but a goddamn piece of shit!"

The monster woke up.

Screaming...

Kicking him in the gut, she forced him to release her.

"Fuck you! Fuck you! You fucking murderer! I hate you! I hate you!"

"Goddamn it, JoJo! Did you even hear me!? Ben Shimmers killed your fucking parents! BEN killed your dad! I told you a dirty cop killed him. It was BEN. Ben is the mother fucker that destroyed your family. He burned them all alive... everyone..."

She didn't understand.

Parents? What the fuck was he saying?

Her rib was tormenting her and suffocating her. Bending over, she grabbed her abdomen, crumbling to one knee. She couldn't fucking breath!

Parents?

Several guards had quietly entered the room, filtering in around them. The gunfire had drawn them.

They were watching the interaction carefully without interfering, yet waiting for the green light to intervene. With a slight nod, Yang turned his back on her and they moved in quickly, grabbing her and picking her up off the ground like they could somehow read his mind.

"You asked me... no, you begged me to help you kill your dad's murderer and I did. I fucking shot him right in front of you. Right next to the dumpster, because that's what he was! Trash. A piece of shit! Ben Shimmers was the fucking asshole who started *Red Fever* and he came back to LA to finish it. I warned you what revenge would cost. But you're so goddamn hellbent you missed the truth. Ben Shimmers wasn't even your fucking dad! Are you listening? Jesus Christ! Get her the fuck out of here! Get her out NOW! I don't want to look at her!"

He was right. She couldn't listen and she couldn't understand. She was blinded by rage and pain... and guilt.

Mindlessly, she attacked his men as they tried to drag her out. Her nails ripping into flesh, her foot nailing someone's groin. It was unfair. The henchmen knew they couldn't really defend themselves without incurring Mr. Choo's wrath.

But JoJo was beyond reason now, she was like a rabid dog attacking anything that moved – clawing, punching, kicking, biting...

"Enough!" Yang's booming voice commanding everyone's attention. Her rage instantly dissipating as she watched Yang pick up her gun and a couple of the stray bullets. All eyes were glued to the Triad king as he loaded the weapon.

"It would take me nothing to pull this trigger and bury you in the ocean. Is that what you want?"

It was.

"It should be you, Yang. It should be you." Pushing the last guard off her, she slowly walked up to him, letting the barrel of the gun dig into her abdomen. Slowly, she slid it up to her heart.

"Please," she begged. Yang's eyes widened with genuine surprise and the room went deathly quiet. She could hear a pin drop, or a drop of blood. Yang and JoJo simultaneously looked down at her side. Beneath the jacket, her shirt had turned bright red from reopening the wound. And in the silence, there was nothing but the sound of her blood hitting his wooden floor. She looked back up, eyes pleading.

"Make it happen, Yang. Finish your revenge on Ben Shimmers. Kill his only child. Do it. They'll throw you a fucking parade." Holding his eyes, she slipped her hand over his, gently caressing it. Putting her finger over his finger on the gun's trigger, and squeezing…

It was his turn to lose it.

"Goddamn it! What the fuck is wrong with you? Stop it! Just stop this shit!"

JoJo was fighting with his hand, finally sucker punching his throat and ripping the gun away. Yang was gagging and gulping to breath while his men surrounded her.

"Get back! I said get-the-fuck-back, assholes! Move!" she screamed, backing up toward the exit. Yang was motioning toward her but she hit him hard enough that it would be impossible to give a verbal command anytime soon. She partially crushed his windpipe. And his men were momentarily disheveled when their leader fell to one knee, gasping for air.

Stopping long enough to say goodbye, she locked eyes with Yang Choo, leader of the LA Triads one final time, and JoJo Sparks silently said goodbye to the man that gave her everything… and took everything.

She was leaving the same way she arrived, wearing a ridiculous outfit and walking through the streets of LA. And just like Ben taught her to do a thousand times before, she grabbed her run bag and disappeared.

Dr. Joan M Savage

Chapter 36

Epoch of Belief. Back to the Beginning

Do you think it's a sin if I don't want to live anymore? JoJo wondered endlessly.

It was the road less traveled in reality, but mentally, she ran grooves into the ground. Should she dump all the self-stock while she still could? Sell the money pit that was her life? Cut the dead weight?

Charles Dickens had it right when he wrote,

"It was the best of times, it was the worst of times, it was the age of wisdom, it was the age of foolishness, it was the epoch of belief, it was the epoch of incredulity, it was the season of Light, it was the season of Darkness..."

JoJo had been in her season of Darkness. Was she finally in the season of Light? A season of Truth? As she stumbled down a nameless road, an ancient proverb ran through her head,

There is a time for everything, and a season for every activity: A time to plant and a time to uproot, a time to tear down and a time to build, a time to search and a time to give up, a time to love and a time to hate, a time to tear and a time to mend, a time to live and a time to die...

...a time for peace and a time for war...

JoJo was born for such a time as this.

Made in the USA
Las Vegas, NV
27 July 2024

93005219R00187